Before
I Saw
You

Before I Saw You

EMILY HOUGHTON

G

GALLERY BOOKS

NEW YORK   LONDON   TORONTO   SYDNEY   NEW DELHI

G

Gallery Books
An Imprint of Simon & Schuster, Inc.
1230 Avenue of the Americas
New York, NY 10020

This Gallery Books trade paperback edition May 2021

GALLERY BOOKS and colophon are registered
trademarks of Simon & Schuster, Inc.

For information about special discounts for bulk purchases,
please contact Simon & Schuster Special Sales at 1-866-506-1949
or business@simonandschuster.com.

The Simon & Schuster Speakers Bureau can bring authors to your live event.
For more information or to book an event, contact the Simon & Schuster Speakers
Bureau at 1-866-248-3049 or visit our website at www.simonspeakers.com.

Manufactured in the United States of America

1 3 5 7 9 10 8 6 4 2

Library of Congress Cataloging-in-Publication Data
Names: Houghton, Emily, 1991– author.
Title: Before I saw you / Emily Houghton.
Description: Gallery Books trade paperback edition. | New York : Gallery
Books, 2021. | Summary: "For fans of How to Walk Away and Me Before You
comes a poignant and moving novel about two people recovering from
traumatic injuries in the same hospital ward . . . and who begin falling in
love without ever seeing each other"—Provided by publisher.
Identifiers: LCCN 2020018977 (print) | LCCN 2020018978 (ebook) | ISBN
9781982149505 (trade paperback) | ISBN 9781982149529 (ebook)
Classification: LCC PR6101.H875 B44 2021 (print) | LCC PR6101.H875
(ebook) | DDC 823/.92—dc23
LC record available at https://lccn.loc.gov/2020018977
LC ebook record available at https://lccn.loc.gov/2020018978

ISBN 978-1-9821-4950-5
ISBN 978-1-9821-4952-9 (ebook)

*For Rebecca, who believed in me and
this book before I ever could. I carry your words
and support with me in my heart every day.*

Before I Saw You

Chapter 1

ALICE

As she slipped in and out of consciousness, all Alice could process were the stark white lights overhead, the acrid smell of burning, and the searing heat that ripped through her entire body.

"Good God, she's lucky to be alive." A strange voice drifted above her.

She wanted to try to work out where she was. Find out who these voices belonged to and, more important, who on earth they were talking about. But it hurt to just be, let alone think. Plus those lights were blinding.

"Lucky? You think she's going to feel lucky when she looks in the mirror for the first time? She's been burnt pretty bad, the poor girl."

She tried to force her brain into action, fighting desperately against the pull of sleep. Just as she was about to give up and allow the cool safety of darkness to take her, Alice started to piece it all together.

The "poor girl."
The smell.
The *burning*.
It was Alice who was lucky to be alive.
It was Alice who had been on fire.

Chapter 2

ALFIE

"There he is! Alfie Mack, the luckiest son of a bitch I know!"

He didn't need to pull the curtain back to know who had come to visit him—he would never be able to forget that voice even if he'd wanted to.

"Not *quite* so lucky when they chopped my leg off, but you win some, you lose some, right?"

"Can't argue with that one." Matty shrugged. "Anyway, how have you been, buddy? By the way, I can't stay long today, got to pick the missus up and go for lunch with the in-laws."

It was normal for everyone to make their excuses to leave before they'd even taken a seat, and Alfie was grateful to Matty for at least asking how he was first.

"Yeah, no worries, I've got a pretty packed day too."

"Really?"

Alfie could tell he was only half listening.

"Oh yeah, it's relentless in here. The main challenge is trying to guess the number of times Mr. Peterson will get up and go to the toilet this morning. Normally we average a good seven, but if he has a sip of that apple juice it could be anything up to ten."

A disgruntled voice rang out across the ward: "When you're ninety-two and your bladder is about as taut as a dead duck's arse, you'll be pissing constantly too."

"It's all right, Mr. P., there's no judgment here. Although, are you sure you weren't a writer in another life? Your vocabulary is downright poetic."

The old man across the way in bed fourteen broke into a smile, then very quickly shoved his middle finger up at Alfie and returned to reading his newspaper.

"Seriously though, mate, how are you doing? How's the physio going? Any idea yet when you'll be out of here?" Matty's eyes were wide with hope.

Everyone asked the same questions with the same concern. It was strange—on the one hand, he knew that they all just wanted him home and out of the hospital; but at the same time he couldn't help but sense their slight apprehension. He supposed that while he was in the capable hands of St. Francis's nursing staff, it was one less thing they all had to worry about.

"No idea, if I'm honest. The infection seems to be all under control now. Physio is going well, and they are going to measure me for a custom prosthetic soon. I just need to keep building my strength up. It's small progress, but, as the nurses say . . . every step is a step closer to the end!"

"That is the *worst* motivational phrase ever. It sounds like you're walking to your bloody death."

"Well, isn't that what we're all doing, Matthew, my friend?" Alfie reached over and patted him on the arm.

"Oh, give over, you're still a dark-humored bastard even with one leg, aren't you!" Matty slapped his hand away affectionately.

It was around now when most people usually took their cue to leave—they'd checked in on him, cracked a few jokes, asked the questions they thought they should. There was usually only so much time being surrounded by the sick and vulnerable that a person could take.

"Right, buddy, got to dash. Mel and the kids send their love. Let me know if you need anything, otherwise I'll see you same time, same place next week?"

"Don't you worry, I'll be here! Take care of yourself and give the little ones a kiss from me."

"Sure thing. Love you, mate."

"Yeah, you too, Matty."

The declarations of love were something Alfie was still getting used to. They had only started after Matty had thought his best friend was gone forever. The first time, Alfie could have sworn he'd misheard.

"What did you just say?"

"Nothing." Matty had shuffled uncomfortably, his gaze fixed to the floor. "I just . . ." His eyes flickered up briefly to meet Alfie's. "I just said 'I love you,' is all."

Alfie had burst into laughter. "Oh, come on, mate! Don't be ridiculous. You don't need to say all that stuff." But Matty was definitely not laughing. In fact, he was looking even more uncomfortable. His head had dropped lower; his fists were tight by his sides.

"Look, it's not ridiculous, okay?" He was painfully forcing the words out through gritted teeth "When I thought I'd lost you, I realized I'd never said it to you once. Not in the entire fifteen years of our friendship, so I promised myself that if you survived I'd tell you. Thankfully, here we are, so you better get used to it, okay?"

It was all Alfie could do not to cry "I love you too, mate."

Since then it had become the full stop at the end of their every good-bye. Of course it was said in a very nonchalant, testosterone-filled manner, but Alfie knew how important those few words were to both of them now.

Alfie had been a patient at St. Francis's Hospital for nearly six weeks. Since he'd moved to Hackney three years ago, he'd had the pleasure of seeing St. Francis's regularly. Its murky pebbled façade loomed over the trendy, gentrified streets as a reminder that there was a shabby history that couldn't be ignored.

"Jesus Christ, if I ever end up in that place, Mum, promise me you'll get me transferred?" he used to joke every time they'd walk past it during one of her visits.

"Oh, don't be so morbid. I've heard very good things about that place," she'd retorted.

"Really? You're telling me you've heard good things about a place that looks more like a multistory car park than a hospital?"

"Stop it! If you were at death's door, trust me, you'd be begging them to take you in." She'd smiled at him in that infuriating self-righteous way. "And what have I always taught you? Never judge a book by its cover."

But continue to judge it he did. Right up until the very moment the unsightly building and the people within it saved his life. As soon as he was admitted, they'd known it was serious. Just one look at the wreckage would have told you that—but more than a month in the hospital? Nobody could have predicted that.

Chapter 3

ALICE

"Hey, honey . . . can you hear me?" The voice was quiet, hopeful, and cautious.

The smell was the first thing to hit her.

Bleach. Blood. Human decay.

"You don't even need to say anything, Alice, love. Maybe blink or wiggle those fingers of yours, we just want to know if you're awake."

In order to get this human and her nauseating kindness away from her, Alice forced her fingers to move. The effort alone felt strange. How had she forgotten how to use her own body? How long had it been since she'd told her brain to work?

"There you are, Alice, my girl. Well done, you're doing brilliantly!"

It didn't feel like she was doing brilliantly. It felt like someone had stretched and pulled at her skin, trying to fit her into a new body that was the wrong shape altogether, and then to top it off they'd run out of material and had given up halfway through the job. She felt unfinished and in a hell of a lot of pain.

"You've been in a serious accident, Alice, but you're on the mend now. I'm going to call for the doctor so he can come and explain what's been happening, okay? Sit tight, sweetheart, I'll be back in a moment."

Alice's head was pounding. Broken fragments of memory kept swirling around her mind, making it impossible for her to think. She blinked her eyes open and saw two people hurrying towards her bed.

Please just tell me where the hell I am.

"Hi, Miss Gunnersley. Do you mind if I call you Alice?"

The doctor stepped a little closer to her. He had a face that Alice presumed had once been filled with hope and enthusiasm for the work he was doing but now appeared a little jaded and somewhat wary. Here stood a man well and truly hardened to death.

She shook her head very slightly. The only act of acknowledgment she could muster.

"Fantastic. So, Alice, as the nurse has probably already explained to you, you've been brought into St. Francis's Hospital because you've been in a pretty serious accident. There was a fire in your office building, and unfortunately you were caught in it. You've suffered some quite substantial injuries; we estimate about forty percent of your body has been burnt to varying degrees. We've already performed one surgery in an attempt to minimize the damage, but there's still a long way to go. For now I want you to know that you're receiving the best possible care and we have a plan in place to support you." An awkward smile appeared momentarily on his face.

"Do you have any immediate questions that I can answer? I know it must be a lot to take in."

The words washed over her, flooding her with a deep sense of dread. Surely this couldn't be real? Was it some cruel joke? Her brain desperately searched for any alternative other than the one staring her in the face. But the pain was real. She knew that for certain. She looked down at her arm. The damage was unavoidably real.

Alice snapped her eyes shut immediately.

Don't look. Don't you dare look at it again.

She heard the doctor shift at the end of her bed. "It may be uncomfortable for a little while, but we are giving you pain relief to help. I'll let you rest some more, Alice, but I'll be back in the morning to check in on you again, okay?"

She nodded and then, without needing to be told twice, fell back into a deep, ignorant sleep.

Over the coming days, as she grew stronger, Alice found herself able to stay awake for more than a mere scattering of time. Her brain had slowly come round to the idea of working, which in turn meant she was finally able to take in her surroundings.

Bleak.

That was the first word that came to mind. *Soulless* was a fast follower. For a place that was constantly brimming with noise, it felt empty. There were always people busying themselves with one thing or another. Checking this. Reading that. Talking constantly. Alice knew she was alive only by the grace of the machines she was attached to. There were so many wires feeding into her she started to forget where the flesh ended and the mechanics began. She let herself be prodded and poked and discussed, all the while taking her mind and most important her gaze elsewhere. Every time she looked down, the evidence was there. It was as if the fire had been so incensed that she'd managed to escape with her life that it wanted to leave its mark on her indefinitely, and it had done its job well. The entire left side of her body was charred. Eaten up and spat out by the flames. In a bid to block out the state of her, she spent most of her time looking at the ceiling or at the insides of her eyelids. Sleep became the only place that felt familiar. The only place she didn't feel pain and the only place left for her to escape to.

Sleep also meant that she avoided the influx of people constantly checking on her like clockwork. Throughout her life she'd often wondered how it would feel to be looked after. How would it feel to be cared for with no questions asked or conditions to be met? Now that had become her reality, and it made her want to scream until her lungs bled raw. She knew they were just doing their jobs. She was fully aware that the nurses and doctors were *obliged* to care, but what wasn't required were the tears that would well up in their eyes every time they saw her. Nor was staying after hours to try to talk to her because for days in a row there had been no visitors by her bedside. A bitter resentment ignited inside her, flooding her body with poison and spilling out onto those around her. She recoiled at their touch; she despised their pity. It was nobody's job to take pity on her.

Often if sleep hadn't carried her away, she'd close her eyes and pretend during rounds. She couldn't stand looking at the same faces trying desperately to disguise their shock every single time they saw her. The same faces desperately trying to coax even a hint of a word from her mouth, but still she said nothing. At first it genuinely was too painful to try to speak. She'd breathed in so much smoke during the fire that as well as a melted face she'd also won a pair of lungs fit for a forty-a-day smoker. No matter how many liters of oxygen she was forced to inhale each day, the entirety of her throat still seared with pain. Alice was charred from the inside out. A truly well-done piece of meat.

Chapter 4

ALFIE

When he'd first been admitted into the hospital, everything felt strange. He didn't belong there. Nothing fit. Everything from the chlorinated smell of the air to the feel of the scratchy starched bedsheets to the sounds of the people was wrong. There was no space that was his, and he was constantly being walked in on, interrupted, or woken up by the doctors and nurses. He could feel the frustration mounting with every passing hour and the unfamiliarity was overwhelming. Every night he prayed he could be back in his home. Back in his little one-bed flat in Hackney surrounded by the safety of his life. Now he wasn't sure how he could ever go back to it. How would he sleep without the meditative beeping of the heart monitors? How could he wake up in his bedroom alone? Where would the faces of the other patients be when he needed company?

One of the rare perks of being a patient for so long was that you got pretty familiar with the dos and don'ts of hospital life. Six weeks was long enough to know what to eat and what to avoid from the menus every day, long enough to know which porters had a sense of humor and which could barely even blink, let alone crack a smile. It was also long enough to know which of the nurses would slip you an extra pudding at dinner and which of them you needed to be on your best behavior for. Luckily the Moira Gladstone ward contained more of the former than the latter. And none were kinder, more protective, and larger than life than Nurse Martha Angles, a.k.a. Mother Angel. There was nothing small about her; she was a woman who could fill a room with just her bust and her sense of humor, and she oversaw the rehab ward with a keen eye and an open heart.

"Good morning, my Mother Angel, how are you today?"

For the first time in a long time, Alfie actually enjoyed waking up early. You couldn't help but want to absorb every moment you could with Nurse Angles; she was one of those shiny people who you only really found once in a lifetime.

"Good morning, my love. Same old same old for me. Hank took me to the cinema last night—apparently I was asleep twenty minutes in! No clue what the film was about, but it was a wonderful sleep, I can tell you that for sure."

Hank was the love of Nurse Angles's life. Childhood sweethearts, married at eighteen, and with four lovely children. She adored him with every piece of her being, which also meant she moaned about him every waking hour.

"He really must love you to put up with your snoring on date night! Also, when are you going to introduce us? I need him to teach me how to find a woman like you."

She gave him a sharp, affectionate slap on the wrist. "Trust me, honey, finding them is the easy part—it's trying to keep them that's the hard work!"

"Amen, Nurse!" Sharon shouted from her bed. She was a recent divorcée and even more recent feminist.

Nurse Angles laughed a deep and chesty laugh. "Anyway, let's see how we're doing today." Her eyes glanced down at his bandaged stump.

"Really? Again?" Alfie knew he was being petulant, but quite frankly he wasn't in the mood to have his wound pulled and poked at today.

"Oh, so you want the swelling to come back, do you? You want the scar to burst and that thing to get infected again? Don't make me call orthopedics and have you transferred back. You don't think I'll do it, but I will!"

Alfie might not have been in the mood for his checks, but Nurse Angles was clearly not in the mood for his answering back. He'd been moved to the Moira Gladstone rehabilitation ward after completing his stints in intensive care and orthopedics. Alfie had been around the block a bit, and he knew this was the best place he could ever hope to end up. There was no way he was going to risk moving again.

"Sorry. Be my guest. I just don't like looking at it, that's all."

"I know, baby, but I'll be quick." She gently started to unwrap him. His skin lit up with sensations. It didn't hurt as such, although sometimes he wondered whether he'd experienced so much agonizing pain in the days after the accident that his threshold was much higher now. It was a bizarre feeling, like red-hot pins and needles coursing up and down his body. He flinched a little, and Nurse Angles rested her hand on his. "I know it's annoying, but this little bit of fuss far outweighs the risk of losing you. Not going to let that happen on my watch."

He knew she was right, so he lay back and closed his eyes. No matter how much time passed, seeing the wound still sent ripples through his body. He'd take all the pain in the world over looking at his scars. Those thick white lines represented everything he'd lost and would never be able to get back.

"Right, all done. Now, are you ready to storm that runway in physio this afternoon?" Nurse Angles had finished the wound checks as quickly and painlessly as she'd promised.

"Oh, you bet, big momma. Today's the day I nail it."

She gave him another of her gentle slaps and continued going through her routine assessment. Vital signs checked, measurements noted, and, most crucially of all, pillow fluffed.

"Now, Alfie, I need to ask you a favor." There was a slight change in her voice.

"Of course, what is it?"

She sat most of herself down on the edge of his bed. "There's going to be someone new moving in next door to you soon."

Alfie's heart leapt.

"Before you go and get too excited, I need to warn you: she's severely traumatized and hasn't spoken a word since she was admitted to the hospital."

Alfie's heart sank.

"How long has she been here?" Alfie couldn't imagine being silent for even an afternoon.

"A few weeks now." Nurse Angles inched a little closer to him. "Look, Alfie. I know you'll want to talk to her and try to become her friend, but please, I'm asking you to just leave it be for a while. Let her settle in. Give her some space until she's ready to start talking—okay, honey?"

Alfie was still perplexed by the idea that someone could be silent for so long. He was quite intrigued to witness how that could even happen!

"Alfie?"

"Sorry, of course. I won't say a word."

"There's a good boy." She patted the space on the bed where his left leg used to be, an unintentional reminder of what he lacked, and heaved herself out of his cubicle.

Alfie wondered how on earth this person had survived so long without talking. Surely that was an exaggeration? No one in their right mind could possibly volunteer to be quiet for that long. Throughout his life, numerous people had challenged Alfie to be silent. Once, in high school, he'd gone as far as to raise three thousand pounds to do a sponsored forty-eight-hour silence. He'd barely lasted the morning—but people were so proud of him they'd donated anyway! Alfie lived for conversation. He thrived on connection. In fact, one of the only things that got him through his days was annoying Mr. Peterson or catching up on the gossip with Sharon. Conversations were the fabric of existence on the ward, and without them Alfie could only imagine what a desperately lonely place it would be.

She won't last long.

How could she? He knew how adamant Nurse Angles was about this, but Alfie couldn't help his sneaking suspicion that the moment this mystery patient got sucked into the goings-on here, she wouldn't be able to resist joining in. That was the beauty of the Moira Gladstone ward. It wasn't like the ICU or the emergency room. People weren't in and out a revolving door. They stayed. They recuperated. They became family. It was only a matter of time before his new neighbor would follow suit.

Chapter 5

ALICE

One thing that Alice had managed to achieve during her time in the ICU was to piece together an idea of what on earth had happened to her. It had taken a while for her to sieve through the haze of her memory, move aside the broken debris of heat, smoke, and screaming to remember her movements that day.

She'd worked late the night before, so hadn't made her Pilates class first thing. She remembered that had annoyed her: missing even one was the start of a downward spiral of complacency. Two double espressos and a quick shower later, she was out the door and on her way just before 6 a.m.

Alice had worked long enough and hard enough to have earned herself a very comfortable salary and a very senior role in financial consultancy. She was fortunate enough, therefore, to have a choice when it came to buying her flat. She'd forced herself to look in the suburbs, at the beautiful homes that people had poured their creativity and love into. She went through the motions of requesting properties with preened gardens that drank in the sunshine and provided a green sanctuary in the concrete jungle of London. She insisted on extra bedrooms for future guests and potential offspring. And then she caught herself using the word *offspring* instead of *children* and dropped the pretenses. Alice Gunnersley prided herself on being one very independent, very single, and very cynical human being. She was never one to believe in anything that she couldn't see with her own eyes, measure with a stick, or at the very least read in a textbook. Alice was not the person with whom to engage in deep spiritual conversation; she quite frankly didn't give a shit about your hopes and dreams, and she certainly wasn't one for relying on anyone for anything. All Alice Gunnersley needed was convenience and solitude. And so came the purchase of a penthouse flat in Greenwich. She didn't have neighbors; she had views of the river and just enough of the park to convince herself she was surrounded by nature. Best of all, she could see her office from her flat, which always brought her a perverse sense of calm.

The day of the accident had been an especially stressful one at work. There was a big report that needed to be finalized before the end of the week, a report that if successful would cement Alice in the minds of the board when it came to identifying future partner talent. Unfortunately, standing between her and writing the extremely important report were endless meetings, project reviews, and financial budgeting tasks, plus an hour-long review with her boss. Alice often wondered why Henry insisted on having these meetings every month considering they pretty much had the exact same conversation every time.

"Alice, you are no doubt a phenomenal asset to this company. I've never met anyone with a work ethic and ability to deliver like yours. But you know that's not all that we value here at the firm. If you want to make it all the way to the top seat, you have to start taking people with you."

Taking people with you.

Another stupid HR phrase, she thought. *What does that even really mean, Henry?* She wanted to bite back, but instead she took a deep breath and smiled.

"I do take people with me, Henry. Look at the stats. I've promoted five members of my team this year alone and have the highest staff retention of everyone on the floor."

"I know." He shook his head in exasperation.

Alice knew that she wasn't exactly easy to manage, but she also knew that you couldn't argue with facts. So facts she always gave him.

"But that's not the point," he persisted.

"Well, Henry, I don't mean to be rude, but I've got a hell of a lot to do today, so I'd be grateful if you could get to your point quite quickly. . . ."

She knew her comments wouldn't surprise him. They'd worked together for more than ten years now, and Alice's ruthless commitment to her job had remained very much the same.

"The *point* is that there is more to life than this office. I just worry sometimes that you don't see that. You're here all hours of the day and night, and I'm just not sure it's particularly healthy. Plus, you rarely attend social events here, and I hardly ever see you interact with anyone other than to talk about deadlines. "

Alice frowned. Was he having some sort of emotional breakdown on her? She began to laugh.

"I see what this is. It's some new HR policy about employee health and well-being, isn't it? Look, you don't have to worry about me at all. I sleep, I eat, and I have some friends that I see from time to time. And I do talk to people here."

His eyebrow shot up. "Oh, really?"

"I talk to Lyla."

"She's your PA. You have to talk to her."

"Fine. I talk to Arnold."

Ha. She'd got him with this one.

"Arnold? Who the hell is Arnold?" His eyes narrowed as he desperately searched for the answer. He always squinted when he was thinking. It was a habit Alice couldn't stand.

Suddenly the penny dropped. "Oh Jesus, Alice. Not the old man on reception?"

"The very same one." She smiled smugly.

Henry rolled his eyes; she could tell his frustration was hitting new heights. "Right. Well, if you're really telling me that you have deep and meaningful conversations with Arnold, then who am I to judge?"

"Exactly." Alice stood up. "Are we done?"

Henry shrugged his shoulders; the man had all but given up. "Apparently so."

"Thanks, Henry." She didn't even bother to look at him as she left the room.

How strange, she thought. Why on earth was he so concerned with what she did with her life outside of work all of a sudden? Surely all he cared about was getting the best possible value for money out of her. And so what, Arnold wasn't exactly a *friend*, but as her role grew progressively bigger, he was the person she'd found herself seeing more than any other human being in her life. Five days a week, Arnold Frank Bertram manned the reception desk during the night shift at Alice's office. It was common practice for Alice to be the only remaining colleague in the building after 9 p.m., meaning that she and Arnold were the only breathing souls in the entire forty-floor office tower. Every night when she finally found the discipline to tear herself away and leave for home, there he'd be, waiting patiently at the front desk, eyes fixed on the front door. As soon as he saw Alice, his face would break into a smile.

"Another late one tonight, miss? Not worth doing if it's not done properly, ain't that right?"

For a long time, Alice would simply placate the man with a smile. It was a genuine, grateful smile, but nothing more. She could sense he was the talking type, in a wonderful, grandfatherly, storytelling kind of way, but at 11 p.m. on a Wednesday night with a 7 a.m. start the next day, Alice would challenge anyone to be up for a conversation. A smile would have to do.

But as time passed and her late nights often turned into early mornings, Alice found it harder and harder to ignore the old man and his continuous attempts at conversation. During one particularly hellish week after Alice had decided, at the godforsaken hour of 2 a.m., that she needed some fresh air, Arnold had been waiting for her with a cup of hot chocolate on her return.

"Got to keep your sugar levels up, miss." He smiled and nodded.

"Thank you." She didn't have any energy to protest and simply took the gift, realizing she in fact hadn't eaten since lunchtime that day. "How much do I owe you?"

"Nothing." He held his hands up. "You can get them to-morrow night." He winked, then returned dutifully to his desk

And so the strange nightly ritual began; alternating hot chocolate purchases and snippets of conversation with Arnold had become a standing agenda item in Alice's working day.

The night of the fire was no different, although for some reason the sugar rush hadn't done much to energize her. Alice had been working on the report since 10 p.m., but something wasn't quite sitting right with the tone of it. She distinctly remembered closing her eyes in the hope that a quick power nap was all that was needed to reenergize her brain. She'd drained the dregs of her hot chocolate and laid her head on the desk.

The authorities had later informed her that while she was sleeping, between 2 and 3 a.m., an air-conditioning unit on the floor above had caught fire and ripped the top of the building to pieces.

"You were lucky, miss," the police officer said after his fruitless attempts to gather as much information as possible from her for his reports. Even though she was getting stronger physically, her recollections were still based on other people's versions of events. A patchwork quilt of stories that she'd been forced to adopt as her own.

If this life was lucky, she dreaded to think of the alternatives.

"You have a very diligent receptionist. That man would have all but dragged you out himself if the fire rescue teams hadn't arrived when they did. The poor guy was distraught."

Arnold.

"He pretty much saved your life, Miss Gunnersley." The second officer looked imploringly at her, his desperation for even a hint of emotion or response blatant. She gave him nothing but a nod.

"All right, well, we will send you the full report when we've written it up. If you do have any questions, please don't hesitate to call."

Apparently Arnold really had been a friend. In fact, overnight he'd turned out to be one of the most significant people in Alice's life. He had saved her.

Now she wondered if it would have been better to let the fire take all of her instead.

Chapter 6

ALFIE

"Mr. P., you know what time it is!" Alfie heaved himself up and reached for his crutches.

The old man frowned. "Jesus, it's worse than being on a Butlin's holiday with the amount of activities you have planned. I'm not one of your bloody schoolkids, you know?"

In his old life, before the accident, Alfie had been a sports therapy and physical activity educator at a high school in South London. Back in his school days, he would have been called your run-of-the-mill PE teacher—but politics and status had firmly infiltrated the education system, and titles soon became a reflection of self-worth and ego. Alfie didn't care, he didn't need prestige or glory; he simply loved every second of his job. In fact, one of the hardest parts of being on the ward was how much he missed being surrounded by his pupils. Sure, he'd cursed them continuously throughout every waking moment he spent with them, but he wouldn't have changed them for the world.

"One day your misery will be the death of you," Alfie said. "Now, hurry up before they run out of all the chocolate brownies."

Despite Mr. Peterson's complaining, Alfie noticed he'd already got his slippers on, ready for their walk.

"Hurry up! That's rich, coming from you. Don't forget you're the one without a leg, son—I move at lightning speed compared to you."

"Are you two ever nice to each other?" Sharon's voice cut across the squabbling.

"Pipe down, Sharon," Mr. Peterson retorted. "Or I won't buy you that hot chocolate you've been moaning at me to get you for the past hour."

The bickering never stopped. Alfie sometimes wondered if without it everyone would be forced to remember that they were stuck in a hospital ward desperately fighting their own pain without the comfort of their families around them.

"You're worse than my Ruby, and she's just turned six! You should be ashamed of yourselves," Jackie called out from across the ward, her words still slightly mumbled from the stroke. Jackie was the only resident on the ward who had children and Alfie loved how even just the mention of her daughter would seem to momentarily ease some of her suffering. "But while you're there, Alfie . . . I'd kill for a cinnamon bun."

"Jesus, it's not a delivery service," Mr. P. mumbled.

"You know if you don't ply them with sugar they're even worse!" Alfie smiled at his friend, who had hooked his arm through his. He was a stubborn, strong-willed man, but at ninety-two Mr. Peterson was, understandably, physically frail.

Their twice-weekly walk to Costa Coffee was an excuse to escape from the ward and alleviate some of the cabin fever. Alfie knew he needed to keep practicing his walking, and

Mr. Peterson was a sucker for a hot chocolate, so it suited both parties perfectly.

"I had an interesting chat with Mother A this morning." Alfie tried to sound casual, knowing any hint of gossip would hook his friend in immediately.

"Oh yeah?" The old man's eyes lit up.

"Turns out I'm getting a new neighbor. A silent one."

"You what?" Mr. Peterson's face crumpled in confusion.

"There's someone moving into the bed next to me. Apparently she hasn't spoken in weeks, completely refuses to and has done ever since they admitted her. Nurse Angles says she's pretty traumatized." Alfie shrugged, still puzzled by the silent determination of this patient.

"I think she must be hurt pretty bad."

"Sure seems that way, doesn't it." Silence hung heavily between them as each focused intensely on their slow, shuffling steps.

"Well, give it a week or so, I reckon. These things always pass. And if not, then maybe she can teach you a thing or two about being quiet! Give us all some peace for a bit." The old man laughed loudly at his own humor.

"Or . . . most likely, I'll get her to cave, and in no time we'll *both* be spending our days irritating you." Alfie nudged his friend gently in the ribs, grateful for the lightness returning to their conversation.

Mr. Peterson rolled his eyes. "Good God—in that case, I pray the lady never speaks again!"

Chapter 7

ALICE

When Alice had first been told that she'd be moving wards, part of her was relieved. It meant progress was being made. She was no longer deemed in critical condition, and she was finally on the road back to her old life. Although her skin grafts had started to heal, the burnt flesh beneath them slowly recovering, she still hadn't spoken a word. What was there to say? All anyone wanted to hear from her was that she was "doing okay." That she was "feeling much better, thanks." Yet all they needed to do was take one look at her to know that was a lie. Not that *she'd* actually taken one look at herself since the accident. She had point-blank refused to open her eyes when the doctors had encouraged her to look at her reflection. All she had to do was look down at the congealed skin on her arms to get an idea of the damage done to her face. She didn't need a mirror to know that she was significantly damaged goods.

And still the overfriendly, overemotional, and incessantly

positive nurses carried on with their "weren't you lucky" bullshit.

"Weren't you lucky it only really affected one side of you, Alice."

"It's lucky you were rescued when you were or the damage might have spread to your right side too."

Oh, wonderful, she would have been *completely* fucked up then. How lucky she felt that she was only disfigured down one side of her body.

Lucky, lucky fucking Alice.

"Good morning, Alice. How are you?" the doctor said flatly. Why people persisted in asking her these questions baffled her. Silence continued to be her only answer, yet they kept trying.

"I've been looking at your notes, and I'm happy with your progress. The grafts are healing well and all the vital signs are stable." The doctor looked up from his clipboard and smiled, his weak attempt at positivity somehow more awkward than encouraging. "The next thing we need to do is build up your strength and mobility—you've been lying down for quite some time, and we need to prevent any further muscle waste. That's why we want you to move to the Moira Gladstone ward. It's a rehabilitation facility based in this hospital. It's one of the best in the country. You'll have a physio plan put in place and they'll continue to monitor the wounds, and when we know the extent of the scarring, we can discuss other options."

Nothing you do can give me back what I had.

"The only thing we're concerned about is . . ."

The fact I haven't spoken in weeks or looked at my own face? Alice strangely enjoyed watching this man struggle to find the appropriate words.

". . . we don't feel like you've made much progress on the

path to accepting the accident. We need you to start communicating, Alice. If you're going to get out of here, we have to be confident that you've accepted what's happened and can make positive steps forward."

Positive steps? Why don't we swap places, Doctor, and see how many positive steps you take.

She raised the corner of her mouth as a poor offer of acknowledgment.

"Alice." He inhaled a deep breath and took a step closer to her. "There *are* other options for you, but first we have to let the skin heal more. This isn't the end for you, I know it may feel like it now, but it isn't." The doctor reached his hand out momentarily, then let it fall limply by his side. "In order to make you feel most comfortable, we will move you tomorrow night. Any questions, you know we're here to answer them."

Unfortunately, it hadn't been possible to transport the curtains along with the bed, but at least the darkness just about hid her face as she was wheeled along the corridors. The moment she arrived on the Moira Gladstone ward, she sensed the change in energy. It was calmer. No rushing. No fear of immediate danger. People weren't running off of extreme adrenaline and caffeine twenty-four hours a day. As she rolled between the two rows of beds, Alice could just about make out the picture frames, multicolored bed throws, and trinkets. It seemed that the people occupying this space were no longer patients, they were residents. That was another stark difference from the ICU: all of these people had been given back the gift of time. In theory, they weren't going anywhere anytime soon.

Alice was woken the next morning by one of the nurses. This woman was big and bold and not afraid to confront the elephant in the room.

"Morning, baby."

Alice physically recoiled. She was definitely not this stranger's baby. Alice Gunnersley was, in fact, no one's baby.

"I'm Nurse Angles and I'll be overseeing your treatment while you're here. I know you're not comfortable talking, so whenever I ask you something all I need is a simple nod yes or a shake no, can we at least manage that? Otherwise it's going to be pretty hard for me to make sure you're comfortable."

Maybe she could forgive the terms of endearment if this nurse wasn't going to try to force her to talk. Alice nodded.

"Wonderful. Well, welcome to the Moira Gladstone ward. Let's do a quick change of your dressings, and then we can discuss the treatment plan."

Alice glared at Nurse Angles, keeping her arm just out of reach.

"I know it's uncomfortable, but I will need to change the dressing."

Uncomfortable? Just lying still was scarcely bearable. The itching of the skin as it tried to heal itself, knitting together with the foreign slabs of flesh they'd stitched onto her . . . any movement, even breathing, would tug and pull at the skin, making her wince in pain. Sometimes it was a sharp pain, like a hundred knives slashing and tearing at her; other times it was a deep, dull ache that would sit in her bones and weigh her down.

"I need to make sure your dressings are clean, Alice." The nurse tentatively reached for her arm again. "Please."

Reluctantly Alice allowed herself to be taken and tended to. She hated it when they did this. Not only did she have to feel the covering being peeled off her raw flesh, but also it meant she had to see the damage in all its glory. No hiding. No masking. A melting pot of skin and bone, fighting to heal but still falling short. Yet the exasperation in the nurse's voice pulled at something inside of her. She didn't mean to cause a fuss, but she had gone too long without saying anything and it felt too hard to break the silence now.

"I've been given the hand-over from your doctor, and there's a lot we need to start doing to get you fit, healthy, and out of here." Nurse Angles scanned the sheet of paper on her clipboard. "You're off the oxygen now—which is great—wound care will remain pretty much the same, pain relief can start to be decreased slowly, and we'll have to start physio." She squeezed herself into the chair next to Alice's bed. "And that, honey, means you're going to have to get yourself up and out of this bed."

Fear drenched her like ice-cold water. She couldn't. She wouldn't get up. Alice started to shake her head furiously; adrenaline made her stomach churn and her fists clench tightly. Nurse Angles rested her hand on the bed.

"It's okay, Alice. I'm sorry, I didn't mean to panic you." Alice felt her breathing slow just a little; the weight of Nurse Angles's hand next to her was having a strangely calming effect. "I know it's a lot to ask of you, but we do need to get you moving. You've been lying down for so long it's important we build your strength up quickly. Let me speak to the physio and see what we can do, okay?"

Alice closed her eyes and drew a long, deep breath into her lungs.

It's okay. It's going to be okay.

"I'll let you rest now, sweetie. Like I said, leave it with me and we'll work something out."

Just work out how you can stop this hell. Please.

Chapter 8

ALFIE

He knew his neighbor had arrived the moment he'd woken up. The curtains around the bay next to him were fully closed, and from inside he could hear the familiar sound of Nurse Angles running through her routine introduction. It was a rare occurrence to transfer people at night, so everyone on the ward knew the red carpet really was being rolled out. Alfie could see the familiar faces of the other patients craning their necks, trying to sneak a glimpse as Nurse Angles expertly extracted herself from the curtains without revealing an inch of what lay within.

Did you see her? Mr. Peterson mouthed, waving at him from across the corridor.

Alfie shook his head; it was too early and he was too tired from a rather disturbed night's sleep to respond properly. He tried to settle himself back down, longing for a few more hours of rest to help him get through the day. But just as he closed his eyes, he heard it.

A cough. A ragged, heavy, and painful cough coming from behind the tightly closed curtains.

He bit his tongue and resisted asking if everything was okay. The sound alone told him it was a no. The rest of the morning followed the same pattern: silence punctuated by that excruciating cough, over and over. It took Alfie a huge amount of self-control to stay quiet. It was in his nature to care; in fact, all Alfie ever wanted to do was help. That desire coupled with his uncanny ability to connect with people was the main reason why Alfie was so good at his job. "Those who can't, teach," everyone would joke. "Fuck that," he always said. "Those who can change lives, teach." But he had promised Nurse Angles to stay clear, so he needed to be cautious.

For the rest of the day Alfie did his best to distract himself. He managed to pass a good hour or two with his puzzle books, but it was hard not to get caught up in the hushed excitement that was mounting in the ward. The nurses would come and go, talking at her as they went, but still the lady behind the curtain said nothing. The other patients became so intrigued as to who the mysterious new guest was that they started to gather in small groups, whispering their suspicions and throwing wild guesses around like confetti.

"Do you think she's even in there?" Jackie asked.

"This isn't some elaborate joke they're playing on us! Of course she's in there." Mr. Peterson laughed dismissively.

"I'm going to ask the nurses about her. The young ones always let slip things they shouldn't." Sharon's voice rose in excitement.

Alfie lay in his bed half listening to the mutterings of his friends and half worrying that the woman next to him could hear them as they hovered next to her curtains. Maybe she was asleep? Maybe that would explain her silence.

"Can we not just stand around blocking the corridor, please?" One of the nurses strode through the ward. "Surely you have better things to do with your time?"

His friends shifted a little uncomfortably.

"There is one thing we need to discuss . . ." another of the younger, more enthusiastic nurses chimed in. "What film are we going to watch for movie night tonight?"

"*Pretty Woman!*"

"Oh, give it a rest, Sharon, you know you're the only one who wants to watch that god-awful film. Plus it's not exactly pro-feminism, is it?"

"Stop being such a grumpy old git and instead of moaning about everyone else's choice, why don't you suggest something?"

"Yeah, Mr. P., why don't you pick something tonight?" Alfie piped up, sitting a little taller in bed.

"Ach, no, I can't be doing with all that decision-making. Is Ruby coming in tonight, Jackie?"

"Yeah, Mum and Dad are bringing her in after school. She should be here soon." Jackie checked her watch anxiously.

"Well, then, the decision is made for us, isn't it?" Mr. Peterson said, looking around at the other patients.

"*Finding Dory* it is then!" The younger nurse laughed.

"I am going to be able to recite that film word for word by the time I leave this place," the old man grumbled, making his way slowly back to his bed.

"Oh, come off it. You know you love it, even if it's just to see the look on Rube's face when you tell her we're watching it," Alfie called out to him.

Jackie and Ruby's story was one of the most tragic Alfie had come across during his time in the hospital. Despite her only being a visitor, everyone on Moira Gladstone seemed to go out of their way to make the hospital feel like home for Ruby. Even the nurses didn't mind making more work for themselves if it meant making Ruby's smile a little bigger. It took a certain kind of person to say no to a twelve-year-old girl whose dad had died from cancer a year ago and whose mum, Jackie, was currently in a rehabilitation unit recovering from a stroke.

"Hey, old man, while you're up, do you fancy going for a stroll?"

"Old man! The bloody cheek of it!" Mr. Peterson grumbled. "But fine, I could do with a muffin anyway. I'm starving."

"I'm not sure Agnes would agree with that. Aren't you meant to be on a new health regimen?"

Mr. Peterson didn't even bother to respond; the murderous glare was enough. Agnes was the love of his life, but apparently not even sixty-four years of marriage could keep the old man away from his cake.

"Noted. No new health regimen." Alfie chuckled to himself as he swapped his crutches for his prosthetic. He'd thought that over time he'd get used to it, but even the sight of the plastic limb made him angry. It had hurt at first, so badly that he'd cry out with every step. Hours and hours of ruthless physio had taught him well, but his walk was still marred by signs of discomfort. He was slow and uneven, and often had to stop for breaks. His strength was up but by no means back to normal, plus his whole body had to constantly adjust and shift its weight to accommodate the new addition attached to him. He tried not to think anymore about how he looked when he walked, instead choosing to focus on how lucky he was to have the privilege to even take a step.

As the two companions returned to the ward, steaming cups of sickly sweet hot chocolate and blueberry muffins in hand, they saw Sharon waiting for them at the entrance.

"You won't *believe* what I've just heard." Her green eyes were wide with excitement. The joy that gossip brought to this lady's life was quite unbelievable.

Mr. Peterson rolled his eyes; as much as he'd deny it, he loved the pieces of information Sharon offered—he just didn't like her to know that. "What is it this time?"

Sharon smirked. "It's about that lady in bed thirteen. The mute one."

"She's not mute, Sharon, she's traumatized." Alfie sighed.

"Okay, well, you know what I mean. I heard that every time she gets up out of her bed, we all have to stay hidden away in ours with the curtains closed. Can you believe it? It's like a mini lockdown!"

"Where on earth did you hear that?" Alfie loved Sharon, but he had to admit he didn't always trust her.

"I overheard the nurses talking about it just now. So not only is she refusing to speak, *but* she's point-blank refusing to let anyone see her. They didn't sound best pleased. I'm not surprised, though, who does this woman think she is!" Sharon suddenly gasped so loudly that Alfie nearly gave himself whiplash looking behind him. "Maybe she's *royalty*." Her eyes were so wide they occupied half of her face.

"Give over. What planet are you on?" Mr. Peterson looked genuinely pained by her wild fantasy. "They wouldn't send a member of the royal family to this place!"

"You don't know that for certain." Sharon folded her arms, clearly a little put out.

"No, but I would bet the rest of my years left on this planet that she isn't royalty." The old man turned to Alfie. "Find out what the hell is happening, will you? I can't be dealing with all this fussing. Now, come on, let's get back inside. My drink's getting cold."

Alfie wasn't filled with quite the same confidence, but he knew it couldn't hurt to ask. "Fine, but I can't promise you I'll get anywhere. This patient might turn out to be the hospital's best-kept secret!"

The three of them made their way back through the ward.

"Agnes is visiting later and I need to finish all this before she gets on at me again about my sugar levels." Mr. Peterson took a giant swig from his cup. "In the meantime, kid, you better hurry up and get to work on uncovering this bloody mystery. If anyone can get information out of Nurse Angles, it's you."

"Yes, and the moment you find out anything, you better tell me!" Sharon smiled sweetly, poking Alfie hard in the chest before making her way back to her bed.

"Let's give it a day at least and then I'll start asking questions."

His friends didn't look satisfied by Alfie's proposal, but he knew this would be a waiting game. A test of patience. Something Alfie found incredibly difficult, but something he knew he'd have to get good at pretty quickly.

"One step is a step closer . . ." he muttered to himself.

Chapter 9

ALICE

"Who's in that bed, Mum?"

Alice woke lazily from her sleep and could see the shadow of a little figure standing outside of her bay.

"What, sweetie?" A voice from the other end of the room drifted past.

"Next to Alfie. The curtains are closed. Is someone in there?"

Then the girl started to raise her hand. Alice saw the tiny pearl fingertips grip the material that was keeping her hidden and safe. Everything was moving in slow motion. How on earth was she going to get this little girl away? Should she scream? She wasn't sure her voice could take it, but she had to do *something*.

"Ruby! No!" one of the nurses barked. The little girl dropped the curtain immediately. "Sorry, honey, I didn't mean to shout. It's just there's someone behind there who doesn't want visitors today."

Alice could see another silhouette steering Ruby away. Beads of sweat had appeared on her forehead and her heart was thumping in her chest.

"But who doesn't want visitors?" The surprise in Ruby's voice made Alice's heart sink. "Everybody wants friends, don't they?"

"Yes, of course they do. Just not right now. Come over here and show your mum that card trick I taught you yesterday, okay?"

Alice watched as the silhouettes faded away, but the little girl's question rang loudly in her ears.

It was her third day on the ward, and Alice realized that her "lie back and let the days pass you by" plan wasn't going to be as easy to execute as she'd hoped. In fact, from the very first morning she could see the outlines of other patients strolling past her curtains, subtly lingering in the hope that they might snatch a look at her. Failing any sightings, the whispers had started, and she'd definitely heard "have you seen her yet?" float past more than a couple times. Clearly this wasn't a ward where you could keep yourself to yourself. Mostly she managed to ignore it, relying on her old friend sleep to take her away; but sometimes, if the shape of someone lingered a little too long or stood a little too close to her curtain, her heart rate would spike and anxiety would begin to course through her veins. This, however, had been the closest call yet, and Alice's breath had barely steadied before she heard someone else approaching.

"Alice, dear, I'm coming in, if that's okay?" Nurse Angles's face was already poking through the curtain before she'd finished talking. Alice knew it wasn't going to be good news by the way Nurse Angles hung tentatively at the foot of her bed, quite the opposite of her normal brash entrance.

"I know we discussed the importance of physio the other day, and I also know how intimidating being up and about in front of the other patients is for you. So we've made a compromise. This is only temporary, just while you build up your confidence, and it's important you understand that. We can't do this forever, okay?"

Alice wasn't quite sure what she was agreeing to just yet, so she didn't dare make any movement of acknowledgment.

"When you have your sessions, we'll ask everyone on the ward to remain in their bays with the curtains closed while we transport you to the female lounge, which we've managed to reserve for an hour. It will be just you, the physio, and a couple of the nurses, okay?"

Relief and fear swirled in her stomach.

"We have to get you up and moving, Alice. There's no room for negotiation about that part." Her face was stern. "We start now."

Tears filled her eyes and she shook her head in resignation. Why? Why were they making her do this? Hadn't she been through enough?

Nurse Angles placed her hand gently on Alice's feet. "I know this is hard for you, honey, but I cannot let you rot away in this bed forever. The sooner we start, the quicker it's over with."

Alice didn't even look up; she could hear the nurses outside the curtain waiting for the green light from Nurse Angles. She was being moved whether she liked it or not.

On any other day, the sight of a wheelchair being presented to her would have caused Alice to revolt. Right now, however, she had much bigger concerns. The dissatisfied moans from her fellow patients barely registered with her. The nurses flocking to her bedside waiting and watching her failed to anger her. All Alice could think about was Nurse Angles's hand on the curtain ready to pull it back.

"Everyone's in bed and all curtains are closed," the young nurse reported dutifully. If this weren't happening to Alice right now, she probably would have enjoyed the absurdity of the situation. A military operation just for her. Because she was too bloody stubborn and too goddamn scared of her own face to get out of bed.

"Right, Alice, can you swing your legs over the edge of the bed and we can help lower you into the chair?"

What if she said no? If she refused to move, what was the worst that could happen? Were they really going to force her out of bed? Judging by the look on Nurse Angles's face, Alice didn't want to know the answer to that question.

Alice shifted ever so slightly to sit up taller. Slowly she began to slide her right leg across the bed and down. She didn't know what the fuss was all about—sure, it felt a bit stiff, but she was fine. Then came the left leg. The first attempt at movement set her nerves alight. The wound coverings shifted across her skin, sending shivers down her spine. How had she become so weak?

"Try to use your arms, honey." Nurse Angles was watching her with such intensity it hurt to look.

Alice planted her hands down on either side of her hips. Her face had tightened in concentration, and she could feel the frown lines digging deep into her forehead.

Come on, just lift yourself up.

Alice pushed down as hard as she could, but immediately felt her arms give way.

She felt the room hold its breath.

"Do you mind if I help you?" Nurse Angles stepped forward cautiously. What else could Alice do? Hang off the side of the bed until she practically fell onto the floor? The humiliation of it burnt a hole inside her chest. What had she become? This accident had taken more than just her looks: it had sucked away every last drop of pride and strength that she had left. The shame of it all was too much to bear. Reluctantly Alice nodded her head.

"Okay, sweetie. I'm just going to really gently move this leg, okay? Just squeeze my arm if I'm hurting you."

Slowly and ever so gently, Nurse Angles lifted her left leg up and round. It felt so foreign to be held like this. Sadness and repulsion collided, making Alice's head swim with nausea.

Let it be over, please, God, let it be over.

"Wonderful, you're doing amazingly. Now, I'm going to ask you to shift your weight onto me and I'm going to lower you into the chair, okay?"

It was like being a child again—helpless, useless, and entirely dependent on someone else. The whole ordeal made Alice want to rip herself apart and scream until the entire hospital felt her pain, but instead she surrendered, falling limply into Nurse Angles's arms and allowing herself to be carried into the chair.

"Perfect. Now, let's wheel you out quickly and get you with Darren." Her calm, controlled voice was the only anchor keeping Alice from losing it completely. "Sally, open the curtains, please."

And just like that, Alice was rolled out into the big, wide world of the ward.

Chapter 10

ALFIE

Alfie had tried not to listen to the sounds of the scene next door, but it was impossible not to. He winced, listening to the encouragement of Nurse Angles, remembering all too well how it felt to struggle to hold yourself upright. The unbelievable amount of strength it took to move even an inch. How demoralizing it was to be carried like a defenseless infant. Alfie knew how any scrap of pride or ego could be completely shattered overnight as in the blink of an eye your survival was placed in the hands of a team of complete strangers.

Guilt and, as much as he was loath to admit it, pity started to rise up inside of him. How unfair they'd all been. Sharon had been wrong. His neighbor hadn't demanded anything; this had all come from Nurse Angles as a desperate ploy to help her. He vowed to put the record straight and tell Sharon as soon as he could.

The sound of the wheelchair being rolled back across the floor was the signal they'd all been waiting for. The session had finished. It was over. But no one dared move an inch until Nurse Angles had spoken.

"Right, everyone, you're free to get up," Nurse Angles's voice rang out over the ward a little while later.

"About bloody time too!" Mr. Peterson groaned loudly.

"Until next time you herd us all back in like cattle again!" Sharon barked.

"How long are we going to have to do this for, Nurse? I'll make sure I've got snacks next time," Jackie called.

"Every other week until I say otherwise. So you better get the food supplies sorted sharpish."

Disgruntled mumblings and restless shuffling rippled down the ward, but despite the green light, no one moved. Curtains remained firmly closed and the patients stayed dutifully in their beds. Whether it was out of lethargy or protest, Alfie couldn't be sure; all he knew was that even his trusted puzzles couldn't distract him. No matter how hard he tried, his thoughts kept wandering back to her. When he'd heard her being wheeled through the ward, an overwhelming urge had come over him to take a look. All he'd have to do was take a small peek through his curtains. All he wanted was a glimpse of the person at the center of the whole drama. Who was this woman? How badly was she hurt? Even to see the back of her head would have given him some strange satisfaction—but he knew better. The nurses would be on red alert for any peeping Toms, and Alfie didn't fancy being called out as the rule breaker in front of everyone. Plus curiosity was no excuse for disrespect.

Taking a deep breath, he hauled himself up, reaching this time for his crutches rather than the dreaded prosthetic. After walking his stump would often be sore and sensitive, so he'd allow himself to take a break. Even though the confinement had officially ceased, he still felt nervous about leaving his bay. An old childish fear of being told off lingered over him.

"Mother A, have you got a minute?" Alfie approached the nurses' station cautiously.

"Of course." She looked flustered and a bit out of sorts.

"What's going on?"

"What do you mean, what's going on?" Her eyebrows began to knit themselves together in the center of her forehead.

"With the lady in bed thirteen."

Nurse Angles stopped her filing and turned to face him square-on. "I told you that she was traumatized, Alfie, before she'd even got here. I warned you."

"I know, but I guess I didn't realize quite how badly. Surely this 'shut everyone away while she finally ventures out into the big, wide world' debacle can't go on forever."

"Really, Alfie? I'm surprised! I thought you of all people would be up for helping her come out of her shell."

"I am. I just don't quite understand why she's getting all this special treatment?" He loathed how childish and spoilt he sounded.

"It's not your job to understand, Alfie. But if you really want to know, the poor girl hasn't spoken a word since she got here, plus to top it off she hasn't had a single visitor either. Her emergency contact is all the way in Australia, apparently, and nobody can get hold of her. There's no one else, okay, Alfie? No one. So if it's all right with you, we've taken the decision to give her some extra support."

Nurse Angles had never spoken to him like this before. Her eyes were wide in defiance and her breathing had grown heavy. She looked like she was readying herself for a battle that not even Alfie was foolish enough to fight. The shame started to swell up into his chest.

"No one has been to see her?" The words were only really starting to sink in.

"I shouldn't have told you that—sorry, I forgot myself for a second." She shook her head in frustration. "It's just . . . she needs our help, Alfie, and I'm doing the best I can."

The exasperation in her voice hit him the hardest. The indestructible Mother A suddenly seemed so helpless and lost.

"Trust me, if anyone is going to help her, it's you. She's the luckiest person to have landed in your care, and I promise, I'll do whatever I can to support you." He felt relief flood into his body as he saw the smile return to her face.

"Thank you, Alfie. Now, get on your way, I'm sure you've got better things to do than accompany me round the ward."

"Oh yeah, you know me, too busy for my own good! The choice of activities in this place is just *endless*."

"Behave yourself, will you, and go! I've got work to do," she said, shooing him away.

As he made his way back to his bed, he stared at the closed curtains of bed thirteen. The guilt bubbled up inside of him as thick and heavy as tar, coating his chest and stomach.

"Who are you?" he whispered.

All he got in response was her silence.

Chapter 11

ALICE

Within an hour she was back in the safe confines of her bay. It had been an emotionally and physically exhausting sixty minutes, and Alice felt as broken as on the day she'd woken up from her accident. Every muscle ached but none more so than her heart. How would she ever be able to do this again, let alone every other week as the doctors had ordered?

"You did great today, Alice. The first one is always going to be the hardest, but give it time. It will get easier, I promise," Nurse Angles cooed as she tucked her back into bed.

Alice closed her eyes and let the weight of her head hit the pillow.

"If you need anything, you know where I am, just buzz me, okay?"

The only thing Alice needed was to be alone. To try to erase that shameful hour of her life from her mind and pretend nothing had ever happened. If she'd thought the journey to physio was mortifying, then actually *doing* it was a whole different level. Trying to stand unassisted was impossible. Moving farther than three inches was a no-go. How had she regressed to this? Any ounce of ego she might have had left had been officially squashed. Any self-respect or dignity she'd clung to had been firmly ripped out of her grasp. She'd become so weak, so fragile. All that remained of her was an empty shell, ready to be blown over by the lightest breeze. Every time she moved, the entire left side of her body protested. The skin would pull at the seams, and at any moment Alice was certain she'd tear apart. It was as though someone were rubbing her down with razor blades, peeling away layers of her until she'd be reduced to nothing.

Luckily the rest of the day passed like clockwork. It turned out that this ward followed a very similar routine to the one she'd come from. In fact, practically everything about the place was the same. As she was being wheeled across to physio, she'd been able to take her first proper look at the space in daylight. There were the same beige walls, the same plastic furniture, the same harsh strip lighting. There were the same eight beds, four on each side of the room, separated from each other by the same blue cloth curtains that offered as much privacy as a piece of paper. Every room was a near-perfect replica of the one next to it, all designed with the sole intention to be sterile and inoffensive. Unfortunately, there was nothing inoffensive about the smell that lingered. It was a heady mix of human effluence and bleach, as though someone was desperately trying to clean away the sweat, blood, and tears that exuded from the inhabitants. It turned out that grief, fear, and death weren't easy to remove. To her relief, sleep came quickly that night, gathering her in its arms and taking her away from the reality of her day. In her dreams she could slot easily back into her old life, with her functioning limbs and smooth, unblemished skin. For those few hours, Alice could be free at last.

"Cornflakes for breakfast again this morning. The most boring cereal on the planet."

Alice stirred, roused by a voice coming from the bed next to her. It was soft and almost gentle, just loud enough for her to hear. There was lightness to its tone, a boyish mischief that sang of careless days and freedom. Maybe she was still dreaming—surely no one could feel anything but despair in a place like this.

"Who on this entire earth actually enjoys eating cornflakes? I get that they are a classic staple of the cereal population, but I'd like to meet one person who would actually choose them for breakfast."

Alice, fully awake now, shifted in bed. Surely he wasn't talking to her?

"Out of every other sugar-coated carbohydrate you could select for breakfast, why would you pick cornflakes? I just don't get it. Do you know what I mean, neighbor?"

Oh God, he's talking to me. . . .

"Maybe we'll be lucky and they'll surprise us with Coco Pops tomorrow. God, I used to love those. The kids at school go wild for them. Actually, they go wild for anything smothered in chocolate."

Please stop. For both of our sakes, stop talking.

"Look at me talking at you without even introducing myself. I'm Alfie."

Hi, Alfie, guess what? I don't care.

"On behalf of everyone here, I'd just like to say welcome to the Moira Gladstone ward! We do hope you have a pleasant stay here. Just some admin before you settle in: to your right are the female washrooms and to your left are the male. Please don't get them confused, otherwise you'll probably experience a whole new level of trauma. Entertainment will vary throughout your stay, but you'll see that as part of your deluxe room you have your very own television set. Unfortunately Sky isn't included, but I find Channel Five has a surprisingly good selection of documentaries in the afternoons."

He just about paused for breath.

"In all seriousness, we're a bit of a mixed bunch here, but we're all just trying to get ourselves back on our feet. Or in my case, foot! I don't know about you, but I find it so weird how quickly you get used to hospital life. How long have you been here in total now?"

Jesus, man, will you stop?

". . . Anyway, probably long enough to get used to people prodding and poking at your body every day. When I get out of here, I think I might actually miss it! Waking up won't be the same without Nurse Angles giving me the once-over, you know?"

She did not know. In fact, she was actually counting the seconds until no one had to touch her again.

And right now she was counting the seconds until he left her alone.

"I don't know how you do it, to be honest. The not-talking thing, I mean. It would drive me *crazy*."

The only thing driving me crazy right now is you. . . .

"Hey, neighbor, do you like puzzles?"

He wasn't even pretending to wait for her response now. She rolled over and closed her eyes, praying harder than ever for sleep to come and drag her away.

"I've always been obsessed with them. Never go anywhere without a puzzle pocket book with me just in case, I don't know, I find myself stuck on a long-term-care hospital ward with every day full of nothing to do. It's good to keep the brain active."

She hoped that his brain would shortly become very much inactive. She didn't know how much more of this she could take. The silence seemed to be egging him on, as if she were challenging him to try harder. But despite the constant stream of words bombarding her, she remained stoic and mute.

"Alfie, what the hell are you doing?" A nurse's voice interrupted his monologue.

"Nothing. Just talking to myself." He didn't sound even a tiny bit embarrassed to be caught out. Alice rolled her eyes and silently praised the nurse for her timing.

"Sure . . . well . . . you have physio now, so I need you up and out of here."

"Okay, I'm coming. Give me a second to put my leg on, will you?"

"Of course. Darren is waiting for you in the normal spot." Alice heard the nurse's footsteps fade away.

"I'll be back in a bit, neighbor. Don't get too lonely without me," he called back as she heard the curtains swish closed behind him.

Alice bathed in the glorious silence once more, allowing her thoughts to roam as they pleased, something she'd never really been afforded in her old life. There was always something to do, somewhere to be, lists to be worked through. God, how she missed being busy. Now the only activity on her list was keeping an ear out for the sound of her neighbor's returning footsteps. A mere two hours later, and she was greeted once again with the sound of him.

"Christ, that was a tough one." He was trying to sound up-beat, but Alice could hear the weariness in his voice. "Darren doesn't go easy, does he?"

He's tired. He'll shut up in a minute.

Luckily, this time Alice was right. As the day wore on, his attempts at conversation grew few and far between until eventually, as night fell, the only sounds she heard from his side were the deep sighs and yawns of someone on the cusp of dreaming.

"Wake up!"

Her eyes snapped open. What the hell was going on?

"Please."

Alice was wide awake now, struck with the sharp realization that the cries were coming from the man next door.

"Ross, please."

His mumbling was growing more urgent and desperate. He seemed to be reliving something awful. Alice held her breath as she bore witness to the pain. The moans and the cries. It was all just muffled noise. Terrible, heartbreaking noise until—

"Ross. Ross. Please, God, wake up!"

The murmurings were getting louder and more panicked. Alice prayed that someone would come and shake him awake, but no respite arrived. What the hell was she supposed to do? She couldn't wake him up. Wait—what if this was some sick joke he was playing? What if this was his twisted way of getting her to talk?

Then she heard it.

"Ciarán, no! No. No. No. Please, no."

It was a cry that shook with horror, a cry that rang out with such pain that it reduced Alice to tears. This was anything but a joke.

Chapter 12

ALFIE

He woke with a start.

"Jesus Christ, pull yourself together." He couldn't help the words coming out. Tired of going through his own version of hell and back, Alfie felt his fear morph into deep frustration. Why was he doing this to himself again?

Such a weak, stupid idiot.

As he said the words over and over in his head, his fist started to punch his surviving leg hard on the thigh. He wanted to fight this stupidity out of him, drum in some sense and logic.

"Don't do that, it's the only one you've got, remember." A quiet voice lingered just outside his curtain.

"Mr. P.?" Shame flooded him. Thank God his face was hidden from view.

"Aye, kid. Now, try to get some rest, got some tricky crossword clues for you in the morning and I need you in top form."

"Okay." A tear escaped down his face. Alfie closed his eyes and swallowed down the ball of sadness that had lodged itself in his throat. He heard his friend's footsteps shuffling back across the room. If he'd woken up Mr. Peterson, there was no way his neighbor was still sleeping. Still she'd not said a word.

As he lay there coated in sweat and barely able to breathe, he grew frustrated at how regularly he was finding himself back here. He'd spent so long trying to block out the flashbacks and bury what he couldn't bear to remember about the accident. It seemed that just when he thought he'd done it, his brain served him a cruel reminder that the battle wasn't over just yet.

When he'd first come around after the crash, he hadn't been able to recall much. The serious head injury he'd sustained had wiped most of the details from his mind. This, he often thought, was a small blessing. Then the episodes started. Thick and fast. He couldn't believe it: just as he was starting to feel more stable, it was as though his brain had decided to flick the switch and take him right back to square one. His mind would visit the wreckage regularly, sometimes multiple times a day. No sleep needed. It would just take him over, at random and without permission. He'd never felt so out of control in his life. This wasn't your average nightmare. This was real. This was time travel. His nose would burn with the toxic mix of petrol, humans, and rubber. His ears would be filled with the deafening crash, the screaming and the crying. He could see the broken remains of their car from where he'd been thrown on the tarmac. Crumpled like paper. Trapped under the lorry whose path it had been forced into. Then he'd see them, and his world would come crashing down around him all over again.

At first he thought something specific might be triggering the flashbacks—a smell, a word, a time of day. He drove himself mad trying to pinpoint the exact things that dragged him back kicking and screaming to that night. No matter how hard he tried, Alfie soon had to accept that no amount of analysis would give him an answer. His brain had decided to throw rhyme and reason straight out the window, and it was simply hijacking him as and when it felt like it.

The worst part always seemed to be the morning after. His entire body would hurt and the sleepless night would leave him drained of all energy. But he knew that, no matter how exhausted he felt, he had to find a way to drag his positivity out of the closet and put the mask on.

"Fake it till you make it, honey," his mum had always told him. "Trust me, during the dark days, it was the only thing that got me through. I'd put a smile on my face and force a couple of laughs, and then one day, I didn't have to pretend anymore. If you believe something enough, if you tell yourself it every moment of every day, then soon enough it will come to be."

He knew that if anyone had the means to survive the curve-balls that life threw at you, it was his mum. And so he faked it. He faked it every single day until it started to become normality. Some days were harder than others, of course, but no matter how he was feeling on the inside, he made sure to wear a smile on the outside. Today was no different.

"Morning, Mother A!" he called, forcing his voice to be bright and breezy.

"Hi, Alfie." She looked distracted and almost concerned. Who was that with her? Alfie watched as the two women made their way past his bed to hover just outside of the closed curtains of bed thirteen.

"Alice, guess what—you have a visitor today!"

Alfie's eyes widened. Oh God, it was really happening! Someone had come for her.

"Alice, sweetheart, did you hear me? Your mum has arrived!"

Chapter 13

ALICE

Alice didn't even acknowledge what the nurse had said at first because there was absolutely no way on this earth she could be talking to her. Her best friend, Sarah, was still safely in Australia, and she'd given no one else as an emergency contact.

"Alice, sweetheart, did you hear me? Your mum has arrived!"

Fuck, fuck, fuck, fuck, fuck.

Was she dreaming? She'd barely got any sleep last night. Maybe she was hallucinating?

"Alice, can we come in?"

No way. There was no way in hell her mother was standing outside her curtain right now. The only people in the world who could possibly know where she was were work and Sarah. Alice knew that even if Sarah had miraculously found out about the accident, she wouldn't dare betray Alice in such a way. But why the hell would her mum contact her work? Did her mum even know where she worked? Too many questions were firing through her brain, but there was no time to seek the answers.

"Now, remember, Mrs. Gunnersley, Alice has been through a lot, but it's still your little girl in there. Don't forget that."

That was probably the bit her mother would hate the most: that underneath all that scarring, it was still the same old Alice. The same little girl she hadn't seen in fifteen years. It was the very same daughter she'd resented for being alive ever since the day they lost him.

Unfortunately for Alice, it was also the very same mother she'd left behind. When the curtain was drawn back, Alice found herself looking into the same soulless eyes she'd known as a young girl. Nothing. No reaction whatsoever. As much as she despised the flinching and wincing when people saw her for the first time, she was surprised how much more the blank stare hurt. Her mother didn't even care enough to react.

"Right . . ." Even Nurse Angles was reeling from the distinct lack of emotion. "I'll leave you both to it. Alice, honey, you know how to reach me if you need anything?"

Nurse Angles took Alice's hand and gave it a slight squeeze. Fixing her gaze on Alice, she whispered just loudly enough for her to hear, "I'm right outside if you need me, okay?"

Alice managed a weak smile, appreciating the understanding that passed between her and Nurse Angles. If she needed her mother gone, all she had to do was buzz. Alice could be saved if she needed to be.

As Nurse Angles turned to go, Alice sneaked a quick look at her mother, who was clearly unsure whether she would be staying long enough to warrant sitting down, or if in fact she should just stay standing. Standing it was.

"Well, I can't say I was surprised that you didn't tell me. But seeing you like this, good God, Alice, how could you?"

Hold on, how could she what?

Where the hell was her mother going with this one?

"At least look at me, for Christ's sake!"

Alice lifted her gaze and stared at her defiantly.

"How could you nearly *die* and not tell me? Don't you think I've been through enough? You think it's okay to let your mother lose another child without telling her? When would I have found out? Would I have even been invited to the funeral? Jesus, Alice how could you? No reply to my texts, what was I meant to do? I had to call your office. How mortifying that a mother doesn't know where her daughter is. Luckily your boss thought it *was* appropriate to tell a mother that her child was nearly dead."

It was quite amazing how much resentment words could carry. Her mother never raised her voice or changed the expression on her face, but it was there, spat out with every single word that came from her mouth.

Alice could feel a fire starting to rise up inside her. It felt just as destructive as the one that had claimed her body, but this time it was working its way from inside out. A part of her wanted to bite back—hit this hateful woman standing in front of her with a thousand spiteful words—but all she had in her arsenal was silence. She closed her eyes and tried to steady her breathing.

You're not a little girl anymore, Alice.

She repeated the words over and over in her mind until she had regained some control. She opened her eyes and smiled.

"Really? They said you weren't talking, but you won't even speak to your own mother now? Did the fire take your voice as well as your looks?"

Alice clenched her fists, fingernails digging so deeply into her flesh that she had to bite down on her lip to stop herself from screaming. Their eyes were still locked; it was clear that her mother was not willing to give up. Maybe it would be easier to just speak, but Alice's silence was clearly more enraging to her mother than an onslaught of insults ever could be. She wouldn't give her the satisfaction.

The standoff lasted for what felt like hours until finally Alice tore her eyes away and closed them.

"Well, if you really have nothing to say to me, I guess I'll just go."

With a slight bow of acknowledgment, her mother turned and left. And for the first time since she was a little girl, Alice Gunnersley shed tears for her mother.

Chapter 14

ALFIE

If following a complete stranger weren't considered such a taboo, Alfie would have been tempted to go after the little Irish lady just to make sure she was real. He couldn't quite believe the words he'd overheard had come from the mouth of the woman he'd seen walk in just twenty minutes ago. She had looked so small and withered it was as though she were merely a paper cutout of a human being. A small, crinkled head peeped out of the collar of her jacket, revealing a face lined with desperation and exasperation. Alfie had assumed it was hearing that her daughter had nearly been killed in a fire that had knocked the wind out of her—how wrong he'd been. Even when she'd turned back momentarily and caught his eye, there was no emotion in her expression. She was cold through to her core.

Should I have said something?

He'd spent the rest of the morning restless. He couldn't seem to erase the conversation he'd been privy to from his mind. He knew that incidents like this were often best left alone; family drama was difficult to navigate when it was your own, let alone trying to get involved in a complete stranger's! He didn't even know this woman, but to simply ignore it went against everything he strived to be as a person. Maybe he'd say something tomorrow morning. Let the dust settle and allow the silence to continue for just a little longer. The silence that had now become a permanent fixture, hanging heavy between them like the faded blue curtain itself.

As a way to remove the temptation, Alfie spent most of his morning up and about, hanging out in other people's cubicles and finding every opportunity to annoy Mr. Peterson.

"Why are you over here again, boy? Can't you see I'm trying to read?"

"Agnes has bridge today, so I thought you might fancy the company. Plus you've been on the same page for the last hour, Mr. P. Don't pretend you're finding it interesting."

The old man slammed the book down on his bedside table. "Well, I definitely can't concentrate with you nattering away in my ear, can I?"

"Nope! That was my plan!" Alfie grinned, pulling out a thick puzzle book.

"Don't you ever get sick of doing those things?"

"Nope."

"Fair enough. Make it an easier one today, though; my brain hurts already from dealing with you."

An hour of sudoku and crosswords later, Alfie's mind kept drifting back to the same thought.

How was that her mother?

Alfie had always felt lucky. He'd always been surrounded by love and, naïvely, he'd assumed so had everyone else. Sure, there were hard times. There were moments when he all but wanted to disown his two older brothers; but despite the scuffles and the bickering there was always love. Alfie felt sick at the thought of what he'd do if that went.

"Oi. Are you even paying attention, lad? I said four down is ROTARY."

"Sorry, sorry." Alfie hurriedly scribbled the letters down.

"You better be. You come over here, disturb my reading time, and then you don't even have your head in the game!" The old man tutted.

"Luckily for me, I don't need to concentrate. My brain isn't addled with age like yours, remember?" He flashed a wicked smile.

"You're too cheeky for your own good, Alfie. One day it will bite you in the arse, and when it does I'll be there rubbing my hands with glee!" The old man's face lit up. "Now, tell me, what more have you found out about her majesty your neighbor?"

Alfie shuffled uncomfortably. "Not much."

"Pull the other one, will you? I saw that visitor lady going into her cubicle! Didn't hang around long, did she? What were they *saying*? You must have heard them!"

For a man of ninety-two, Mr. Peterson was exceedingly sharp. Alfie knew those beady eyes and drooping ears never missed a trick.

"Nothing gets past you, does it?" He moved closer; he didn't fancy anyone, especially Sharon, overhearing. "It was her mum."

"It what?"

"It was her *mum*. The visitor."

"Interesting. . . . So she isn't completely on her own then." His face twisted in thought.

"Based on what I heard, I'd say she's not far off it, be honest."

He didn't want to pity her. He would hate the thought of anyone feeling sorry for him or discussing his private life so publicly, but he couldn't help himself. He would challenge anyone to overhear that conversation and not feel bad for her.

"I know that look, boy." Mr. Peterson prodded him in the arm. "You're going soft on her, aren't you?"

"No." Alfie's voice was less than convincing. "Let's just say if I had a mum like that, I think I'd have a few issues too. I reckon there's more to her than we think. . . ."

"Hmm, whatever you say, kid. Seems to me she's more trouble than she's worth, but hey, who am I to judge?" He held his hands up in acceptance.

"You, Mr. P., are a grumpy old man who is rubbish at crosswords, that's who!" Alfie laughed and thrust the puzzle book under his friend's nose. "Five across is HUMOROUS, and twelve down is DISCOMBOBULATE," he declared smugly.

"I'll discombobulate you in a minute. . . ."

Luckily for Alfie, the afternoon came around quickly. It was Sunday, and Sundays were Alfie's favorite day. They had been since the dawn of time because Sundays meant one thing and one thing only: Jane Mack's roast dinner. A meal that was cooked to absolute perfection and seasoned with more love than one person should be capable of holding. He'd witnessed old men tear up at the taste of his mum's potatoes. He'd seen raging children silenced by a lick of her gravy. The family would swear that just a morsel of her chicken could cure any illness. Alfie could practically taste his mother's desperation rubbed into its skin as a cure to his disability.

Pre–hospital life, Alfie would show up at his parents' house without fail at 3 p.m. He would be able to smell the garlic and onion from the driveway, and his stomach would be screaming as he knocked on the door. His mum knew that there was a strict fifteen-minute window during which the food needed to be plated up or she risked an onslaught of whining and grumbling.

That first Sunday when she turned up at the hospital with a silver tray packed with her finest roast dinner, Alfie couldn't help but cry. He loved his mum so deeply that it sometimes took his breath away. In a whirlwind of operations, tests, technical terminology, and limb loss, all Alfie had wanted was the comfort of home. His wonderful mother, without even needing to be asked, gave it to him quite literally on a silver (foil) platter.

At first Alfie had assumed that this was a one-off treat. A gift to remind him of how loved he was and how life on the ward could still feel like home. It was only after the fourth weekend in a row of roast dinners that he realized this was a regular feature. Like clockwork, at 3 p.m. Jane Mack would show up with piles of delicious treats. As is customary for mothers to do, she always made too much, and soon, along with the mountains of food came extra plates and cutlery.

"Do us a favor, would you, Alfie, and see if anyone else would like a plate? We really have got too much for the three of us."

Alfie would look at his dad, who would simply roll his eyes and shrug. There was no use fighting her, especially when food was involved, so off Alfie would go, handing out portions to the other patients, with Mr. Peterson often charming his way into getting seconds. Every week, the moment the smell of gravy sneaked in from reception the energy in the room would lift. It was that same unique fervor that often bubbled up at Christmas: excitement and anticipation. And it was all thanks to his parents. He knew then that every bit of goodness he had inside of him came from them.

This week was no different. Hidden behind platters of food, his mum and dad stormed into the ward to raucous cheers. Commotion ensued with spoonfuls of food being dished out here, there, and everywhere. It was only when everyone was in that wonderful contented silence of eating that his mum noticed the curtains drawn around the cubicle next to him.

"Do you have a new neighbor, Alf?" She was already reaching for a spare plate to pile high with food.

"Yeah, but we've been told to steer clear. She's not one for talking." He tried to keep his voice as low as possible.

"Hmm. Talking maybe not, but eating is a different matter entirely."

Alfie knew it was pointless trying to stop her. He watched as his mum knocked on the curtain. When she realized that rapping on cloth was a fruitless exercise, she plucked up the courage to speak.

"Excuse me, dear, I don't want to disturb you, but I've got a plate of Sunday roast here if you'd like it?"

Nothing.

"I could always leave it with the nurses for them to bring over?"

Silence.

"No? Are you sure, sweetheart? It's my special chicken!"

Not even the whisper of a breath.

Dejected, Alfie watched his mum turn back to face him. He was about to open his mouth to reassure her when, as if by magic . . .

"No, I'm okay, but . . . thank you for asking."

Chapter 15

ALICE

It took her a moment to register the words as they came out of her mouth. How unsettling it was to talk again! Everything felt alien, the vibration in her throat, the movement of her jaw, and most of all the sound of her voice. Any softness had gone. It was scratchy and harsh as though her vocal cords were clawing at one another in protest. She didn't know whether it was the dire interaction with her own mother that had made her nostalgic, or whether it was the delicious smell of roast chicken, but she couldn't help but be moved by the kind lady and her offer of food.

Somewhere, deep in the recesses of her mind, there was a memory of what family was. It was faded and weak from being ignored for so long that sometimes Alice forgot it even existed, but in that moment it sprang back to life in full color. She remembered how it felt to be part of something. A protected tribe. Then she remembered the woman who had stood before her only hours before, and she was reminded why she hid the memory in the back of the cupboard. Out of sight and out of mind.

After *it* happened she couldn't help resenting those who still had a "stable," "normal" family. When she would leave school and see the children running into their parents' arms, she couldn't keep the acidic envy from bubbling up inside her stomach. They looked picture-perfect. Puzzle pieces fitting together so seamlessly that she wanted to rip them apart and break them so they didn't go together any longer. She wanted to take one for herself and never give it back. Where did she fit in now? All the pieces had gotten lost or destroyed or forgotten.

As she grew up, the anger had subsided. It took too much energy to hold on to it, and so slowly but surely, she let it go. As long as she didn't have to be involved with her own family, then other people's no longer bothered her. In fact, they almost intrigued her. It was like a riddle she needed to analyze and solve. She'd firmly convinced herself that she didn't need a family to be happy. Why did she need family when she had Sarah?

The image of her best and only friend flashed up in her mind.

Alice knew it was stupid not to give the hospital Sarah's mobile number, but the thought of facing Sarah looking like this, with her life in pieces and her independence gone, was too painful. Alice had planned to have absolutely no visitors during her time at St. Francis's; to her mind, it would be far easier to deal with this alone. She'd been forced to give a next of kin, but had conveniently only provided an old landline for Sarah, who was living halfway around the world in Australia with her husband, Raph.

Every morning the nurses would ask her if there was anyone else they could call—other family members, even work colleagues? Alice refused. No need to bother anyone else. Although as the days passed, she did wonder if Sarah was getting concerned. They usually texted back and forth every few days, often her friend sending through pictures of ridiculously beautiful beaches to make Alice jealous. Where was her phone anyway? Before the accident, she'd never been without it—in fact, Sarah used to joke that Alice's iPhone was the only real relationship she'd had in her adult life.

She racked her brain trying to remember if any of the doctors or the fire officers had mentioned its whereabouts. Suddenly she felt lost without it; what if someone had been trying to get hold of her?

Don't be silly, Alice. They don't tend to make severely burnt employees work while in the hospital.

Without the focus of a project or a couple hundred e-mails to sift through, her rest was quickly becoming restlessness.

Then it struck her cold in the chest. Would she ever be able to go back to work?

Right now she could barely get herself up and out of bed without the help of other people. Would she ever get the full movement back in her left side? What if she couldn't use her hands properly again? Her fingers twitched, longing to feel the keys of her computer keyboard tapping furiously underneath their tips. Would she be able to muster the confidence needed to walk into a boardroom of thirty uninterested men and grab their attention in less than a minute? God, how good it felt to be totally in control and in command. She dared to look down at her broken body, raising her hand in front of her face, wiggling her fingers in hope that the skin wouldn't twinge in agony. But it did. It always did.

Chapter 16

ALFIE

What a turn of events! In the last twenty-four hours, Alfie had gotten more insight into his silent neighbor than he could have ever hoped for. Sure, the meeting with her mother hadn't been a very pleasant experience to witness — but she'd spoken! She'd actually spoken to him. Well, technically to his mum, but still, it was progress. Alfie knew he had to seize the opportunity and strike while the iron was hot. This was a tricky situation to navigate, but if anyone could do it, Alfie was confident it would be him.

The next morning, as soon as he clocked Nurse Angles with her short dark curls and unapologetically large frame entering the ward, he was up on his crutches and hobbling towards her. He'd been up before dawn after another night of particularly vivid flashbacks had left him unable to settle.

"Alfie, honey, what the hell are you doing up? It's not even six a.m."

"I know, bad dreams again, I couldn't sleep."

She gave him a knowing look that he desperately wanted to avoid. "Are you speaking to the doctors about these properly, Alfie?"

There was no point getting into it right now—the dreams would come again, meaning there would be plenty of time to discuss them in the future.

"Yes, of course I am. Anyway, listen, you'll never guess who spoke to us yesterday." He didn't even give her the chance to think. "Alice! The lady in bed thirteen!"

"Really?" She couldn't hide her surprise.

"Really really." Alfie was so proud of himself, his chest felt full to bursting.

"Well, that is good news." Her voice was measured, almost flat.

"Good news? It's amazing news! This is a woman who hasn't spoken in weeks!"

Why was she looking at him like that? Why wasn't she exploding with excitement? Surely this was what the whole nursing staff had wanted?

"Alfie, I know that look in your eyes. Of course it's great that she's started to speak, and over time, little by little, I'm sure she'll start to say more. But don't go obsessing over this, okay? You can't force it. Let her be, honey. Please, we spoke about this, remember?"

Alfie dropped his gaze to the floor. His shoulders slumped as all of the enthusiasm fell out of him. His childish excitement now felt a little embarrassing.

"I know. I just thought it was good progress." What was he expecting, a gold star?

"It is good progress, of course it is!" She placed her hand on his shoulder, delicately steering him back to bed. "But like I said, it's up to her to make the progress, we just have to be there when she's ready. Plus you need to focus on looking after yourself. Try to get a little bit more sleep, will you?"

With the wind firmly knocked out of his sails, the exhaustion from his sleepless night hit him hard. He climbed back into bed and allowed his mind to drift aimlessly.

"Pssst. Alfie." He heard a whisper close to his ear. "Alfie, wake up!" Ruby's high-pitched voice screeched in his ears.

"Yes, Ruby? You better have a good reason for waking me up, young lady!"

"You're going on a walk. Mr. Peterson told me to come and tell you," she said decidedly.

"Now, Ruby, that's not what I said, was it?" The grumbling tones of Mr. Peterson grew louder as he approached. "I told you to tell him to get his lazy arse up and out of bed."

Ruby giggled. "But Mum says I can't swear, Mr. P.!"

"Because swearing is for naughty children and grumpy old men!" Jackie called out.

"Ach, you people are too soft on children these days. Anyway, you coming, boy?" His old friend was standing over him now, and Alfie knew there was no answer other than yes.

"Fine, but give me a second. I may be younger than you, but I'm still a little rusty."

Soon they were ambling along the corridors. Sharon had unceremoniously invited herself yet again, and Alfie knew that could only mean one thing. She wanted gossip.

"So how are your attempts at befriending the silent one going then, Alfie?" He knew everyone found it hilarious that he was trying to speak to his neighbor, especially Sharon.

"Well, she's actually speaking now, so it's obviously doing something, isn't it!" he replied smugly.

"I'd hardly call it speaking, she's said, what—less than ten words?"

"To be honest, Sharon, if I had the choice I'd probably say less than five to that annoying git." Mr. Peterson jabbed Alfie with his elbow. Alfie knew he found Sharon's incessant questioning mildly frustrating too.

"Look, I'm not trying to put a downer on anything, I just wonder how long it's going to take for her to act like a normal human being and for everything to go back to how it was."

"You mean for you to get all the attention again?" Mr. Peterson winked at Alfie. My God, this man was a professional pot-stirrer.

Sharon whipped her head round and shrieked, "How dare you!"

"You know I'm only kidding." A knowing look passed between the two men. "Anyway, I reckon Alfie can get her dancing down the corridors in the next two weeks."

"Hmm." Sharon folded her arms unforgivingly. "I'd like to see you try."

"I'm not playing this game with either of you. She's a person, not a toy. I said I'd help Nurse Angles with making her feel more comfortable, and that's it."

"Ooooh, look who's getting all high-and-mighty." Sharon let out a piercing cackle. "Don't worry, Alf, I wasn't asking you to lower yourself to our standards. Now, do you want a hot chocolate or not?"

Chapter 17

ALICE

The fact that her neighbor had not even attempted a hello the next day was not just a massive relief but also quite a surprise. Alice had been certain that he would jump at the chance to get her to speak again—but no. For the entire day, her neighbor stayed clear of her, spending most of his time up and about with the other patients. Normally Alice didn't mind listening to the comings and goings of people on the ward; as long as they left her alone, it didn't matter too much. But today she felt a pang of separation. Maybe the thoughts of Sarah yesterday were making her nostalgic, or maybe the impending physio session she had coming up in a few days was making her more emotional than usual. Whatever it was, Alice craved to be anywhere in the world but in this depressing hospital bed on her own.

If she were to die tomorrow, who on earth would be sad that she was gone? Of course there was Sarah, but she'd upped and left her two years ago to move to Australia. Technically she had a new life with Raph. Maybe her mother, but only because Alice probably hadn't died quite in line with her expectations. Arnold? Lyla? She was really pushing it now. Could she really call them friends?

The thoughts consumed her afternoon, eroding the time with their cruelty. Heaviness grew in her chest, and she willed sleep to come and relieve her of the day. She'd barely closed her eyes before her neighbor's dreaming woke her again that night. Alice hadn't got used to the nightmares, and it was always chilling to hear a grown man moaning, even if it was in his sleep.

"Ross, I need you to wake up. *Please.*"

Alice was so tempted to try to wake him. Surely it would be better to stop the pain? Plus she wasn't quite sure how long she could stand listening to it. On the other hand, waking someone in the midst of a flashback like that could turn out to have significant consequences. So she lay there and waited.

"Someone help me. God, help me."

Please wake up, she begged. He was thrashing around so violently that Alice wondered if he was at risk of throwing himself out of bed. She hoped not, because there was no way in hell she'd be helping him up.

"HELP ME, GODDAMN IT. *PLEASE!*"

She couldn't bear it any longer. The last cry was so loud that Alice reached for her pillow to cover her ears. Luckily it was also the scream that woke him up. She could hear the subtle change from dream state to reality in his voice.

"*Goddamn it, Alfie.* Get a grip."

His heavy breathing was punctuated by small groans.

Then came a quiet shuffling of footsteps and quiet whispers.

"It's all right, Nurse, I'll go."

The outline of the old man across the way came into view. "Alfie, son." Mr. Peterson's gentle voice cut through the silence.

"Sorry. I didn't mean to wake you."

"Don't be an idiot. You think I can sleep with Sharon snoring next to me? I just came over to see if you wanted anything, I'm going to get one of those piss-poor cups of tea from the machine."

"No, I'm all right, thanks. I'm just going to try to get my head down again."

"Right you are. Good night, son."

As the footsteps of Mr. Peterson slowly faded, Alice was struck with a memory of Arnold: another old soul whose stiff upper lip couldn't keep his kindness away. A pang of longing struck her; Arnold had saved her life and she hadn't even thanked him. Maybe she could call him on reception one day and check in to see how he was?

No, she told herself, she'd been fine on her own this long and she would be fine on her own now; not even a life-changing near-death experience would alter that.

Alice could barely open her eyes when Nurse Angles came the next morning. Her sleepless night had really taken its toll. But none of the nurses were expecting any conversation from her anyway, so she simply rolled over and tried to fall back asleep.

"Morning, neighbor. How are we today?"

How on earth could someone in so much pain be so upbeat and *happy* every day? Alice found it tiring to even smile when she didn't want to, let alone be the life and soul of the party.

"It feels strange calling you 'neighbor' all the time. It's Alice, isn't it?"

She sighed, loudly enough for him to hear, then turned onto her side away from him.

"I'll take silence as a yes, then. . . ." He barely even paused for breath. "So the thing is, I know you think you managed to escape my mum the other day, but I feel it's my duty as her son to warn you that the battle is far from over. *Determined* doesn't even scratch the surface when talking about my mum. Just a heads-up, she'll be back with more roast chicken and ploys to feed you next time."

The thought of his mother forcing piles of food through her curtains made Alice laugh and panic all at once.

"Anyway, I thought I'd let you know. It's better to be prepared when facing these things, isn't it—"

"God, do you ever stop talking?" the disgruntled voice of Mr. Peterson snapped from somewhere across the ward.

Alice smirked. She did have to admit she enjoyed hearing their little back-and-forth every day. Maybe she just liked hearing someone put this Alfie character in his place every now and then!

"I'm trying to do my duty as a patient of this ward and let our friend Alice here know what she's let herself in for by rejecting my mum's roast dinner."

"It meant more food for me in the end, so I'm not complaining."

"As long as you're okay, Mr. P., that's all that matters, isn't it?"

"Too damn right." The old man chuckled.

"Anyway, I'll leave you all alone now and get on with this puzzle book."

Alice turned onto her back. It seemed the only times he really was quiet were when he was distracted by food or puzzles. Perhaps she could do an anonymous order of the world's hardest puzzle books and get them delivered directly to him? *Does Amazon deliver to hospital beds?* she wondered.

"Oh, for God's sake, why don't they make these things easy?" A sigh, followed by a frustrated groan. "Don't suppose you're any good at puzzles, are you?"

Really? It had literally been five minutes.

"I mean, *come on*, who in their right mind is meant to solve these things!"

His words hung in the air, knocking louder and louder at the barrier between them.

Maybe if you answer him, he'll shut up for a bit?

Don't you dare. . . .

"I think I'm too close to it. If only there was someone who could help me. . . ."

It's the morphine and the boredom, Alice.

You give him one word and he'll take a mile.

ALICE . . .

Chapter 18

ALFIE

"Is there a clue, then?"

If you'd blinked you would have missed it. One cough from Mr. Peterson and it would have been lost. But Alfie had heard her. It was as though his senses had been poised ready to snatch her words from the air.

She'd spoken. She'd actually spoken *to him*!

He wanted to shout it out loud so the entire ward knew what a groundbreaking moment this was. But instead he smiled and waited, biding his time. His whole brain buzzed with excitement.

"Is there a clue or not?" The voice, a little louder now, was tinged with frustration. Her voice had an intriguing lilt to it; the shadow of an Irish accent lurked gingerly in the background. It spoke of wide-open spaces, of luscious greenery and bracing winds. There was a beauty to it, but he could also sense the defense, the anger and the fiery edges waiting to attack.

"Sorry, I got lost in my thoughts for a second. No, there isn't a clue. It's not a crossword puzzle. It's more of a . . . visual challenge." He couldn't stop the smile on his face from seeping into his voice. Thank goodness the curtain was drawn, or he could see a bedpan being thrown in his direction very shortly.

"Well, how can I help when I can't see it?" The fire licked her every word—he could feel the heat in the air.

Suddenly, through the curtain a hand appeared. Just one pale hand with nails bitten down to their red raw beds and friendship groups of freckles scattered across the surface. If it hadn't been only one inch from his face, he would have told himself he was dreaming.

Slowly he reached over and handed her the book. "It's on page one thirty-six."

He waited. Listening.

A scratch of the pen maybe? Or was that Mr. Peterson rearranging his paper underwear again?

Just as he was about to offer more words as an olive branch, he heard something hit the floor on his side of the divide.

The puzzle book lay on the floor by his bed. In normal circumstances he would have made a sarcastic comment about respecting the disabled, but he knew he needed to tread carefully; so, resourceful as ever, he used one of his crutches to drag the book closer before reaching down silently and picking it up.

He opened the book to page 136.

Alfie couldn't stop the laughter erupting out of him. On his dot-to-dot, she'd carefully and very artistically joined the dots to spell the word ARSEHOLE.

"Oh, I see. Well yes, of course, when it's right in front of you like that, it suddenly becomes very obvious."

"Good-bye, Alfie." The fire in her words had receded, and what was left was a warm glow.

He folded the page with a sweet satisfaction. Just as he was about to tell her that he wasn't going anywhere so there was no real need for good-byes yet, Alfie stopped himself. Enough had been said already for today.

One step towards the end and all that.

Chapter 19

ALICE

What on earth had just happened?

The feeling that overcame her was reminiscent of the wine worry that would plague her every morning after a night out at university. The dread. The panic. That neurotic feeling that screamed in your ear while fear and embarrassment knocked loudly on your door: *What did I do? Oh God, what did I say?*

This time she couldn't even blame Sarah for forcing her to be sociable and the three bottles of five-pound wine from Wetherspoons for her actions. She could potentially have forgiven herself for asking the question, for indulging him in a small bit of conversation. After all, he'd had a pretty harrowing few nights, and if a couple of words exchanged here and there would cheer him up, then it would be no more skin off her nose.

But to reach out her hand! Seriously. Was she mad?

Obviously, she had made sure to use her undamaged

hand, reaching over just enough so that no other part of her was revealed. But for a brief second Alice had allowed herself to do what she wanted without restrictions or barriers holding her back.

As Alfie placed the book in her hand, she had recognized a little fluttering rising in her chest. Why was she feeling nervous about this? She told herself it was the fear of him tricking her, maybe he would grab her hand and force back the curtains to take a look at her. Hindsight would tell her the nerves were actually excitement, a deep knowing that a barrier had been crossed. Her arm was the unwittingly given olive branch.

She'd leafed through to page 136 and forced herself not to curse out loud.

Staring back at her was a dot-to-dot.

Of a cat.

A puzzle fit for a two-year-old.

The little shit!!

She should have known it wouldn't be straightforward! Was the court jester really going to hand over a genuinely hard puzzle to solve? No. He was going to provoke and push her to her limits. He wanted her to crack.

Not this time, Alfie.

Even though she knew saying good-bye was a ludicrous way to end the conversation, Alice wanted to stop the interaction before it got out of her control. She'd been sucked in once, and she sure wasn't going to let herself be played a second time. She'd crossed a line, and her instinct was telling her to retreat immediately.

Don't let him in, Alice.

You don't need a friend; you need to get yourself out of here.

Her defiant independence had taken over again. Put up those walls and don't let anyone in.

"Get over yourself, Alice, it was just a laugh. . . ." The voice of her best friend drifted into her mind.

Sarah.

This was exactly the type of thing she would have done to get Alice out of one of her bad moods. It was so ridiculous and infuriatingly childish, but it always seemed to work.

Alice's chest started to throb with longing for her friend.

But talking to him once doesn't mean I'm committed to him forever. . . . There's no harm in conversation. . . .

The absurd thoughts were cut short by the appearance of one of the nurses.

"Hello, Alice, how are we today?" The nurse didn't even bother to look at Alice as she started her checks. She was on autopilot, anticipating more of the same sweet silence that had been present since day one.

"Okay. How are you?"

The nurse did a double take.

"Oh, wow! Erm . . . yes, I'm fine." She shook herself out of her stupor and carried on with her checks. "I'm doing good, thank you. Very well, in fact."

The nurse's face flushed with pride. Here was one of her children finding her words for the very first time.

"Can you tell her to stop talking so much please, she's been nonstop!" came Alfie's voice from next door. "Some of us are trying to rest."

The nurse rolled her eyes. "Don't worry, I'll make sure to change his dressing very vigorously today." She winked at Alice as she turned to leave. "Right, Alfred Mack, I hope you're ready for a cold, firm hand."

"Oh well, your husband is a very lucky man. I'm surprised he lets you out the house in the morning with that bedside manner."

"If Nurse Angles heard you, she'd have you off this ward in a second with that cheek!"

Alice smiled affectionately.

Suddenly the nurse leaned in close to her, whispering for Alice's ears only: "What have you gone and let yourself in for, young lady!"

Alice couldn't help but laugh. She'd been asking herself the very same thing.

The nurse had barely left before the entertainment started up again.

"Hey, Mr. P., do you think we should put our new friend to the test with some of your crossword clues?"

"I think you should learn when to stop and keep quiet."

"Don't spoil the fun, old man! Right . . . I'm looking for a nine-letter word meaning 'lively or enthusiastic,' starts with a *c*."

"Couldn't-care-less."

"No, Sharon, that's why we don't ask you to play. Sarcasm isn't welcomed in this serious game of intellect. Alice? Any thoughts?"

Oh, trust me, there are many, but none that would be pleasant for you to hear. . . .

She had to lay down some boundaries early. Draw a line in the sand and manage expectations.

"Look, just because I can talk doesn't mean I'm going to, okay?"

Chapter 20

ALFIE

"That taught you, didn't it, kid."

Alfie shrugged his shoulders nonchalantly as he made his way over to Mr. Peterson's bed.

"One step is a step and all that. Rome wasn't built in a day, my friend." He hoped the disappointment at her rebuff wasn't leaking out into his voice. "Anyway, I've got the joys of physio now, so you get a break from me for at least an hour."

"Praise the Lord. He's going!"

Alfie mustered his best glare, but no matter how rude or sarcastic his friend was, he couldn't help but admire him. He really was one of the best gifts being in the hospital had given him.

"You and Alice can celebrate my absence together." He made sure his voice carried all the way to her bay.

He couldn't give up on her now.

She'd only just started to let him in.

If any of his fellow teachers had been here, they would have scoffed and rolled their eyes, dismissing Alice as "another one of Mr. Mack's projects." So what if he tried harder than most people would with the children written off as "difficult" and "resistant." He'd tried many times to keep his distance, but his heart simply refused to let him. His desire to help took over and pushed rules and procedure to the side.

He needed to remember that this was going to be a marathon and not a sprint.

Not that you could do either now with your one pathetic leg.

He left Alice well alone for the rest of the day, partly because he was exhausted from another intense physio session but also because he was trying to employ his "easy does it" strategy. Therefore when he woke the next morning, he was very surprised to see Nurse Angles standing over his bed, arms folded and giving him a look he knew all too well. He'd been on the receiving end of that same look for the majority of his life. Most of the time, including this occasion, it was given with a healthy dose of affection.

"What the hell have you been up to, Alfie? What did I tell you?"

Alfie shrugged his shoulders, feigning complete bewilderment. Nurse Angles leant forward on the bed, one hand resting on his remaining leg and the other reaching towards his face. He braced himself for a little warning, maybe a gentle finger wag to go with it—the other nurses on shift must have told her of his continued efforts to get Alice to talk.

"I'm sorry, it's just I—"

But before he could finish, Nurse Angles placed her hand gently on his cheek.

"Thank you, my love, you did good," she whispered.

"So you're not about to kick me off the ward and banish me back to orthopedics?"

"No, not *quite* yet, baby." She laughed.

"Phew. I think I've got a bit more work to do before I go."

"Yes, like getting yourself well enough to get out of here, okay?" This time the finger was pointing at him, and with one raise of her eyebrow, she disappeared off down the ward.

Spurred on by Nurse Angles's delight, he waited less than ten minutes before grabbing one of the puzzle books next to his bed.

"So it's that time again, ladies and gentlemen. I'm looking for a five-letter word for annoying."

Mr. Peterson didn't even look up from his book.

"Try A-L-F-I-E." The old man still hadn't lifted his eyes from the page but he was now wearing a wry smile.

"Agreed," came that faded Irish voice from next door.

"Aha! She speaks again! Now, I want to get one thing straight: if this is going to become a regular thing, I don't want it to just be an excuse to insult me, okay? I have feelings too."

"It's not going to become any type of *thing*," she replied. *Tread carefully, Alfie.*

"Okay, neighbor, noted." He reached for his TV remote and switched on *This Morning*.

"Alfie, when are those gorgeous friends of yours coming to visit again?" Sharon called out from her side of the ward.

Sometimes Alfie wondered if Sharon got more enjoyment from his visitors than he did.

"Shit. I think they're coming today. You're in luck, Shaz."

He'd been so caught up in his own head that time had simply flown past him. He looked back up at the television screen and clocked the date immediately.

Of course they were coming today.

Today was the day that Lucy left the country. The day the woman he'd loved for three years would disappear from his life altogether.

Chapter 21

ALICE

One of the benefits of never seeing anyone was that Alice's hearing had started to elevate to whole new levels of incredible. Even after just a few days of isolation, it felt almost superhuman at times. Not only could she identify the residents on the ward from just their footsteps, now she was even able to name visitors just from their hello.

She had to admit, having Alfie in the bed next to her had given her a lot of practice. Being one of the most popular residents on and off the ward meant he was rarely left alone. A stream of friends passed in and out regularly. There was a Matty, who was sometimes accompanied by a guy called Alex, a Ben, a Simon, a Johnny, and a Jimmy. Alice found it hard to keep track of them all, especially as conversations seemed to all follow a similar theme, namely: football, nights out, rugby, football again, and moaning about their families.

Today was a little different.

Today there was a distinct lack of unnecessary banter being thrown about among them. Thinking about it, everything seemed a little too subdued—almost polite.

"Hey, Alf. How you doing today?" Caution, there was definitely a hint of caution in the guy Matty's voice.

"Yeah, I'm doing all right, same old same old with me. How about you? What's been going on?"

"Oh, nothing really. Just the usual, right, Alex?"

"Yeah, yeah, nothing major. Same old same old with us too."

Alice could picture the scene playing out just behind the curtain: the two men standing awkwardly around the bed, hands in their pockets, desperately avoiding eye contact. Shoulders slumped, shifty looks between them, and a slight rocking back and forth in preparation to run at any minute.

"Look, it's fine, boys. Just tell me how last night was, I'm guessing you went?"

A small intake of breath.

Alice could feel their guilt seeping out of the cubicle.

"Honestly, it's fine, she was your friend first, I get it." Alfie's voice was a little more forceful now. "Did she have a good send-off?"

"Yeah, it was all right, she had a good time, I think." Matty was the one to speak first.

"Good, that's all that matters."

"The thing is—" Alex started.

"You were missed, everyone said so," Matty cut him off.

"Matty, don't be a prick. Go on, Alex—the thing is . . ." The force in Alfie's voice was making even Alice feel nervous at what was to follow.

"Well, the thing is, Lucy was asking after you. Quite a lot, actually." The more words he used, the braver Alex seemed to get. "She asked me to pass on a message to you. She asked me to tell you she was"—the tiniest pause of self-doubt— "she was sorry."

He delivered this last sentence as though relieving himself of a great weight. The awkwardness was palpable.

"She said what?" Alfie's voice grew louder. Alice couldn't help but wince for his friends on the receiving end of his sudden anger.

"She said . . . she was sorry," Alex repeated.

"She's sorry?"

"Yeah, you know, for everything that happened."

"Well, me too, mate, me fucking too."

Alice felt an odd mix of intrigue and guilt. There was such resentment in Alfie's voice that it made her feel ashamed to be listening, but her curiosity had been piqued and she desperately wanted to know more.

"Anyway, what's going on with you, Alex? Bagged yourself any more disastrous dates lately?" Alfie still sounded weary, but everyone seemed to breathe a sigh of relief at the change in topic.

"Tell him about that one the other night, Al. The one where you made a complete fool of yourself." Matty began to laugh.

"Oh Jesus, please don't make me relive that. . . ."

Unfortunately Alice would have to wait until another time to hear more about this Lucy, but for the rest of the day she couldn't stop thinking about her. She reckoned her boredom must have reached brand-new heights, and it didn't help that her neighbor had fallen into a deathly silence that even Alice would have been proud of. Something must have happened between this Lucy girl and Alfie. She'd never heard him react like that before. Who was she? Had they been together? Had she broken his heart? Did he break hers? Stories and scenarios grew in her mind until she was so close to just asking him outright. Thank goodness the familiar voice of reason stopped her. But she was left with an even more disturbing question . . .

Why do I care?

Chapter 22

ALFIE

At the time, Alfie had told everyone he was fine that his long-term girlfriend had left him. He empathized with the fact that she was "having a hard time coming to terms with everything after the accident." He understood that waking up to a one-legged boyfriend who needed significant care probably wasn't on the wish list when it came to life partners. But not once had she asked how he was feeling or what he needed. It was as though she'd totally forgotten that he was the one who'd been in the accident; he was the one who had to endure the hours of physical therapy and rehabilitation exercises just so that he could walk himself to the toilet. Just like that, three years of a relationship had been thrown away, and he was the one left grieving more than just the loss of his limb.

He was angry with himself for even asking about the party. Often he was angry that he'd even let Alex set him up with her. Angry that she was friends with his friends and that, at the time, that had seemed such a perfect reason to welcome her into his world and his heart. Angry he'd stepped over barriers to love her. Angry he went and got his leg amputated. Angry he wasn't the man she wanted him to be. Angry that he repulsed her. And more than that, angry that he was left to deal with it all on his own.

He knew he couldn't be mad at Alex for passing on the message. The stupid idiot probably thought he was doing the right thing, that in some way hearing those words would dissolve all of the heartache and resentment that had built up after the breakup. It had taken a few moments for Alex to realize that this didn't amend anything. Nothing was fixed. In fact, it just brought everything right back up to the surface again.

Alfie had found it within himself to bring the conversation back to something a little more lighthearted, but he was too tired to pretend for very long. Matty knew him well enough to sense that after a few more embarrassing stories from Alex, it was time to go; and with that, they left Alfie alone with his thoughts.

For the rest of the afternoon, all he could do was stare blankly at the TV. He didn't want to sleep, despite his body begging him to; he knew the dreams would come, and he had nothing left to fight them right now. He didn't want to talk and have to mask the despair from his voice for the sake of others around him. No. Today he would just lie there and be. Everyone on the ward could feel the shift in him. Normally this would have bothered him and he would have sought a way to snap himself out of it. But this time he let them stew in it. A part of him almost enjoyed them knowing he wasn't coming to save them today with jokes. They couldn't always depend on him for fun. He didn't want anyone to depend on him ever again. He was in the midst of a black cloud, and he wasn't coming out anytime soon.

As the ward around him slowed down and everyone tucked themselves in for the night, Alfie's anger began to rage. He'd felt it gradually building in the pit of his stomach all day, growing in intensity, clawing at his insides desperate for freedom. He'd had to use every ounce of strength to keep it under control; but now, as everyone around him slipped peacefully into sleep, it came alive. He could feel it rushing up through his chest and searing his throat. It had to come out. He had to let it out before it ripped him apart.

"AAAGGGHHHHHHHHHHH!" he screamed into his pillow. He buried his head deeper and let the noise scorch the fabric with its anger. His fists were balled so tightly; he wanted to tear the cushion apart and reduce it to scraps. He wanted something to feel as completely broken as he did. Riding that wave of destruction, he threw the pillow as hard as he could.

Then the tears came. Hot and thick and furious. He had nothing to muffle the noise, as his only defense lay flat and lifeless on the floor a couple meters away. Suddenly he started to laugh, louder and louder, until it was bursting out of him uncontrollably.

You've gone and thrown your toys out of the pram and you can't even get them back without help, you one-legged prick.

The irony was too much.

Then he heard something. Something that stopped his slightly hysterical moment in its tracks. Of course he was going to wake someone up with all the noise he was making, but out of everyone on the ward, he really, *really* didn't want it to be her.

Just as he opened his mouth to form some sort of apology, he heard something land by the side of his bed. Looking down he saw that, just within reaching distance, a pillow had been pushed through the gap between the curtain and the floor.

"Just in case you had some more screaming to do." Her voice was gentle and just loud enough for him to hear.

"Thanks. I kind of shot myself in my only foot by throwing mine, didn't I?"

"Yeah. I was going to get it for you, but then I realized I don't like you that much."

"But you like me enough to give me your only pillow? And to talk to me again!"

Aha. He'd got her.

"Don't get too excited. I actually have three spare. I think the nurses pitied me and decided to express their sympathy through extra bedding accessories. Plus, I felt sorry for you."

"Holy shit. And I thought I was liked around here. They won't even give me an extra chocolate pudding, let alone pillows!"

"You're clearly not hurt bad enough. It doesn't pay to be liked, Alfie, it pays to be injured."

Even though he knew she was joking, he didn't really know how to respond to that. He knew she was hurt pretty badly, but the extent of her injuries was a mystery to him. Before he had time to formulate an adequate reply, she floored him with a question.

"Are you okay after what happened earlier? I couldn't help but overhear your conversation."

He could almost feel her wince in anticipation of his response.

"Oh. Yeah. I mean, I thought I was fine, but I guess if you ask that abused pillow I've left for dead over there, apparently I'm not."

She laughed. A shy half-laugh. He wondered if she ever

allowed herself to laugh fully, or was it always a little held-back and contained?

"We've interviewed the victim and they are going to be pressing charges, sir. You want to tell us your side of the story?"

He knew she was just playing but, with the darkness thick around them, he felt a strange urge to tell her things. The feelings and thoughts he'd kept buried deep down were suddenly clamouring to be heard. He wanted to share it all with her. Wanted to let her peek inside his head, even just for a moment.

"Well, Officer, I'll keep this brief as I know you're busy: my girlfriend of three years left me a week after my accident because she couldn't deal with what happened. Apparently it was too difficult for her. So not only did I have my leg amputated; not only did the wound swell, burst, and then become infected; not only did I nearly die from the sepsis, *but* I was also left heartbroken. Please feel free to cry for me now if you wish."

He realized that this was the first time he'd ever really talked about this with anyone. He wasn't ready to let Alice see the full extent of his heartache just yet, but there was a small relief in speaking about it. Everyone had been so concerned about upsetting him that they had either chosen to ignore the situation or would tentatively skirt the issue, keeping to the very edges of the subject at all times. They had been so focused on healing his physical injury that the pain from his heart was left for him to deal with in secret and out of sight.

"Seriously, Alfie, what is wrong with you?"

Wow, he was not expecting that. Sure, he hadn't given her the full emotional breakdown of events, but he was expecting at least a little bit of sympathy.

"Why would you still ask after her when she acted like that?" Alice continued. "You're too nice for your own good. I know you say you loved her, but seriously, she sounds like a selfish idiot to me."

He wasn't expecting that either! No one had ever been so direct with him before.

"Well now, Officer, that's no way to speak to one of your suspects, no matter how heinous his crime."

"Alfie, are you ever serious? Just for one moment."

Twice now she'd caught him off guard with her questions. Something was making her bold tonight, and he realized he was kind of enjoying it.

"No one wants serious, Alice. The world is full of shit as it is, look around you, for Christ's sake! Why make it harder for yourself and everyone around you by just adding to it?"

He heard the flicker of resistance in her tone. "What, so we all have to go around pretending nothing hurts? Pretending that everything is fantastic!"

"No, but what's the point of being miserable all the time? People don't like miserable."

"So you want to pretend to be happy for other people? To get friends? Popularity? At the end of the day, it doesn't matter what other people think of you if you're cut up and bleeding on the inside."

She was coming at him hard now, taking no prisoners with her words. Surely she couldn't know that she was hitting him in the places that hurt most. Was she intentionally trying to tear down the defenses he'd spent so many years meticulously building? Maybe he said what he did because he was tired. Maybe it was because he'd forgotten to close the door on his emotions from earlier. Maybe he was just being spiteful.

"And clearly being so serious gets you a total of fuck-all visitors when you're at death's door." His hand instinctively covered his mouth in a pathetic attempt to take back the poison he'd just spat at her.

Silence.

He didn't know what he could say to make anything good again. He just lay there opening and closing his mouth like a fish out of water.

"I think you're forgetting the delightful visit from my mother."

Laughter erupted from both sides of the curtain. Full, real, unapologetic laughter that shook his body and brought tears to his eyes. It was so loud that he could see Sharon stirring across the room, but he didn't care. There was no way of hiding when you felt this alive.

"Oh yeah, that one must have slipped my mind."

"Good night, Alfie."

The deliciousness of their moment had breathed a bit of lightness into her words. He closed his eyes, held the scratchy nylon pillow close to his chest, and breathed in the calm that had hung itself across them both.

"Good night, Alice."

Chapter 23

ALICE

The moment he'd said it, she'd known he was right. There was no point in objecting or fighting over it, and although she'd managed to respond with humor, that didn't stop it hurting. Through her own decisions, careless ways, and strong will, Alice had successfully orchestrated it so that no one would be coming for her. Alice Gunnersley was alone, and for the first time in a long time it didn't feel okay.

She wasn't sure why she'd decided to reach out to him last night, but she knew she couldn't keep blaming boredom. There was definitely something hard to ignore when witnessing someone's raw, uncensored pain like that, hearing him crying out night after night. Alice might be stubborn and independent, but she wasn't made of stone. Here was a man who by day provided so much life for everyone else around him, being reduced to a whimpering, vulnerable shell every night. It wasn't easy to listen to, let alone live through. Maybe she had felt sorry for him? Her wounds were painful and repulsive, but at least they were only skin-deep.

She wasn't sure if either of them slept that night, but by the time morning greeted them, they were both back to playing the part of a well-rested individual.

"Hey." Alfie's voice was quiet, no hint of bravado. It was clear he wanted only her to hear him, not the whole ward.

"Hey."

"Look, about what I said last night. I'm sorry. It was out of order—"

"Alfie, it's fine." She didn't want to get into apologies. In fact, she wanted to erase the whole thing from her mind.

"No, listen. I know you're going to tell me that I was right so there's no need for me to say sorry, but I wasn't right. I was very, *very* wrong. And look, if I get out of here sooner than you, I'll come back and visit whether you let me in behind that goddamn curtain or not!"

The sincerity in his voice tugged at something in her chest, and soon her cheeks were damp with tears. God, she must be really tired. Tiredness and hangovers were the only two legitimate excuses Alice ever allowed herself for emotion.

"Well, there's no way in hell I'd let you in to see me, but thank you."

She had a strange urge to reach her hand across the divide and squeeze his. Instead she settled for holding her own. The texture of her skin felt so different from what it had been before. Sometimes she forgot that there was a brand-new broken version of her to get used to.

"You say that now, but trust me, I can be very determined when I want to be."

"You? Determined? Never!"

"Sarcastic now as well, are we?"

"Go away and annoy someone else, will you?"

He let out a loud gasp. "Challenge accepted! Hey, Mr. Peterson, you heard the woman. I'm coming for you."

Alice shook her head.

"No one is coming for anyone just yet." Nurse Angles's voice cut through their conversation. "Beds, everyone, and curtains closed, please."

Alice's heart started racing. Despite her protests, she'd actually found herself looking forward to her day on the ward. Now that she was facing another grueling and humiliating physio session, any scrap of potential excitement had been destroyed.

"Alice, honey, we're going to have to get you up and out again. Give me two seconds to check we have the green light, and then I'll come and help, okay?"

Nurse Angles had gone before she had a chance to even open her mouth.

"Curtains closed, everyone—the quicker we do this, the quicker it's over with," she barked.

"How long is this military operation going to go on for? I thought I'd left the army forty years ago."

"Mr. P., stop moaning and take a nap, will you?" Alfie quipped.

Hearing his voice come to her defense gave Alice a strange feeling of relief.

"Okay, we are good to go." One of the nurses had accompanied Nurse Angles back inside Alice's bay, with the formidable wheelchair.

"No pain, no gain, neighbor. You got this."

She didn't know whether to laugh or cry at the sound of him.

There was no time for either. Nurse Angles hooked her arms underneath Alice's and started to lift her up gently.

Here we go again.

Once again Nurse Angles had pulled out all the stops. All the patients were confined to their beds, and the small female lounge to the right of the ward had been cleared to allow her full privacy. Darren was already there waiting as they wheeled her in, as cheery and upbeat as the last time she'd seen him.

"Alice! So good to see you. How are you doing?"

"Okay," she muttered, terrified at what grueling exercises he had in store for her.

"Right, let's get you up and out of this chair. Trust me, it won't be long until you don't need it anymore." He winked encouragingly as he helped lift her up to standing.

"Okay, we are going to continue with the simple mobilization exercises we started last week. Take it slow, and we can rest whenever you need. . . ."

It proved to be another humiliating hour of her life—but strangely, instead of wanting to crawl into a hole and disappear, Alice found a small spark of determination igniting inside her. The fiercely stubborn and ruthless competitor she'd been before the fire had begun to rear her head again. The old Alice was still in there, it seemed. As she forced her trembling, stiff body to complete the minuscule movements that Darren was instructing, it dawned on her that this was the only way she was getting out of here, so she'd better find a way to do it, and do it quickly.

Finally she was back in bed, her entire body burning with effort. A little voice crept into her consciousness.

I wonder if anyone's bothered to contact you.
Has anyone even checked to see if you're alive?
Is work the only thing you're needed for?

Her phone! She still didn't know where the hell it was. In a rush of nervous panic, Alice reached over and buzzed the nurses. How funny—even when she'd been in the most pain she'd ever felt in her life, Alice had never called for help; but now when it came to finding her most prized possession, it felt like an emergency.

A spark of guilt ignited in her when she heard a nurse sprint over to her bay.

"Alice, is everything okay? Alice, what's happening?" Flustered, the young nurse appeared between the curtains.

"Sorry. I probably should have just waited until rounds, but I just realized I don't have my phone. I haven't seen it since I arrived. Do you know where it is?"

"Oh. I see." The look of relief and annoyance on the nurse's face was quite a picture. "Let me check—one second."

Nice to know the old Alice hasn't disappeared completely. Pushing the help buzzer for your phone . . . really?

In a few moments the nurse was back, holding a ziplock bag of items: purse, keys, phone. Alice recognized them instantly as hers.

"Sorry we didn't give these to you sooner—they had to cut away your clothing when you were first admitted, someone must have filed them away in the process. Here you go."

An image of someone desperately trying to separate her suit trousers from her molten skin flashed across her mind. She felt sick at the thought, and instinctively felt the dressings along her left leg, grateful she was freed from the mess. "Thanks," she murmured.

Here was another piece of her that had survived the blaze. The cold metal weight in her hand felt alien. She took a deep breath and hesitantly turned on her phone.

Nothing.

Brilliant. Literally not one single—

One message: Mum.

Two messages: Lyla.

Holy shit—three . . . four . . . five messages. . . . The sharp ding of the message tone rang out across the ward. Alice tried to switch the sound off, but her fingers were stiff and aching from physio.

"What the hell is going on over there?" Mr. Peterson called out.

"Ruby, are you playing on my phone again?" Jackie scolded.

"No! I promise!" she whined.

"Alfie, is that you?" Sharon asked.

"Obviously it's not me. If I had that many friends, I would have bragged about it long before now, trust me! Wait— Alice, is that *you*?" There was blatant surprise in his voice. "Is everything okay?"

Alice was too in shock to care what was going on around her. As she scanned the incoming texts, she couldn't believe it.

Message from Lyla • April 24, 9:02 a.m.

Holy shit. Arnold just told me what happened. Are you okay? Do you need anything? DO NOT FOR ONE SECOND WORRY ABOUT WORK. I know it's pointless telling you because you never stop worrying, but hey, I can try right? I've got everything covered. Please let me know you're okay. Lyla x

Message from Lyla • April 25, 5:35 p.m.
Okay, so apparently you're stable but I know that when
you come round you'll be at high risk of having a heart
attack if I don't send you some form of update re:
Hunterland Project. Tim has taken it on, I'm watching him
like a hawk and will be on his ass constantly. Really hope
you're okay, Alice. Lyla x

Message from Mum • April 27, 8:55 a.m.
Hope you're well. M

Message from Lyla • May 2, 12:15 p.m.
Dear Alice, it's Arnold here. I hope they are giving you
lots of hot chocolate and taking good care of you. We all
miss you here in the office, my day isn't the same without
seeing you! Get well soon. Yours sincerely, Arnold

Blinking back tears, Alice had to laugh at that last line. Of
course Arnold would sign off his text as if it were a letter. Her
heart felt so full in that moment it was fit to burst. These people whom she had so often taken for granted, and had so
often deprioritized in life, cared about her. They cared
enough to message her, and it blew her mind ever so slightly.

There were more texts from Lyla and Arnold just checking in and giving updates on life at the office. Then Alice
saw the message that made her heart leap.

Message from Sarah BFF • May 28, 7:50 a.m.
Hey, Al. ARE YOU OKAY? I called your work because you
have been completely MIA recently and I was starting to
worry and they told me about the accident. Why the hell

didn't you give them my mobile number?! Holy fuck—
seriously are you okay? I'm working on getting a flight to
you ASAP. I love you so much it hurts. Sarah x

Message from Sarah BFF • May 28, 9:30 a.m.
Okay so Raph keeps telling me to calm down and that
you're probably not even allowed your phone on, but
please Al just let me know you're okay. I've called the
hospital but they aren't saying much. I love you. x

Message from Raph BFFs Husband • May 28, 1:35 p.m.
Hi Alice, it's Raph. Sarah's kind of losing her shit over here
and has asked me to message to ask you to message her.
We've rung the hospital a bunch of times and they've
reassured her you're alive, but you know what she's like.
We are both thinking of you and praying you get better
soon. We love you. R x

Message from Sarah BFF • May 29, 4:00 a.m.
Al, I hate you so much right now for ignoring me, but I've
called the hospital and they've told me you're doing
okay and after many arguments they've reassured me
you haven't actually been on your phone. We are still
coming to see you, will send details as soon as I have
them. I love you. x

Alice couldn't get her head around what she was reading.
Sarah was going to be traveling halfway around the world
just be to with her.

She couldn't hold it in any longer. The reality was hitting
her hard and the emotions that came with it were uncontrollable.

No. You can't let her see you like this.

Alice slowly tried to type out a response to her friend, but every stroke of the keypad felt like a gigantic effort. How the hell had she managed to fire off hundreds of e-mails a day without a pause? This was why she couldn't let Sarah visit. This wasn't the Alice Gunnersley she knew and loved.

Message to Sarah BFF • June 25, 1:27 p.m.
Hi Sarah. I am so so sorry. I've only just got my phone back. No need to worry about coming to visit. Flights will be stupidly expensive and it's so far! Please. All okay here. Will let you know when I'm out. Love you. x

Suddenly there was a movement to Alice's left. Startled, she turned and saw a hand reaching through the curtain.

She dropped the phone and grabbed it, squeezing him tightly. She didn't even bother using her good hand.

Chapter 24

ALFIE

And so they lay, holding hands across the curtain. Alice hadn't even spoken to him until a few days ago! It was funny how long that brief period of time now felt, how quickly they had fallen into sync with each other, and how normal—no, not even normal, how *good* it felt to be holding her. He realized straightaway that it was her injured hand clasped in his, he could feel the gauze wrapped around her creating a rough second skin. Suddenly he was afraid—had he hurt her? Was he holding too tightly? Then she squeezed him hard, and he let the panic settle in his chest.

"Thank you. Sorry, I just need to wipe my face," she whispered, and then let go. "God, crying is disgusting."

"Lucky there's this big old curtain between us so I don't have to see it." Alfie let his hand linger momentarily before pulling it back across to his side.

"One of the many benefits," she replied, half laughing.

They sat in contented quiet for a few minutes. Alfie's brain was buzzing with excitement, his skin tingling from the memory of her hand in his.

"For someone who doesn't get many visitors, you sure have a hell of a lot of texts. You're not hiding secret friends back there?" He prayed he hadn't overstepped the mark.

"No." She laughed. He breathed a sigh of relief. "It's only a couple of people from work and Sarah."

"Who on earth is Sarah?"

There was a slight pause.

"I guess you could say she's the greatest person I've ever met in my entire life."

Why did his stomach sink a little when she said that? Surely he wasn't feeling jealous?

"Wow! I'm afraid you're going to have to give me more with a statement like that! Who is this person?"

"I mean, no matter what I say, it won't do her justice. She's one of those people you have to meet in the flesh to really get the measure of. She's my best friend."

"Do you think she'll come and visit?" Alfie assumed this must be the mystery emergency contact Nurse Angles had mentioned who was currently unreachable and halfway across the world.

"She lives in Australia now so it's not exactly the easiest trip to make. She said she'd fly in to see me, but I've told her not to come." Her voice was resolute.

"Well, she sounds incredible."

"She's the best." He could hear her voice cracking again. "God, I swear I've never cried this much in my entire life."

"Spare pillows but no tissues over there? I'd complain if I were you."

He could hear her laugh muffled by some vigorous face-wiping.

"You want to complain about something, honey? I'll come and give you something to complain about!" Nurse Angles's voice rang out across the ward.

"At last! Give him one from me too." Mr. Peterson was clapping enthusiastically.

"Alfie's in trouuuble. Alfie's in trouuuuble," Ruby repeatedly sang as she danced up and down the ward. Sharon whooped and cheered her on in delight.

Alfie sat bolt upright. "Hold on a second, since when did it become gang up on Alfie day? You got to give me at least a little bit of warning, team!"

"Let's all gang up on Alfie. Let's all gang up on Alfie." Ruby's singing was getting louder and louder as the dancing grew more and more spirited.

"Ruby, enough!" Jackie half attempted to control the wild child dancing up and down the ward.

"I see. I guess I'll just be silent for the remainder of my time here then, should I?" Alfie folded his arms in defiance.

"At last the penny drops!" Mr. Peterson slapped his hand to his forehead in mock exasperation while Alice sniggered next door.

"Perfect. Let me just grab my prosthetic and I'll be out of your hair immediately. That's right, my *prosthetic* because I only have one leg and you're all abusing a very disabled young man. I really hope you can find a way to live with yourselves!"

"You're both idiots, the pair of you. Now, Alfie, let's get you ready, the physician wants to see you before physio today, baby." Nurse Angles was already trying to lift him out of his bed before he had a chance to protest.

"Wait, why does the physician want to see me?"

"Maybe he's going to answer all our prayers and get you discharged!" Mr. Peterson chuckled.

He couldn't go now, surely?

Not yet. Please, not just yet.

"Come on, Alfie, concentrate. I know you're tired, but you're doing so well. We're so close to nailing this. I reckon you only need a couple more rounds."

Alfie was unceremoniously snapped out of his daydream by the familiar motivational tones of Darren. The physiotherapist was a sweet guy who really cared about his patients. You could see it in the way he picked people up off the floor, dusted them down, and pushed them to try again and again. He was the light when no one was home and the energy when the tank was running on empty. Darren was the kind of person you wanted to do well for as a patient. You'd try doubly hard just because you couldn't stand the thought of letting him down. However, his kindness sometimes backfired, making him both a cheerleader and a punching bag. God, it made Alfie cringe to think back to how he used to behave at times.

When he first started treatment, Alfie, being Alfie, had assumed it would be over in a few weeks. But apparently being thrown from a moving vehicle at seventy miles per hour, sliding across the tarmac, and having one of your limbs amputated really took it out of you. The physical exertion was one thing, but no one could have prepared him for the emotional toll of it all. The embarrassment of having to relearn the most basic of things was enough to reduce him to tears. A twenty-eight-year-old man crying from the sheer difficulty of lifting a weight he would have previously blinked at—it felt extremely emasculating. At first he was able to keep the emotion tightly bottled up, drowning out the negativity with the words of encouragement from those around him. Everyone told him it would get easier, that it would take some time but things would soon get better.

Except they didn't.

They got harder.

There were times when he couldn't even get himself out of his wheelchair, couldn't even lift his leg up, didn't even have the energy to cry. It was then that he cracked, and out poured the torrent of emotions he'd kept so carefully contained. At first the outbursts were directed at himself.

You stupid, weak idiot.

Look at what you've become.

You're a joke.

Try harder, you fucking loser.

Like a vicious snake, the anger writhed and twisted in the pit of his stomach, its fiery tongue licking at his flesh until he seared with the pain. When it had gorged on all of him, the creature had to look elsewhere for fuel, directing its venom at anyone close to him. It hurt to remember the times he'd collapsed into Darren's arms too exhausted to move another inch. It was even more painful when he remembered how he'd lashed out, punching and screaming into Darren's torso at the shame of falling once again.

He would have liked to say he'd managed to turn it around himself, realizing how ineffective his behavior was to his recovery and how detrimental his outbursts were to his healing. But once again it had taken the great insight of his mum for it to hit home.

"The doctors and physio team have told me you're acting up. What's going on, Alf?"

"Nothing. I'm just tired. It's hard, and I'm done with it."

"You're done with it?" Her eyes widened in disbelief.

"Please don't start, Mum. Do you have any idea what it's like living like this? Like a fucking freak?" He had never spoken to her like that before, but he was so full of hate he couldn't control it.

"Alfred Mack, never in my life have I ever been disappointed in you. Never." She'd bent down to look directly into his eyes. "Until right now."

He'd tried to turn his face away, but she'd reached out and held it in front of her. "Are you telling me you're a quitter? That my own flesh and blood is someone who gives up? I did not raise you to be 'done with it,' Alfie, no matter how hard things get. Because guess what? Life is hard. I can't imagine the hell you're going through and I won't pretend to, but, my God, I've known pain. I know what it's like to feel there is no hope left anymore. You think it was easy for me? You don't think my heart broke every single day during that time?"

He winced and went to speak, but she cut him off. "I'm not asking for your sympathy—I'm just telling you that there's always a way out. Even when you're in so deep you can't see anything but the darkness. Alfie, there's a whole life out there waiting for you. It might not be the life you had before or the life you dreamed of having, but it's there. There's an opportunity for you that right now you're throwing away. I'll be here every minute of every day, and I'll support you in any way I can, but I won't stay around and watch you throw your life away. I promise you that." Her eyes were fierce and wide. "So, what are you going to do?"

With that, he had stopped fighting everyone around him and started fighting for his life.

"Alfie, buddy, are you okay? You haven't been in the room all session. Something you want to talk about?" Darren was standing right in front of him now, hand on his shoulder.

"Sorry—it's just that I met with the physician earlier and he said that, if all goes well in our sessions, I should be out of here in a couple of weeks."

Alfie knew it sounded absurd. Why would he be sad about the prospect of leaving this place? He was getting the thing that everyone who walked into St. Francis's wanted, the chance to leave with their life still ahead of them.

"Ah." Darren signaled for Alfie to sit down on the bench. "I mean, that's got to be pretty scary, right? You've been here, what—eight weeks or so now?"

Alfie nodded.

"That's going to be a hell of an adjustment, buddy. I'm not surprised you're a little thrown! Come on, let's sack this session off and get a coffee?"

Alfie smiled. Of course Darren would understand. How many patients had he seen come through those doors, all with their own physical and emotional damage to deal with?

"Darren, are you ever not a nice person? Please tell me you're not one hundred percent great at all times? Like, surely you must get angry sometimes!"

"Of course I'm not nice all the time. For example, I'm going to make you get me these coffees for all the shit you put me through, and then I'm going to get two slices of cake just for the fun of it. And yes, you're paying for those too!"

Despite only doing half a physio session, Alfie was exhausted by the evening. Speaking to Darren had been a big help, but it hadn't erased his anxiety completely. He'd been reassured that it was 100 percent normal to feel worried about leaving—going back to reality was a big deal and something that a lot of patients worried about—but Alfie was still having trouble picturing what his life would be like outside the ward. In the end the thoughts became so depressing that the prospect of a turbulent night filled with flashbacks became a more welcome option. He closed his eyes and prayed that tonight his dreams would go easy on him.

Turned out, Alfie wasn't *always* so lucky.

"ROSS, NO!"

He sat bolt upright in bed. Sweat had drenched his T-shirt, and his heart was pounding so fast he could barely distinguish one beat from another.

The ward appeared empty. None of the nurses were going to be checking on him tonight, and neither was Mr. Peterson, it seemed; Alfie could hear his snores ringing out above the humming of the machines. Maybe everyone had grown immune to his cries now; he'd become just another background noise in the soundtrack of the Moira Gladstone ward. How could everything around him continue as usual when Alfie's world felt like it had been tipped upside down?

Alone in the darkness, he let his heart slow and his breathing grow deeper. Then he heard it.

"Who are they?"

Chapter 25

ALICE

"Sorry. I didn't wake you up, did I?" He sounded groggy, as if he were coming round from a thick hangover or a punch in the face.

How anyone could sleep through that noise was beyond her. This time the cries had felt more panicked and piercing than ever before.

"No, don't worry, I was already awake," she lied.

What the hell had she been thinking, asking him that?

Thank goodness he'd ignored her question and changed the subject. She wasn't sure if he'd done it knowingly, but she wasn't willing to force the issue.

"Okay. Good. That's good."

Every word sounded like a huge effort for him. She closed her eyes and tried desperately to fall back asleep, but everything around her sounded ten times louder than before.

The sound of her breathing.

The sound of his breathing.

Restless rustling of starched bedsheets.

Heart pounding on her side.

"They were in the car accident with me. . . ." He paused as if uncertain whether to continue. "Ciarán and Ross. My two best friends. They died. I survived."

Her cheeks burned as her face flushed with embarrassment. "I'm so sorry, Alfie, I should never have asked. I just—"

"Hey, stop that. You have a right to know who I wake you up moaning about every night."

"I mean . . . it's not every night!"

He tried his best attempt at a laugh. Strangely, she felt the urge to know more, but she stayed quiet. It wasn't her place to ask, and she'd already let her curiosity get the better of her once tonight. If he wanted to tell her more, he would.

"I think I've been kidding myself that the flashbacks are getting better. There have been times when they've become less intense and less frequent, but then they always come back. They're so real. So real it's like I'm there all over again, Alice."

The way he said her name caught her in her chest, and she was filled with a rush of affection.

"Have you spoken to . . . anyone about them?" She was trying to tread carefully here.

"By anyone, you mean a psychiatrist, right?"

She cringed at her lack of subtlety.

"For someone who doesn't say much, you're very tactful when you want to be."

"Eurgh. I'm sorry."

"It's fine. And in answer to your very generic but specific question, yes and no. I mean, people here obviously know, the nurses do the obligatory 'are you okay' every time the dreams happen, plus Sharon has the hearing of a bat so there's no fooling her. I spoke to the doctors about it briefly when they put me on antidepressants, and I've mentioned it in passing to my mum. But no, I haven't spoken to anyone about them *properly*. People have tried to encourage me to but, in all honesty, they are bad enough to experience when asleep, let alone recounting them to a stranger."

Another stab of guilt. If Alice could remember being in her accident, if she were repeatedly taken back to the moment when she was almost burnt alive, then she was pretty sure she wouldn't want to be regaling an audience with the tale either.

This is why you don't have more than one goddamn friend anymore, because you have the emotional capacity of a piece of wood.

"I'm sorry, it's none of my business. I didn't even think."

"Honestly, it's fine. Unless you say sorry again and then it will be anything but fine, okay? I've kind of wanted to talk to you about it since the first night you pretended not to be woken up by me. You may be many things, but you are no actress!"

"Oh well, fuck you very much. I happen to have had a budding theatrical career before the whole face-melting thing happened."

"I don't think it's the 'face melting,' as you so beautifully put it, that would be the stumbling block, more like your insane stubbornness. There is no one on this earth who would be capable of giving you direction."

She couldn't argue with him. Digging her heels in and sticking to her guns was just what she did. "I'll give you that one, BUT only because challenging you would confirm your accusation."

"You really are something else, Alice. I don't quite know what yet, but you're definitely something. Give me some time, I'll work you out sooner or later."

The affection that had been sitting in her chest surged again, but this time she felt like his eyes were on her. It was suddenly too intimate, way too personal, and she had to deflect.

"So . . . do you want to talk about them? The dreams, I mean?"

She heard him rearranging himself in bed and imagined him sitting up a little straighter.

"Most of the time it's exactly the same, I just relive the accident. I literally go through everything that happened that night over and over. Sometimes there are differences, small nuances that change, but mostly it's a detailed replay."

She was so scared of saying the wrong thing or pushing too hard that every word felt like a precarious step on a very thin tightrope. "Do you mind me asking what happened?"

She'd allowed her curiosity to get the better of her again.

Silence.

God, this is excruciating.

She had to fill the gap quickly. "You don't have to say anything if you don't want to."

No wonder Alfie used to just talk at her all the time. Filling the space with something felt much better than sitting in the silent vacuum.

"I do want to. I really do. I guess it's just harder than I thought."

He took a deep breath and then started his story.

Chapter 26

ALFIE

For so long he'd wanted to find someone he could open up to. Someone he could talk to without feeling uncomfortable or awkward. Now, at last, someone was asking, and he couldn't find one single word to answer. The doctors had always put him on edge. He couldn't work out if they found the act of witnessing his grief awkward or whether in fact they were immune to the pain after hearing thousands of similar stories, but either way he found talking to them impossible. There was no eye contact, just endless scribbled notes and the occasional "How did that make you feel?"

So like them, he'd simply shut down. The regular mental health support sessions continued, but the degree to which Alfie opened up shrank over time. In their minds, the flashbacks had got better, and therefore no more questions were asked. In reality, the trauma was simply being buried deeper and deeper within the recesses of Alfie's mind.

As Alfie lay there in the dark searching for a starting point, it struck him how vulnerable he felt even though Alice couldn't see him.

"We'd been at a friend's wedding just outside of London. We thought we'd be clever and save money by driving home that night, it made sense as we were only a couple of hours away from home. Ciarán knew he was driving, so he didn't drink."

The pain throbbed at the back of his throat.

"I had to tell the police *so* many times that he didn't touch a drop. He would never do that to us. Ever."

The words came out more forcefully than he'd intended, but she had to know the type of guy Ciarán was. He took a deep breath and let the anger subside.

"I was so tired I was pretty much asleep the moment I got in the back of the car. I remember waking up to the two idiots arguing over what song to play next. Ross was insisting on Ariana Grande for like the fifteenth time, it was his new girl-friend's favorite song apparently, and Ciarán just kept switching the track back. 'It's my phone,' Ciarán kept saying. 'But it's my turn to choose,' Ross kept whining. They were going at each other like this for ages, back and forth, over and over. I couldn't be bothered to deal with them because I knew this would go on for the rest of the journey, they ar—were both stubborn bastards."

Past tense, Alfie.

"I reached forward and took the phone off of them. They both looked round to try to grab it back. It was my fault: I took the phone, so no one was looking at the road. It was such a brief moment, but he didn't see it coming. He didn't see it coming because I'd distracted him."

His words were falling out of his mouth so quickly he couldn't catch his breath. The guilt that had been building up inside of him was forcing its way out.

"Some drunk arsehole a few cars up had swerved into the wrong lane and thrown a lorry off course. It came right at us and no one fucking saw it. All I remember is feeling the weight of everything hitting me all at once. It was like someone was ripping me inside out. There was so much pain I couldn't work out where or who I was anymore."

He paused. His hands were clenching the bedsheets so tightly he could see the whites of his knuckles glowing in the dark.

"They say I was thrown five meters from the car. That's where the dreams always start. Me waking up, facedown on the road with a knife in my stomach telling me something is very wrong. Then I look up and I see it. The car. It's crumpled like it's nothing more than paper. There's smoke everywhere. I can hear screaming. I'm trying to find the others, and then I see Ross's face. He's still in the goddamn car. It's like I'm so close, but every time I try to drag myself towards him he just gets farther and farther away. I'm screaming for him, begging him to get out of the car. But it's like someone's muted me or turned the volume up so loud on everyone else that my words just disappear into nothing. And then. Fuck. Then it burns. The heat is hitting my face but I don't care because I just want to go in there and get him out. But someone's grabbing me, trying to pull me away, and I can feel their hands gripping me so tightly, but the harder they hold me the more I'm pushing them away. I try to get up and walk but I can't. My leg is a dead weight underneath me, completely and utterly useless. Every time I push myself up enough to try to stand, the pain grabs hold of me completely and it's so intense that I almost black out again. I'm stuck. I'm stuck, unable to save my friend who is so fucking close to me. I can't think or feel anything but rage, as if I'm on fire too. And then out of the corner of my eye I see Ciarán. I see him just lying there. He's so broken. Just in a heap of human mass left on the road. But it's Ciarán. I know it's Ciarán. I start screaming for him, pleading for him to wake up. But he just stays so still. I need him to wake up. Why isn't he waking up? We need to go and get Ross. I'm so mad at him for just lying there, and I'm so scared, I just want to hold him, but there's more people pulling me away and I can't hold them off any longer. I want to hold on so badly. I can't leave them. I can't fucking leave them there."

When the tears started, they hit him with such a force he could barely keep himself upright.

Suddenly he saw her hand come through for him. He was too scared to reach out and grab it, so certain that if he released his grip from his bedsheets he would fall and never come back.

"Alfie, I'm here. Take my hand."

He didn't need to see her to know there was no pity, no awkwardness or repulsion. She would hold him. She would anchor him. He held her hand, and she squeezed him tightly.

"I woke up in the hospital adamant that they would be just a couple of beds away from me. I wouldn't believe them when they told me. It was only when I saw the look in my mum's face that I knew they were really gone. I didn't even care that they took my leg. They could have taken all of me. I just needed to not be the only one to survive. Seeing the resentment in their families' faces became unbearable. They loved me like a son but wanted me to be the one they were grieving for. I suppose that in the end the only way I could get through it was to bury it. Shut all the pain off. But the honest truth is that sometimes I wish I were the one they put in the ground."

They held hands as if it were all they could do just to keep on breathing; he couldn't tell who was holding on more tightly. Tears from both of them ran down their arms to meet in the middle.

The silence unfolded around them, bringing with it a sense of peace. Alfie could feel the tightness in his chest melting away as his breathing grew deeper and more considered. He had survived the storm, and someone was next to him picking him up from the rubble.

"I know what it's like to be the one they want dead," she whispered.

Just as he felt he was back on solid ground, it shifted beneath him again.

Chapter 27

ALICE

It was such a powerful feeling, holding someone. Being there for someone. Being *wanted* by someone. Had she gotten so caught up in the magic of the moment that she'd let a part of her escape in the hope of being held back? Shame coursed through her body, and even though she knew he couldn't see her, she found herself burying her head in her hands.

Why the hell had she said that?

She'd opened her mouth to apologize for making it all about her, when his voice broke the silence.

"Do you want to talk about it?" His hand was still outstretched on her side of the curtain.

"I don't even know why I said it. This was your time to talk about stuff. I just . . . I just wanted you to know that you're not alone in the way you feel."

"To be honest, I'm pretty done with talking. There's only so much I can relive in one night. I'm all ears if you want to tell me your story."

"There's not that much to tell."

"Really? You're saying that a story that starts with 'I know what it's like to be the one they want dead' doesn't have much to it? Come on!" He was laughing. She imagined him shaking his head and rolling his eyes at her.

"I set that one up fairly dramatically, didn't I?" She snorted. His laugh really was infectious. "I've never really spoken to anyone about it properly before, so I'm not even sure where to start."

"You can start anywhere or nowhere. It's totally up to you."

He was right. It *was* up to her. She could tell as much or as little as she wanted. At the end of the day, it wasn't really for him. She was telling the story for herself.

Twenty years was a long time to carry around something as heavy as this; maybe it was time to let go of some of the pain.

She closed her eyes.

"I was born a twin. My brother, Euan, was four minutes older than me. He was so full of life that I wouldn't be surprised if I'd actually had half my leg out before he hauled me back into the womb and pushed himself out first. You couldn't stop him doing what he wanted, and you were a fool if you tried. There was such a fire in him that you could feel the heat just by looking at his face. He was a whirlwind and shook up everything in his path, except for me. It was as if he held those four minutes like a gift. He was my big brother and he took it upon himself to protect me as though his life depended on it." She paused as a suffocating lump rose in her throat. This was why she always stopped herself from thinking about him.

"He sounds like he was more stubborn than you—and that is an incredible feat!" Alfie squeezed her hand reassuringly.

"He was. He was brilliant. The best." She paused again, allowing the space to hold her in her thoughts. "But in reality, he was the one who needed looking after. He was born with a congenital heart defect—it's not uncommon in twins, sharing the same placenta there is always a risk that one baby doesn't receive as much oxygen as the other. Unfortunately, I took the lion's share and left him without."

The guilt surged through her heart and hot tears pricked her eyes.

Another squeeze. *Go on, don't stop now*, it said.

"We had a relatively normal childhood. Euan was determined that his condition wouldn't get in the way of anything. He didn't seem to have a care in the world. Maybe we all carried the fear for him. My parents were strict with him and even stricter with me. I had to look out for him at all times. Make sure he was okay. Anytime we were out of the house and away from them, he was my responsibility. I would have done anything for him. I loved him with every cell of me. He was a part of me."

She took a deep breath. She knew she was waffling, buying any semblance of time she could before she had to tell the real story.

"We were eleven years old when it happened. It was a Saturday in late October and the weather was turning. We'd begged our parents to let us go and play outside for the afternoon; by the cliffs was our favorite spot. I knew he was feeling restless that day. He had been trying to push boundaries, desperately seeing how far he could stretch my parents' rules and his limits. As we got to the edge, he began to run. I screamed after him to stop, but he kept going. I can see him now, like a caged wild animal that had finally been set free. He was laughing manically, throwing his head to the sky in pure joy. He ran and ran all the way down to the beach. I followed him as quickly as I could, but he was so fast."

She could feel herself speeding up as she spoke, almost as though she couldn't wait to just spit the story out and be done with it. The toxicity was sour and she no longer wanted the taste of it on her tongue.

"By the time I reached him, he was already in. He'd taken off his clothes and run into the sea. I screamed so loudly my throat burned. In the end I had to run in after him and drag him out. He kicked and screamed and clawed at me, shouting over and over how unfair his life was. I held him so tightly, both of us crying with the pain of it all. He begged me not to tell Mum and Dad what he'd done. He knew we'd both be in trouble. And for some stupid, *stupid* reason, I didn't." She shook her head in frustration. "When we got back, I sneaked him into the house, made him have a warm bath and sent him to bed. I told my parents he was tired from running, and everything seemed fine the next morning. By the evening, things were bad. He was sweating. Drenching the bedsheets and his pajamas, but when I put my hand on his head he was like ice. I told him over and over that it was going to be okay, but I knew everyone was scared. My parents were so confused as to how he'd gotten so sick so quickly. He pleaded with me not to tell them, but I had to. I had to do *something*."

The memory of it all was whirring in her mind. Jagged edges of sounds and colors pierced her consciousness. Closing her eyes didn't help; it just brought everything into clearer focus. She didn't want to see his face again. She couldn't bear to replay the memory anymore. The pit of her stomach started to lurch as the nausea hit her. *You let him die. You should have saved him.* Those poisonous words echoed over and over until she wanted to scream them out of her head.

"They were so angry when I told them. So angry that they couldn't even shout at me. I wished they had, I wanted them to scream at me, tell me off, but instead they were silent. My mum wouldn't look at me. They called the ambulance, but . . . but by the time they came it was too late. He'd been so cold. His body was in so much shock that his heart just gave up."

Her fingernails were digging so deeply into his hand she was surprised he was still holding her.

"I should have done more. I shouldn't have let him run off. I should have told my parents straightaway. But I didn't. I didn't do anything." The tears were sticking in her throat, leaving little room for breath. Why had she even started telling this story? She was losing control and she hated it. She needed to focus.

"You did. You did everything you could."

"But I should have done more. They blamed me. They both blamed me. I know they did. They could barely look at me afterwards. Every time I tried to explain or go near them, they'd walk away in tears. I just wanted him safe. That's all I ever wanted, I promise." Sobs were starting to rack her chest. The thread that had been holding her so tightly for so many years was loosening quickly.

"Alice, it wasn't your fault. Do you hear me? It wasn't your fault. You were just a little girl."

She tried everything possible to maintain control, but it was becoming harder and harder to hold on.

"Alice, it's okay not to be okay. You can cry and be angry and scream and shout if you want to."

"If I start, I'm scared I'll never stop." Her voice sounded so small and childlike, yet the fear came through loud and clear.

"You will. Eventually you will. I'm right here, and I'm not going anywhere."

With those words, the final stitch in her armor was cut. The thread fell to the floor as the wave of grief took her breath away. She leant into the sobs that rang out from deep inside her. She didn't try to quiet the pain anymore. There was no point. It was coming out, demanding to be heard. The air was so thick with sorrow she half expected to see it hanging as fog in front of her eyes. Instead, she saw nothing but his hand holding hers. She couldn't remember when she fell asleep, or even if she stopped crying as she dreamed, but she knew he was holding her.

Chapter 28

ALFIE

There were so many points during the night when Alfie wanted to tear down the curtain and just take her in his arms. He was scared to fall asleep in case she needed him. Even as he heard her sobs fade into the sounds of sleeping, he fought to keep his eyes open. Mostly he ended up staring at the curtain, telling himself that one look at her wouldn't hurt anyone. She wouldn't know. The voice urging him on would grow louder and more convincing to the point where he would be reaching over to pull the fabric back just a tiny bit, and then—

No.

This is her choice.

You can't just take without asking.

They had come so far; was he really willing to risk her trust in him already? No. He would wait. He would ask her when the time was right.

Thinking back on everything she'd told him, it was no

surprise she was so closed off. It must be pretty hard to let people in when you'd been hurt that badly, and as much as Alfie wanted to believe that last night's conversation would change everything between them, he knew better. The walls she'd built for most of her life weren't suddenly going to come crashing down. Their conversation wasn't going to be the magic key that unlocked everything, and he knew he had to prepare himself to be pushed aside again.

As the new day dawned on the ward, he waited silently. He wanted to give her the freedom to choose her reaction. How did she want to play it today?

"Hey." Her voice was drowsy and hoarse from the crying, but it was welcoming. It said, *I'm tired and I'm weary and I'm feeling vulnerable today*, but what it definitely didn't say was *Get away from me* or *Leave me alone*.

He let out a sigh of relief. "I'm not even going to ask how you are because I think I can guess."

"I'm not feeling my best, I won't lie." She laughed. It was that tentative, shy laugh that warmed his soul a little. "Thank you for last night. I don't quite know what to say except thank you."

"You don't need to say anything else. Like I said, I'm not going anywhere."

Silence.

Good silence.

Accepting, understanding silence.

"Everything all right over here this morning, being as annoyingly adorable as ever, Alfie?" Nurse Angles was making her way across the ward straight towards him.

"You know me. Can't help something that comes so naturally, I guess." He winked at her as she burst into a blinding smile.

"We're going to miss you around here when you leave us, Mr. Mack. You're the sunshine of this place."

He laughed to mask the panic that quickly pierced his stomach.

"Isn't that right, Mr. Peterson?" she called across the ward.

Silence.

Not a good silence.

A worrying, unusual, alarming silence.

"Mr. P.? Didn't you hear that? Mother Angel over here was just being especially nice to me. I'm surprised you're missing out on an opportunity to take me off that pedestal." Alfie tried to make his voice lighthearted, but there was a definite edge to it.

Nothing.

"I'll go check on him, sweetheart. I'm sure he's just sleeping." Nurse Angles crossed the corridor, and he heard her closing the curtains behind her. "Mr. Peterson, is everything okay over here?"

Say something, please.

"Okay, honey. Okay, sure. I'll get your breakfast then ask the doctor to come and just check in on you."

A faint grunt of acknowledgment, followed by the curtain being drawn.

"He's not feeling too well, Alfie. Says he's okay but just a little tired. I'm going to get the doctor to check in, just in case."

He smiled and nodded, very aware of how discreet she was being.

It's okay. He's a ninety-two-year-old man. He's allowed to be tired.

The reassuring words played in a continuous loop until he saw the doctor appear. Alfie quickly analyzed his approach. As a semipermanent resident, you soon became able to assess the severity of a situation by the way the doctors walked. This guy was in no hurry. He sauntered across the ward, distracted by his notes and saying hello to the nurses on his way. There was no rushing, no urgency. Everything was going to be fine.

"Bloody fuss about nothing. Just a bit of dehydration. Probably because they put about a liter of salt in every god-damn meal in this place," scoffed the old man after the fifth time he'd been checked on by the nurses.

"Oh, please, Mr. P., don't you dare pretend you're not en-joying all the attention."

"Ach, give it a rest will you, boy. And do me a favor? Go and annoy someone else today, will you? I'm in a bloody awful mood as it is."

Alfie looked at his friend; was it really just a bad mood? Or was there something else?

"Get away with you, kid. Stop giving me that look. I'm fine!"

Alfie did as he was told and left Mr. P. alone. He seemed like the normal grumpy old man he'd come to know and love, but something was telling Alfie not to be so sure.

Maybe he wasn't the only one who wore a mask in this place.

The rest of the day held nothing new or out of the ordinary, which, to Alfie, felt like a blessing after the unwelcome ex-citement of the morning. He didn't even mind that Alice had gone quiet; he assumed she was still processing their conver-sation last night. Which reminded him that he should proba-bly be doing the same thing.

It was, after all, because of Alfie that Alice's emotional outburst had happened. He'd spoken about the most harrow-

ing night of his life—and to his surprise, he wasn't embarrassed or ashamed about it. In fact, the only thing he felt was
an overwhelming relief. Storing all of that noise in his head
had been more of a burden than he had known. He hoped
that eventually Alice would feel the same way.

Alice. Alice. Always thinking about Alice.

No matter how hard he tried to keep focused on himself,
Alfie found his mind constantly drifting back to her. There
were so many questions he wanted to ask, but none appropriate so early on in their friendship. He wanted to know what
had happened after her brother died. What had caused so
much tension between her and her mum? Where was her
dad in all of this? Most of all, he found himself wondering if
she was lonely. This last one he found too upsetting to think
about for too long. Or maybe it was because he already knew
the answer.

"You're worried about him, aren't you?" Her quiet voice,
almost a whisper, crept through the curtains.

"Huh?" Her question caught him off guard.

"Mr. Peterson . . . you're worried about him."

How had she known?

"Yeah, maybe. I know everyone is saying he's fine, but
something just feels off and I can't seem to shake it."

"If he's not fine, at least he's in the best place."

"Yeah, I know."

Logically a hospital ward was the safest place to be, but Alfie
couldn't quite convince himself that he didn't need to worry.

"Can I ask you something?" Her voice was still a little tentative.

It was a strange feeling, being the one on the receiving
end of the questions—nice, but still strange.

"Of course."

"Are you scared about leaving this place?"

Had she literally been inside his head?

"Honestly?"

"Yes."

"I'm terrified."

"Do . . . do you know when you're going?" If he didn't know better, he would say she almost sounded nervous.

"No. Well . . . soon, apparently. It all rests on me being signed off by the physio team, and they are pretty happy with how I'm doing. Then it's my final assessment. Maybe I should start being a little less awesome in my sessions from now on."

"I think everyone on the ward would appreciate that."

Even you? he wanted to ask.

"Not sure Mr. Peterson would always agree with that, but maybe I'll stay just to have the pleasure of annoying him some more."

"Do you think you'll go back to what you were doing before?"

"What, being the happy-go-lucky, lovable, yet incredibly infuriating human being that I was? I'm sure I can still manage that with one leg!"

"*Alfie.*"

He'd forgotten for a moment that she'd seen underneath his humor. He couldn't easily laugh his way through the serious conversations anymore.

"Sorry." He paused to think. What was he going to do when he got out of here? "I mean, I guess I assumed I would slot back into life before I left. My flat's waiting and ready for my grand return, and I can't imagine doing anything else with my life except teaching. I wouldn't *want* to do anything else with my life. Those kids are the best and worst things about my every day! But is it possible to be a PE teacher with one leg? I really don't know. I hope so."

"Aha." She chuckled. "You're a teacher. That makes a lot of sense."

"I'm taking that as a compliment." He smiled, turning himself over to face the curtain.

"Have you spoken to the school yet? Surely they can't discriminate against you for having a disability. That would be illegal, not to mention setting an awful example for the kids."

He sensed an organized, practical Alice joining the conversation. Perhaps this was a small glimpse of the woman before the accident, a woman he imagined storming the office floors and taking absolutely zero prisoners.

"All right, *Mum.*" He'd had these thoughts over and over, yet he still hadn't actually done anything about it. Was he lazy? No. Was he terrified of hearing something he didn't want to? Hell yes.

"Sorry, it's just—"

"It's fine. I will speak to them. I know I'm avoiding it, but right now holding on to the hope that I can still go back is helping me cope with the thought of leaving this place. Ideally I'd go back home, adjust a bit, and when I've dealt with not being fed and watered twenty-four/seven, then I'll face it. If I think about doing everything all at once, it becomes impossible."

"I can understand that." She sounded deep in thought.

"Have you had any ideas about what you're going to do?" He tried to keep his question casual and lighthearted. He was very aware that, without seeing her properly, he had no idea of the extent of her injuries, both emotionally and physically. He'd seen the dressings on her hand, heard the snippets of conversations with the doctors. The physio regimen. The wound care. But he knew it was still a very sensitive subject and one that he'd have to navigate carefully.

"Considering the fact that I can't even look at my own face in a mirror right now, it doesn't bode well for me returning to work."

She hasn't even seen her own face?

Jesus, how bad is it?

"What was your job? I'm guessing something ridiculously high-flying and important?"

Alfie prided himself on being a good judge of character, but he reckoned anyone who spent even two minutes with Alice could guess she had a very prestigious and very well-paid job.

"I was a director at one of the big financial consultant firms. I led teams of fifty people, and now I'm scared to even go to the toilet in case someone sees me and runs away."

"Well, luckily for you they close down the whole bloody ward when you want to go anywhere. It's like living with Beyoncé."

She snorted out a laugh. God, he really loved it when she did that. "Oh, please, I am way more demanding than her and you know it!"

He was so tempted to pull back the curtain and see for himself who this complicated, wonderful stranger really was.

Just one look.

"Until I see you forcing Nurse Angles to give you only the red M&M's, I'd say the jury is out on that one."

"Red? I'm a blue kind of girl every day! Way more food dyes in them." The lightness suddenly dropped from her tone. "Seriously, though. I feel like such a completely different person sometimes that I don't even know if I could ever fit back into my old life. Some days I lie here and dream about giving everything up and leaving London behind me. A part of me just wants to escape to Australia, make Sarah build me a granny flat in her apartment, and see out my days there."

"Okay, so, why don't you go? After here, book a ticket and just go!"

"Maybe." Her voice went quiet.

"How did you two meet?" He hoped it was a long and intricate story. He wanted to keep her talking for as long as possible.

"First day of university."

"Ah, I bet you two were at some wild, raucous party, bonding over copious amounts of cheap alcohol and terrible dance moves. Am I right?"

Alice burst out laughing. The sound made Alfie's face instantly beam into a wide grin.

"Not quite."

"Go on . . ." He longed to be able to see the expression on her face right now. But all he had was the plain blue curtain staring back at him.

"We met at the vending machine in our hall. Both of us were trying to secretly swerve the first night of Fresher's Week by buying copious amounts of snacks and hiding in our rooms. She made a comment about my poor choice of crisps, which to this day I defend and love dearly, and that was it. We spent the night hiding away from both our sets of hideously drunk flatmates, watching movies and drinking wine."

"Wow. I don't know what to ask first. Why you were hiding or what crisps you chose."

Her laugh floored him again, this time with a warm feeling in his stomach.

"They were paprika McCoy's."

"And you were hiding because?" He leant a little closer to the curtain.

"I don't know really. I came to university to get away from home. For me, it was a fresh start. A chance to get away from the life that I wanted so desperately to forget. I wasn't there to make friends and lose my mind to alcohol and hormone-filled boys. I think Sarah was the same. She had her head screwed on. She was as determined as I was to get her degree and get out of there into the adult world. We were insepara-ble after that night."

"So when did she leave for Australia?"

"About two years ago now. It had always been a dream of hers to live abroad, and after she got married to Raph they decided to just do it. So that was that and off they went. Ever since she moved, she's been telling me to come and visit. Funny how I never seemed to have the time; everything was more urgent or important."

"You should go!" Alfie couldn't believe she was even hesi-tating.

"I'm thinking about it."

"No offense, Alice, I'm not too sure what there is to really think about."

"You haven't seen me, though, have you?"

Her retort was quick and cutting. He'd forgotten just how easily her words could sting.

"No, you're right, I haven't. I would love to, though. And if I did, I'm sure it wouldn't stop me wanting to see you again."

Silence.

Please, God, not the silence again.

"Good night, Alfie."

Chapter 29

ALICE

"Alice." A voice drifted into the realms of her consciousness.

"No, don't tell her yet. She'll refuse to see me. I need to be close enough that she can't say no."

"I'm not sure that's the best approach with a patient like Alice."

"*Trust me*. If anyone knows how to deal with Alice, it's me."

"Right, okay, if you say so. Let's go in and see if she's up for visitors."

Alice was vaguely aware of a conversation happening about her. It was taking place somewhere just out of reach of her full consciousness. The voices sounded so familiar, but they didn't quite make sense being here. They didn't fit. Maybe she was still dreaming.

"Alice, honey."

The voice was definitely louder now.

"Alice, dear. Are you awake?"

She really had spent too long on this ward if Nurse Angles was now appearing in her dreams.

"Alice Gunnersley! I have traveled halfway around the world to come and see you, and you can't even wake up!"

Her eyes snapped open. Holy shit.

"Sarah?"

"I'm glad you haven't forgotten the sound of my voice. Can I come in?"

She was really here.

"No! Please. No. Sarah, what the hell are you doing here? I told you not to come!"

She was so confused. What was happening? It was only last night that she'd been talking about her friend, longing for her to be here, and now she was standing just outside of her cubicle. She had gotten exactly what she wanted—yet right now all she wanted was for her to disappear.

"Alice, please? It's me."

"If you aren't feeling up to seeing anyone today, that's totally okay," Nurse Angles interjected.

She appreciated Nurse Angles's attempt at protecting her, but she knew there would be no telling Sarah to go. Plus deep down she didn't want her to leave—she just needed a minute to compose herself. It had been such a long time since she'd seen her friend in the flesh, but she couldn't bear to watch Sarah's face crumble into pity as she saw Alice for the first time.

She took one deep inhale and closed her eyes.

"It's fine, she can come in."

Suddenly the weight of Sarah was next to her. She didn't even think twice as they wrapped their arms around each other and Alice held her friend close.

"There's my Alice. God, I've missed you."

Alice opened her eyes and through the tears started to bring her best friend's face into focus. She took in Sarah's blond hair, still fine and short, framing those elfin features and those eyes. The eyes that were colored the deepest, brightest, kindest blue that she'd ever seen. To look at, you couldn't have found two more opposite people. For all of Sarah's lightness and brightness, Alice had an intense darkness. A guy at work had once kindly described Alice as "one of those earthy types. You know, a Stonehenge type of beautiful." Despite her pride being just a little wounded, she had to admit she knew what he meant. Still didn't stop Dan from accounting from being an absolute arsehole, though.

The thing was, Alice had a presence about her. Her frame was strong and sturdy, and there was no hiding her, standing tall at nearly six feet. Sarah, on the other hand, was small in all directions. Barely tall enough for her head to graze Alice's armpit, she was slight and dainty.

"Sarah. Why the hell di—"

"Don't even start. My best friend in the entire fucking world has been seriously injured, in fact nearly *killed*, and on top of that isn't replying to one single message I send her. Obviously I'm going to fly to be by her bedside. And don't bullshit me, because I know you'd do exactly the same for me."

As she said, there was no way she'd want to go up against Sarah in a fight.

"Now, move up and make some space for me on this tiny piece-of-shit bed and tell me what the hell happened."

"Jesus Christ. You're literally here for less than a minute and you're already telling me what to do."

"Yes," Sarah said defiantly, swinging her legs up onto the bed without waiting for Alice to move. "What did you expect?"

Alice looked her friend square on in the face and was filled with such affection it made her heart want to burst. "Absolutely nothing less."

"I thought so. Now, please move up, my arse is pretty much hanging off the side here."

Strangely, considering that Alice had not voluntarily let anyone this close to her since the accident, it didn't feel uncomfortable having Sarah lie next to her. It felt like coming home.

"So, now we're sitting comfortably, are you going to tell me what happened?"

Alice closed her eyes and began reciting all the information about the accident she'd managed to piece together. The only way she was going to get through it was to tell the events of the accident as if they belonged to someone else. There was no emotion left in her voice. Sarah listened patiently — she did not flinch or gasp or react, she simply allowed Alice to tell her story in its wholeness. The only sign that she was present was the hand that clasped Alice's tightly.

". . . as soon as I was stable, they moved me to this ward, I guess to kind of rehabilitate me before they eventually discharge me."

There was a long pause. Saying it out loud had really brought the enormity of what had happened to life, and Alice could see her friend trying to digest it all at once.

"I can't believe you went through all of that by yourself!" Sarah nestled her face into Alice's neck. "If you weren't in the hospital right now, I'd be pretty mad you didn't demand I come over sooner. In fact, I am pretty livid you didn't give the hospital my mobile number, but I'm not surprised. It was a very clever move, Alice, but it didn't work, did it? When will you realize you can't do everything on your own? Anyway, that's by the by—I'm here now, aren't I? Have they said anything about when you might be ready to leave? What's the treatment plan? Are they helping you enough? Do you want me to speak to one of the doctors? Someone told me you had barely spoken until recently? It's not good enough if they aren't supporting you, Al."

Hurricane Sarah had officially hit, and Alice wasn't quite sure the Moira Gladstone ward was ready for it. Remnants of last night's conversation floated through her mind. It seemed that Alfie would actually get the privilege of meeting Sarah in the flesh.

"Just breathe for a second, will you?" It was what Alice always used to tell Sarah when she got herself worked up. "They've been amazing. Truly."

"Okay." Sarah deflated before her eyes. "I'm just trying to make up for lost time here. So tell me, what have they done so far?"

Alice could feel her friend's entire being slow down to a normal rate of existence. It was important to get her to switch gears when she was in these moods; otherwise she had the potential to upturn everything in her path. "I've had one operation, and depending on how the wounds heal and how bad the scarring is, there may be a potential for more. At the moment I'm doing physio to get me moving again, and they are treating the wounds every other day. It's a bit of a waiting game, to be honest with you."

"Fine. Well, you know I'll help you with whatever you need." Sarah seemed satisfied with her answer, but Alice knew this was only temporary. Sarah liked action; she practically lived on to-do lists and tasks, and Alice was willing to bet big money that more questions were just around the corner.

"And how . . . how are you feeling about it all?"

There it was. The one question she really didn't want to answer.

"I was talking to Alfie about this last night. It's all still pretty overwhelming, if I'm honest. The thought of leaving here feels way too big right now. I can't even look at myself in the mirror; how am I going to be able to walk down the street, or leave the flat!"

She felt Sarah squeeze her hand tighter.

"There are so many things about what you just said that need addressing, but first I want to know who this Alfie is?"

Alice laughed a deep belly laugh. Of *course* Sarah would latch on to that.

"Alfie is the lucky son of a bitch who gets to lie next to your friend every day and night! Hi . . . I'm guessing you're *the* Sarah?"

A familiar hand shot through between the curtains. A smile of sheer delight erupted across Sarah's face. Alice groaned. She knew that smile meant one thing and one thing only. Trouble.

"Pleasure to meet you, Alfie." Sarah smirked as she shook his hand.

"Come by anytime, Sarah, my cubicle is an open curtain."

"I'll be sure to, don't you worry."

Alice practically disappeared under the covers as Sarah flashed her a knowing wink.

Chapter 30

ALFIE

As much as Alice had tried to convince him that Sarah wouldn't come for her, Alfie had known deep down it was only a matter of time. A part of him thought he might be jealous that Sarah was allowed inside Alice's cubicle, but all he felt was relief that someone was going to be by her side. He tried so hard not to listen to their conversation. It felt intrusive and slightly inappropriate. At one point, Alfie was tempted to turn the TV up as loud as possible, but then he thought that in itself was intrusive, so he'd turned to his faithful puzzle books. He managed quite well for a while, engrossing himself in a particularly hard sudoku, but when he heard his name mentioned he couldn't help but listen. How could he not? They were talking about him!

After his and Sarah's brief introduction, he forced himself to remain quiet. He knew they needed space, and luckily he had another physio session in the afternoon to take him away from any further temptation to make conversation. Just as he was making his way out the doors, he heard someone running up behind him.

"Hey, hold up a second, will you. It's Alfie, isn't it?"

"The very one."

Sarah looked him up and down, cocked her head to one side, and then broke into an approving smile. He appreciated how she barely stopped when she saw his prosthetic leg. No lingering stare, no quick aversion to pretend she hadn't seen what he was lacking, just a steady gaze taking him all in. Apparently he'd passed the test.

"Do you want anything from PizzaExpress?"

"Pardon?"

"PizzaExpress. I'm going to get some food for Al, did you want anything? I'm hoping you're the kind of guy who knows exactly what he wants or else can make a decision in about thirty seconds."

Wow, this woman took assertive to the next level. He definitely approved.

"I'll have the American Hot, extra pepperoni, and a share-size plate of dough balls." He couldn't help but smile a little smugly at her. "Please."

"Nicely done." She nodded, turned, and walked off without saying another word.

His physio session with Darren turned out to be extremely successful, which did nothing to put Alfie in a good mood. He knew he should be celebrating his achievements, but every ounce of progress took him closer to leaving the ward and towards the reality of the outside world. Darren wanted to talk about it. What plans was he putting in place, how were his parents preparing for his return? He knew he'd have to face it soon, but every time he began thinking about it he conveniently found something much more important and interesting to focus on. Although, he had to admit, seeing that pizza box by his bedside when he arrived back helped cheer him up a lot.

"Sorry, we ate the dough balls—we got hungry and you were taking ages!" Sarah called out.

"Are you kidding me?!

"Obviously she's joking. They're in the box." There was a hint of exasperation in Alice's voice, as if she were dealing with two unruly children.

"Thank God for that. Don't you underestimate me, Sarah—I may only have one leg, but you get in between me and food and there will be trouble."

"Don't play the one-leg card with me. It won't get you anywhere!"

"Doesn't get me very far now anyway, to be honest."

"Ha! Touché."

"I'm really not sure how I'm going to be able to deal with the two of you together. I thought having Alfie's relentless joking was tiring enough."

"Jesus, Alice, when did you get so serious?"

"Perhaps when I went and got forty percent of my body burnt in a fire?" Alice shot back.

"Ah, there she is!"

It was so funny having two voices to deal with from behind the curtain. He felt like he was back at school, trying to get on the good side of the popular girls. Alfie sat back in bed, pizza in one hand and dough ball in the other.

These next few days are going to be really fun.

Chapter 31

ALICE

The moment Sarah arrived at Alice's bedside, it was as though she'd never been away. Everything just felt so familiar that for a moment Alice would forget about her burns and the bitterness and the bleak hospital surroundings. She felt like her old self again, the unstoppable, unflappable Alice Gunnersley. One look down at her arms, though, would bring reality crashing down around her.

"Alice. You know that visiting hours are finished, please could your guest leave." Nurse Bellingham stood stony-faced at the end of the bed. "Quickly." Of course everyone else on shift had managed to turn a blind eye, but not her.

"Sorry, Nurse, I'm going now, I promise." Sarah hurriedly gathered up her belongings, which had already spread themselves over every available surface. "I'll be back tomorrow, okay, Al?" She leaned over and planted a gentle kiss on the top of her head.

"Where are you staying tonight? How long are you even here for?" Questions bombarded Alice's mind. The day had felt like a dream and there had been no space for logistics and practicalities until now.

"Staying with Mum tonight, God help me, and then will get an Airbnb or a hotel sorted tomorrow." Sarah looked at Alice apologetically. "And . . . annoyingly, I could only manage to get ten days off work. They said that with me still being quite new, they couldn't afford to give me much more. I'm so sorry, Al."

Ten days.

A hard lump was forming in her throat, tears pricking her eyes.

Just enjoy it. Day by day.

Since when had she got so goddamn needy? Had she underestimated the extent of her damage after all? Perhaps nearly dying had left its emotional scars too. She swallowed down the disappointment and dragged a smile onto her face.

"Don't be silly. It's amazing you're even here." She prayed the sincerity had masked the disappointment. "Honestly."

"Miss Gunnersley, if I come in there and find that your friend has not in fact left yet, I will be extremely unhappy."

Sarah's eyes widened as she tried her best not to laugh. She lowered her voice to a whisper. "Seriously? It's like we're back at school again! Right, I'm going, I love you, and I'll see you tomorrow. Unless, of course, this woman murders me on the way out for breaking her rules."

"Just run really, *really* quickly."

In one mad dash of bag, blond hair, and swearing, Sarah was gone. Alice couldn't stop herself from laughing out loud when she heard her friend's cries.

"Alfie, I'm bringing pain au chocolat tomorrow for break-fast, hope that's okay?"

"Hell yeah, it is!" her neighbor shouted back.

It turned out that Alice wasn't going to be the only one benefiting from Sarah's arrival. Alice didn't mind. Before Sarah's arrival, Alfie had started to become the closest thing she had to a friend. It might have changed her thoughts on him if Sarah hadn't liked him. As brutal as that sounded, Alice knew how important Sarah's opinions were to her. If she didn't like someone, it would be hard for Alice to either.

"I can see why she's your best friend. My God, she's a whirlwind."

Alice grinned; he sounded like an awestruck little boy. "Yeah. I think she might even have more energy than you."

"Absolutely not! There is no way I'm accepting that. You can't judge her performance on one day; the real test is how she fares after spending ten days in this place."

"This is very true, although I still back her."

"How predictable. Always underestimating me, aren't you?"

"I wouldn't dare, Alfie. . . ."

"Hmm. I'm not quite sure I believe you, Miss Gunnersley."

"Good night, Alfie." A smile lingered on her lips.

"Good night, Alice."

"Ladies, I need your help."

"I'm sure you need many people's help. What's up?"

The next day the rapport between her two friends was so natural that Alice had to remind herself that they'd only just met.

"Sarah, don't even ask—it's going to be a stupid crossword clue."

"Well, I won't be asking for your expertise in the future then, will I, Alice? No more puzzle fun for you."

The thought of him turning his nose up in defiance made her smile.

What do you look like, Alfie Mack?

Would Sarah laugh at her if she asked? Of course she would!

Why do you even care?

She didn't care so much as she was simply curious.

Sarah's voice cut her daydreaming short. "Come on, then, what's the clue? And if it's simple, I'm going to be really pissed off."

"It's probably simple to a mind like Alice's, to be fair."

"Flattery will get you nowhere, Alfie. I'm not going to indulge you in this game." She wasn't in the mood for his charm.

"Fine, be like that. So, Sarah . . . we are looking for a five-letter word, clue is 'long-term prisoner.'"

"A-L-I-C-E." Sarah laughed at her own joke.

"That's a good one! But unfortunately not *quite* the answer we were looking for."

Alice scowled at her friend.

"What? Don't give me that look. You're the one who apparently refuses to leave this bloody cubicle."

"Excuse me?"

Who the hell told her?

"The nurses told me this morning on my way in."

Alice's eyes widened.

"I wanted to know how you were really getting on." Sarah nudged her affectionately. "There's nothing stopping you getting yourself up and out! You know I'll be right by your side if you want me to."

Here they were, the first signs that Sarah wasn't going to go quietly.

Alice looked at her friend with all the *don't start this now* she could muster.

Sarah raised her hands. "Okay, we'll leave it for now!" she whispered, and then kissed her on the forehead. "Alfie, if I'm honest, I don't give a shit about your crossword, but if you really want to know then the answer is LIFER and I suspect you've already guessed this because it's pretty bloody obvious, *but* what I am interested in is how you're going to keep Alice in the manner she's now accustomed to after I leave?"

God, Sarah was relentless. And quick. Without breathing, she'd changed tactics and was charging full speed ahead without giving Alice any time to rein her in.

"You've only just arrived!" Alice exclaimed.

"I know, but I want to give Alfie here adequate time to make arrangements." There was a devilish glint in her eye that made Alice's heart sink.

"And what manner is that?" There was a playful note in his voice that Alice was not a fan of.

"Well fed, entertained, and completely and utterly adored."

"Right. Duly noted. And, yes, LIFER is correct, well done"—both girls rolled their eyes at each other—"and in answer to your question, I'll have to get back to you on that one. Even if I had two legs, I wouldn't be able to go out and get takeout for breakfast, lunch, snacks, and dinner—but leave it with me. I have other skills that can be of use, don't you worry."

"I'm actually kind of worried now," Alice cut in. She punched her friend in the arm, whispering, "What the hell are you doing, he is going to go to town now!"

"Of course he is. That's the whole idea, my love."

"Alice?" The nurse's voice from outside her curtains still sounded cautious. Although Alice was now speaking and, God forbid, laughing, the team on the ward still seemed wary of her. How difficult had she really been to look after? she wondered.

"Yes?"

"The doctor is here—can we come in?"

"Of course." Alice felt her body stiffen as she sat up a little straighter. She never liked it when he visited.

"Hi, Alice, how are you doing today?" Mr. Warring had his gaze fixed firmly on the notes in front of him and hadn't quite clocked the new visitor on the bed.

"I'm okay, thank you. Is it okay if my friend Sarah stays for this?"

His head jerked upwards. His face twisted with shock, confusion, and delight all at once.

"Yes, certainly." He shook Sarah's hand earnestly, and Alice couldn't help but register a genuine sense of relief in his demeanor.

Sarah didn't even pause for breath before the interrogation began. "So, what's the latest? How is she healing? There was mention of another surgery, I believe?"

"Oh, right. Yes . . . well . . ." His eyes darted back and forth between the pair of them; he was clearly unsure to whom he should be directing his answers—the patient or the protector. "In terms of your healing, the physio reports are showing good improvement in your physical strength, which is encouraging. Although we really need you to start moving more frequently to keep the momentum up; even just walking to the toilet will help."

"I can't." Her voice was thick with panic. She needed to find a way to stay in her protected bubble for as long as possible.

"Okay, well, until you feel confident enough for that, walking around your cubicle bay will do. We need anything to get you up and about. It's important, Alice."

She nodded reluctantly.

"Anyway, I'll check the wounds myself now, and if all is okay then we can discuss . . . other options."

Sarah was practically pulling off the dressing herself when Mr. Warring started to shuffle uncomfortably.

Something's not right.

"What is it? Is something wrong?" Alice's voice was firm. This wasn't one of Alfie's stupid puzzles; she didn't have time for guessing games.

"Nothing is wrong per se." He lowered his voice and moved a little closer to the bed. "I'm just a little concerned about the emotional aspect of your recovery. The nurses tell me that you still haven't seen yourself properly and that your interactions with other people continue to be limited."

"So making friends with other patients is now a measure of my emotional stability?"

The anger rose surprisingly quickly; she could feel her palms sweating and her teeth clenching together. How dare he? How dare he decide what she was fit enough to do? It was her body after all.

"No, but I can't recommend you for future surgery if you haven't seen the extent of your current injuries, Alice. Any further operations would be optional, and I have to be sure that you've made a sound and informed decision. Right now I don't think I can confidently say you have. There is a huge amount of support here for you if you need it. We have a fantastic team of counselors if you want me to refer you to speak to someone?"

Been there, done that, and it did sweet fuck-all.

"Thank you, Doctor." Sarah, sensing Alice's tension, took control. "I think Alice might need some more time to think this all through, but it's important information that we needed to know."

"Of course, take your time. You know where I am if you have any further questions. I'll do my examination quickly and then be out of your way—but remember, we are all here to help you."

She didn't need their help. Alice had everything she needed right here. It wasn't that she couldn't; she just didn't *want* to face up to her injuries yet. Her arms and legs she could cover up, find ways to mask and deflect away from the disfigured scar tissue. But her face—now, that was a whole different story. Coming to grips with what she'd be stuck with for life was too big a task to comprehend, but it seemed to be one that was unfortunately unavoidable. Not that she'd been fixated on her physical appearance before the accident—it had never been something she'd focused on much. Looking back, she wondered whether that was because she didn't need to. She knew she wasn't unattractive and she'd had enough propositions throughout her life to know she was blessed with a good set of features. Features that she'd taken for granted. A face that she had unknowingly underappreciated until the moment it was taken away from her. Now she had no idea what she was left with; reality had come knocking and it was refusing to go away.

Chapter 32

ALFIE

Well fed, entertained, and completely and utterly adored.

As soon as Sarah had said the words, his mind went into overdrive.

Maybe it was the teacher in him, or maybe he was grateful for a task other than learning to walk again, or *just maybe* he was excited at the possibility of creating something especially for Alice. Whichever it was, there were fireworks going off in his head and ideas sparking everywhere.

Before he got too carried away, he remembered that there were some clear boundaries he had to work within. Things had to be small-scale and possible to execute without her having to get out of bed: rule number one.

Rule number two was obvious. Whatever he planned had to be fun. Alfie knew, from his mother's extensive research, that happiness and laughter could improve a patient's recovery significantly. He was pretty confident he could nail this one.

Think like Alice: rule number three.

In all his creative excitement, the conversation happening next door hadn't escaped him.

Another operation?

The thought filled him with a strange sense of unease. Surely that was a big step to take? He knew from his own injuries that there were creams that could help reduce scarring. But then again, the mere sight of her hand had told him that these weren't your run-of-the-mill surgery scars. Her injuries were in a totally different league — but still . . . to resort to another surgery?

Then he stopped.

He barely knew this woman. From the outside, it was an absurd situation. Two strangers talking all day every day but never actually meeting face-to-face? Could you even call that a friendship?

His head started to pound from all the thinking, his feelings blurring into one another until his insides felt like one giant melting pot.

"Alfie, you've gone awfully quiet." Sarah's voice sounded concerned, not so much about his welfare but more, he supposed, about what he was planning.

"Geniuses need time to think. I'm taking my new role very seriously."

"New role?"

"Yes, chief entertainment and recovery officer."

"Let me guess — you're an only child, right?"

"Wrong! But I'm the youngest of three boys. To avoid being beaten up and teased every day, I had to find ways to entertain myself. My imagination was a godsend."

A short, sharp longing clawed at his heart. The three Mack brothers were so alike in looks but so different in nature. He loved them all the more for it, but neither of Alfie's brothers had been able to visit him since the accident. The corporate sellouts had both relocated halfway around the world, making it even more difficult for them to escape their already demanding offices and drop by.

"Well, now it's our godsend." Sarah suddenly appeared in front of his bed. She silently mouthed the words *thank you* and blew him a kiss. It was nice to be relied on again. He'd forgotten how great a responsibility it was to take care of another person's loved one. That was one of the parts of his teaching job that he loved the most. You were in possession of someone's greatest gift, and it was your duty to look after them.

"Well, I'm glad to see my talents are appreciated by someone on this ward. Are you totally sure you can't stay here forever? Do you have to leave us for the golden sands and sunny climate of Australia?"

"Unless I want a divorce and/or unemployment for a Christmas gift, then yes."

"Can't argue with that one."

"Right, I'm going to go and do the obligatory family lunch with my dad and stepmum. It's a good job they don't know that you're not in critical condition anymore, Al. I'm unashamedly using you as an excuse to get out of there in less than two hours."

"Charming." Alice's voice sounded flat. She'd retreated to near silence ever since the doctor's visit that morning.

"What are friends for, hey?"

A memory flashed through his mind. That was the exact same phrase that Ciarán would say to Ross whenever he'd annoyed him. They were always getting at each other with nonstop pranks and teasing, but no matter how far they pushed it, they would always end up laughing about it a moment later.

Fuck.

Even the good memories had that familiar stab of grief and guilt associated with them. Would he ever be able to think about them without wanting to rip his own heart out and scream?

Distract yourself, Alfie.

Fortunately his attention was caught by a conversation happening across the room.

"Arthur, you may be over ninety, but if you don't start doing what you're told and looking after yourself, I swear to God I'll leave you," Agnes chided. Normally her nagging of Mr. Peterson was purely playful, but Alfie could tell instantly that today she was dead serious.

"Oh, give it a rest, will you?" Mr. P. huffed. "I'm fine. The doctors say I'm fine. The nurses are checking on me every five bleeding minutes now you've been on at them. What more do you want?"

Alfie didn't want to listen in, but it was hard not to, especially when it concerned Mr. Peterson's health.

"Are you eating properly? Are you taking all your medication?" Agnes was relentless in her questioning.

"Yes, woman, I am! Now please, can we just enjoy our time together, because I'm honestly fine. . . ."

Mr. Peterson had his curtains open just enough for Alfie to see the old man reach out for his wife's hand. Alfie racked his brains to see if he'd noticed any further decline in Mr. P.'s health since the morning that he supposedly overslept—and only then realized that he had barely spoken to the old man in the last few days. Stung by guilt, Alfie made a mental note to check in with him more regularly. It wasn't okay to get caught up completely in Alice and Sarah and forget everyone else around him.

"Got any more crossword clues for me then?" Her voice was magnetic, drawing all his attention back to her.

He smiled. "I knew you'd be back for more."

Alice's hand shot through the curtain, middle finger pointing proudly up.

He wanted to reach out and grab it. To pull back the curtain to reveal more than just her pale, scarred hand. The same question that had been plaguing him since her arrival burned fresh in his mind.

Who was the girl hidden behind the curtain?

Chapter 33

ALICE

It was funny—minus the encounter with the doctor that morning, and despite still being hospital-bound and scarred, Alice hadn't felt this happy in a very long time. Having Sarah by her side was the biggest gift she could ever have asked for. She was also very aware that their time together was short, and after today there were big decisions to be made.

A small voice started to niggle at her.

Make the most of her being here.

There was no doubt in Alice's mind that, even before Mr. Warring's visit, Sarah was already planning ways to get her to look at herself in the mirror. If it was inevitable, then why not go with it? Did she really have the energy to resist and fight her? As she'd said before, only a fool would try to go up against Sarah.

Plus you're going to have to face yourself at some point.

It seemed that point in time was growing ever closer.

For the first few days after the accident, she'd spent most of her time thinking about ways she could end it all. Life just didn't bear thinking about. How could she ever be accepted with injuries like this? It hurt to think, let alone move. She didn't need to look in a mirror to know that she wasn't the same woman anymore. Her life had been turned upside down and she'd been burnt inside out. The thought of reestablishing herself in a world that she knew could be cruel at the best of times felt too exhausting to bear. Alice wasn't naïve about how critical human beings could be, and she didn't fancy being on the receiving end of their constant judgment. It was only recently that those thoughts had quieted and the impending dread and anxiety had lessened. Was she really going to live as a recluse, hiding away in her flat at the age of thirty-one? Afraid of everything, even her own reflection? Was that what she really wanted for her life?

Can you even call that a life?

Sarah was a stark reminder of the best of her. Maybe she really could move to Australia! She'd said it half jokingly to Alfie before, but now it didn't seem so ridiculous. Maybe she could emigrate and live with Sarah. With her experience, she could walk into any job she wanted, perhaps a smaller firm with less pressure and more time to relax. She could be Sarah and Raph's on-call babysitter whenever they decided to have kids. Every day she could feel the sun on her skin and salt in her hair.

Will moving halfway around the world actually make you happy? Or are you just running away?

All this thinking was only making Alice more confused. Her brain felt heavy. The only thing that was becoming clearer was that if she wasn't willing to die, then she had to find a way to live. And if she was going to live, she damn sure needed to know what she was dealing with.

The next morning Alice woke with the fire of determination raging inside her. She had to do it today. If she waited too long, the flames would subside and her confidence would most certainly evaporate. The moment Sarah came in, she said it. In fact, she pretty much shouted it at her.

"I need to look at myself. Today. With you."

Sarah froze—coffees in one hand and pastries in the other. It was a rare thing to stun Sarah, but the force of what Alice said seemed to take the breath from her lungs.

"*Please*," Alice added quietly.

And just like that, Sarah snapped back into life. "Of course we can, Al. Like, a million percent yes. Do you want to do it right now? Or do you want to have some food? I could go out and get some vodka maybe?"

Her friend was by her side holding her hand.

"As much as I'd like to be completely drunk, I feel like this is something I need to do sober. If I can't face it now with you by my side, I don't think I ever will. I need to see *me*, Sarah. I need to know who I am now."

"Alice Louise Gunnersley." Sarah became instantly serious. Her eyes locked on Alice's and her grip became viselike on her hand. "Before we do anything, I want you to listen to me. First, and most important, you are not defined by what you are on the outside. Do you hear me? Whatever you see in that mirror will never, *ever* reflect the incredibly special person that you are. You are pure fucking gold, Alice, and anyone with half a brain can see that. Second, I think you'll be surprised; it's really not as bad as you think. "

"Breakfast first." It was all she could manage.

"As you wish, my love."

Neither of them spoke the entire time they nibbled on their pastries. Alice's mouth was so dry and her appetite wasn't exactly high. There was a knot in her stomach that seemed to be getting tighter and tighter with every second that passed.

Sarah turned to look at her. "I'm going to have to ask the nurses for a big mirror, if that's okay? The one in my bag is tiny and we need to do this justice."

"Okay." The knot had decided to migrate up into her throat, making it hard to speak.

"You're the bravest person I know," Sarah said, as she left Alice to sit with the reality of the decision she had just made.

This was really going to happen.

It's time to see who you really are, Alice.

Sarah took much longer than Alice had expected to come back. How long did it take to find a mirror?

It was when she saw the small bottle of champagne in Sarah's left hand that she realized where she'd been.

"Before you say anything, I asked the nurses and they practically forced me to get it. And it's for after, not before. This is special, Alice, we couldn't let the occasion go unmarked."

Before Alice could even start to say thank you, Nurse Angles popped her head around the curtain. "I told her to do it! Enjoy, baby."

Tears started streaming down her face. It was all getting too much; what with the building anticipation, the kindness of these near strangers, and the love of her best friend, Alice's heart felt fit to burst.

"Oh, Al." Sarah wrapped her arms around her and kissed the top of her head. "It's going to be okay. Like I said, I'm right here next to you the entire time. You just tell me when you're ready. No rush. And you know what? We don't even have to do it today. We can just put the mirror in the corner and drink the champagne. It's all completely up to you."

"Now. Please. Let's just do it now."

Sarah nodded, sensing the urgency in her voice.

Alice closed her eyes and took some deep breaths. Her heart was pounding so hard that her entire body vibrated with the force. Her mouth went bitterly dry. Her breath flapped wildly in her throat like a trapped bird. Suddenly she felt the warmth of her friend next to her. Their hands found each other without thought.

"Whenever you're ready, tell me and I'll hold the mirror up to you, okay?"

Alice squeezed Sarah's hand so tightly she could almost feel her circulation stop. "Hold it up."

Alice kept her eyes closed. She must have stayed like that for a good three minutes, mirror positioned, eyes shut.

"I'm going to open my eyes now." Saying it out loud was the only way that she was able to hold herself accountable. Sarah remained silent, knowing no reply was needed. "I'm opening them."

The smallest crack of light broke through the darkness. The blurred background of her curtained cubicle started to appear. Slowly she allowed more and more light to enter. She could make out the figure of Sarah on her right side and the curtain that separated her from Alfie on her left. She blinked. Sudden focus. The outline of the mirror. A reflection. The shape of a face. Half of a person she recognized. Long auburn hair, thick and wavy, framing her freckled face. Same full lips. Same dark-chestnut eyes. Same fine bone structure. Same Alice that she'd seen a thousand times over. But wait. Someone had altered the other half of the picture. As if she were a candle that had been left to melt on one side. No hair. Red, thick, scarred skin stretching over lips and nose and eye. Mottled. Damaged. A patchwork quilt of flesh that had been crudely stitched together using other people's materials.

Bile rose in her throat. She wanted to scream. To cry. To be sick. She wanted that mirror out of her face and to never see this reflection again. But she was frozen. Frozen staring at this poor broken version of herself. The tears came, but she didn't even notice. Alice was transfixed.

"Al?" Sarah was trying to bring her round from her stupor. There was nothing Alice could do but stare. "Alice . . . do you want me to do anything? Are you okay?"

Alice shook her head. Her pillows were sodden with tears, but still she didn't move. For more than twenty minutes she stayed there staring, trying desperately to absorb and process the reflection that now belonged to her. It was an unwelcome gift that she was now burdened with. No return policy. No exchanges.

She was staring into the new face of Alice Gunnersley. And it broke every last piece of her heart to look at it.

Chapter 34

ALFIE

"Alfie, where the *hell* have you been?" Sarah was standing just outside the entrance to the ward.

"I went for a walk, why?"

"Can we talk?"

As much as he loved Sarah, all he could think about was crashing out on his bed with a trusted puzzle book for company. "I'm pretty tired, can it wait until later?"

"I don't have long." She looked nervously over her shoulder. "She thinks I'm on the phone to my mum."

Alfie's stomach turned to ice. "What's going on?"

"I'll explain outside."

"Okay, let's go."

They made their way in silence down the tepid beige corridors and out into the fresh air. The courtyard acted as a refuge for patients, visitors, and hospital staff alike. Alfie often wondered what conversations the plants were privy to in this tiny corner of the world. What pain had they breathed in through their leaves, and what miracles had their flowered faces shone upon? It was fairly empty today; the rolling gray cloud cover was keeping people safely inside the sanctuary of Costa.

"Do you want to sit?" He pointed in the direction of a swinging bench in the corner.

"Sure."

The moment she sat down on the seat, the sobbing began, racking her body so strongly that the entire swing shook. Alfie rested his hand on her back, willing himself to be patient.

"I'm so terrified to leave her, Alfie. I'm scared of what she'll do."

"Come on, Sarah, she'll be okay. You know better than I do how tough she is—she's a fighter. She's not going anywhere." He was desperately trying to strike the balance between positive and supportive. It was a fine line to tread with someone you barely knew.

"You don't understand." She turned her gaze away from him and fixed her eyes on the ground. "She looked at herself for the first time today."

Oh God.

He felt the beads of sweat break out on his forehead.

"It was awful. It was like I could feel her heart break the moment she saw her reflection. There were no words. Nothing. All she did was just sit and stare." Sarah's breathing was getting quicker and her body was shaking more violently with the tears.

This was bad. This was really bad.

"I imagine she's just in shock. It must be completely normal." He clutched desperately for words of comfort. "It will pass, though, just give it time."

Even as he said them, the words felt empty.

"No!" Her voice hit him hard. "You didn't see her, Alfie. It was like she became someone else, a shell of a human, there was nothing left inside of her." She shook her head vigorously. "And for the first time in my life, I don't have a clue what to do to help her."

Alfie pulled her close to him. How could he not have seen the signs? His attention had been so focused on Alice that he'd missed them all. The constant upbeat humor, the distracting busyness, the ever-optimistic attitude—all of these were the exact same tactics that Alfie employed in difficult situations to deflect the pain away from him. Sarah's friend had nearly died. Her best friend had been through the most traumatic and terrifying experience of her life, and she'd been halfway across the world when it happened.

He'd never even asked if Sarah was okay.

Eventually her breathing started to slow. Her body stilled, and a strange calmness flooded them both.

"First and foremost, you can wipe your face on this. My gift for being such an unaware, self-absorbed idiot." He handed her his jumper.

"Thank you." She buried her head in the fabric.

"Second, you have to trust that it will be okay. She *will* be okay. Losing a part of yourself is hard. It took me months before I could look down at my wound without wanting to vomit, or scream, or cry. Sometimes I'd do all three at once. It gets better. Slowly and often painfully, but it does."

Sarah smiled weakly.

"Third, you can keep that if you want." He nodded at the jumper. "Not sure I like you that much to wear your snot just yet."

"Thank you, you're so sweet." She flashed him a sarcastic smile; then the façade dropped again. "Seriously, though, thought I was going to explode in there, so thank you for listening. The last thing Alice needs is to see me cry."

"Actually, maybe it's exactly what she needs to see. Maybe she needs to see the fear to realize how important it is that she lives. Be honest with her. You're probably the only person she'll listen to."

He only realized when the words were out how sad it made him to say that last part.

"Was." She nudged him gently. "I *was* the only person she'd listen to. Don't forget, now there's you too." She smiled at him with such gratitude it caught him off guard. "I want you to promise me that you'll look after her when I've gone. No matter how much she pushes you away or tries to convince you she doesn't care. She needs you. She wants you to be there. She's just not very good at knowing it."

Electricity sparked inside his stomach. "You didn't even need to ask. I'm not going anywhere."

She reached out and hugged him. "Thank you. Now, let's get back before she thinks we've run off and had an affair. Plus it takes you fucking ages to move anywhere anyway."

Sarah was back—the mask in place, the warrior poised for battle. Alfie had to hand it to her, she was even better at this than he was.

"Sure thing . . . although you might want to take my jumper off if you don't want people to think that we've spent the last twenty minutes having wildly passionate sex." He winked at her, pulled himself up, and walked away as quickly as he could.

Alfie was hoping that by the time they returned to the ward the shock would have miraculously worn off and Alice would give them an earful for disappearing, but she didn't speak a word for the rest of the day.

Without her, time seemed to pass at a pace that was slow even for Alfie. With nothing but his thoughts for company, he found himself feeling very claustrophobic and anxious. As much as he tried to distract himself, Alfie couldn't take his mind off her. He found himself trying to imagine her reflection; different faces with different levels of damage kept flashing through his mind. Part of him wished he'd asked Sarah what Alice looked like when they were outside, but a bigger part of him knew that was not the point.

It was getting too much. The thinking. The hypothesizing. He needed to do *something*.

Alfie craned his neck to see if Mr. Peterson was sleeping, but to his surprise the old man was sitting upright and staring blankly at his TV.

"Hey, Mr. P., mind if I come and sit with you for a bit?"

"Oh, so you still remember who I am then?" The old man feigned surprise.

"Trust me, it would take several lifetimes to forget you."

"Ach, do me a favor, you couldn't give two shits about me now you're smitten."

"What on earth are you talking about?" Alfie pretended not to know, but there was a panicked feeling rising in his stomach as he hurriedly made his way to his friend's bedside.

"Don't play dumb with me, kid." He nodded his head in Alice's direction. "Look at you, pink as a bloody lobster! It's all right, boy. There's only so much fun you can have with an elderly git like me. Now, do you want to sit down or are you going to hover at the end of my bed like a bloody fly on shit?"

Alfie could feel his cheeks burning red.

"You've done a good job with her though, I have to say."

"What do you mean?" He was trapped in his own blur of thoughts.

"I *mean* you've done a good job at getting her to talk. She's really opened up around you. Everyone can see it. Well . . . hear it."

They both laughed. Alfie couldn't ignore the purr of contentment that had settled in his stomach.

"I thought I'd give annoying you a break for a while and focus my energy into something else. Now it's paid off, I reckon I can spare some time to aggravating you again. I know you've missed it."

"Trust me, without your constant flow of inane bullshit bombarding my eardrums, I've been able to watch *Homes Under the Hammer* in peace every day. It's been an absolute delight."

Suddenly and very subtly, his expression changed. He reached for Alfie's hand and held it gently. It was like clasping a tiny bird, so fragile and small that its bones felt dangerously breakable in his grip.

"Alice is lucky to have you, boy. In fact, we all are." The old man's eyes lingered on Alfie's momentarily before turning to look at the TV.

There were so many things Alfie wanted to say, yet he couldn't find the words. All he could do was softly squeeze the paper-thin hand that remained resting in his palm and join him in pretending to be interested in the terrible daytime TV show. He managed to keep Mr. Peterson awake for a good hour before the old man dozed off. Alfie sat with him a little longer before resigning himself to his own bed and boredom.

The silence behind the curtain continued into the night. He could just about make out a couple of grunts and mumbles, but they were few and far between. Sarah remained dutifully until Nurse Bellingham decided enough was enough.

"Sarah, how many times do I have to tell you, visitors are *not* allowed to stay beyond four p.m. I don't care how special you consider yourself or how many of the other nurses allow you to break the rules, if I catch you again I will have to report you."

"I'm sorry, it's just been a really tough day and I ju—"

"Just was getting your things and leaving? Yes, please do that."

As she left, Sarah popped her head around to say good night.

How is she? he mouthed silently.

The look in her eye told him all he needed to know.

He nodded in acknowledgment.

She tried to smile, but the sadness wouldn't let her.

And there he was. Back to square one, drowning in the silence again.

Chapter 35

ALICE

Get me out of this body.
   Get me out of this fucking useless disgusting body.
   You're a freak, Alice.
   You're a damaged, twisted-looking freak.
   You're not okay.
   You're anything but okay.
   They lied to you.
   They all fucking lied to you.

Chapter 36

ALFIE

"Hey, can I come in?"

Sarah's voice was barely a whisper, but somehow it roused him from his sleep.

"Yeah. You okay?"

He was careful not to speak too loudly; he didn't think it would be a good thing if Alice overheard them talking about her. Sarah had opted for a strange half-whisper half-mime tactic.

"Did she say anything last night?" The tiny flicker of hope in her eyes made Alfie's heart sink.

He shook his head. He'd known that last night was not the right time for conversation. He'd had to endure listening to Sarah's painful attempts to get Alice to speak all afternoon; if she'd failed, then there was absolutely no hope for him. He might be optimistic, but he definitely wasn't stupid.

Maybe this was a chance for him to wean himself off her.

You're getting too attached, Alfie.

No. That wasn't it. Despite what Mr. Peterson had said and regardless of how he felt hearing her voice every day, Alfie knew that all he wanted to do was just help. She was his friend. And besides, he knew what it felt like to wake up one day and feel like a completely different person overnight. Alfie could instantly recall the first time he'd seen his wound properly. It wasn't so much the blood and gore of it that shocked him but the realization that something had been taken from him. Something that he would never get back. It was the pain of lacking that tore him up. The knowing that forever more he would be incomplete. It was more overwhelming than anyone could have prepared him for, so he'd stayed silent last night. He needed to give her space, time to breathe, time to accept.

"Right. Well, wish me luck. I'm going in."

He attempted his best consolatory smile and watched her leave. It was almost as though his entire being was on red alert. His ears strained to hear every sound she made, praying Alice's voice would join in the noise.

"Hey, Al, it's me. I'm coming in."

Silence.

"You okay this morning?"

Nothing.

Alfie's heart was beating so loudly now he was scared it would drown out any potential signs of life. Much to his dismay, all that followed was the scraping of a chair and the sound of Sarah sitting down on it.

"I'll let you sleep if you want, I'm just going to sit here and read for a while."

Was she really not going to say one word, not even to her best friend?

As the day wore on, the silence became stifling. He found himself torn between getting up to distract himself and staying put in case she decided to speak. With every wordless hour that passed he found a strange sense of pressure building inside of him.

Do something.

You have to do SOMETHING.

No.

Just wait, he told himself over and over.

But he wasn't good at waiting.

Then the idea struck him.

"Right, ladies. I've got an extremely difficult crossword puzzle and it's got your names written all over it."

"Alfie, what the hell are you doing?" Sarah didn't even bother to lower her voice.

"I'm doing my puzzles—what does it sound like I'm doing?"

"It sounds like you're doing something no one asked you to do."

He heard her get up and storm round to him. Why didn't she trust him? Had she forgotten that he was the one who got Alice to speak in the first place?

Her face was all kinds of angry.

"I told you. I'm doing my puzzles." He looked at her, hoping it was all about to click into place. It clearly wasn't. He lowered his voice to a whisper. "It really helped last time, remember?"

"That was different. *She* was different."

"We can't just sit here and do nothing." Alfie crossed his arms like a petulant child. Who was she to tell him off?

"Yes we can. And we will. Okay?"

He knew that wasn't a question.

"Fine, I'll do these by myself, shall I?" He wasn't whispering any longer. He wanted Alice to hear that he was trying and that he hadn't given up on her. He wanted her to know that it was Sarah stopping him.

"Oh, don't be a selfish idiot all your life, will you?"

"Selfish?" Alfie's voice was raised now. "How the hell am I the selfish one? I'm trying to help."

"*Help?* You think this is helping?"

"Stop it. Both of you, just stop it!" Alice's voice hit him square in the chest. "I'm not deaf and I'm not some sick little child who needs looking after. I don't want your fucking pity and I don't need your help. So do me a favor and leave me alone. Both of you."

She was venomous, spitting poison at them with every sound she let out.

"Sorry, Alice, we didn't mean to upset you." Sarah immediately ran to her.

"I was being stupid, it's my fault, I wasn't thinking." The words were falling out of Alfie's mouth so quickly he barely registered them.

"I said leave me *alone.*"

"I'm sorry, Al, plea—" Sarah's voice was thick with tears.

"Didn't you hear me? I said GO."

Suddenly the silence didn't seem such a bad option.

Chapter 37

ALICE

Not once in the entirety of their friendship had Alice spoken to Sarah like that. In fact, Alice struggled to remember a time when they'd even argued.

The worst part wasn't the look on Sarah's face afterwards.

The worst part was that Alice quite enjoyed it.

"Alice, *please*. You know it's not like that. All we want to do is help. I'll do anything. I'll delay my flight, I'll tell Raph I'm never coming back if that's what it takes, but I refuse to leave you like this."

"Unless you're willing to help me die, then you might as well go."

"What?" Sarah's eyes were so wide they were practically bursting from her skull. Her shock was repulsive.

"I *said*, if you're not willing to help me die, then go."

Sarah turned and ran. It seemed even watching her best friend leave in floods of tears did nothing but add even more fuel to the fire inside of her.

Maybe she was now the monster inside and out.

Chapter 38

ALFIE

The moment he heard Sarah running, he had reached for his crutches and scrambled his way out of bed. There was no time for his prosthetic; he needed to catch up with her and fast. Despite the adrenaline coursing through him, Sarah was a pretty quick mover, and even just keeping her in sight was a challenge. He needed to focus—with so many people milling about on the wards, he knew one lapse of concentration could result in losing her completely.

He'd known there was a side to Alice that could cut people out and push them away. He'd been on the receiving end of her deathly silences before—but that? That was downright cruel.

"Sarah!" He had to resort to shouting after her; he was tiring slightly, and the crowds in reception were making it difficult for him to keep up. "Sarah, stop!"

She turned her head briefly, but carried on.

Although she was short, her bright-blond hair marked her in the crowd like a lightbulb. He eventually spotted her at the very edge of the outside smoking area, bent over, head in her hands.

"Christ, you're fast."

He rested his back against the wall and paused for a moment to recover. Now that he was out here, he wasn't quite sure what to say.

"Are you okay?"

Suddenly she jerked her head back to the sky and screamed so loudly that everyone within a two-meter radius took a step back. How could such a small human make so much noise? Alfie had to admit he was a little impressed.

"Sarah, it's oka—"

"She wants to die, Alfie. Did you hear her? She wants to *die*."

Suddenly she was collapsing into his arms, her little frame heaving with sobs. Alfie pulled her close, holding her as tightly as he could. All he could hear were the muffled cries against his chest repeating the same words over and over.

There was nothing Alfie could say. He'd heard it too, and to deny it would simply be insulting.

Soon her voice grew fainter and the sobbing slowed. Alfie felt the tension leaving her body, as her frame grew limp in his arms. Carefully, he tried to lower them both to the ground, cradling her as though she were a sleeping child.

You can do this, Alfie. Just lower down slowly.

Sweat started to bead across his forehead. He was now stuck halfway, limbs bent awkwardly and shaking under the strain of it all.

Don't drop her. Whatever you do, don't drop her.

What with the running and the standing, Alfie's leg was starting to cramp. He inched himself down a little farther and was so close to managing his graceful descent until, at the very last moment, his leg gave way and they both fell in a crumpled heap on the ground.

"Shit! I'm so sorry, Sarah. Are you okay?" His face burned with embarrassment as he reached for his crutches, which had spilled into the road. "I'm an idiot. I should never ha—"

"Look, I know you want me to stay, Alfie, but don't try to get me admitted to the ward as well, you sneaky bastard."

God, what a relief it was to laugh again! Sarah shuffled herself to sit beside Alfie.

"Cigarette?" She was holding out a half-empty packet of Marlboro Red.

Alfie smirked. "Aha! So this is why you insist on going out to get us food every hour. You're using us to hide your dirty smoking habit."

"You bet! Your insatiable appetite is the best excuse ever."

For a little while they simply sat there, side by side, in comfortable silence, Sarah chain-smoking her way through the rest of her cigarettes while Alfie provided the perfect headrest.

"What am I going to do, Alfie?" She stubbed out her last cigarette on the ground and looked at him.

"I think you just have to give her some time. Remember, it only happened yesterday. She's probably still in shock."

"But I don't have time. I've got to go in less than a week. I can't leave her like this."

He leant his head back on the wall and let the sun warm his face. He'd been racking his brains desperately for ways he could help the situation, and the thought he kept coming back to was of his own experience.

"I know, and that must be pretty scary for you. But trust me, it will pass. Maybe not all of it, but some of the anger will." He took her hand tentatively in his. "Plus, you know that when you go, she's not going to be on her own, right?"

She looked at him and managed a very faint smile. "I know."

"Right, come on. I need to move or I'll be stuck here forever, and you'll have to winch me up to standing. Also it's movie night tonight, and I *need* to make sure we don't end up watching *Finding Dory* again."

"Movie night?" She stood up and started to pull him up from the ground.

"Oh, you are going to have to stick around for this, it's right up your street. Enforced fun, you'll love it!" He threw his head back and laughed at the mix of fear and repulsion on her face.

"I think I'm suddenly busy tonight." She linked her arm through his and sighed. "Alfie, what the hell are we going to do?"

"Something. I'm pretty sure we'll think of something."

Unfortunately, even that eternally positive part of Alfie couldn't quite make his words sound convincing.

Chapter 39

ALICE

The anger hadn't left her. It still lay curled up deep inside, poised to strike at the next helpless victim that crossed its path. But now it was joined by something else. A sickening feeling of guilt had crawled in and taken up residency too, its cold claws sinking into her chest, a constant reminder of its presence.

What the hell have you gone and done?

All at once she felt faint with claustrophobia. Her little cubicle felt too contained, too confined. She was trapped in her own version of hell—a version she'd created for herself. It was complete and utter torture, yet she didn't have the energy to do anything about it, not even to cry. She simply lay locked in her own mind, letting the nurses come and go and the sounds of the ward wash over her. It was only when she heard his footsteps returning that her ears pricked up.

She sat a little straighter.

It's him. Definitely him.

But where is Sarah?

Her stomach lurched.

Maybe she could ask Alfie? Maybe he'd tell her what had happened. Maybe, if she asked nicely enough, he would go and find Sarah and tell her how sorry she was.

But the moment she heard him drop down onto his bed, the words disappeared from her mouth. The shame of her behavior snatched any possible conversation from her, and she was forced back into her silence. A silence not even Alfie seemed willing to break anymore.

Time seemed to drag its heels even more than normal. Restlessness coursed through her, but her bones were too tired to move. She was stuck waiting and wishing for her friend to come back.

You could always go and find her.

No. After what she'd seen in that mirror, there was no way in hell Alice would be going anywhere. The awfulness of it burned in the back of her throat, and no matter how tightly she closed her eyes all she could see was her new reflection. The mangled version of herself that she was stuck with lingered permanently in her mind.

What if she doesn't come back?

Those few words made her heart sink. Why was she so good at this? Pushing people away seemed to come so easily to her, it was right up there on her CV with financial planning and strategy. Alice Gunnersley's top skills that got you anywhere you wanted but with no one by your side. She needed Sarah more than ever. Her wonderful friend who hadn't even batted an eyelash at her injuries, who since arriving hadn't flinched, cried, winced, or even commented on her wounds, had now disappeared. Alice let the tears come as she willed herself into a deep, unthinking sleep.

The sound of Sarah's voice woke her instantly.

Alice opened her eyes just a tiny bit.

Sarah smiled as she caught Alice peeping out from under her sheets.

"Hey." She sounded cautious, and Alice couldn't blame her.

"Hey," she managed to whisper.

Sarah sat down in the chair beside her and leant in close enough so no one else would hear them.

"I'm so sorry about earlier, Al. I just . . . I just want to help you. That's all."

Alice turned so their faces were almost touching. "I know. I'm just so scared." Tears formed rivers of salt down her scarred cheeks. Alice resisted the urge to flinch as Sarah gently wiped them away. "I'm sorry too, I didn't me—"

"Stop." Sarah cut her off mid-sob. "If there's one time in your life I'll forgive you for being a total bitch, it's now."

Alice snorted. God, she really did hate crying.

"Can I come in?" Sarah nodded to the bed.

Alice wriggled over to make room. How lovely it felt to have the warmth of her friend next to her again.

"You scared me earlier." Sarah's voice became so small it barely reached her ears. "When you talked about dying. Alice, I can't . . . I can't lose you." The words were swallowed by the sobs that came thick and fast. Alice pulled her friend closer and held her while she cried.

"I'm sorry," she breathed into the top of Sarah's head. "I just feel like I've lost myself and I have no idea how to get me back." Saying it out loud for the first time lifted something from her heavy chest. "I don't know what to do, Sarah."

The two friends lay intertwined, cocooning themselves in their pain.

"I know, but this is the first and most difficult step done." The positivity was creeping slowly back into Sarah's voice. She turned over and stared at the ceiling, still clasping Alice's hand tightly in hers. "Let's speak to the surgeon as soon as we can and see what the options are, okay?"

"Okay." Unlike Sarah's, Alice's positivity was still missing in action. Could anything really make that much of a difference? No one would be able to give her her old face back. No one was able to turn back time, and she was pretty sure that no one, as hard as they might try, would be able to make something good of the mess she was left in.

"I'll speak to the nurses on my way out." She sat up straight and folded her arms. That was that. There was a plan, and that meant Sarah was happy. "I have to go a little earlier today, by the way—I'm on family duty *again*."

"That's what you get when you fly halfway around the world and don't come back and visit!"

"Thanks for the sympathy as always, Alice. Speaking of family, have you heard any more from Patricia?"

Patricia was Alice's mum. Sarah could never quite bring herself to use the term *mum* or even *mother* when referring to her. Alice loved her all the more for that.

"Nope. Not even a courtesy 'Hi. Hope you're okay' text. Think our last meeting may have been a little too much for her."

"Meeting? Wait. What? She came *here*?" Sarah's face was an absolute picture. Her mouth hung wide open in disbelief.

"She sure did. Let's just say it wasn't enjoyable for anyone involved."

"Alfie, did you get the pleasure of meeting Patricia?"

Seriously, did she really need to bring him into *every* conversation they had? Alice still felt awkward about the way she'd acted earlier, and she hadn't yet had a chance to apologize to him. Although why she cared that much, she still didn't know—but it seemed Sarah really was grooming Alfie to become Alice's stand-in best friend when she left.

"Erm . . ." He hesitated. "I didn't meet her in the traditional sense, although I did have the pleasure of overhearing a little of the conversation, and I think that was enough for me."

Alice laughed. The way he was trying to be tactful was cute, but it was very clear all he wanted to say was, *Wow what a fucking coldhearted bitch your mum is.*

"Isn't it such a wonder how her daughter is one of the best human beings ever known to man when she has a mother like that?" Sarah kissed her on the forehead.

"In that case, maybe we should be grateful to Patricia."

Sarah physically recoiled at Alfie's words. "Excuse me? She's an absolute nutjob. Sorry, Al, but it's true."

Alice smiled; there was never any need to apologize when it came to insulting her mother.

"Well," Alfie continued, "if you think about it, without her we wouldn't have Alice, and a life without Alice would be too sad to think about."

No one said anything for a minute. Even though they'd had emotional conversations before, it still took Alice some getting used to when Alfie was being sincere. Sarah squeezed her tightly, and Alice refused to look her in the eye. She didn't want her friend to see the warmth his words brought to her heart or the swell of affection she felt for him in that moment. It would be written all over her face, and she wanted to keep it for herself for a while longer.

"As cute as you guys are, please stop talking about me like I'm not here!" She hoped she wasn't too dismissive of his kindness, but she also didn't know what else to say. "And enough about my mum, there's more important things to discuss."

"Like?" Sarah looked at her, confused.

"Like . . . when are you going to make yourself useful and go get me some food? I'm starving."

"Maybe when you decide to get out of bed and come with me?"

"I can't leave the hospital, you know that!"

"But you can leave your bed, Alice."

"Not now, Sarah. You've just got back in my good books, so don't push it." She gave her a wry smile.

"Charming. Alfie, I'd get out while you can, otherwise she'll have you running around after her twenty-four/seven!"

"Trust me, with one leg there will be little to no running happening. I'm safe to stick around, I think."

Another burst of warmth and a tingling in her stomach.

Christ, pull yourself together.

"Seeing as there's nothing better to do, and you're my best friend in the entire world, I guess I'll go get us some food. What do you want?"

Alice was quickly pulled out of her self-pity by the mention of food. "Anything full of carbohydrates and garlic."

"Really? You want PizzaExpress again?" She looked at Alice and shook her head. "I'd totally forgotten what a creature of habit you are. Didn't you eat the same meal every day for lunch and dinner for about four months at university?"

"Yes, and it was absolutely delicious."

"You're the boss!" Sarah saluted and closed the curtain behind her as she left. "Alfie, do you want anything while I'm out?"

"I'm good, thank you. One of the nurses sneaked me in a chocolate brownie earlier so I'm done for treats today."

"I'm glad you decided not to share any of it with us!" Her footsteps receded.

Alice loved listening to Sarah and Alfie. A small part of her wished they could remain in this microcosm of life forever, safe and sound and entwined in their own strange routines.

"So, may I ask what this same meal for four months consisted of then?" Alfie's voice was thick with mischief.

Goddamn it, why was Sarah always dropping her in it?

"How did I know you would ask me that?" Alice grumbled.

"Because I'm the most curiously annoying person you've ever met?"

"That could be it, made more annoying by the fact you openly admit to your annoyingness."

"You have to be proud of what you've got, right? Come on, then, stop distracting me. What was this gourmet meal you so lovingly consumed twice a day for four months?"

She closed her eyes and smiled in anticipation of his reaction. There were many justifications she wanted to reel off, but she knew they wouldn't make any difference to his judgment. "Pasta with baked beans, cheese, and ketchup—and if you haven't tried it for yourself, then I accept absolutely no judgment or bullying from you about it."

"Interesting addition of the ketchup. For me it was always barbecue sauce," he said casually.

"AS IF you used to eat that too!" Alice couldn't help but get excited, slamming her hand down on the bed in disbelief.

"Hell yes, I did. What's not to love about the warm cheesy mix of that bowl of carbohydrate goodness? A childhood staple for me, in fact."

"I wasn't expecting that."

"Don't write me off just yet. I'm not sure we are as different as you may like to believe."

"Trust me, Alfie, I *know* that we are different, but I still wouldn't write you off in a million years."

She smiled as the silence settled over them once again.

Chapter 40

ALFIE

He didn't care that Alice had gotten so mad. That her talk of dying had sent both him and Sarah into distressingly dark thoughts. All that mattered now was that Alice was talking again and she seemed okay. Her words lingered in his head, filling him with a warm buzzing that seemed to radiate from somewhere deep inside his stomach.

It was odd to think he still hadn't seen her face. Some days this bothered him more than others. In reality, did it matter? He'd never judged his friends on their appearances—in fact, most of the time he barely even registered what they looked like. Other days, though, he felt desperate to see her. To look into her eyes when they spoke, and see her face shape itself into a hundred different expressions. A longing to know who she was, as if somehow her face would hold all the secrets. In those moments, he would scold himself.

Looks aren't everything. Stop being so shallow.

Of one thing he was certain: with the majority of his focus

assigned to Alice, his own recovery had taken a back seat. Everything just felt less important compared to making her laugh. He was in deep with this latest crusade, and he often wondered whether his efforts were because it was her that he cared about so much or because he simply had to save someone.

Come on, Alfie, you're in a hospital ward full of sick people all waiting to be saved. It's definitely her.

He knew now more than ever that the plans he'd been formulating to keep her entertained were important. If he could find some subtle ways to get her to open up, then maybe the likes and life of Alice Gunnersley would be demystified at last! So far in their friendship he'd been privy to small glimpses of her life before the accident, but that didn't feel like enough anymore. The deeper their connection grew, the more Alfie wanted to know about her. He set to work immediately.

"Nurse Angles. Hey, Nurse Angles!" He tried not to shout, but he needed to get her attention. Trying to catch up with the busiest woman on earth while negotiating walking with a prosthetic was no easy task.

"Come on, baby, walk with me if you got to talk, I've got a long list of stuff to do." She didn't even look up from her clipboard, but he knew he had her attention.

"Okay, okay! Basically I need to ask a favor. Well, two actually. First, I need an oversize sheet of paper and a thick black pen. Second, I need you to stick what I'm going to write on said paper with said pen to the inside of Alice Gunnersley's curtain."

Immediately she started to shake her head. "Oh, no no no! What the hell are you up to? I can't be shoving things in patients' faces without permission! We've only just got her talking and cooperating—I'm not doing anything to jeopardize that. You know better than this, Alfie."

"But she's asked me to do it . . . kind of." Technically that was a lie, but he knew some things were worth taking a risk for. "And you know there's no way she'll let me inside her cubicle! Please, Mother A. I know how much this will cheer her up."

She stood there for a moment, clearly thinking deeply about her answer. Alfie hoped that she could see how important this was to him. How important this would be for Alice. Suddenly a noise erupted from her trouser pocket— she was being beeped.

"I have to go. Look, if I say yes and this turns out to be one great big mistake, then I will make your life hell on this ward, Alfie Mack, you do know that, right?"

Oh, he knew. He knew that Nurse Angles meant every single word.

"I know that, and I also know this won't be a mistake. I promise you that."

"Fine! I'll get you the paper and pen, and you leave whatever you want me to put up on the desk." She patted him on the cheek and sped off to deal with the ever-growing list of demands being thrown at her.

"Remember, it needs to be put there overnight so she sees it in the morning!" He didn't want to push his luck, but it was an important part of his plan.

"Jesus, Alfie, the things I do for you," she called back over her shoulder.

His bubble of excitement was quickly followed by a sharp pang of nervousness.

Please, God, don't let this be a massive mistake.

Chapter 41

ALICE

"Right, Big Al, it's ten a.m. You know what that means?"

"You're going to never call me Big Al again?"

"Incorrect. It's the quick-fire questions game. One hour of relentless questioning—no time for thinking, just the first answer that comes to mind. Them's the rules, remember!"

Much to Alice's surprise, she'd woken up that morning to a handwritten "Daily Fun Schedule" attached to her curtain. The moment she saw it, she felt sick.

How the fuck did that get there?

Did he come inside my cubicle?

No, he wouldn't have.

But who else would have put it there?

"Alfie, what on earth is th—"

"Before we go any further, Alice, I want to reassure you, I did not step one foot inside your curtain. I promise you. I pulled a few strings and got one of the nurses to help me."

For some unknown reason she'd trusted him on this one.

"Okay . . . but still, what the hell is it?"

"It's our daily fun plan. A regular schedule to keep you entertained courtesy of *moi*. It's pretty great, I won't lie."

Alice had scanned the sheet of paper.

The early morning was assigned to the nurses' rounds, and then there was time allowed for breakfast and washing, a generous one hour and fifteen minutes, before the supposed fun and games began. She sensed the extra fifteen minutes had been added in a slight panic. Alfie probably wasn't sure how much time a badly burnt woman needed to get herself ready for the day. Bed baths with burns wasn't a fast or enjoyable experience.

The rest of the day was laid out and time-boxed to within an inch of its life.

10 a.m.–11 a.m.: quick-fire questions

11 a.m.–12 p.m.: reading [She wasn't quite sure if this
    was out loud to each other or silently. She prayed for
    the latter.]

12 p.m.–1 p.m.: lunch

1 p.m.–3 p.m.: physio for Alice and Alfie (depending
    on the day)

3 p.m.–4 p.m.: puzzle books

4 p.m.–5 p.m.: nurses' afternoon rounds

5 p.m.–6 p.m.: musical round [Give her strength.]

6 p.m.–7 p.m.: dinner

7 p.m.–8 p.m.: group walk [In his dreams.]

8 p.m.–9 p.m.: bedtime stories

9 p.m. onwards: sleep or DMCs

"Do I even want to know what a DMC is?" Alice could only imagine what he was going to come out with.

"It's a deep and meaningful chat. You know, sharing is caring and all that."

Alice couldn't help but scoff. "Only *you* could plan for an emotional conversation."

They hadn't even started the schedule, and she was nervous. She didn't want to put a damper on something he'd clearly spent a lot of time on, but she didn't think anyone other than Alfie would have enough energy to complete this timetable, certainly not her.

"So as it's the first day, I'll choose the topic. I'm going for food."

Alice let out a moan.

"Wait—don't tell me you're not a foodie? I had so much hope after the pasta, cheese, and beans! Please don't break my heart and reveal that you only eat beige food like digestive biscuits and potato waffles?"

"Try existing only on coffee and takeout sushi." She grimaced, knowing what was coming.

"Oh, for Christ's sake. Every day?"

"Every glorious day. I took the decision to upgrade from my pasta dish when I got my first real job."

"Wow. You really did take a step up in the world, didn't you?"

"It hasn't exactly worked in my favor. Why do you think it's taken me so bloody long to recover? My body was made of caffeine and raw tuna."

He laughed. "Now, if you ever try to tell me you're not an attractive lady—"

She reached across with her unblemished hand and slapped him hard on the arm. Over time, their beds had seemed to grow closer and closer together. On some mornings, if the light shone just right, she could almost make out his silhouette lying next to her.

"Fine. Well, this will be a short and very boring game then, won't it? Let's go!"

She let out another groan.

"Oh yes, my friend, we are still playing, don't you worry about that. Remember, this is just the first activity; you're going to need more enthusiasm if you're going to last the whole day."

She wasn't sure it was enthusiasm she needed, more like a heavy dose of Valium.

"Okay. Pizza or pasta?"

"Erm . . . my heart says pasta because, well, it kept me alive for a good four years, but then again pizza is so god-damn good. You know what—for old times' sake, I'm saying pasta."

"First, good answer; second, this isn't an opportunity for a monologue, Alice. You can't think about it, it's got to be instant!"

"Give me a break—that was the first one. I bet you're more competitive than your kids at school, aren't you?"

"Don't start deflecting or distracting by asking me questions, Alice, I know your game. But yes, of course I am. The kids never stand a chance against me. Now, question two . . ."

And so it went, back and forth for a good half an hour until Alfie finally agreed to let Alice ask some questions.

"I'm not doing food because clearly I have no real knowledge of it. Ohhhh, I know. My category is people."

"People?"

"Yeah, people."

"As in . . . ?"

"Don't start deflecting or distracting, Alfie. I give you two people and you choose one."

"Someone is feeling sassy today, I like it! Fine."

"Okay, so . . ." She paused. "I know. That TV presenter lady on *This Morning*, what's her name? Holly Willoughby or—"

"HOLLY!"

Alice actually jumped as he screamed the name. "Jesus Christ, I hadn't even said anyone else."

"No one will ever be more important to me than Holly. Ever."

Alice rolled her eyes. A petulant part of her wanted to say, *Even me?* but strangely she wasn't quite ready to hear him say no.

"Fine. Okay. Maybe that was too easy. . . . Nurse Angles or your mum?"

Alfie burst into laughter. "What kind of question is that?"

"Well, I don't know how to play your stupid game! You do one then."

"Okay. Me or Sarah?"

"You."

Oh.

Shit.

Laughter erupted from behind the curtain.

Shit. Shit. Shitting shit.

Alice buried her face in her pillow, desperate to erase that last minute of her life.

"Well, well, well! Me? Oh. My. God. You picked me? I mean, I can't believe it. Luckily for you, Sarah isn't here yet—but just you wait when I tell her." He paused, and Alice could tell he wasn't done yet. "ME! I want to shout it from the rooftops. You picked ME!"

"Argggggh" was all she could muster out loud.

Obviously she didn't mean him.

She'd been caught off guard and he was the first option.

Surely there was some science to say that you always picked the first option?

"Don't be shy about it now, Alice, you're the one who said it. It's always important to be honest about how you feel."

He was going to be absolutely insufferable.

Why wasn't this bed just swallowing her up?

"Will you just *leave it*, Alfie? Jesus, grow up!" she spat, surprised by her own anger.

Where had that come from? Alice felt like a child who'd had her diary read out loud in all its embarrassing detail. But this wasn't embarrassing, surely? This was just a stupid game, and a stupid mistaken answer.

"Okay, I will say no more."

"Thank you." She hoped he could hear the apology in her voice.

"So, fancy another round?"

"NO!"

"Okay . . . your call." His voice was still thick with glee.

Alice, Alice, Alice, what the hell is going on with you?

At least he had the grace to let her cool down a bit and regain some composure before he moved on to the next item on the list—which, much to Alice's dismay, was reading out loud.

"Now, you're lucky that my mum brought in the entire series for me just last week. Otherwise we'd be stuck with Mr. Peterson's *Daily Mail* to read from."

"Really?" They were only thirty seconds into page one, chapter one before she cut him off.

"Sorry, is there something the matter?"

"First, you're expecting us to actually read out loud to each other?"

"Correct. And second?"

"You're going to read me *Harry Potter*?"

"Correct. Have you read it before?"

"No, because I'm not seven years old." She smiled, feeling pretty smug about that comeback.

"Well, you're about to experience one of the greatest works of fiction ever written, then. And you can thank me later. Imagination doesn't have to stop at seven, you know. Grown-ups can be fun too."

Touché.

"Fine." She sighed. "Go on."

And so he did, with intense enthusiasm. Every character was given an individual voice, there were dramatic pauses left right and center, plus he even adopted a very good Stephen Fry–like narrator voice. She soon realized there was no stopping him, so she lay back, closed her eyes, and brought his words to life in her mind. *How lucky those kids are to have someone like him as their teacher*, she thought. How lucky she was to know him.

"So, what do you think, Miss A? Did your old-woman brain manage to enjoy it?"

"The jury's out, I'm afraid. I'll have to hear more." As loath as she was to say it, three chapters in and she was hooked.

"What a lame excuse to get me to read to you again. Don't you worry, I see right through you."

She had to laugh.

"Shall I continue?"

"If you have to . . ."

"Ah, look, lunch is coming. What a shame—you'll just have to wait until tomorrow."

She could picture the Cheshire cat grin wiped across his face. "You're a tease, Alfie Mack, you know that, don't you?"

"But you wouldn't have me any other way."

"Gosh, aren't you two so cute!"

"Sarah!" Alice must have been on a completely different planet—she hadn't even heard her friend approach, and nearly jumped out of her skin when Sarah's head popped round the curtain. "Where the hell did you come from?"

"Well, I walked through the entrance, turned left, and followed the corridor—and, *bam*, here I am."

"You're so *annoying!*" She threw a pillow at her friend but missed, which only made her more frustrated.

"Sorry, my love. Maybe Alfie's childish behavior is contagious."

"Hey, why the hell am I being brought into this? I'm just an innocent bystander," he called out from beside her.

They looked at each other, rolled their eyes, and laughed. Sarah took up her usual position lying next to Alice in the bed.

"You can't stay mad at me for long, especially when I've brought you . . . pain au chocolat!" Sarah held out a warm paper bag of sweet-smelling pastries. One surefire way to melt any of Alice's negative emotion was to hand her something buttery and full of sugar.

"God, you know me too well. I love you, hand them over."

Sarah leant in and kissed her on the head. "I love you too."

Alice took the bag and in less than one second had already stuffed half a pastry in her mouth.

"You're actually quite lucky you can't see this, Alfie. Let's just say Alice is a bit of an animal when it comes to eating."

Alice, too distracted by the heavenly sensation of warm flaky pastry and oozing chocolate in her mouth to care, half-heartedly nudged her friend in the ribs.

"She must be enjoying it to be so silent," Alfie remarked.

"So, what have you kids been up to today?" Sarah asked.

"Well, I'm *so* glad you asked actually. . . ."

He wouldn't dare tell her.

". . . Alice and I have been testing out my new schedule!"

"Ooh, is that what this thing is?" Sarah reached to the curtain and pulled down the piece of paper. "Very good work, Chief Entertainment Officer—this looks like an incredibly detailed and full-on schedule! How was it? Did you learn anything new about each other?"

Alice realized she'd stopped chewing her pastry.

"I certainly learnt a lot about Alice . . ."

NO.

Please, Alfie, don't be a complete dickhead.

". . . mainly that she has an extremely limited knowledge of food and isn't too seasoned on how to have fun."

She didn't even care that he'd insulted her; she was simply grateful that he hadn't revealed her ridiculous answer to that ridiculous question. Alice swallowed her mouthful, wanting to shut down this conversation very quickly. "Just because I've never played some stupid game before does not make me not fun."

"It was more the fact you had never read *Harry Potter*, actually. Can you believe that, Sarah? No concept of Hogwarts. No idea about the Boy Who Lived. Nothing." He sounded genuinely shocked and even a little bit offended.

"Yeah, *Sarah*, can you believe that?" Alice turned to her friend with a knowing look.

"Oh no—don't tell me *you* haven't either?"

"Look, Alfie, I'll be honest with you. I haven't read it." Sarah was holding her hands up in confession. "I'm not proud of myself for it. Neither do I have anything against the books, I just never got round to it."

"Have you watched the films at least?"

"Erm . . . no," Sarah said, wincing slightly.

"Who am I even dealing with here?! I've never met any-one in my life who hasn't at least watched one *film*. And here come two of the most incredible women who haven't got a clue about anything! Does this mean I'm going to have to blow your mind too and introduce you to a world of purely joyful yet deeply dark magic?"

"I suppose it does." Sarah shrugged her shoulders in defeat.

"Sit back and relax, ladies, we are going to take a little di-version from the planned schedule and dive straight back into story time. Prepare yourselves for what you're about to hear."

"Do I need a catch-up?" Sarah asked.

"Don't worry—we weren't that far in, and I'm sure Alice won't mind that we start all over again."

Alice groaned but couldn't keep the smile from creeping onto her face. "Fine, but be quick!" she shouted.

And so he began again, painting the walls of the ward with the colors and sounds and smells of this other magical world. Sarah curled up against Alice, her warm body encas-ing her in its curve. How wonderful it felt to be held by them both, each in their different ways.

"Ladies. Sorry to interrupt." The voice of one of the nurses jolted them out of the world of Muggles and wizard duels. "Mr. Warring just called, he said he'll be down to speak to you within the hour."

"Thank you!" Sarah practically launched off the bed. "Sorry, Alfie, but we might have to cut this story time a little short."

"Oh. That's okay." He hadn't quite mastered hiding his disappointment just yet.

Alice's insides twisted over themselves.

"It will be fine," Sarah reassured her. Clearly Alice hadn't quite mastered her anxiety just yet.

"I know." She smiled.

You're still a good liar, though.

Chapter 42

ALFIE

Alfie had hoped the schedule would work. He had prayed that it would help open her up and not push her further away, and this time his luck had come through. Although there was a slight hairy moment when she'd picked him over Sarah (much to both their surprise!), all in all it had been a wonderful interlude. He'd loved reading to Alice and Sarah. For a while he was transported back to his school, surrounded by eager, wide-eyed kids all desperately hanging on his every word. He loved losing himself in books, and the art of creating worlds and characters from sheets of paper never grew any less exciting. As much as he wanted to carry on, he closed the book and turned to his other trusted pastime, puzzles.

Just as he was about to finish a particularly good arrow word, Alfie noticed the doctor arriving on the ward. He recognized him from his previous visits to Alice's cubicle, tall, wiry, and angular. There was nothing soft about him. Even his eyes were sharp and piercing. Did all doctors grow a sharpness over time? Maybe it was the only thing that stopped them absorbing all the grief that lingered in the air. Alfie didn't envy them at all.

"Hello, Alice, it's Mr. Warring—may I come in?"

For some reason, watching the doctor enter Alice's cubicle made Alfie feel very nervous. What was he going to say to her? Would they be able to help her? He shuffled over in his bed to edge closer to her side. So what if someone caught him? He needed to hear what was going on next door.

"I understand that you saw yourself for the first time the other day." Mr. Warring's voice remained calm and steady. "I know that must have been hard for you, Alice. How are you feeling about it now?"

"I want to know what my options are."

Alfie's heart strained at the hurt in her voice.

"Of course. First, you can never underestimate the value of time. In six to twelve months, your scars could look very different depending on how well you heal and look after yourself. In the short term, there are also a variety of topical solutions that can help reduce scarring—but if you are looking for significant improvements quickly, I'm afraid it will have to be another surgery."

"I don't want to wait. I want results. I want the surgery."

"Okay, if you do want to proceed down that route, then I first need to make you aware of what the surgery involves and also make you aware of the risks. Essentially we will be performing another graft but taking a large portion of skin from your shoulder area. We will try, if we can, to also rebuild some structure back in." Mr. Warring was clearly trying his best to explain in layman's terms. "The risks are the same as with any major operation. First, we can't guarantee the results you want; it depends on how the skin graft takes, how you heal, and if we can harvest enough healthy skin in the first place. Second, there is always the risk of . . . complications. Your body has been through a lot, Alice, so we need to be mindful of that."

The more he spoke, the quicker Alfie's heart raced. Surely she wouldn't be willing to put herself through all this?

"Whatever you say to me, Doctor, I'm going ahead with the surgery, so just tell me what I need to do and how quickly we can get it scheduled."

He knew that Alice could be stubborn—anyone who could be silent for weeks on end clearly had extreme willpower—but he was shocked at how forthright she sounded and how determined she was to have this operation in spite of the risks.

"Al, maybe give it a day or two just to think it over. We can discuss it and see how you feel in the morning."

Thank you, Sarah.

"I think your friend is right. This isn't a small undertaking, and I would ask that you take some time to think about it. I'll check back in a couple of days, and we can work out a plan from there, okay?"

"Fine."

"Great. I'll see you both soon. Have a good afternoon."

All of a sudden Alfie felt very uneasy.

"I know you want this, Alice, but please just at least sleep on it. In fact, why don't you do what we used to do—write it out? The pros and cons list. We can review tomorrow morning, if you like? You're never one to make a rushed decision about anything! Don't let this be the one time you do."

"You're right. I know you're right." Alice's voice was thick with defeat.

"Now, why don't we get Alfie to take us all back to Hogwarts again, hey?" Sarah shouted across to him. Alfie quickly slid back to the middle of his bed. The last thing he wanted was for anyone to discover him eavesdropping.

"Were you asking me or were you telling me?" The odd sensation of anxiety was still rumbling in his stomach, but he managed to inject lightness into his voice.

"Telling," Alice and Sarah confirmed in unison.

"As the ladies wish . . ." And so he began to lose himself in the wonder of words yet again.

Chapter 43

ALICE

She knew she wasn't going to sleep a wink that night. There was so much going on inside her head that keeping it all in was becoming unbearable. She grabbed the piece of paper next to her bed, switched the reading light on, and searched frantically for a pen.

When in doubt, write it out.

Sarah was right. It was always her solution whenever Alice was faced with a problem she couldn't easily solve. Do I take this job? Do I buy these shoes? Do I spend three thousand pounds on a kitchen I am never going to cook in?

Pros and cons—write them down. It was always the same advice, and nine out of ten times, it worked.

As Alice snatched the clipboard from the end of her bed to write on, she couldn't help but smile at seeing the piece of paper she'd grabbed. It was the schedule Alfie had made for her. The wonderful attempt he'd crafted to help her get through the days.

Don't think about that right now.
Focus.

And so for the next hour Alice created a pros and cons list: to have the surgery or not.

Pros:

- Look like less of a freak

Come on, Alice, be serious.

- "Reduced scarring and more even skin tone"—says Mr. Warring
- Potential to look more "normal"
- Help me gain more confidence
- Less afraid to be seen

Cons:

- Might not work as well as I hope
- Complications of surgery—could I die if it went wrong?
- Have to go through recovery all over again
- More time in the hospital

But more time in the hospital could also mean more time with Alfie.

But who was he—the man behind the curtain? The complete stranger who had now become such an integral part to her every day. There was so much she wanted to know and so much she realized she was afraid to find out.

"Alfie? Are you awake?"

"Yeah, are you?"

She laughed. "Surprisingly, yes."

"Good. Everything okay?"

"Yeah. . . ."

She took a deep breath. Her mind was spinning and it grew harder and harder to focus on a single thread.

"It's just . . . I mean . . . I don't know . . ."

He remained faithfully silent.

"I guess I was wondering . . . how does it feel to be in love?"

"Wow. I won't lie to you, I wasn't expecting that. . . ."

"Sorry"—she was mumbling, desperately trying to gather the words back into her mouth—"I just thought, because of your ex-girlfriend, that maybe—"

"It's fine. It was just a bit out of the blue."

God, she wished she'd never asked. The silence seemed to stretch out for hours.

"Do you want the honest answer?"

"Yes."

Do you really, Alice?

"I don't know. I thought I was in love with Lucy. She made me laugh, I made her laugh. I fancied her so much. Sometimes it hurt to look at her because I wanted her that badly. We'd been together three years, so I thought she must be the one. The one I was going to marry, have kids with, grow old with—but now, now when I really think about it, it feels like there was something missing. I think I got so caught up in the idea that someone wanted me back that I let it override my true feelings about it all. It was as though I felt like I *should* have been in love with her, because on the surface everything was so perfect."

"It sounds pretty perfect to me." She closed her eyes and let the feeling of longing drench her in sadness.

"It was—but like I said, it was only surface-level. I loved her, but I wasn't in love with her. There wasn't any deeper connection. I mean, look at us now. I lost my leg, and she left me. She didn't even want to try. And looking back, neither did I. I could have fought for her, but I didn't. I didn't wake up every morning needing to know if she was okay, how she was feeling, or if could I do anything to help. I didn't waste hours upon hours just thinking about her, or ways I could make her world brighter, or things I could do just to hear her laugh one more time. Hearing her name didn't make the hairs on my entire body stand up on end. Something was missing. There was nothing that bound us together. Do you know what I mean?"

"No, Alfie, that's the whole point. And I'm scared I never will." She shook her head. How stupid had she been for even bringing this up?

Never finding love—now, where would that go on your pros and cons list, hey?

"Sorry for asking such a ridiculous question—I didn't mean to start such a deep conversation in the middle of the night."

"Well, they are a key agenda item on our schedule, so I'm glad you're taking it seriously!"

She forced a laugh that seemed to disappear as quickly as it came. "I guess I'm just starting to realize how lonely I've been my whole life. Before I didn't care so much, but now I think I really do."

"You have Sarah."

"True, but the reality is she's moved away. Her life is on the other side of the world now with Raph."

"Do you think you would ever try to reconcile with your mum?"

"Ha!" If only he knew the half of it. "I've tried, I really have. When I first left home I swore I would never contact her again, the anger was so intense that I couldn't see past it;

but over the years I found that there was a hole inside of me that I couldn't seem to fill. Not with academia, not with food, not with men. I wrote her so many letters telling her how she made me feel, how it was growing up in a house like ours and how desperately I wanted to hear her say 'I love you.' But it was pointless. I burnt the letters and made peace with it. My family is elsewhere, and I don't need her validation to be happy."

Now that the words were flowing, she knew she couldn't stop even if she'd wanted to.

"Sarah is my family. I have acquaintances and people who care about me, but I don't let anyone get too close. I used to think that it was a choice. Being independent was a sign of strength, and it was a badge I wore so fucking proudly right in the middle of my chest. *You can't hurt me because there's no way in hell you'll get close enough to try. The only person you can count on is yourself. Other people let you down — even those who are meant to take care of you and love you unconditionally. The most important relationship you'll ever have is the one you have with yourself.* All this bullshit I fed myself just so I didn't have to face the reality that I'm scared about being vulnerable and intimate and God forbid falling in love with someone. In the end I either pushed or let everyone fall away, and now, with this hideous body and face, no one is going to even want to come close."

"I'm still here." His voice was so quiet and timid, like a little boy's.

"Only because you're stuck in the bed next to me."

"Yeah, because it's mandatory for me to spend my whole day speaking to you because I'm stuck in the bed next to you." Through the sarcasm, the resentment was unmistakable.

"Okay, sorry, I didn't mean it like that. What's wrong?"

"Nothing, I'm sorry. I'm tired, my mum is coming tomorrow, and it's going to be a tough day, so I just took it out on you."

"That's okay. Why is it going to be tough? Is everything all right?"

"Yeah, yeah, all fine. Ignore me. I'm just tired."

"Okay. . . ." She wasn't convinced, but she didn't push it. Maybe she was starting to know his boundaries too. "Good night, Alfie, sorry for keeping you up."

"Good night." She heard him sigh, and pictured this faceless man closing his eyes. "And just so you know . . . I love being stuck in the bed next to you."

Her breath caught in her throat, and for one glorious moment she felt her heart flutter. "I love you being stuck in the bed next to me too, Alfie."

Chapter 44

ALFIE

When he woke up the next morning, Alfie instantly felt the regret of last night. Why had he said all those things to her? There was something about the darkness that made it feel safer to talk honestly—no one to stare or judge you as you let fragments of your heart pass between the curtains. It was the first time he'd ever admitted his realizations about Lucy. In fact, he hadn't even known himself until he'd reflected a few days ago. He had cared for her, deeply and truly, but he had never had conversations with her like he did with Alice. As he was describing all the things that were missing from his relationship with Lucy, it had dawned on him where he now sought them. Sometimes his connection with Alice felt more real and precious than three years with his ex-girlfriend. Had he revealed too much of his feelings last night? Had he given away any hint of where his thoughts were going? He prayed not. He didn't want to give Alice any reason to push him away again, not now that they'd come so far.

The conversation hung around him like thick smog. His head was cloudy with lack of sleep and his body ached with frustration. Alfie concluded that it could be nothing else but an emotional hangover. And what was the worst thing to do when you were hung over? Deal with your parents.

He hadn't lied last night when he said today would be a tough day, although he knew that his mother would strive not to let her pain show through. In fact, he presumed she would go in the complete opposite direction and be overly energetic and full of joy. She would definitely have been baking. The small silver lining to his mother's grief was always the copious amounts of baked goods that would appear. Selfishly and very inappropriately, he found himself praying for brownies.

"Oh, wow, Mrs. Mack, you've got enough there to feed the entire hospital. Are you sure you don't want any help bringing it in?"

Alfie rolled his eyes at the sound of the nurses greeting his mother that afternoon.

"No, no, not at all! You've got enough on your plate without carrying all this stuff in. I can manage—and if I can't, that's why I bring Robert along." She laughed at her own joke.

Yes, she's definitely sad today.

"I'll make sure to save you some, though. I've got lemon drizzle, oat squares, and brownies. Knowing my Alfie, there won't be a crumb of brownie left, but I'll try to wrestle one off of him."

"Thank you, Jane, you're a good woman, and a brave one to go up against that cheeky so-and-so!"

"Oi! Ladies, stop talking about me and come and share some of this baked goodness you're hiding over there," Alfie shouted across the ward in the hope of piquing the interest of

Mr. Peterson, who remained very quiet and rather lethargic these days.

"Don't forget to serve the elderly first, please," the old man replied. His voice was strained and almost cracking. "We have to make the most of these pleasures before we snuff it."

"No thank you, Mr. P. None of that talk. If anyone is going to live forever it will be you, if only just to continue being my favorite person to annoy!" Alfie hauled himself up out of bed and saw his mum sneaking a plateful into Mr. Peterson's cubicle. "Mother! I'll have you know he's on a strict diet. You can't be feeding a fragile old man that sort of thing." Alfie waggled his finger at them both.

"Fragile? I'll give you fragile in a minute, son, if you stand in the way of me and this cake!"

Alfie was glad to hear a bit of bite in the old man's voice. He walked over to his mum, kissed her on the cheek, and held out his arm in readiness. "Can I accompany you to my cubicle, madame?"

She squeezed his arm gently, looping hers through as she handed the cake tin to Robert, who was already balancing five in his hands. "Certainly. Lead the way."

He knew that showing her the progress he'd made in his walking would cheer her up, so he was vehemently pushing down the pain of using his prosthetic. He wanted to keep her mind distracted and the topic of conversation light. It was important not to leave too many silences or she'd find a way to fill them with memories. Memories were always the start of a slippery slope into despair.

Once they were across the ward and Alfie had settled back in bed, he realized just how many tins his dad was carrying.

"Mum, how many people are you feeding? How long did it take to bake all of this?"

"Don't even ask, Alf. She had to go and use next-door's oven because we ran out of room. I swear, I've never seen Tesco run out of butter as a result of one single person."

Alfie loved the way his dad moaned about his mother's ridiculous habits while simultaneously looking at her with such complete adoration and love.

"Well, if you don't want them, I will happily take them back and give them to the ladies at the salon."

"Oh, come on now, Mum, let's not make rash decisions here." Alfie reached across for one of the tins. "I'm very grateful for the cake, especially the brownies. Thank you."

"Don't be silly, I know how much you love them. And you know I always like to bake a little something to try to honor today." Her face dropped, and his dad immediately reached for her hand and gave it a squeeze.

"Come on, love, why don't we see if anyone else wants some of these?"

Before she could reply, Robert was already pulling her to her feet, cake tins in hand, and leading her out onto the ward floor.

As they were finishing their rounds, Sarah walked in. "Oh my God! What the hell is going on, Alfie? Have you hired people to bring better food than me?"

There she was. A small, blond, bright ball of energy hurtling towards him.

"Hello, love. I don't think we've met yet. We're Alfie's parents, Jane and Robert."

Sarah ignored his mother's outstretched hand and went straight in for a hug. "I'm Sarah, Alice's friend. I'm guessing you haven't delivered the mystery woman any cake yet? Pretty hard to when she's stuck behind this bloody curtain."

"Oh, well, we were just about to, act—"

"Don't worry, I'll take some in for her, if that's okay?"

"Of course! Take as much as you want."

Sarah fished out a handful of the lemon drizzle and disappeared behind the curtain.

"Thank you!" Alice called from behind her curtain.

"THAT'S OKAY, LOVE. THERE'S MORE HERE IF YOU WANT."

Why his mother was shouting at her, Alfie had no idea. "Mum, it's just a curtain, not a stone wall. You don't have to shout."

"Oh, right. Yes." Redness flooded her cheeks. "Well, just be quiet and eat your brownies."

The afternoon passed surprisingly well—probably a result of the extremely high blood sugar levels and numerous cups of tea that were being delivered because "a slice of cake isn't right without a cup of tea," according to the nurses.

"So come on, tell us. Is there any news yet on when you'll be out?"

His mum was desperate to have him home; every day that passed was one too many, in her opinion.

"No. They keep saying soon. It all depends on when the physio team is happy to sign me off."

"Do you want me to talk to them? Maybe get them to give a firmer timeline? I'm happy to go and speak to them if you want."

Of course she was. If you needed an answer from someone, it was highly recommended that you send in Jane Mack. No man, woman, or child could survive a grilling from her.

"No, it's fine. Thanks, though. I'm having a review next week—if I still don't have any answers after that, I'll call you in for backup."

"You're just too laid-back. If this was either of your brothers, they'd be asking every minute what was happening. But knowing you, you could be in here for another ten years if someone doesn't get involved! You get that from your dad."

"Don't go comparing me to my idiot brothers, *please*. And I think you'll find I've seen our Robert over there stressed and highly strung on many occasions. Don't lump me in with him!"

"No, Alfie." She looked exasperated. "I don't mean Robert. I mean your *dad*." Her voice was tired. She sounded exhausted by life today. "I remember so many times everyone would be tearing their hair out or shouting and screaming, and your dad would just be sat there, not fussed at all. Calm as anything. Sometimes we asked him if he had any cares in the world. Life was just water off a duck's back for him."

Robert wore a mixture of joy and grief on his face. Somehow they'd landed right in the center of where Alfie really didn't want to go today.

"Mm-hmm. I remember you saying this before." He didn't want to be rude, but he was frantically looking for a way to steer the conversation away from here. Sometimes if he just sat quietly, they would run out of steam and move on themselves.

"I remember this one time, we were all going on this stag night, and th—"

"Can we not? Please? I just can't hear it today," Alfie snapped, stopping Robert in his tracks.

He couldn't help himself. He didn't want to look Robert in the eyes because he knew what he'd be faced with: deep regret, grief, and longing to educate a boy he loved so dearly about a friend he'd loved just as much.

"Of course, son, of course. I guess just today being the anniversary and all, it's easy to get caught up in reminiscing. But you're right, we can do that at home."

Then came the familiar wave of guilt. Alfie didn't mean to be so sharp with them. It just came so naturally whenever they started doing this.

"Sorry, I know it's hard. I just—"

"No need to be sorry, darling. Let's talk about something else, shall we?" His mum patted his hand reassuringly. "Have another brownie, it always makes things better."

"No, Mum. *You* always make things better."

He leant over and kissed her on the cheek. Neither of them managed to stop the tears from welling in their eyes.

If there was a world record for number of cakes eaten in a day, Alfie was pretty sure he would come close to claiming the title with his performance that afternoon. His parents left earlier than usual, he assumed to go and visit the rest of the family, but conveniently forgot to take with them the remaining piles of sweet treats. Sure, it was probably emotional eating, but it felt so good stuffing his face with rich, sugary brownies that he couldn't even pretend to feel guilty about it. Sarah and Alice were chatting away as usual, and despite many attempts to bring him into the conversation, Alfie didn't feel like talking. He just wanted to sit there, eat, and then go to sleep.

"See you tomorrow," Sarah said as she popped her head around the curtain to say good-bye. "It was lovely to meet your parents today. Your mum is a magical baker."

"Yeah, she's pretty special. They both are." Alfie looked down at his hands. Why did he still feel so guilty for his behavior earlier? And why was Sarah looking at him like that?

"Makes sense that they created someone as special as you, then. Night, Alfie."

And just like that, she left.

And just like that, he started to cry.

Chapter 45

ALICE

As hard as she tried, she couldn't ignore the sounds of him crying next to her. Muffled sobs and gulps of air punctuated the relative silence of the ward. And as much as Alice wanted to reach out and ask if he was okay, they'd been through enough of these episodes now for her to know that space was key.

It had been a strange sort of afternoon; she'd felt something had been off the moment Alfie's parents had walked onto the ward. A tension in their conversation, Alfie's tone slightly harsher and blunter than usual. But for now she'd wait; they had all evening to talk, so her curiosity could be silenced for a little longer.

Surprisingly, it was Alfie who started the conversation. To say she was relieved was an understatement; navigating her way skillfully into emotional conversations was still not her strong point.

"Hey, Alice, do you want some more brownie? I think for the first time in my life I've reached my limit."

"Alfie, it's ten o'clock at night."

"And? Brownies are good twenty-four/seven, it's a scientific fact."

"Well, in that case, yes, hand some over. Plus Sarah ate most of the lemon drizzle cake we had, I barely got a look in."

An entire cake tin suddenly appeared through a gap in her curtain.

Alice reached for a couple to find it stuffed full with cake. "Honestly, how much did your mum bake? There's still so many!"

"Please, Alice, just take the whole lot—I still have two tins here, if you can believe it."

"If you insist."

Without hesitating, she started making her way through the brownies. Maybe she could eat herself into oblivion and avoid the reality of the outside world. She supposed it wouldn't be a bad way to go. *Burn victim escapes fire but dies by chocolate.*

"Was there any particular reason your mum decided to give us all diabetes today?"

"You can always tell when something bad has happened, or if someone's sad, when my mum starts to bake obsessively."

"Is . . . is everything okay?"

"It's a bit of a weird one, to be honest. I'm not really sure where to start."

"You can start anywhere or nowhere. It's totally up to you." She held her breath; would he remember he'd said those same words to her not so long ago?

"Ah, someone very wise must have said that to you once."

"Oh yes, he was very wise—wildly inappropriate and laughed at his own jokes a lot, but he was one of the wisest . . . and the kindest."

"Well, then, in his honor I guess it's only fair that I tell the story."

"I'm right here, with a hell of a lot of brownies and ready to listen."

"Today was the anniversary of my dad's death."

Had she really heard that right?

"But I th—"

"You thought Robert was my dad? Well, of course you did, I call him Dad. To me he is my dad. I've never known anyone else. But biologically he isn't."

"Oh right, I see."

She wanted to know more immediately, but she didn't dare push him.

"Basically my real dad, Stephen, got cancer when my mum was only a few weeks pregnant with me. It was in his kidneys. They operated and he went through chemo, all with the prognosis that he could have years left to live. Years left to meet me and see me grow up and live a relatively normal life. Unfortunately, they got it wrong. Or maybe the cancer just decided to show us all who was boss. He was dead within three months. So not only did my mum have to nurse my dad through some really dark times, she had to look after two young boys all while being pregnant with me. Then to top it off, the love of her life went and died on her only weeks before she gave birth. It was really shit, apparently—I mean, I only know this from my brothers and Robert, of course."

"Wait, so Robert was around even then?"

"Robert was actually my dad's best friend. They'd known each other since school. They came as a package, apparently, you rarely saw one without the other. Robert was like an uncle to my brothers—they grew up with him too. With Mum being so heavily pregnant and pretty much dealing with all of this on her own, he was around a lot to help us out. Plus he kept Dad's spirits up and helped with taking care of him. I don't think my family would have survived without him, to be honest. Nothing romantic happened for a while after my dad passed. Robert just wanted to make sure he looked after us—I think Dad made him promise to be there for us after he'd gone. Over time things started to change between him and Mum, and turns out they found love. It's pretty amazing, to be honest, and I love Robert like a father. Like I said, to me he is my dad. I've never known any different."

He paused, although Alice knew there was more.

"It just makes days like the anniversary of Stephen's death hard, because everyone is grieving, even my brothers, and I'm just there going through the motions. I know I should feel sad, but I can't miss a man I never knew. Robert insists on telling me stories about him, I think he's desperate for me to love the man like he did. Everyone says I'm a lot like him, I have his laid-back attitude, his humor, and of course I'm the only one who got his eyes."

"His eyes?"

He laughed. "I forgot you wouldn't have seen them! I have different-colored eyes. One is hazel and the other is bright green. It's pretty cool, to be honest, although growing up people used to tease me about it. Every time I'd come home crying after school, my mum would say to me, 'It's a piece of your dad, Alfie. What's not to love?' That made me hate him even more. It was hard for my mum to watch her youngest son pretty much try to forget his real dad ever existed. As I grew up, I realized just how important he was to both Mum and Robert, so I made a special effort to listen more to their stories. To ask questions. To study the photographs of them all as a family. It's just hard when it's not the family I know."

"That's a hell of a lot for you to deal with as a kid."

He was silent.

"Sorry, I didn't mean to imply anything bad towards your family—it just seems like that's a lot of pressure for you to take on as a child."

"No, it's okay. I'd never really thought about it like that. Growing up in a family that carried so much sadness and had been through so much pain, all I wanted was to make them smile. I guess I've just never grown out of it. I hate the thought of ever upsetting anyone."

Instinctively she reached her hand through the curtain. His hand was warm and firm in hers. "Sorry, there's probably a load of brownie on my fingers."

He squeezed her harder. "Just how I like it."

It was strange: once again she had that urge to share something of herself with him in return. Not out of duty or because she felt she had to, but because she really wanted to.

"My dad left us after Euan died."

Wow, there it was. Just like that.

"Really? How come?"

"Didn't want to be around the sadness anymore. That was the exact line he wrote in the letter he left for me. He didn't even have the guts to say good-bye to me face-to-face. I was twelve by then, and he left me at home with a psychopathic mother who could barely look after herself, let alone a child. He was a coward." There was so much venom in her voice that she could feel the acid burning her tongue as she spoke. Her dad was a subject she rarely spoke about, even to Sarah.

"Has he ever been in contact?"

"He wrote a few times. Always apologizing and trying to

explain why he had to get away—and the worst thing is, I understand. I couldn't have stayed married to my mother after what she became. But still, to leave me there with her, I find that really hard to forgive."

"I can imagine."

"The funny thing was that I convinced myself he was coming back. Every night I would leave the hall light on, a glass of brandy out on the sideboard, and a portion of dinner I'd saved in the oven for him. Every night for almost a year, until one night my mother, who had drunk more than her usual liter of whiskey, woke up on the sofa and saw me leaving the drink out. She laughed and told me how pathetic I was for thinking he would come back for me. That he didn't love me. He couldn't wait to get away from me. Euan was the only one he cared about, and how he'd told her he wished it was me who got sick instead. I got so mad I threw the glass at her head. It missed, fortunately or unfortunately, but after that I gave up on him. And her. Told myself he was never coming back and shut myself off from that life altogether."

Silence.

Hands squeezing even tighter than before.

"Alice, I'm so sorry that happened to you." His voice was so soft it barely kissed her ears.

"I haven't thought about that night for years. I kind of forgot it ever happened, actually."

"People do say I'm like therapy, but better and free."

He was joking, but he was right. Not that she'd been to therapy as an adult. Her dad had tried to make her go after Euan's death; she'd gone maybe three times before her mum pulled her out of it saying it was a waste of money.

"Thank you." She squeezed his hand again and let go. It was suddenly too much for her and she had to break free.

"You know that not everyone is going to hurt you, right?"

His words hit her hard. A sob escaped from her mouth as she buried her head in her hands. All of a sudden the pain was pouring out of her and she didn't know how to make it stop.

"I didn't mean to make you more upset. I just needed you to know that. Not all of us are going to leave you. You don't have to push us all away."

She looked down to see his hand still outstretched on her side of the curtain. She reached for him once again, just briefly. A wave of heat flooded her body.

Maybe Alfie was right. Maybe she didn't need to push everyone away to survive. Maybe love didn't need to be feared. She remembered the words that had come to her before.

If you're not willing to die, you have to find a way to live.

Chapter 46

ALFIE

He didn't know what was more exhausting, waking up after a night of vivid dreaming or waking up after having late-night conversations with Alice. Both seemed to pull deeply at his heart and leave him more than a little drained the next morning. This morning, though, alongside the heavy tiredness there was a giddy feeling, an excitement in his stomach that hummed from deep inside. How much she had shared with him last night! He couldn't believe how much she had opened up, and also how deeply painful her life had been growing up. That story alone would explain the walls she put up and her deep-rooted independence. The mystery of Alice Gunnersley was slowing unraveling.

"Morning, Alice. Mr. Warring said he would be down to see you this morning—I wanted to let you know in case you need more time to think." Nurse Angles didn't even ask permission to come into her cubicle these days. Alfie watched as she walked straight in without thought or apology.

"That's fine, thank you." Alice's voice sounded thick with sleep.

Did this mean she knew what she was going to do?

Please, Alice. Don't rush into this.

Luckily he didn't have long to wait before the figure of Mr. Warring appeared striding down the ward. Was she really going to do this without Sarah here?

She's not a child, Alfie.

He was panicking and he knew it.

"Hello, Alice. It's Mr. Warring, may I come in?"

"Sure." She was quiet; maybe some uncertainty had crept back in. Maybe she would ask for more time.

Alfie shifted his weight over again to listen in.

"So, it's been a couple days since we last spoke, and I wanted to get a sense of where you were with our conversation."

Just say it bluntly, Doctor: "Do you want to undergo major surgery all over again for the sake of a few scars?" He knew he was being unfair, but the anger was appearing out of nowhere.

"I want the surgery, and I want it as soon as possible."

Her assurance was loud and clear. There was no hint of doubt.

"Okay then, we will get you scheduled in. I'll let you know dates and we can talk details then."

And so it was done.

He knew he couldn't be here right now. If Alice dared to try to talk to him, he was afraid what emotional outpouring would escape him. He needed space to breathe and to think and to be.

Hauling himself up, he reached for his prosthetic and attached it as quickly and quietly as possible. Now was not the time to draw attention to himself. Slowly he extricated himself from the bed and was out into the ward without any word from Alice.

Half-consciously he found himself standing outside in the courtyard again. This little patch of outdoors was quickly becoming a place of refuge for him. Slowly he made his way over to the little swing bench in the corner and allowed himself to sink down and wallow in his thoughts.

There was one he just couldn't seem to let go of.

Why am I so against the surgery?

If he really cared about Alice, then surely he would just want her to be happy?

Alfie closed his eyes and let the answers bubble up from within.

There they were, clear as day, the lifeless bodies of Ciarán and Ross staring up at him.

He couldn't save them. Nearly every night, his dreams showed him how he had failed to save the two people in the world who had needed him most. Despite his best attempts, despite dragging his body across the road to reach them, he'd been too weak, too hurt, too pathetic to get to them in time. He could have done more. He should have done more. For the rest of his life he would have to live knowing he had let them down. Would protecting Alice somehow make up for his previous failings? Had his natural inclination to help morphed into something more intense? He knew the risks of surgery were low, but after the pain he'd endured he didn't want any possibility of loss in his life, no matter how small the odds were. He couldn't lose her. Not on his watch. He simply wouldn't.

"You all right, buddy?"

Alfie jerked his head up so violently he gave himself head rush; he had been so lost in his thoughts he hadn't heard anyone approach. He breathed a sigh of relief when he realized that it was Darren standing over him.

"Oh hey, yeah, I'm okay." His voice betrayed him with a slight wobble.

"Mind if I sit?" Everything inside of Alfie wanted to say no—wasn't it obvious he needed space? But then again, this was Darren, the nicest man on the planet. He shifted over, making a little room for him on the swing. "I saw you as I was walking past, you seemed a little off, so I thought I'd check in."

Alfie's gaze was fixed determinedly on a group of ants in front of him.

"You want to tell me what's going on?"

Alfie bit his tongue and dropped his head lower.

Darren was playing the waiting game, and Alfie realized the only way to get him to leave was to give him what he wanted.

"One of my friends is thinking about having major surgery to correct her face. She was badly burnt in a fire. I don't know how much damage there is. I haven't seen her—she won't let me see her—but I do know it would be purely cosmetic."

"Ah." It suddenly dawned on Alfie that Darren knew Alice. He'd treated her. He'd *seen* her. "And you don't think she should have it?"

Ever the professional, Darren didn't acknowledge that Alice was the subject of their conversation. Alfie couldn't ignore the pang of guilt that spiked through him. He felt himself grow suddenly defensive. "I just don't think she should put herself through all of that risk and uncertainty and *stress* for no reason." His fists were balled tightly now.

"But that's her choice. Not yours."

He should have known Darren was not the person to talk to about this. Of course he wouldn't get it, he was too nice for his own good.

"Don't you think I know that?" His voice came out louder than he intended, but it felt good to shout. Alfie didn't care that people were staring at him. Let them stare. "I just keep thinking, what if she *dies*? What if she dies and I didn't try to stop her?"

He felt Darren's hand on his back. A warm, comforting, solid hand. Alfie shook his head as the tears came.

"It's not your job to save her, Alfie."

Alfie was so tense that he could feel his fingernails making cuts into his palms.

"I'm sorry if it's not what you want to hear, mate, but you know I'll always be honest with you."

Alfie knew he was right, but a part of him still wanted to scream in Darren's face. Instead he chose to remain stubbornly wordless.

"Right, buddy I have to run to my next appointment. You know where I am if you need me." He gave Alfie a gentle pat on the back, then stood up to leave, pausing for a moment.

"Thanks, Darren."

The words were so small, but he knew Darren had heard them.

Another gentle pat and he was gone.

Chapter 47

ALICE

As she watched the doctor leave, Alice felt the urge to tell someone. To let someone know that she'd made this decision, that she'd taken back control. The feeling of wanting to volunteer her news was a foreign one. For so long the only person she'd concerned with her business was herself. The act of sharing felt new and exciting. Just as she was about to turn to call for Alfie, she heard the familiar sounds of him going: the rustle of the bedsheets, the small groan as he prepared to lift himself up, the solid sound of his prosthetic footsteps.

Where on earth is he going so early?

No matter. He'd be back, and until then she would just sit patiently and soak up the sounds around her. The sounds that she hoped she wouldn't have to endure for very much longer.

I'm getting my life back.

This is the first step to getting my life back.

"So it's a pain au chocolat for the lady, of course. . . ." The voice of her best friend cut through the ward. "And I went wild with an almond croissant for the gentleman. Wait. Al, where's Alfie?" Sarah poked her head around Alice's curtain.

"No idea, he left quite early this morning." Alice shrugged. "I'm sure he's not gone far." She had more important things to discuss than Alfie's whereabouts.

"Yeah, true. In the meantime I'm starving, so I'm going to eat his croissant as punishment for him being missing in action. Don't tell him, though, I can't handle the stress of his moaning today." She'd already taken a bite before the sentence was finished.

"Mr. Warring came round this morning to talk about the surgery."

"Oh?" Sarah paused, pastry hanging from her lips.

"I'm going ahead with it. They are scheduling a time as we speak. It's actually happening, Sarah." The combination of relief and excitement made Alice's stomach somersault with hope.

"I'm so happy for you, Al." Sarah wrapped her arms tightly around her. "I'm going to be scared shitless and worried about you from the moment you go under, but if it's going to help you, then I support you all the way." She nuzzled her face in closer.

"Thank you."

Sarah pulled back and faced her with a serious look in her eye. "Now, there's something else we need to discuss. . . ."

Jesus Christ, what more is there?

"Tomorrow is my last day, and we need to celebrate in style. I don't want any tears. We need to go out with a bang, okay?"

Shit. How could I have forgotten that?

Alice had been so wrapped up in everything else that she had completely missed the fact her best friend was leaving so soon.

"No. Enough of that." Sarah pulled her closer. "What did I just say, Al? We are going to celebrate tomorrow. No more sadness, *please*, for the love of God. I think we've both had our fair share of that."

Alice managed a weak smile. "Sure."

Why was it that everything always seemed to happen at once? As Alice lay in her friend's arms, a thought struck her: Was she going to be able to go through with the surgery without her? The decision had felt so easy a moment ago—but that was when she had Sarah by her side. Could she face putting herself through all of that stress alone?

You're not alone.

You have Alfie.

Where was he anyway?

"For someone so meticulous about this agenda, he's not taking his duty very seriously today, is he? We need our chief entertainment officer back, it's nearly puzzle book time!" Sarah was peering round the curtain into Alfie's empty bay. Alice managed to snatch a glimpse of where the voice next door inhabited every day. It felt extremely personal and a little too intimate. Seeing where he slept, laughed, and cried next to her was the closest she'd probably ever come to seeing Alfie.

Maybe not, if the surgery goes well.

No. She couldn't think like that right now. She didn't want to pin all her hopes on this one operation bringing her back to life, even though she had to admit a part of her wanted it to.

"Oh, hallelujah, here he comes!"

"Sarah! Close the curtain." Alice snatched the material from her friend's hands and drew the tiny gap shut. There was no way in hell she was about to reveal even an inch of herself.

"Sorry, I didn't think."

"It's fine, I just panicked." Alice knew she'd overreacted, but the ferocity just seemed to burst out of her. These days her emotions were free-falling, coming and going as they pleased, and she hadn't quite got the hang of controlling them.

"I know." Sarah kissed her hand. "Alfie! Where were you? I was about to send the troops out looking for you, but then Alice reminded me that you probably wouldn't be able to get too far."

He laughed. It sounded forced and a little flat. "No, unfortunately I'm not quite fit for a prison-break scenario yet."

He'd avoided the question. Alice knew better than to push it, so she adopted one of Alfie's very own techniques: distraction.

"I don't want to be a stickler for the rules, *but* someone did promise me a very in-depth entertainment schedule, and so far today we haven't covered one single element of the itinerary!"

"Ah yes, of course!" Sarah chirped excitedly. "And as it's my penultimate day here, I think I should be able to choose what we do."

"Wait, what?" The shock was audible in his voice.

"Tomorrow's my last day." Sarah pulled Alice in closer. As they lay there side by side, Alice wondered if she'd be able to find a way to imprint every sensation of her friend onto her skin. How could she keep this moment forever?

"No way! That's gone quick!"

"I know, and so tomorrow we are celebrating. I've already told Alice here that it's not going to be a day of crying and commiserating—it's not a final farewell, it's just a temporary good-bye. So guess what? We are going to have a goddamn party, okay?" As she spoke her voice grew louder and louder until she was practically preaching her demands.

"A party?" Sharon called eagerly from across the ward. "Did someone say party?"

Alice rolled her eyes at Sarah. "Look what you've done!" she hissed.

"Don't you worry, Sharon, no one in their right mind would think about having a party without inviting you. Nothing could get in the way of you and some Lambrini, and anyone who thinks otherwise is an idiot! We all know that," Alfie shouted back.

"Too right!" she remarked, clearly content with Alfie's flattery.

"You can thank me tomorrow, ladies, with an invite to this exclusive party of yours," he whispered.

With that, his wonderfully familiar hand burst through the curtains, and he gave them a quick thumbs-up.

"You're a smug bastard, aren't you, Alfie." Sarah laughed.

"Wouldn't have me any other way, though, would you?" Alice smiled.

Not in a million years.

Sarah hadn't been joking when she said that they were going to celebrate. She arrived the next morning hidden under bags of food and drink.

"Marks and Spencer's finest party collection! Don't say I don't treat you." Alice rolled her eyes. "And don't you dare look at me like that, young lady. I told you we were celebrating."

Alice knew there was no point in arguing. Sarah did as Sarah wanted.

"Salmon blini?" She stuck the plate right under Alice's nose.

"Absolutely not."

"Don't tell me you're too good for a canapé?"

"Sarah, it's half ten in the morning."

"And?"

Her entire being flooded with love as she watched her friend shove five little pancakes into her mouth at once.

"You go wild, I'll join you later."

"Well"—her mouth was still half-full of salmon and cream cheese—"how about a little Buck's Fizz, then?"

Alice stared in disbelief as Sarah pulled five mini bottles of the champagne and orange concoction out of her handbag. "You absolutely cannot be serious right now?"

"I am deadly serious. And guess what? These are just for starters! Look in that bag over there."

Alice shook her head. She couldn't bear to see what other contraband Sarah had sneaked in. "Go on, but don't make a song and dance over it. If Sharon gets a whiff, she'll be on us like a rash."

"Did someone just call me?" Sharon's confused voice rang out across the ward.

Sarah's eyes were so wide they were practically popping out of her face. Like two delirious schoolgirls, they crumpled into a heap of laughter.

"What the *hell* is going on back there?"

"The party has officially started, Alfie." Sarah sat up straight, grabbed a bottle of Buck's Fizz, and winked daringly at Alice.

Don't. You. Dare, she mouthed. It was bad enough Sarah had bought the stuff in the first place, but to hand it round like chewing gum, that was too far.

"Show me what snacks you've got back there then!" He sounded so childish that Alice couldn't resist.

"No!" she declared defiantly.

"Aha, I see. Like that, is it? Well, how about I tell the nurses that Sarah over there has smuggled bottles of prosecco into the ward illegally?"

"You wouldn't dare!" Sarah fired back.

"Oh, I would. Now, give me some sweets and I'll keep my mouth shut."

Reluctantly Sarah reached in the bag and pulled out some Percy Pig gummies. "Fine. But that's all you're getting from us."

His hand reached through to grab his reward. "Let's see about that, shall we?"

The rest of the day was a heavenly mix of eating, laughing, and Sarah trying to force-feed Alice illegal alcoholic goods. The nurses came and went, and every single one of them conveniently happened to miss the bag of bottles lying on the floor in front of them. Alice was beyond grateful at how amazing everyone had been by allowing Sarah to pretty much move in as a resident while she'd been here.

As the night drew in, Alice's mind started to switch into panic mode.

How long do we have left?

When does she have to go?

Surely she can't stay all night?

Her fears were confirmed when their safe little bubble was burst by the presence of Nurse Bellingham.

"What have I told you about being on this ward after hours? Am I not making myself clear?"

"I'm sorry, Nurse Bellingham, it's just tonight is my last night with Alice and I wanted to spend as much time with her as possible."

"But once again you're breaking protocol, and if you don't leave in the next minute I'll be forced to call security."

"As much as I find it hard to believe you're going to waste precious hospital resources over me, I'll go—just give me five minutes and then you'll never have to see me again. Deal?"

Nurse Bellingham gave one final defiant look, turned on her heel, and left.

"Argh, how can someone be so *mean* all the time?" Sarah shook her head in disbelief. Alice could feel the anger bubbling out of her friend. Not exactly the best note to leave things on.

"It's fine. Maybe it's better this way; otherwise if it were up to me, I'd be keeping you here all night and then you might miss your flight tomorrow morning. And that wouldn't be good for anyone."

Alice reached for Sarah's hand. One last chance to feel the lifeline that had been her anchor these last ten days."

"Since when did you turn so positive?"

"Since I don't fancy you being escorted out by security as my lasting memory of our good-bye."

Sarah kissed her hand. "I love you, Alice Gunnersley. And I meant what I said. We will see each other very soon. I'll make sure of it, okay?"

Alice smiled. She looked at Sarah—her wonderful, incredible, beautiful friend. How blessed she was to know her. "I love you too, Sarah Mansfield."

Alice finally took a deep breath and let go.

"Don't forget . . . he really is one of the best." And with a slight cock of her head towards the curtain, Sarah blew her one last kiss and walked away.

Alice's heart broke, and Alfie's hand was there immediately holding hers.

Chapter 48

ALFIE

Alfie didn't let go of her hand even after she fell asleep. It had been an exhausting day for everyone, and he wasn't surprised to find that barely an hour after Sarah left, Alice was fast asleep. There was so much he wanted to say to her, so many things to ask, that his mind was still spinning when he eventually closed his eyes.

Alfie woke with a start. Sounds of hurried footsteps, machines, and panicked orders rang out across the ward. It was disorientating to be woken up suddenly and it took Alfie a few moments to come round and realize that something was very wrong.

"Mr. Peterson, I need you to try to keep your eyes open for me."

Was that Nurse Bellingham?

"I need some help over here, please, he's not breathing."

What?

Alfie sat up suddenly. Then he heard it: the coughing, the cries for help lost amid the gasping.

"Mr. Peterson!" he cried out, frantically searching for his prosthetic. "Mr. Peterson, are you okay?" The fear was building rapidly inside of him.

"Alfie, what's going on?"

At first he didn't register the voice drifting from behind the curtain next to him. He was too busy searching for his leg.

Where the hell is it?

"Alfie?" Alice's voice was bleary, still dusted with remnants of sleep but firmer now.

He paused from his erratic search. "Alice, please, you have to help me. It's Mr. Peterson. He can't breathe." The words tumbled out of his mouth so quickly that he could barely understand himself. He had to get her to help.

"What do you mean?"

"Alice, I need you to come and pass me my crutches. I can't find my prosthetic and I need to get to Mr. Peterson *now!*"

"But . . . but I can't."

Why isn't she here already?

"What do you mean?" Alfie tried to shift his body closer to the edge of the bed, but it was no use. The dread was weighing him down so much that every move was excruciatingly slow.

"I . . . I just can't come round there."

Alfie stopped struggling; he couldn't quite believe what he was hearing. "Yes you can, Alice. Please!"

He heard the familiar rustling of her movements next door. The sound of her sitting upright, positioning herself on the edge of the bed, and preparing to stand. Then silence.

"I *can't*, Alfie."

"No, Alice. You just won't."

There was no time to argue—Alfie knew he had to move quickly. He could see the crowd of nurses growing around bed fourteen.

"Sharon!" His cry rang out across the ward. He didn't care if he woke anyone up; no one deserved to be sleeping while Mr. Peterson was in danger.

Maybe she couldn't hear him above the chaos of the crisis?

"SHARON," he was practically screaming.

"I'm coming, honey, just one second."

Alfie couldn't wait one second; he managed to haul himself right to the edge of the bed and was just on the verge of toppling off when Sharon was suddenly by his side.

"What the hell are you doing, Alfie? You think you're going to be good for anyone laid out on the floor with a concussion?"

Without another word, she'd grabbed his crutches from the floor and was helping him move as quickly as possible towards the old man. The closer he got, the tighter Sharon gripped his waist. The closer he got, the more ragged Mr. Peterson's breathing sounded.

"What's happening?" He reached out for Nurse Bellingham's shoulder.

"Alfie, you can't be here right now. We need space to work on him." The flash of panic in her eyes made Alfie's stomach drop.

"Work on him?"

Alfie's heart was pounding. His body was sweating, his breathing shallow. He felt like he'd been running at a million miles per hour, yet he was rooted to the spot.

"MOVE, ALFIE. We need to get to him." Nurse Bellingham pushed him aside.

"Honey, come over here, you don't need to see this." Sharon was trying to pull him away.

"No." She had his hand and was dragging him. "No, Sharon! I can't leave him. I can't."

"At least move over here a bit more. Make sure the doctors have enough space to help him, okay?"

He didn't even care that she was treating him like a child. In fact, all he wanted right now was someone to hold him and soothe him and to tell him everything was going to be okay. Instead all he had were his own words, repeated over and over like a mantra:

"Please be okay. Please be okay. *Please* be okay."

And then the sound cut through.

The eternal, unbroken sound of a heart that had stopped beating.

Alfie didn't even bother to watch as they tried to resuscitate him. Mr. P. wasn't the kind of man who did things by half. If he'd decided to go, there was no way in hell he was coming back no matter how much electricity someone passed through his body. Slowly Alfie started to make his way back to his bed, and it was only when he began to move that he realized how numb he'd become. He saw his hands move in front of him, but had to question to whom they belonged. In an act of protection his body and mind were shutting down, and he was truly grateful for the void.

He didn't cry. He tried. He really fucking tried. He didn't cry when he heard them announce the time of death. He didn't even cry when someone mentioned breaking the news to Agnes. The thought of this woman hearing that her soul mate, her life partner, her entire world had just died without her even being able to say good-bye was beyond painful, yet still no tears came. All he could do was lie there, stare at the ceiling, and allow the commotion of the night to settle down around him.

"Alfie? Can you hear me?" Alice's desperation was unmistakable. He finally understood how satisfying silence was as a way to shut people out.

"Alfie, please?"

He was strangely enjoying listening to her worry. He wanted her to feel bad. She *should* feel bad.

"Alfie, I'm sorry. I just—"

Something suddenly snapped inside of him. Rage flooded him, tearing through every part of his body until he wanted to rip his own skin off to escape the heat. For the first time since they'd met, Alfie prayed to be anywhere other than in this bed next to her tonight.

"You just what, Alice? You just couldn't get up to help me? You just couldn't get up out of bed for one minute to help me get to my friend? My dying friend. After everything that's happened, you couldn't even fucking get up! For once I actually don't want to hear what you have to say, so please just do me a favor and leave me alone."

As he turned over to face the other direction, he could have sworn he saw some movement from the curtain. Funny how something you'd been thinking of obsessively for days could instantly become insignificant. He didn't care if she was looking through at him. He didn't care if she'd pulled back the whole goddamn thing. Some things were just too little too late.

Alfie had assumed that by morning at least some of the shock of the night would have worn off. How wrong he was. He woke, still very numb and very empty, unsure whether he was even awake or still dreaming. Luckily, Alice didn't try to talk to him. There was no way he had the energy for it today. It was hard enough to try to smile when Nurse Angles came to see him.

"Alfie, honey." She placed her hand gently on top of his. "I'm so sorry for your loss." He couldn't stand to look at her; he didn't want to see any kindness this morning, not when life kept proving how cruel it could be over and over. "I know it looked traumatic, but the doctors have assured me he didn't feel any pain. He was an old man, sweetie, it was simply his time to go."

There was nothing he could say. Nothing he wanted to say. All he could do was curl the corners of his mouth into what he hoped resembled some sort of smile of acknowledgment.

"I'll leave you to it, but I'm here, we all are, if you need anything."

As she turned to go, he was suddenly struck with a devastating thought. "Does Agnes know yet?"

"We told her this morning. She's coming in to see him this afternoon."

The rest of the day passed in a blur. Alfie was vaguely aware of people moving around, staff cleaning and talking amongst themselves, but he didn't care enough to notice the details. When Alfie looked over at Mr. Peterson's cubicle at the end of the day, he was stunned. There was no evidence that the man had existed at all. Everything had returned to its original sterile state. How quickly every trace of a person could disappear, wiped away and collected up to be replaced with fresh bedsheets and a brand-new resident.

Before his own accident, Alfie could never really understand why people got so worried about forgetting their loved ones when they passed. Surely you could never erase those memories or moments from your mind? How could you ever forget a person who had meant so much to you? But you could. And you did. One of the hardest lessons he'd had to learn was that time didn't stop for anyone. If you didn't go with it, there was a risk people would move on without you too. But to take that first step felt so much like betrayal, it rooted you to the spot. Watching the ward prepare for a new body to move into Mr. Peterson's space was another stark reminder of how quickly the world carried on without you.

"Alfie. Are you awake in there?" The voice of one of the nurses cut through his stream of thoughts. It was tentative and barely audible over the whirring in his head. It seemed everyone was treading on eggshells.

"Uh-huh."

She pulled back the curtain. "Agnes is here. She'd like to talk to you, if you don't mind?"

Panic raced through him, stealing his breath as it went.

"It won't take long, dear. I know you'll want to be by yourself today." Agnes's voice sounded so strong and calm. Was she still in shock? Had it hit her yet that her husband was dead?

"Of course, come in." He sat up a little straighter, rearranging himself in the hope of masking the creases of grief that had folded themselves into him.

She looked smaller than the last time he'd seen her, although maybe that was just in his mind. Her crinkled face was etched deeply with lines of laughter, of tears, of sun-kissed days and freezing nights. This was a worldly woman. Alfie got the impression that there wasn't much that could shock her anymore. Today it seemed she was using everything she had inside of her to keep upright and strong.

She shuffled towards him and sat down in the chair by his bed. Her hands were clasped around her handbag, clutching the worn leather so tightly that the knuckles on her paper-thin hands were turning white.

"Agnes, I'm so, so—"

"Alfie." She stopped his words dead in their tracks. "It was his time to go and we must respect that."

Alfie sat, eyes and mouth wide open, looking at the incredibly calm woman before him.

"Of course, it doesn't stop it hurting any less." She coughed, and her gazed dropped briefly to her hands. "I want to thank you for being there with him. Not just last night, but ever since you came to the ward. I'm not sure if he ever told you, because he was a stubborn old bastard at times, but he loved you. It's funny; so many people would ask me if I found it hard being apart from him for so long, did I find it difficult knowing he was left in this place without me—but whenever I thought about it, I came back to the same answer. I never felt worried or guilty, because I knew he was surrounded by love here. He had you. And he was so grateful for that."

Alfie shook his head. He was the one who had stopped checking on his friend as much because he'd got too caught up in another silly side story. Alfie couldn't bear the compliments. He didn't want the affection. Niceties made the pangs of guilt more intense.

"But I let him down." The words came out so small and quiet.

"You did nothing of the sort." Alfie was a little taken aback by the slap on the wrist she gave him. "Stop that nonsense. I knew my husband for over sixty years, and I saw the way he looked at you. You were a good friend to him, and I am very thankful for all that you did for him. In fact . . ."

She reached into her handbag and pulled out two worn, shabby-looking books.

"I know he'd have wanted you to have these. I can't stand the things, but I know you both loved puzzles so much. These are two of the hardest, apparently—he tried over the years to finish them but never got round to it. Now it's your turn to try."

Only then did Alfie manage to cry.

"Oh look, don't get yourself upset now." She handed him a tissue from her bag. "He'd want you to be happy."

"Thank you. I'm really going to miss him, you know?"

She patted his hand one last time and shuffled her way up to standing. "You and me both."

Chapter 49

ALICE

She'd messed up. She'd messed up really, really badly.

Straight after it happened, she tried to convince herself that she'd simply been too confused to do anything. Being woken up by the shouting had been disorienting, and she couldn't be sure if she was still dreaming or not. Confusion. That was why it took her so long to react, and by the time she'd worked out what was happening, it was all too late.

It was a hard pill to swallow to admit it was all bullshit.

Ultimately she was a coward. A selfish, unforgivable coward.

It *was* true that she was disoriented when she first woke up; however, the moment she heard Alfie's voice she knew that this was very real and something was very wrong. Yet despite his desperate cries for help, she couldn't go to him. Fear was holding her down against her will. The most ludicrous part of it was that no one would have been looking at her anyway. The only thing anyone cared about was saving the life of a man who was dying before their eyes. It was all in her head. She was the only one who cared. She was the only one standing in her way, and now she was suffering the consequences.

At first she couldn't work out which was worse, his anger or the silence. Hearing the disappointment in his voice was devastating, but it was the edge of repulsion that she couldn't seem to shake off. He was disgusted by her actions. Well, her lack of; and no matter how many excuses she tried to find, Alice knew that he was completely and utterly justified in his feelings towards her. Knowing that seemed to make it hurt all the more.

Even though she was still hidden away in her cubicle, Alice decided to wait until the evening to try to talk to him again. Being rejected in broad daylight was never a nice feeling, even when you'd tried to make yourself completely invisible.

"Alfie?" Her voice was tentative but definitely audible.

Silence.

"Alfie, please?"

Nothing.

"If you don't want to talk to me, I completely understand, but please at least hear me out."

She took his silence as a green light.

"What I did, well, what I didn't do . . . It was unforgivable. I didn't get up. I didn't get up because I'm stuck in this ridiculous minefield of fear. I wanted to, I really wanted to be there for you, to help, to do something, but I just . . . I just couldn't. Do you know how sick that makes me feel? How ashamed I am? I don't want to live my life as a coward anymore, Alfie, I *refuse* to live my life like this. That's why I've agreed to have another operation. A second surgery to fix my face. I know it doesn't make up for what I did, and it doesn't bring Mr. Peterson back but . . . I want you to know that I'm going to change."

She waited, straining her ears for any sound of acknowledgment.

"Alfie, I'm going to be better, I promise."

She heard him take a breath.

Her heart rose slightly.

She knew he'd still be there, as he'd always promised.

"Well, good for you." His sarcasm coated every word.

Alice felt her heart fall through the floor.

I'm sorry, Alfie. I'm so, so sorry.

Turned out living in silence wasn't that fun anymore. Alfie still hadn't so much as breathed in her direction since Mr. Peterson's death, and in fact the entire ward seemed to have descended into an eerie stillness. The only signs that there was life beyond her curtains were the faint shuffling of feet and nondescript noises of human existence. Grief had made its home here, and there was no sign of it leaving. Even Nurse Angles was struggling to find a smile.

"Morning, Alice. I have some good news." There was not one shred of joy in her voice. "Mr. Warring has confirmed the date of your surgery. You're scheduled for eight days' time."

Wow. That soon?

"Amazing, thank you so much." Alice's cheeks hurt from her overcompensating smile. "I'm also so sorry for your loss. Mr. Peterson was a good man, and I know how much he meant to you."

God, you really are trying, aren't you, Alice?

All she received for her efforts was a tiny nod of acknowledgment, and then Nurse Angles was gone.

Every day Alice thought about trying to make conversation with Alfie, but each time she opened her mouth the sting of potential rejection closed it tight. There were so many moments when she wanted to cry out or scream just to get some sort of reaction. Life was definitely less vibrant without him in it. She missed all of his annoying quirks, his jokes, his laugh, his incessant determination. Without him, her days were painfully quiet—a quiet that, ironically, Alice no longer welcomed.

There had to be a way to make him see how sorry she was. There had to be a way to get through to him.

Then, just like that, a flash of inspiration took hold.

It was time to play Alfie Mack at his own game.

Chapter 50

ALFIE

He knew she'd been battling with herself all day about whether to talk to him. The interesting thing about not being able to see someone was that you became incredibly attuned to the sound of them. Every time she opened her mouth to try to speak, he would stop what he was doing to listen. Despite the small sparks of enjoyment that he relished from her anguish, there was a much bigger part of him that just wished they could go back to the way they were, back to how it was only a few days ago. In the space of a few hours, he'd lost two of the most important people in his life on the ward. Loneliness was not a familiar feeling for Alfie, and he was starting to understand how one could die from the pain of it all.

Normally Alfie would find the silence unbearable. Previously he would have been the one lightening the mood, desperately trying to find a way to cheer people up and make them laugh—but not anymore. Instead, Alfie ended up spending his day staring at the blank pages of his puzzle book while trying to push all thoughts of Mr. Peterson out of his mind. The only person he wanted to talk to about what had happened was exactly the same person who had let him down so badly. The conflict was too much to bear.

He couldn't quite believe the relief that washed over him when it was time for his physio appointment. At last! Something to take him away and distract him. When Alfie arrived in the little side lounge, he was in such a daze that it took a moment for him to register the scene before him.

Did I miss something? What's going on?

Standing in the center of the room was Darren holding a massive CONGRATULATIONS! balloon and wearing an overwhelmingly large smile on his face. Alfie glanced behind himself.

"Alfie! Buddy!" Darren approached him, obviously sensing his confusion. "Guess what?"

Alfie continued looking around, attempting to piece everything together. "What's going on?" he mumbled.

"We're signing you off, mate! We're happy to let you loose on the outside world!" Darren wrapped him into a firm embrace. Alfie just stood there, frozen.

Sensing the awkwardness, Darren stepped back. "Okay, so maybe the balloon was a bit over-the-top."

"Hey, no, not at all! It's great, it's really great . . . thanks!" He forced a smile and gave Darren a slightly more accepting embrace.

His performance clearly went some way to comforting Darren, who shrugged sheepishly. "Well, it was the least we could do. I know it hasn't been easy, and with everything else that's been going on lately . . ." Alfie avoided his gaze. "I just wanted to give you some good news."

"Wait, does this mean no more physio?" Alfie joked, praying that he wouldn't be forced back to the ward so soon.

"Absolutely not, my friend. We have one more proper session, and then you'll see the doctor for a final assessment. And while I have you I am going to make every single second count, so hurry up and get yourself in there before we change our minds!"

It turned out Darren wasn't joking. That afternoon Alfie was subjected to one of the most grueling sessions he'd ever had, and it certainly wasn't helped by the continual "things won't be this easy on the outside, Alfie" commentary. Even though life on the ward well and truly sucked right now, the thought of actually being outside and dealing with real life was still more terrifying. Everything felt like it was suddenly happening all at once—a sequence of events crashing into one another so quickly that by the time he'd tried to stop one from falling, two more had already been knocked down.

He had been signed off.

He had reached the final step to getting out of here

He couldn't believe it.

He would be going home soon.

Are you really going to leave things like this with her?

He couldn't think about that right now. There were too many factors involved. First of all, he was still so goddamn *angry* with her; and second, it was hard to concentrate on anything when Darren was going all boot camp on him. But no matter how much Darren admonished him, or how hard Alfie tried to ignore it, the question refused to leave his thoughts.

By the time he got back to the ward, he was exhausted. The moment he set eyes on his bed, relief surged through him. At last! Rest! But just as he was about to throw himself down, a piece of paper on his bedside table caught his eye.

That had definitely not been there when he left for physio earlier this afternoon. Intrigued, he reached across to see what it was.

It was a letter-size piece of paper that had been folded in half. On the outside someone had simply written his name and nothing more. He opened it, and found that he was looking at a hand-drawn crossword puzzle.

He allowed his heart to leap just the tiniest amount before quickly analyzing the clues.

UP
1. Organ of the body you use for sight (3)
2. Abbreviation used to describe a time in the morning (2)
3. Present; current state (5)
4. Disastrous, awful (8)

DOWN
1. First letter of the alphabet (1)
2. Square root of 16 (4)
3. Common name for *Homo sapiens* (5)
4. Apology (5)

The more clues he answered, the harder his heart started to beat. When he finished, he looked at the words and couldn't help but burst out laughing. Rearranging them a little, the sentence was revealed to him:

Eye Am Sorry Four Being A Terrible Human

Chapter 51

ALICE

She knew it had worked when she heard his laugh burst through the silence. She couldn't stop the smile curling the corners of her mouth with relief.

"I am so sorry."

"It's okay."

She took a deep breath. Now was the time to tell him, it had to be now. "I meant what I said about being a better person. They've scheduled my operation for the end of next week. It's actually happening, Alfie."

Silence.

Not quite the reaction she was expecting.

"Alfie? I thought you'd be pleased for me."

"I'm sorry, I am, it's just been a long day. In fact, it's been a long few days. I guess I'm just tired."

"You don't exactly sound thrilled about the idea."

"Well, I think it's a big thing to put yourself through. I'm not trying to be negative, I just want you to really know what you're getting yourself into with this."

"Of course I understand what I'm getting myself into," she snapped.

"Do you? You seem to have made the decision pretty quickly. I guess . . . I guess I don't understand why you'd voluntarily open yourself up to those risks again."

"No, Alfie, it's you who doesn't seem to understand, and you know what? I guess you wouldn't unless you knew what I was stuck with." Her voice was razor sharp. Why didn't he *get it*?

"Okay."

"*Okay*? That's all you're going to say?" Her voice was getting louder, but she didn't care. He was being a complete arsehole about this whole thing, and she needed him to realize how unfair he was being.

"I don't know what you want me to say, Alice. I'm not going to lie to you."

"Really? After *everything* you've preached to me about, you're saying that you'd rather I spend the rest of my life hiding? Hiding away from people, from new places, new experiences? Hiding behind these fucking hideous curtains? I want more, Alfie. I never thought I'd say it, but I do."

How had they gone from not speaking, to making up, to arguing? All Alice knew was that she was so full of rage that nothing else mattered.

His voice was so soft she barely caught the words. "I guess I just wish you could see what I see."

"But you haven't seen me, have you?" The uncontrollable fire burst out of her. "You lie there day-in day-out creating this weird ridiculous fantasy of me behind this fucking curtain, but you have no idea. You have *no idea* how damaged I am, Alfie. So stop pretending that you know me!"

Chapter 52

ALFIE

He barely slept that night for all the thinking. At some point in the early hours he must have drifted off because when he woke it took him a couple of moments to remember that it hadn't all been a dream. The dynamic had shifted, and Alfie had no idea who was going to talk first.

"Good morning, and how are we doing today?" Nurse Angles's bust was making its way through his curtains and into the cubicle. He was grateful she sounded a little brighter today; the loss of Mr. Peterson had hit everyone harder than expected, but he had a feeling he'd need every ounce of her sunshine and positivity to get him through the next few hours.

"Fine. Tired, I guess."

"Hmmmm." She eyed him warily. "Are you two friends again, or are we still pretending to dislike each other?" She nodded in the direction of Alice's bed. The way she said it reminded Alfie of how some of the teachers would treat the children at school: *Come on now, let's not be silly, kiss and make up*.

"Long story, but I don't think we're friends." Alfie really didn't want to go into detail on the subject. He also made sure his voice was as quiet as possible so that Alice wouldn't hear.

"I don't know what to do with the pair of you." She shook her head in dismay. "At least you'll be able to tell your mum and dad your good news today! That will be wonderful for them."

"Huh?"

"Seriously, Alfie, what's wrong with you this morning! You're more confused than Sharon without a glass of wine in her hand." She laughed at her own joke. She was definitely feeling better. "Physio agreeing to sign you off!"

Alfie feigned a smile. "Of course! Sorry, apparently I'm too tired to think. Yes, I'm sure my mum will be thrilled. Or panicked. Or both."

"She'll just be so relieved to have her baby back. Our loss, her gain." She flashed him one more loving smile and left him to his thoughts. Surprisingly, not to thoughts about being able to deliver the news his mum had been dying to hear for months. Not to thoughts about the delicious crispy roast potatoes that now seemed to be arriving twice a week at his bedside. No, all his thoughts were about the woman lying in the bed next to him whom he hadn't even laid eyes on!

Alice Gunnersley, what have you done to me?

"Oh, sorry we're a little late, Alf, the traffic was awful, and then I needed the toilet so we had to stop and then Robert got a coffee. I told him to wait until we got here, but you know what he's like with his coffees." His mum seemed to be talking a million miles per hour while kissing him on the cheek, patting him down to check for any new limb loss, and eventually settling into the chair by his bed.

"You know the coffee here tastes like it's come straight from a bedpan. You can't berate a man for wanting a decent latte, can you, son?"

"Oh, don't bring Alfie into it. The poor boy has to put up with the food here all day every day! Anyway, baby, how are you?"

"Well, I won't be putting up with it for much longer actually." He smiled, drip-feeding them the news to see how quickly the penny dropped.

"No, no, of course not. That's the attitude to have. It's not forever, you're right." His mum was still flapping, busying herself with unpacking the food and attempting to serve it onto the paper plates they'd brought.

Robert looked at Alfie. "Hold on a second. Are you trying to tell us something?"

"Huh?" Jane paused midway through dealing out a Yorkshire pudding. "What do you mean? Alfie, tell me! Have they given you a date?"

"Calm down, Mum, I only found out yesterday." He'd forgotten what Jane Mack on a mission could be like. "And I wanted to tell you in person, physio has signed me off. They just need the doctor to give a final assessment, and then . . . yeah, if all goes well, I'm coming home."

Before he could take his next breath, he felt his mum wrap herself around him. The weight of her, the smell of her, the warmth of her seemed to bring the reality of the news home to him.

He was going home.

He was really going *home*.

He could feel his shoulder getting damp as she cried tears of relief.

"Come on, Mum. You're soaking me over here!" He gently held her out in front of him and gave her a kiss on the cheek. There was so much love in her eyes he felt it physically wash over him.

"Can't a mum be happy that her boy is coming home?"

"Not when you drop a perfectly good Yorkshire on the floor in the process." Robert winked at Alfie as he reached for the rogue pudding that had escaped in the commotion.

"Your emotional capacity is less than one of my Yorkshires', I can tell you that for certain. Oh, Robert, give me that, don't put it back on someone's plate, for heaven's sake."

The two men smiled at each other. His mother had successfully been distracted.

"Do you want to pass this through to your friend Alice?" She was holding out a plate to him.

"No, don't worry, I'll take that one. She wasn't well yesterday, so I'm guessing she's sleeping. Best to leave her to it." He hoped they didn't notice his voice drop to a whisper.

"Oh dear. Is she okay?"

Shut it down, Alfie, shut it down quickly.

"She's fine, just a bit of a rough night. Give me a plate and I'll give it to her later when she's feeling better."

"Sure. Take this one. Pass on our best, will you?" His mum looked so concerned that he couldn't face lying to her again. He simply nodded and prayed Alice hadn't heard his lie.

"So, how are we going to celebrate your homecoming, then? I'm thinking a family gathering at ours, obviously you can invite the boys too and then we can drive over the next day to your flat and sort any adjustments that need to happen . . ."

Alfie sat back with his food and let his mum talk at him. It was easier that way. Don't push against the tide; just choose the path of least resistance and flow with it. Although he couldn't help but wonder if anything would feel easy without Alice to talk to.

Chapter 53

ALICE

One moment she was being ignored. Then they were talking. And now no one was talking. She couldn't quite work out who was ignoring whom anymore; it had all happened so quickly that Alice barely had the chance to get her head around it all.

The only thing she knew was that he was *so* angry at her for having the operation, and for the life of her she couldn't work out why. Why did it bother him so much?

Wasn't the whole reason he shut me out because I was too paralyzed by fear to do anything?

Now that I'm actually doing something about it, apparently that's wrong too?

She couldn't deal with it anymore. Having other people involved in your life just complicated everything. This was exactly why she had learned to keep herself to herself. Then no one else needed to have a say or an opinion on what you did. You were the only one who got to decide.

Through the night she could hear him tossing and turning.

At first every rustle of his bedsheets sparked more anger; why did he have to be so noisy *all the time*? Then a perverse little voice inside her reminded her that the more he tossed and turned, the more he was struggling with himself. She let herself imagine him so caught up in his own guilt that the more he struggled, the tighter the sheets got. Good. He deserved it.

However, it also meant that she wasn't sleeping either. She was trapped in an endless loop of thoughts that went around and around in her mind. As the hours crawled by, she began to master the technique of ignoring them all, until one practically hurled itself at her.

Sarah.

She'd been so caught up in everything, she realized she hadn't even checked to see if Sarah had gotten back okay. Alice grabbed her phone and switched it on.

Message from Sarah BFF • July 3, 4:58 p.m.

Hey, my love. Landed safe and sound. Pretty much drank myself to sleep with the free champagne so it wasn't a bad flight. I miss you already. So much. Keep me posted on EVERYTHING please. Send my love to Alfie. I love you. xx

Message from Sarah BFF • July 5, 12:04 p.m.

Okay, it's me again, just checking in and being an annoying best friend. I know the ward is super fun and Alfie has probably got you out doing rock climbing or something ridiculous, but please just let me know you're okay? Love you. xxx

Message from Sarah BFF • July 7, 3:42 p.m.

Seriously? Don't make me go all Nurse Bellingham on you. MESSAGE ME BACK. I love you. Although it's

getting less and less by the minute if you carry on
ignoring me. Xxx

Alice typed out a reply as quickly as her injuries would
allow, hoping it explained just enough to excuse her lack
of response but was still bright and breezy to prevent Sarah
worrying.

Message to Sarah BFF • July 8, 1:50 a.m.
Hey, Sarah. Sorry!! Life on the ward has just been so busy
the last few days, time has escaped me. But really, I am
sorry. I know I said I'd be better at keeping in touch. Mr.
Peterson passed away the other day and I've got my
operation scheduled for next week. Will keep you posted
on how it goes. Miss you and love you xxx

Strangely, seeing it written down like that in black and
white seemed to shift something inside of her. She was going
to put herself through a horrifically complex operation. She
was completely alone. Again.

Shut it down and get on with it.

For the first time in months, Alice was rudely awoken by the
sound of buzzing near her ear. God, had she really lived her
life by the beckoning call of this stupid phone?

Message from Sarah BFF • July 8, 9:15 a.m.
Jesus, Alice, that's a hell of a lot going on! Is Alfie okay
about Mr. P.? Send him my love, he must be really
struggling. Can you please PLEASE get someone to let

me know how the operation goes? I love you but don't
trust you to let me know! All is fine here except I have an
Alice-shaped hole in my heart. Love you. x

She reread the words over and over.
He must be really struggling.
Had she been too hard on him?
She couldn't shake off the feeling that being angry with
him didn't feel quite so good anymore.
With no Alfie to talk to and the wind taken slightly out of
her sails about the operation, Alice had been struggling to
find ways to pass the time between physio sessions. She'd
walked around her cubicle, diligently following the doctor's
instructions and Darren's exercise plans until her bones
ached and her skin felt raw. Then she'd be left with pretending to read, pretending to watch TV, or pretending to sleep.
It was a truly mind-numbingly boring existence. Not that her
life before the accident had been full of social events and activities, but never in her life had Alice spent so much time
doing nothing. Work had filled her days. Work was her excuse for not hanging out with friends or making plans. She
used to moan about her triple-booked diary, her relentless
meeting schedules and demanding to-do list, but what she
wouldn't give to have it all back now. The feeling of walking
into a boardroom with such confidence, such certainty of
yourself that nothing anyone could say would affect you. The
adrenaline of a deadline and the perversely sweet exhaustion
that came from trying to meet it. Now, without work, all she
had left was to lose herself in other people's dramatic story
lines on terrible daytime TV shows. At least none of them
would get on her case about her shitty life.

She must have fallen asleep at some point during the afternoon because, the next thing she knew, she was woken by the voices of Alfie's parents in the bay next to her, overcome with joy that their son was coming home.

Alice felt so torn. Never in her life had she felt so many conflicting things at once. Actually, never in her life had she felt so many things, full stop.

She hated him for last night. She hated him for making her let someone in again after all these years. She was mad at him for leaving her.

Without thinking, she reached back for her phone, and in a rare moment of desperation she messaged Sarah again.

Message to Sarah BFF • July 8, 3:25 p.m.
Alfie and I aren't actually talking at the moment and I just found out he's leaving soon. I don't know what to do. I was so angry at him, but now I'm just scared. I know there's nothing you can do and I don't really know why I'm telling you this when you're so far away. I love you and miss you. xxx

Message from Sarah BFF • July 8, 5:00 p.m.
Alice, what happened? Actually, regardless of what happened, and I'm not saying he's perfect or he hasn't done anything wrong, but some things are more important when you look at the bigger picture. Don't let your stubbornness get in the way of this. He loves you. You know he does. So do I. xxx

Her tears were making it difficult to read the screen.

But what was she meant to do? She took a deep breath and tensed every muscle in her body, holding everything so tightly until she was shaking from the pain. Her jaw was clenched shut: teeth on teeth, bone on bone. It was taking all of her energy not to scream the rage out of her. Instead she squeezed her body tighter, screwed her face up, and dug her nails deeper into the palms of her hands. A voice inside her head was howling, ripping the silence apart.

I don't want to FEEL THIS ANYMORE!

All at once her body went limp. The exhaustion hit and she could no longer hold on to the fire. It was burning her from the inside out.

Chapter 54

ALFIE

"Alfie?" Her voice was soft and almost dreamlike. Alfie couldn't quite trust that he'd heard it for a moment, until she spoke again. "Alfie, are you awake?"

"Uh-huh. What's going on, is everything okay?" He was still a little surprised at her making the first move.

"Why didn't you tell me?"

Okay, now he was really confused. "What?"

"Why didn't you tell me you're leaving so soon?"

"Oh. I only found out two days ago. Then we weren't talking, and then we were, and then we weren't again. I just . . . there just wasn't a right time."

A part of him was flattered by her sadness. Another was confused. She was the one who was angry with him. Why would she care if he stayed or went?

"I know, but still, that's pretty big news."

He sighed, rubbing his face with his hands. There was so much he wanted to say, but the fear of being vulnerable with her again was clamping down on his words. He knew he had to be honest with her. If he pushed her away now, the chances of getting her back were slim to none. She'd opened the door, and there was no way he could slam it in her face.

Taking a deep breath, he dived in. "I'm sorry I upset you the other day. It's just, I have lost so many people in my life in such a short space of time, and I guess I'm petrified of losing another one. You nearly died once, and I just can't wrap my head around the fact that you want to risk it all over again when you don't need to. But that's me. That's my opinion and I shouldn't have put that on you. I'm sorry." He took another deep breath. "I really am sorry."

Clenching his hands tighter, he fought back the urge to cry.

He heard her breathing deepen, quicken, then slow again.

"Alfie . . ." Her voice cracked with emotion. "I'm absolutely terrified of what's going to happen. I know you don't think I need an operation to accept myself, and I wish I could buy into that too, but you don't see the way people look at me. Even the nurses, when they try not to stare they can't help it. I see it. Every day." She paused for air. "I need to do this to help myself. I don't ask that you agree. I don't ask that you wheel me into the operating theater singing praises about my decision. All I ask is that you support me. That's all I ever wanted. I just wanted you by my side, in my corner. And when you weren't, I guess I panicked and lashed out."

Alfie took a few moments to let her words sink in.

She wants me to be there for her.

"Will you do me a favor? Just for one second, would you try something for me?" he ventured.

"It depends. . . . Your plans always worry me!"

"All I want you to do is close your eyes."

"Really?"

"Really."

"Hmm. Okay. Fine. They're closed." She sounded suspicious, but there was definitely a hint of curiosity there. "You do know that I could be lying, right? You'll never know for sure if I'm doing what you say."

"I know, but I'm hoping I can trust you." He wasn't in the mood to mess around tonight. He needed to be serious if this was going to work.

"Okay, so what next?"

"I want you to imagine a place in the world that you've always wanted to go. It could be a country, a city, a building, anywhere—just make sure it's somewhere you haven't been yet."

He waited a moment.

"Can you see it?"

"Yes, I can see it."

"Now, I want you to imagine you're there. That you're standing in that place right this second."

"Okay. . . ."

"How does it feel?"

"What?" She sounded confused and perhaps a little impatient.

"If you're really imagining yourself there, I'm asking, how does it feel? What's the air temperature? What can you hear? What does it look like when the sun rises? How does it change when the moon shines? Alice, are you there yet?"

He heard her inhale deeply. His heart was racing.

"It's incredible. It's breathtaking."

"You've never been to this place before in your entire life, yet when you imagine yourself there now, it's making you feel things, right?"

"I guess." She was hesitating; he knew he had to finish this quickly.

"It's making you feel things in your stomach, in your chest, in the way your breathing changes and your mood relaxes. Alice, don't you see? I don't have to *see* you to know that you make me feel things."

"Wait, what?"

He couldn't stop now. "Being around you, speaking to you, even just hearing you breathing does things to me that I've never felt before. You make my heart beat a million miles an hour, you make me smile without even saying a word, my stomach pretty much ties itself in knots when I know you're awake next to me. I don't need to look at you to know how I feel about you."

"But those feelings are based on a fantasy, Alfie. On only half the information." The frustration in her voice was clear. He knew it was a risk; he knew she wouldn't like it, but he had to try.

"I know it sounds insane. And trust me, I've questioned it myself again and again, but let me ask you this. What do you feel when you think of me?"

Silence.

"I don't need you to tell me. I just need you to know. Because I'm guessing when you start thinking about it, you'll realize that you can feel things about people without relying on your eyes to tell you who they are or what they're about. When I close my eyes and I picture you, I see someone so strong. I see someone who's so brave. Someone whose life has forced her to become so fiercely independent that she shuts out pretty much everyone who wants to get close to her. I see someone who behind all those walls and façades is filled with so much kindness and love that it's breathtaking. I feel someone who radiates the most amazing, electric energy that she lights up this very cold, very lonely, and very empty room every single day. So, no—I haven't seen your face. I don't know the color of your hair or the length of your arms or legs. I don't even know if you have any! But I don't care. Do you hear me? I. Don't. Care. I see you. I see you for who you are, Alice, and it's the most dazzling thing I have ever seen."

The silence was excruciating.

Alfie fought hard not to break it.

He tore his gaze away from the ceiling to see if he could make out any of her silhouette in the dimness.

He couldn't.

Instead, he found her very pale, very shaky, very lonely hand waiting for his.

Chapter 55

ALICE

She woke with her hand still hanging off the side of the bed. It felt cold and empty without Alfie's to hold. She wanted to reach through and grab his again, to feel the touch of the man she cared for so deeply. A man who had spoken the most wonderful words to her that she had ever heard. A man who had saved her these last few months.

Just as she was about to close the gap between them, he started to stir.

"Hey. How are you?" His voice was covered with sleep.

"I'm good. Tired, but good." She wanted to let him know how much last night had meant to her, but she was also aware that in the cold light of day, maybe he was feeling a little embarrassed. Or worse, he might even be regretting it. "How are you?"

Do I really want to know the answer?

"Same. Although, if I'm honest, I'm keen to get back to reading *The Philosopher's Stone* now we know we only have limited time left to finish it!"

She laughed. Alfie Mack was back, and Alice felt nothing but relief.

"You're relentless."

"You don't know the half of it."

"Is that so?"

God, if Sarah were here right now, she'd be vomiting at the sound of their flirtatious exchange. But she wasn't, and it was making Alice feel all sorts of lovely.

"Mm-hmm. I'm not sure you could handle it, to be honest."

"No, sweetheart, he'd eat you alive." A new voice suddenly joined the conversation, and Alice almost fell out of bed with shock.

How much had Nurse Angles heard?

The embarrassment crawled over her skin. It felt as though she'd just been caught naked by a stranger.

"Mother A, are you snooping, by any chance?" Trust Alfie to manage the situation without any sign of embarrassment.

Nurse Angles began to laugh in that deep, soulful way of hers. "Chance would be a fine thing. I have ears, Alfie, and you're not as quiet as you may think. Sweet nothings are usually whispered, not barked."

Aaghhh, her whole body was radiating now. She could feel her face turning a deep red.

"Someone is bringing the sass today, aren't they!"

And just like that, he'd sent her off in another direction. Alice had to hand it to him: Alfie was a professional when it came to conversation. The change of subject didn't, however, ease any of her embarrassment, and she was pretty sure that by the time Nurse Angles came to do her morning checks, Alice's cheeks were still shining a strong crimson.

Alfie hadn't been joking about returning to *Harry Potter*. In fact, the full schedule he had so carefully created before

Sarah left had been reinstated with renewed vigor. During the day only easy conversation was welcomed, no serious questions, no reminders of the two big upcoming events, and absolutely no talk of feelings. This didn't stop Alice constantly replaying the words he'd spoken to her last night.

I see you. I see you for who you are, Alice, and it's the most dazzling thing I have ever seen.

She couldn't get them out of her head. At first, she would just sit there smiling from ear to ear. Her heart was so full of him it felt like it would burst. Then, the familiar seeds of doubt started to sow themselves into her thoughts.

Does he really mean that, though?

One look at your face and he'd probably take them all back.

Just as she would start to get sucked in by the negativity, she would reach for Sarah's message: *He loves you. You know he does.*

Did she know? She knew that before this weird and wonderful thing had arrived rather unconsciously in her life, Alice had never been in love. Her dating life wasn't exactly what you'd call a success before the accident, so how it would fare post-burning didn't bear thinking about. Sure, she'd had sex. Dated guys for a few weeks. Dated multiple guys for a few weeks. But that was it. No relationships. No commitment. Certainly no love. The closest she'd ever had was a very convenient arrangement with a man she'd met late one night in her office. He worked for an investment bank that was renting one of the floors in her building, and they had caught each other's eyes a number of times in passing. Both were slaves to their jobs, but both of them had needs. Twice a week they would meet, spend the night together, and then go about their business fully satisfied and without any urge for contact. Aaron was a forty-three-year-old twice-divorced man who didn't have the time, energy, or heart space left for a relationship. He was extremely attractive, kind, and incredibly talented in bed. This situation ran on for a good few months until, it seemed, Aaron found some time, energy, and space in his heart for a relationship. It just wasn't with Alice. After that very amicable ending, Alice had never really tried with anyone else. Her lack of dating experience had never *really* bothered her, to be honest. Sometimes she felt like she did it because that's what she should be doing. It was only recently, when the prospect of being able to meet someone easily if she wanted to was taken away from her, that she resented how flippantly she'd treated it before. Apparently it was okay being lonely, but only when you were lonely by choice.

One thing she knew for sure was just how much was riding on this surgery. A new life. Perhaps even a chance to feel brave enough to meet Alfie at last?

The last part she still couldn't quite commit to. The thought of him leaving the ward and never speaking to her again made her feel sick to her stomach. Yet, could she really find it in herself to meet this man face-to-face? What if even after the operation she was still a disappointment? What if he left and never looked back? What if she was simply a project for his amusement to while away the time?

She'd allowed everyone in her life to leave her in the end, and even Sarah was halfway across the world now. She couldn't take it if Alfie abandoned her too.

"T minus one day, Big Al. How are you feeling?"

"Really still wishing that you wouldn't call me that hideous name!"

"Sorry! It's a bad habit, I know, but stop avoiding the question."

"I'm feeling the same things I felt yesterday when you asked me. And they were the same things as the day before that. I'm absolutely, positively one hundred percent terrified, yet . . . weirdly excited."

"The terrified I understand, the excited not so much. And you're sure you don't want to try some of my scar cream as a last attempt before the big op?"

A little white tube poked through the curtain.

"Oh yeah, because I'm not already using that, am I? Plus that tiny tube would just about cover my arm."

"Just trying to help." He waggled the tube at her one last time before disappearing behind the curtain again. "And you're sure you don't want me to call anyone if anything goes wrong? Not even Sarah?"

"No. If anything really bad happens, the hospital will call. I don't want her worrying unnecessarily. Trust me on this."

Alice didn't want Sarah to be contacted needlessly. There would be no point. Whatever challenges Alice faced, she would deal with them without worrying anyone else. She hadn't completely forgotten how to fend for herself.

"I don't agree at all, but I'll do as you say."

"Good." She paused. "Alfie."

"Yes?"

"I need to ask you to do one more thing for me."

"You've got my full attention, Miss Gunnersley."

If only he knew that this was really not the time for flirting.

"I need you to promise me that, no matter what happens during that operation, you won't come and visit me."

"Hold on. What?" He couldn't disguise the shock in his voice.

"I mean it, please don't come and visit me. Not even if—"

"Alice, stop! You can't be serious. I –"

"Alfie." Her voice stopped him in his tracks. "I need you to promise me that if things don't go to plan, you won't come and see me. I want you to remember me as you know me now. I want you to remember me like all those beautiful words you said to me that night. Please. Promise me."

She hadn't heard him take a breath in what felt like minutes.

"Alfie, please?"

"Fine. I promise, Alice."

"No matter what?"

"No matter what."

Chapter 56

ALFIE

He held her hand until the very last moment he could.

Everyone had been asked, as per protocol, to close their curtains while she was wheeled away. How tempted he was to leave just a crack, a tiny slither of a gap for him to steal a glance at her before she left.

But a promise was a promise. No matter how painful it was.

Please keep her safe.

Please keep her safe.

Please keep her safe.

He whispered the words over and over into his pillow, hoping that if he said them enough times, with enough conviction, someone somewhere would hear his plea.

It must have been around ten o'clock when Alfie heard the padding of footsteps approaching his bay.

"Can I come in?" Little Ruby peeked her face through a gap in his curtains.

"Hey, Rubes. You okay?"

"Yeah. Are you?" She looked at him with a knowledge way beyond her years. "Can I?" She nodded at his bed.

"Of course, unless you're too old and cool for that now?"

"Not just yet." She ran at him, lay down, and cuddled him close. "Especially not when you're so sad."

Her words threw him a little; you really couldn't keep anything secret in this place. He squeezed her warm little frame.

They stayed like that the whole morning, with Ruby insisting that they watch endless episodes of crap on TV to keep him distracted. As soon as Nurse Angles stepped onto the ward, though, there was only one thing on his mind.

"Alfie, honey, I know what you're going to ask me, and I haven't heard anything yet." She hadn't even looked up from her paperwork. "The moment I hear anything, you'll be the first to know, okay?" She stood up and rested her hand on his cheek. "Now, go back to bed and rest. You look like you haven't slept in weeks."

Alfie attempted a smile and made his way back. He couldn't help but sneak a glance at Mr. Peterson's old bed, now occupied by a very hairy, very disgruntled Greek man.

Alfie spent the rest of the day feeling totally and utterly lost.

"Will you stop pacing up and down the ward, please?" The nurses were trying not to sound exasperated, but Alfie knew he was frustrating them.

"Sorry, I just don't know what else to do." Walking helped. Walking made Alfie feel that he was at least doing *something*.

"We get it, we do. But please, can you walk somewhere else other than just up and down? Maybe outside? Get some fresh air? You're putting everyone on edge here."

What does everyone else matter when the most important person here is on the operating table?

He knew it wasn't their fault, so he bit back the words and took his sorry self out to the courtyard.

The sun was blinding, and on any other day Alfie would have relished the warm air and blue skies. Today, however, he wanted solitude and misery.

"Beautiful day today, isn't it." An elderly lady and her husband were walking arm in arm around the garden. Alfie could only just about muster a half-smile.

"Do you need a seat, son?" A gruff middle-aged man had clearly clocked Alfie's uneven gait.

"No, thanks, though." If he sat, he knew he'd be forced to make conversation, and he couldn't face it. Sitting would be far too much commitment.

What if I need to go back suddenly? What if they're looking for me?

Panic rose in his throat.

Alfie nearly ran out of the courtyard and down the corridors. He didn't care who he had to push out of the way to get there. The panic forced him to move quicker and quicker, far too fast for his pounding heart and aching leg. But he didn't dare stop, not even to take a breath.

By the time he reached the entrance to the ward, sweat was dripping down his face.

"Alfie, what the hell has happened to you?"

He shook his head, feeling foolish. Of course they knew where to find him; the nurses had practically sent him packing to the courtyard themselves.

"Nothing, just tired," he mumbled under his breath.

"Hmm, okay." The nurse was looking at him suspiciously. "Well, take some rest, there's still no news. I am checking for you, I promise."

He smiled, the first real smile of the day. "Thank you."

Chapter 57

ALICE

Just breathe, Alice.

The nerves mounted with every door they passed, every corridor they wheeled down, every turn they took.

Could they not just give her the anesthetic now? Knock her out and bring her round when the whole ordeal was over?

No. Apparently they needed her awake and willing until the very last second.

Fortunately she didn't have to wait long until she was moved from the waiting area into the theater.

It was odd how badly she longed for Nurse Angles to be greeting her instead of these nameless strangers. How comforting her life on the ward seemed now that she'd been torn away from it.

"Okay, Alice. My name is Nurse Hoi, I'm going to be prepping you for your surgery today."

Alice simply nodded. If she spoke, she was pretty sure she would vomit.

"I want you to take some deep breaths for me. You're going to feel a small sharp prick and then a slightly cold sensation. It's all completely normal, it's just the anesthetic kicking in. Okay?"

Alice smiled this time. Nodding made her feel even more nauseated.

"Wonderful. I'm going to count down from ten. You'll start to feel really sleepy soon—don't try to resist it, just go with it, okay?"

All at once everything started to fade. The sounds, the shapes all began to blur into one.

Her eyes were heavy.

She could barely keep her head up.

Within seconds, Alice found herself lost to the darkness.

Within an hour, she'd flatlined on the operating table.

Chapter 58

ALFIE

Alfie knew that everyone was doing their best to get information for him, but he couldn't help feeling that they weren't trying hard enough. Alfie knew he was being insolent, but the not-knowing was driving him crazy.

Couldn't they just go to the operating theater and ask?

At one point he'd decided to go and find her himself. Luckily his reason kicked in and told him how stupid the idea was and how it would probably reduce his chances of ever finding out about Alice if he was caught. And so he resigned himself to waiting.

He waited until the afternoon shift clocked off and the night shift clocked on.

He waited until the stars winked at him from the sky.

He waited until it seemed that everyone on the ward was asleep but him.

So many times his eyes started to drift closed and he would force himself to stay awake. Every time he caught the sound of footsteps he would sit upright, praying they were coming towards him; when they changed direction or faded into the distance, his heart would drop once again with the weight of not knowing.

This time, the footsteps came straight towards him.

He didn't dare make a sound; he didn't want to scare them off.

"Alfie, are you still awake?"

Why is Nurse Angles here? Didn't she finish hours ago?

"Mother A?"

"Hey, love." She poked her head around the curtain. He knew immediately that something was wrong.

"Is she alive? Please tell me she's alive?" He practically screamed the words at her.

She was suddenly by his side, all flesh and warmth, holding his hand tightly. "She's alive, baby, but only just."

Only just.

Those words hit him square in the chest. He felt sick. He needed to see her. He needed to go to her right away.

"I need to see her. I need to see her now."

"Alfie, honey, stop."

"No. Get out of my way." Alfie was using every ounce of strength to wrench out of her grasp.

"Look." She held him out at arm's length, forcing him to stop thrashing. "I know you want to go to her, but you can't. She's in critical condition. No one is allowed up there right now. Not even you." He could feel her fingers making marks on his skin.

Alfie couldn't hold off any longer, he couldn't fight anymore, and so instead he collapsed fully into her arms and cried.

"What *happened*?" The words were almost lost amongst the tears.

"They aren't saying much right now." She paused, pulling him closer. "All I know is she lost a lot of blood and . . . and . . ."

She couldn't continue, and he didn't want her to.

He couldn't remember the exact moment he fell asleep, but he was pretty certain Nurse Angles was holding him as he did. He was almost surprised to find she wasn't still there with her arms wrapped around him, pulling him in tightly, when the morning came.

Instead he heard her, already pacing down the ward, busying herself with her rounds. How could everything just carry on as normal when the entire world had just been pulled from underneath his feet? He was grateful she'd closed the curtains around him as she'd left, giving Alfie the privacy to do whatever he needed to process the news. But all he wanted was to see her.

Why did I make that stupid fucking promise to not visit her?

"Alfie, is it okay for me to come in?" He wasn't used to the Nurse Angles who asked for permission; it was touching to hear the caution in her voice.

"Uh-huh." As he went to speak, he found that his voice was still hoarse from crying.

"How are you doing, honey?"

He shrugged. More and more Alfie was realizing that words were often useless in these situations. What could he even say? Where to even start? Maybe that's why Alice had taken her vow of silence for so long.

The news seemed to have marked Nurse Angles too; as she squeezed herself down into the seat next to him, he could see the dark circles framing her red eyes. She leaned in closer and took his hand in hers. "I've been up there this morning, and her condition hasn't changed since last night."

A conflicting mix of guilt and appreciation surged through him. "Thank you."

"I'll do my best to keep checking, but I need you to try to keep those spirits up. It won't help anybody if you start losing yourself too."

Alfie was reminded suddenly of those dark days after his accident. The days when depressive clouds would block him from doing anything but sleeping, Nurse Angles had been there through it all.

"Can I ask you something?"

"Of course."

"Alice made me promise that no matter what happened to her, I would never go and see her. Even if the very, *very* worst had happened."

Nurse Angles couldn't hide the flicker of surprise that flashed across her face. "Well, that's a very big thing to ask of you."

"I know, and I agreed to it at the time. But now . . . now everything isn't okay, and I don't know if I can keep my promise."

Nurse Angles took a deep breath and leant back in her chair. He was glad she was taking this so seriously—he wanted someone else to feel the gravity of his situation.

"And you want my opinion on what to do? Is that what you're saying?"

He nodded.

"Well, baby . . ." He could tell she was choosing her words very carefully. "If it were me—and ultimately it's not, so you can do whatever you like—*but* if it were me and I made a promise to someone I cared deeply for, I would do everything I could to honor it." She squeezed his hand, obviously aware that those were the words he didn't want to hear.

He squeezed her back.

"I'll leave you be now, but you know where I am if you need me. I'm always here. Always." She hauled herself up and started to shuffle her way out of his little bay. "Oh, and don't forget, your mum's coming to visit today."

She probably hoped that would bring a smile to his face, but the reveal of his impending departure had sent Jane Mack even more hyper than before. Alfie cringed every time he heard the nurses speaking to her on the phone:

"Yes, Jane, we'll make sure that's sorted."

"No, Mrs. Mack, there hasn't been any change in the date, he's still on track to go at the end of next week."

"Hi, Jane, still no change!"

"Jane, we will call if something happens, okay?"

He knew that she would all but move in with him in his final week. In her mind, there was simply so much to sort. In reality, Alfie could probably pack all of his things into one small box in less than ten minutes, but he knew there would be no telling her that. Instead he would let her tell him exactly what needed to be done, exactly where he was going to go, and exactly how he was going to get there.

When she arrived later that afternoon, though, even he couldn't hide his surprise at the bags of cleaning products she was holding.

"Morning, everyone." Her excitement was palpable as she breezed through the ward.

Alfie looked at Robert, who was trailing behind with piles of cake tins.

Before he had a chance to even open his mouth, she had begun fussing and flapping. "Not long now, honey! God,

there's so much to do before you go. I've brought some cleaning stuff so we can make this place a little tidier, it's always
nice to clean up after yourself, isn't it?"

"Mum, you know they have professionals who do that for
you? As part of their job."

She had already extracted the antibacterial spray from the
bag and was wiping down the surfaces.

"*Mum.*" He didn't mean to sound so forceful. "Stop."

She turned to look at him, confused. "What's wrong?"

He knew if he told her the truth, it would open up realms
of pain. He wasn't ready for that—but the cleaning and fussing had to stop.

"Nothing, I'm just tired. Can you just sit for a minute?"

"Of course." She dropped the spray and sat down on the
edge of his bed. "I brought some oat squares in for the
nurses, a little thank-you for all their hard work. Do you want
one? They won't notice if one goes missing, I'm sure!"

He shook his head; his normally raging appetite had all
but disappeared since Alice went into surgery.

"Sweetheart, are you sure you're okay?"

Damn it. He should have known his refusal to eat would
be a red flag.

"Yeah, honestly, I'm just really tired."

"Hmm." She always knew when he was lying. "It's a big
change, Alf. It's okay to be worried or feel a little scared by
it all."

Wonderful—the perfect cover-up, neatly wrapped and
handed to him on a plate. "Yeah, totally, it's all just a little
overwhelming."

"Of course it is. But don't worry; we've already started
thinking about things so that you don't have to. The morning
they discharge you, we will come and pick you up in the car

and take you to our house. You can stay there for as long as you want. We've already done the checks on your flat to see if it's suitable for you, and all looks perfectly fine. I've phoned the school and told them you're being discharged, oh, they were so pleased! It sounds like you've been missed terribly."

All Alfie could do was smile and nod while trying not to scream at the ridiculousness of the situation.

I don't care about any of this. I just need to know if she's okay.

Fortunately Robert was a little more tuned in to Alfie and could sense he needed some room to breathe. "Come on, love, why don't we hand these oat squares round? I'm sure people are dying for a little sugar hit!"

"Great idea. Alfie, sweetie, we won't be long." Just before she disappeared, she placed a couple on his bedside table. "In case you get peckish later, hey?"

How incredibly generous this woman was, and how incredibly guilty he felt about wanting her gone. A part of him had hoped that their presence would be a welcome distraction, but instead their small talk and fussing just left him feeling even more stifled than when he was alone with his thoughts. As he lay there staring at the curtain, he felt a deep urge to pull it back and take a peek into Alice's space next to him. Before he knew it, the fabric was between his fingers ready for the reveal. How would it feel to finally see her space? See where she slept, where she dreamed and cried and laughed. Just as he was about to do it, his stomach lurched. Something was stopping him cold.

He'd made a promise, and even seeing this piece of her felt like betrayal.

"Oh, I am going to miss those nurses when you leave, Alfie. They really are a godsend."

He dropped the curtain immediately and prayed that guilt hadn't written itself all over his face. Jane Mack was a social creature and she'd returned over an hour later with empty tins and heaps of gossip to share. Her eyes darted to the two untouched oat squares at his bedside. "Honey, you really must be tired, you haven't even sniffed at those! How about we leave you to get some rest? You really do look exhausted."

"Sure." He wasn't about to argue with that.

"Robert and I will be back to collect you soon. Nurse Angles said the assessment will be in the next day or two, so don't worry about packing your things; we can sort it when we get here. Can you believe my baby is coming home so soon!" She planted a kiss on the top of his head.

Alfie just about managed to construct a half-smile on his face. That mask of his was getting harder and harder to put on these days.

Chapter 59

ALFIE

Alfie Mack had never really been very good at saying good-bye. He didn't like the act of going, and more than that he couldn't bear the thought of people leaving him. He'd struggled to say good-bye to his classes at the end of each term. He found it hard to say good-bye to his mum and dad after dinner every Sunday. Now here he was, staring straight into the reality that he was about to say good-bye to the place and people who had saved his life.

The doctor had come during the morning rounds and delivered the news. It was formal and mechanical, a routine discharge, probably one of millions this doctor had done over her lifetime, but to Alfie it was life-changing.

"Based on our review of your notes and assessments, we have deemed you fit to go. You'll be able to leave as soon as the paperwork has been written up and signed. Do you need me to call your family?" She'd barely even looked at him.

"No, thank you, Doctor. My mum is on standby anyway, so I'm sure she'll be calling any minute to check how I'm doing."

Jesus, how old are you? Three?

"Right." Her smile had pity written all over it. "Well, any problems, you know where we are."

And that was that. It was officially time for Alfie to go home—and yet after nearly three long months, he was desperate to stay.

For the rest of the morning all he'd been able to do was lie on his bed in silence. He didn't even feel the usual pressure to play entertainer or the guilt of being quiet. All Alfie wanted to do was to try to absorb as much as he could of this strange little bubble for as long as he could. Could he commit the sterile smell of the ward to memory? Could he ingrain the pastel-colored walls into the backs of his eyelids so that whenever he needed to take himself back here, all he had to do was close his eyes? How could he capture the sounds of hospital life eternally inside his head? Everything that had once been so harsh and abnormal now felt as integral as the beating of his heart.

"Alfie!" His stupor was broken by Ruby's cry as she ran onto the ward.

"Hey, you! How was Grandma and Grandpa's today?" He loved the chaos this tiny human brought with her every time she came to visit. She was a bundle of noise and energy that catapulted through the beige ward like a firecracker.

"Mum told me you're leaving today." The little girl stood at the end of his bed, wide-legged, hands on hips, and with an almighty scowl on her face.

"That's right, kid. I'm off." He held out his hand to her.

"No." She stamped her foot hard on the floor.

"Oh, come on, Rubes, don't be like that. You can't be grumpy on my last day."

He saw the bottom lip start to go. "But I don't want you to leave me." She ran at him as the tears fell hard and fast.

"I know." He held her close and squeezed her little frame. "But I can still come and visit you and your mum. We're friends, aren't we?" He held her out in front of him and looked into her crestfallen face.

She managed a slight nod.

"Well then. Friends don't leave each other. *Ever.* Never forget that, okay?"

"Okay." A small, toothy smile crept onto her face.

"Plus," he whispered loudly in her ear, "who is going to take care of Sharon for me when I'm gone?"

"Oi! I don't need looking after, thank you very much!"

Ruby burst into laughter as she ran back across the ward and unceremoniously launched herself onto her mum's bed.

He looked across the ward to the bed that had belonged to Mr. Peterson, a man Alfie had grown to care for and admire so deeply. Then he became aware of the absence of Alice's voice next to him—the sound he'd woken up to every morning and fallen asleep to each night. In that moment, it dawned on him why it was so hard to say good-bye. These strangers had become his family.

Even Nurse Angles had taken her break early to come and say her farewells. For a few minutes they simply sat side by side in silence.

"Mother A, I just wa—"

"Hush, baby. Not just yet."

He couldn't bring himself to look at her, and he suspected she was avoiding his gaze too.

"Alfie, honey, we're good to go. Robert's down in the car

waiting for us," Alfie's mum cooed, suddenly appearing in front of them.

No.

Please not yet.

Just a few more moments.

"Jane, sweetie?" Nurse Angles's voice cracked ever so slightly. "If it's okay with you, I'd like to be the one to walk Alfie out. I was the one who brought him in here, and it just seems right that I be the one to take him out. We won't be long, I promise."

"Sure thing. We'll be waiting outside."

Before Alfie could thank her, Nurse Angles turned to him with a fierce expression on her face. "Alfie Mack, you listen to me and you listen to me good. I am so deeply, *deeply* proud of everything you've done here. Not only have you fought so hard for your recovery, but you've also been a life-line for so many people on this ward. You promise me that you'll keep that sunshine burning bright no matter what comes your way. And above all else, you promise me here and now that no matter how hard it gets, you'll keep fighting. Yours is a life worth living, and I'll still be here cheering you on every goddamn step of the way."

Her eyes were glistening and her grip had tightened on his hand. He stared right into her dark-brown eyes and felt his heart swell with love.

"I promise."

"Now, come here and give this old woman one last hug!" And just like that, she was all smiles and warmth again. Alfie reached for her and let her embrace swallow him whole. He nestled as deep as he could and breathed her in. Her gener-osity. Her open heart. Her mothering instinct. He wanted to take as much of her with him as he could.

"Thank you, my very own Mother Angel. I'll hold you in my heart forever." He kissed her cheek before pulling himself upright. "Right, let's do this!"

"Let's do this, baby." She linked his arm and laughed that wondrous, deep laugh.

Together they made their way through the ward, arm in arm, side by side. As they walked through the double doors, the whole ward erupted into cheers.

Just before they reached the exit, Alfie stopped. He'd been waiting until the very last moment possible to ask her one last favor, because he knew when he did, it really would be the end.

"Mother A? I need your help just one last time. . . ."

Chapter 60

ALICE

Alice had lost all concept of time. She didn't know where she was, what had happened, or why. All she knew was that slowly, very slowly, she began to wake up.

It started with the odd flash of light. She'd try opening her eyes to see, but it would be so bright she'd be forced to close them instantly. Then came the sounds. The sounds of people around her, next to her, talking about her. Throwing words around to each other so quickly that she barely had time to try to catch them. At first it didn't matter; all that mattered was that she wasn't alone. She was somewhere other than inside of that fire, and she was no longer alone.

"Alice, honey, can you hear me?"

Without thinking, she moved her head.

"Alice? If you can hear me, can you nod your head again for me?"

Go away, it's too painful.

"Alice, if you can hear me, I need you to make a sign."

God, this woman was relentless.

Using every drop of strength she had, Alice nodded.

"Fantastic!" The pushy woman was almost singing with excitement. "Well done, my love. I'll go get the doctor immediately. Just sit tight for me."

Oh, because I'm really likely to be wandering off, am I?

It was a little surprising to hear her own thoughts again. How long since she'd been able to do that? What had happened to her? She tried to lift her head, but it was too heavy. In fact, her entire body felt as though someone had filled it with lead.

"Alice, my name is Mr. Warring. I'm your surgeon. Do you remember me?"

I'm tired, leave me alone.

Why did doctors always insist on trying to tell you things when you were half-asleep?

"Alice, I need to tell you some very important news, so I have to make sure you can hear me and understand."

She forced her eyes open. One look at his face and everything came flooding back.

The operation.

Her face.

Sarah.

Alfie.

"What happened?" Her voice was so hoarse that if it hadn't come from her mouth she would have sworn it belonged to someone else.

"I'm afraid there were some major complications with the surgery."

Oh God, no.

"You lost an awful lot of blood and you went into cardiac arrest. We . . ." He paused.

Why was he pausing?

Alice could feel the blood surging through her. Why was he looking at her like that?

"We were unable to finish the operation."

Her hands immediately flew to her face. There were bandages wrapped around her.

"What do you *mean*?" The nausea crawled up her throat, making it hard to breathe.

"Unfortunately, we had to abort the operation before it was complete. We think we managed to make some improvements, but we can't be sure until you're fully healed."

He didn't even have the decency to look her in the eye. Why was he talking to the goddamn floor? Could he not stand to see the monster he'd failed to fix?

"I'm so sorry. I'll come back tomorrow to check on the wounds. In the meantime, is there anyone you'd like us to call?"

She shook her head.

How could she tell them it hadn't worked? How could she admit it had all been a huge mistake? It had failed. Nothing had changed. She was still broken, and she needed to get used to the fact that now she always would be.

Chapter 61

ALFIE

Leaving the hospital was one of the most surreal experiences of Alfie's life. As he walked out into the car park, he half expected someone to tap him on the shoulder and tell him they'd made a mistake

Not today, son. Back you go.

Instead all he had was his mum pulling him towards the car, desperate to get her precious gift inside and on the road. She'd been flying high from the moment she laid eyes on him, and he could tell even Robert was trying his best not to cry now. Alfie wished so badly he could join them in their joy, but the only feeling that sat at the pit of his stomach was a cold, sharp anxiety.

The drive home brought back so many memories that Alfie found himself lost in a blur of nostalgia. The streets he'd driven down but rarely paid attention to, buildings he'd walked past but never taken the time to look inside of, restaurants he'd eaten in and never returned to—every one of them so familiar yet so different. It was the same old London, his same old neighborhood, but something had changed. He'd changed. Life had seamlessly gone on without him, yet during that time Alfie's entire world had been turned upside down. He felt like a stranger in his own city, conflicted and confused as to where he belonged. Anxiety spiked in his chest.

Take me back to the ward. I need to go back.

"You okay, Alf?"

His mum's eyes had been dutifully watching him in the mirror.

"Yeah, all good, Mum." He smiled and rested his forehead against the car window.

One step at a time . . . that's all it takes.

Even as he stood outside his mum's front door, he couldn't help but feel apprehensive. It was so surreal that at one point he wondered if he were dreaming.

"Come on, let's get you inside."

He took a deep breath, willing his heart to slow down as he stepped over the threshold.

"Surprise!"

Alfie's entire body was thrown backwards in shock. If Robert hadn't been behind him, he was pretty sure he'd have ended up on the floor.

*"Fuck*ing *hell!"* He didn't mean to shout. He didn't mean to swear, but good God, his heart was about to throw itself out of his chest.

He closed his eyes.

Breathe, Alfie. Just breathe.

Slowly he opened them again. Staring back at him was a roomful of very concerned and very awkward-looking people. Friends and family he knew and loved so deeply that as soon as he saw them, he couldn't stop smiling.

"Are you trying to send me back to that hospital or what!"

"You gave us all a fright there!" His mum nervously grabbed his hand and led him farther into the room.

He'd managed to salvage the situation. Just.

After the shock had worn off, Alfie had to admire the speed at which his mother must have worked. In the space of a few hours since they'd been given the all-clear, Jane Mack had managed to pull together one hell of a party. Balloons filled every possible space left between the WELCOME HOME and CONGRATULATIONS banners that had been strung across the room. Food and drinks covered any surface available, and Alfie noticed that even the furniture had been cleared to make room for the crowd. He knew how much this meant to her. He knew how much it meant to everyone in the room for him to be here. He stopped and pulled his mum in for a hug.

"Thank you." He kissed her warm cheek and felt the skin flush instantly.

"Welcome home, son."

He was loath to admit it, but the party was actually quite fun. For a good three hours Alfie didn't think about the hospital once. He was too busy being passed around with the canapés, from friends to family back to friends again, all so happy that he was back home. Maybe this wasn't going to be so bad after all. Maybe transitioning back to his old life was just like pressing start again after a very long pause. Life had gone on, time had passed, but no one had forgotten him and nothing had changed dramatically.

Except for him.

"Everything all right over here, son?" Robert appeared with another tray of food. How on earth his mum had managed to mass-cater at such short notice blew Alfie's mind, but he reached for a handful of the spring rolls and shoved them unceremoniously into his mouth. The more he ate, the less he had to speak. "Glad to see you haven't lost that appetite of yours."

Alfie smiled and nodded.

Suddenly it all felt too much. There were too many people, and not enough room to breathe. The spring rolls felt stuck in his throat, the wet pastry clinging, refusing to go down.

No.

Surely it wasn't happening again.

They hadn't happened like this during the day in months. *Please, not here. Not now.*

Alfie managed to force his way through the gathering of people and out into the hallway. He needed to be alone and away from all the noise. The voices in his head were growing louder and louder, and it was becoming harder to drown them out. He reached for the front door and sat down on the porch. As the fresh air hit him, so too did the force of the flashback. Uncontrollably and unwillingly, he was dragged back to the night of the accident. The screams, the cries, the burning smell of tarmac and flesh.

No.

Please, God, stop it.

NO!

"Alfie?"

He was back. On his parents' front step. Cold. Shaking. Drenched in sweat.

"Alfie, son, are you okay?" Robert was crouched by his side still clutching the tepid tray of snacks.

"Yeah, sorry, just felt a bit dizzy was all." The words tangled themselves up in each other, and Alfie was surprised they managed to form a sentence.

"I understand. It's a lot in there, isn't it?" He managed to squeeze himself into the tiny gap between Alfie and the doorframe. "Do you want me to start encouraging people to get on their way? We'll take you back to your flat as soon as they've cleared out."

"No, it's fine. I know how much it means to Mum. I'll be back inside in a bit. I think I just needed some air." There he was again, the people-pleasing Alfie who'd rather sit here reliving the day his friends died than risk upsetting the party.

"Sure?" Robert looked at him, desperately searching for any hint of a lie.

"Positive."

Chapter 62

ALICE

Apparently, for Alice, recovery was quicker the second time round. She was healing well, her blood pressure was stable, and she was regaining strength day by day. Although the operation hadn't improved her injuries, it seemed that it hadn't done any further damage either, and according to her recovery plan she was still on track. To everyone around her, this news was miraculous. To Alice, it was just adding salt to the wound.

"You're doing so well."

"Honestly, considering what happened, you've bounced back incredibly quickly!"

Bounced back to what?

The same mess I was before this whole pointless ordeal?

The acid-tongued voice inside her head had returned, and this time it was taking no prisoners. Angry thoughts gnawed away at her, feeding off any hope or trace of positivity that remained. Bitterness crystalized inside her stomach; it sat sour and heavy, weighing her down.

How had she found herself back here again?

What would Alfie say if he knew?

She could hear the sound of his voice so clearly in her mind that she forgot for a moment that he wasn't actually there with her. Her eyes snapped open.

Oh God, how long has it been?

"Excuse me, Nurse." She looked round wildly for any sign of help. "Nurse!" Her voice was strained in panic.

"Yes, Alice, is everything okay?" Someone was by her side. She didn't even register the woman's face; she just needed answers.

"How long have I been here for?"

"Erm . . ."

"Tell me. How long?" She didn't care that she was practically shouting; she had to know.

"It's been just over a week, sweetie."

No.

I can't have missed him.

Not without saying good-bye.

"Has . . . has anyone been to visit me?" Her heart was racing as her body tingled with anticipation.

"No. The nurses from the rehab ward asked after you a lot. Actually, so much that we had to pretty much ban them from coming up here. But, apart from that, no one."

He'd kept his promise.

She couldn't even wait for the nurse to leave before the tears came.

"Alice, what's wrong?"

She buried her face deep into her pillow. "Nothing. Please just go!" This was a private pain. It was all hers, and she didn't want anyone to bear witness to it.

"Okay." The nurse hesitated, lingering for just a moment. "You know where we are if you need us."

"Good morning, Alice."

No. I don't want to exist today, thank you. Let me lie here in the darkness and wallow.

"The doctor has already paged me to say he's coming down later to check on you." Why did the nurse sound so nervous? "It might be time to take off the bandages. . . ."

"Okay." It was all the exhaustion would allow her to mutter.

"There's also someone here to see you."

Instantly her body sprang to life. Her heart leapt to her throat and her stomach twisted in on itself.

"Alice, baby, it's me. . . ."

Confusion and realization collided. It wasn't him. But it *was* her.

"Nurse Angles?"

"Can I come in?" Her caution was endearing.

"Sure."

Nurse Angles had seen Alice at her worst, so there was really no point in hiding from her.

"Hey there, honey." The moment her face appeared from behind the curtain, Alice felt herself inflate with warmth. A deep feeling of love radiated through her so unexpectedly that for a second it rendered her breathless.

"Hi." A tiny whisper was all she could manage.

"We've been missing you downstairs." All caution disappeared as Nurse Angles squeezed herself into the chair next to Alice. "You gave us a fright, going and nearly dying like that!"

Alice smiled. "Yeah, sorry about that."

"Well, you're here and alive and that's all that matters." She reached over and grasped Alice's hand tightly. She'd missed being held more than she could ever have imagined.

"And . . ." The question was dancing on the tip of her tongue. "And how . . . how is Alfie?"

Nurse Angles smiled even wider. "Well, he *was* a complete pain in my backside, asking me to come and check on you every five minutes. I practically got banned from this floor, I was up here so much!" She let out one of her deep belly laughs, and Alice couldn't help but join in. "He also made me promise to give you this. . . ." From her bag Nurse Angles produced a letter and a carefully wrapped package. "I wanted to make sure you were awake and well before I delivered it. Couldn't have it getting misplaced, now could I?"

Alice took the gift and stared at it. It was small, and rectangular, and she was surprised at how neatly it had been wrapped in its brown paper covering. Had he really left this? For her?

"Now, I need to get myself back downstairs, you know what they're like down there, God knows what trouble's been caused since I left."

Alice was still fixated on the parcel and letter in her hands.

"Make sure you come and say good-bye before you leave, okay?" One final squeeze, and Nurse Angles heaved herself up to go.

"Thank you." Alice squeezed back. "Thank you so much for coming."

"Anytime." She turned just before leaving. "I mean that, okay? You need anything, just get them to buzz me."

Alice was still in such shock she barely managed to nod in acknowledgment.

"Right, Mary, I'm off. Keep me posted on everything, will you?" The booming voice of Nurse Angles could be heard even as she was making her way out of the ward.

Alice turned the letter over in her hands and saw his tiny scrawl on the front.

Big Al
A.k.a. the lady behind the curtain

Adrenaline was rushing through her blood and the anticipation became too much to bear. She opened the envelope as carefully as she could and pulled out a single sheet of paper. Her eyes were so desperate to read everything all at once that she found nothing was making sense.

She closed her eyes and took a long, slow inhale.

Slow down.

Take your time.

Breathe.

She opened her eyes and began again.

Dear Alice,

I hope the cute nickname on the front didn't put you off opening this, it was a big risk but one I was willing to take (especially as I wouldn't be there in person to feel your wrath when you read it!).

I'm sorry if you had to wait before receiving this letter, the only person I could trust to give it to you was Mother A. I hate the thought of you waking up and thinking I'd left without a good-bye, but I am hoping it's worth the wait.

Alice, I wanted to start by saying ... WHAT THE HELL WERE YOU DOING TO ME! Going and getting yourself nearly killed again. I won't lie; I probably cursed you as many times as I prayed for you. I'm sure you weren't having the time of your life up there in intensive care, but it wasn't much fun for me down here either without you. But on a serious note, I kept the promise I made to you and never came to see you. I may have sent Mother A up to check on you a few times, but all I asked was to know you were okay.

Second, I really hope that this operation gives you what you need to feel confident in going out and starting your life again. I hope it gives you what you need to feel as beautiful as you always have been to me, and I'm sorry I wasn't more supportive from the start. There are so many things I want to tell you, but instead of me writing them out in my, quite frankly, appalling handwriting, I've left my address at the bottom.

Alice Gunnersley, it would be the greatest honor if you would come and meet me in person whenever and if ever you feel ready to. I appreciate there are probably many things you wish to do when you get out of the hospital, and coming to find the slightly annoying stranger in the bed next to you might not be high up on that list. However, if there is any part of you that wants to, I will be waiting.

Regardless of what you choose to do, Alice, you have to know that wherever I go or whatever I do, I will carry a piece of you in my heart with me forever.

Thank you for being the best roommate (kind of) ever.

All my love.
Alfie Mack, a.k.a. your new BFF

P.S. Enjoy the puzzles.

Her mind was alive with a million different thoughts, but she didn't have any time to let them settle before another voice drifted in from the outside.

"Alice . . . Mr. Warring is here to see you."

"Come in." She clutched the parcel tightly, then slid the precious gift under the covers.

"Hi, Alice. How are we doing today?"

"Okay." Alice felt sick. She wasn't sure how much more she could take this morning.

"Can I take a quick look at the dressings, please?" Mr. Warring was already so close to her face that Alice didn't dare breathe. "I think we are good to go. Are you ready for us to take them off?"

This time there wouldn't be anyone to hold her hand. There would be no one there to tell her it was going to be okay. She was going into this completely alone, and she realized she didn't like it one bit. Alice nodded, holding the letter tightly in her hand, feeling the weight of the present by her side. It was the only piece of him she had left.

You'll have to wait a bit longer, Alfie.

There's something else that needs unwrapping first.

The cold breeze of air was a welcome relief on her skin, and she closed her eyes as the nurse gently cut the remaining bandages loose.

"Right, Alice, I'm just going to quickly clean this last bit up, and then we can take a look, okay?"

She nodded and made some sort of noise of acknowledgment. The nerves had taken hold of her completely, and her throat was so tight it hurt to breathe.

"So whenever you're ready, open your eyes."

Slowly the outline of her came into view.

Her hair, longer now than before but still as richly auburn as ever.

Her right side, exactly the same as it always had been. Average to some, but still perfectly her.

She took a deep breath in as she dared to look at the left side.

"Oh God." The cry unleashed itself from her. She screwed her eyes tightly closed.

"Alice, you need to understand that you're still healing. The skin is still very sore, but there are definite improvements. Please, let me show you."

Stop trying to make yourself feel better.

You've done nothing.

You lied.

The anger licked her insides, unfurling itself quicker and quicker.

"Alice." The nurse reached for her hand. "Trust me, it's going to be hard and it's going to feel completely awful right now, but give him a chance, okay? Let him show you."

She opened her eyes once more.

This time he was right. There were improvements. If you looked closely enough, you could see that the skin was smoother and perhaps a little tighter in places. But it was still obvious she had been hurt badly. It was also obvious that a lot of time and effort had gone into trying to piece her back together. And it was definitely obvious that it hadn't worked. She was still just a patchwork quilt of skin and scars.

"The swelling will reduce quite quickly, and we will give you some topical cream to continue to help the scarring. I know we weren't able to do as much as we wanted to, but I'm still happy with the results. Honestly, Alice, give it a few weeks, and I think you'll be surprised."

She couldn't even look at him. How dare he try to placate her with a couple fewer scars and a slightly smoother cheek?

The shame of it all began to consume her.

This was it. This was what she was left with. The hopes that her self-worth, her self-confidence would return to normal were shattered. She stuffed the letter and the unopened package in her bedside table. She couldn't bear to look at something so hopeful and full of expectation when all she had left was disappointment. How would anyone be able to love someone so broken?

Chapter 63

ALFIE

Alfie had insisted he wanted to spend his first night back in his own flat. His mother had done her very best to persuade him otherwise, but he knew he needed to bite the bullet or risk spending an eternity regressing into a teenager living at his mum's house.

"Here we are, son," Robert declared as they approached his front door.

"And you're sure you don't want to come back with us? You're welcome to stay for as long as you like, Alfie. Honestly, it's no problem at all." His mother was adopting a breezy tone, but Alfie could see the desperation in her eyes.

"Thank you, Mum. It really means a lot, but I like I said, I just want to get in and settled as quickly as possible." He turned the key in the lock and heard the sweet, satisfactory click of the door opening. Alfie had been fortunate once again. His flat was situated on the ground floor of an old Victorian house and so hadn't required any amendments to make it suitable for his arrival. It wasn't much, just your typical one-bedroom, barely-room-to-swing-a-cat, extortionately priced London living space. But it was all his.

He switched on the hall light and inhaled deeply.

Home sweet home.

"I'll drop your stuff in the bedroom and put the shopping in the fridge, and then I guess we'll leave you to it." Robert was playing his usual role of peacekeeper, trying his best to be upbeat. Alfie's heart surged with gratitude for him.

"We made sure it was all in order before you came, everything's been cleaned and there are fresh bedsheets on. It's always nice to come back to clean sheets, isn't it?" His mum's eyes were starting to glaze over with tears.

"Come here." Alfie pulled her into his arms and held her tightly. He knew she wanted him to stay close to her. The thought of letting him out of her sight again and back into the big wide world must be terrifying. He kissed the top of her head, then held her out in front of him. "I'll be okay. I promise." He smiled.

"I know, I know. I'm just being silly." She shook her head and laughed.

"All good to go then, son," Robert announced, striding back into the hallway. "Call us if you need anything, okay?" He patted him firmly on the arm.

"Will do." Alfie felt a strange rush of sadness well up inside him. "And . . . thanks for everything."

"Right you are. Come on, love, let's go." Robert steered his mum out the door before she could try to resist.

"Bye," Alfie called out, but the door had closed and he was speaking, for the first time, to nobody.

Over the next few days it became very clear to Alfie that the surprise welcome-home party was just the start of the celebrations. He hadn't needed to worry about being left on his own, as every day his flat was filled with people popping in and out, bringing an abundance of food, cards, and well wishes with them. Great-aunts, cousins, neighbors, and friends all passed through on an endless conveyor belt, and by the end of his first week at home Alfie had to admit he was exhausted. There was no downtime, and although he'd spent nearly three months surrounded by people on the ward, this felt like it required a whole new level of effort. No time to shut the curtains and disappear into his own thoughts. No space to be alone with himself. Every day there was someone desperate to talk to him, to tell him how glad they were to see him and ask him how great it felt being home.

"It must be such a relief to be out of that ghastly hospital ward at last."

"I don't care how well they looked after you in there, there really is no place like home."

"You must be thrilled to have your own space again."

He nodded and agreed, placating them with smiles and murmurs of acknowledgment, but he couldn't shift the strange feeling that he'd felt more at home in the hospital.

Maybe that was because she was there.

The second that thoughts of Alice crept into his mind, he shut them down. There was simply no point torturing himself any further. It hurt enough hearing her in his dreams each night, let alone allowing his waking hours to be consumed by her. His regular flashbacks now seemed to be continuously interrupted by the sounds of Alice, and every morning he'd wake delirious with the hope of turning over and seeing her hand outstretched waiting for him. Instead, he was met with disappointment and silence. He'd lie in bed staring at his ceiling for hours until the realization that there would be another visitor arriving soon pulled him up and out and into the shower. He had to admit that each day it got harder and harder to get moving, but he knew he had to, for everyone's sake. This was the moment they'd all been hoping and praying for, and he couldn't let them down now.

In between visitors and mealtimes, Alfie spent most of his days immersed in his puzzle books. He sought refuge in the complex sudokus and intricate word searches. He tried to exhaust his brain with the most challenging crosswords and riddles, but not even his most trusted vice gave him peace anymore. It wasn't the same without them. The back and forth between him, Alice, and Mr. Peterson was what had made doing the puzzles so much fun. *That* was why he loved them so much—because they were doing them with him. Now he just had his own thoughts for company, and that wasn't much fun at all.

By the third week he'd had to enforce a strict quota on how many times his mum came to visit. For the first couple of days she'd casually turn up, unannounced, at his front door in the morning and refuse to leave until after dinner. Since then it had been decided: visits once a week only and phone calls in between. But even that Alfie was finding arduous. Every time the phone rang his heart would sink, and every day his patience seemed to grow thinner.

"Hi, Alfie, it's me."

He took a deep breath and willed himself to stay calm this time. "Hi, Mum."

"How are you doing?"

"Same as yesterday."

"Good, good. Have you spoken to your brothers at all? I'm meant to be Skyping them later."

"No. I'll message them in a bit."

Alfie could feel his fists clenching. Why did he find this so hard?

"Well, make sure you do. They miss you."

"Uh-huh."

"Have you heard from anyone on the ward since you left?"

He loved his mum, he really truly did, but sometimes he wished she didn't feel the need to constantly and relentlessly fire questions at him.

"Nope."

"That's a shame—you had some really great friends on there, didn't you?"

"Yeah." In response to the daily interrogation, he'd adopted the terrible habit of offering only one-word answers. Keep it short and sweet with no room for further questioning.

"Why don't you call the hospital, and we can see if we can go and visit?"

"Maybe."

"Well, you let me know. I'm more than happy to drive you."

Then came the guilt.

She's just trying to help.

I don't need help.
Are you sure about that one?
"Thanks."
"Of course. I love you, Alfie."
"I love you too."

Chapter 64

ALICE

Alice was discharged from St. Francis's Hospital a month after the bandages came off. It was a very sobering moment when she packed up her things and walked out into the world completely alone.

"Alice, baby, wait."

Her head instinctively turned at the sound. Alice had to laugh as she watched Nurse Angles willing her curvy frame to hustle through the crowds in reception.

"You can't go without giving me one last good-bye!"

How did she know?

Alice allowed herself to be taken into the nurse's arms.

"How did you even—"

"You think I'd let them discharge you without telling me? What kind of woman do you take me for!" she exclaimed.

Alice couldn't stop herself from laughing. How wonderful it felt to be held like this again. Not quite the firm, muscular frame of Sarah, but with the exact same warmth and care that made her heart soar.

"Thank you for everything," she whispered into Nurse Angles's soft shoulder.

"Like I always say, baby, if you need *anything*, just buzz me."

She nodded, waiting for Nurse Angles to turn and go. Waiting to be left all alone once again. But the woman wasn't moving.

"Don't you need to get back?"

"Not just yet. I'll stay and see you off."

Alice knew there was no point in arguing. The tears came thick and fast as she started to walk away. She could feel the eyes of Nurse Angles watching her even after she'd turned the corner and disappeared from sight completely.

Maybe Alfie was right. Maybe she really wasn't alone anymore.

"Mummy, what's wrong with her face?"

Alice looked down to see a pudgy little finger pointing straight at her. That hopeful thought had lasted all of two minutes.

"Samuel. We don't point at people. And we don't say such things." Horrified, the mother to whom the pointing baby belonged almost pushed Alice out of the way in her attempt to run away.

Get me home.

Please, just get me home now.

One silent and equally awkward Uber ride later, Alice was back. She'd kept her head low as she entered through the main door and, ignoring the kind hello from the receptionist, practically sprinted into the lift, jabbing the top-floor button as hard as she could. She couldn't face any more questions today, and she certainly couldn't risk any more pointing. All she needed was to be in her flat, by herself, completely alone. As the lift carried her slowly upwards, she couldn't help but think how strange it felt to be back here. How could it be that on the surface everything looked exactly the same as always, yet on the inside everything felt different? Alice *was* different. It was hard to believe that this was her life she was going back to.

She opened her front door for all of three seconds before slamming it shut again.

Holy shit—did I get the wrong flat?

Alice checked the door again.

Obviously this is your flat—it's the penthouse, it's the only one on this floor!

Tentatively, she opened the door again, millimeters at a time.

Same beige walls, same bare kitchen, same sterile lounge. Yes, this was definitely hers. An apartment picked straight out of a showroom catalogue—but who were all the cards from? Where had all the flowers come from?

Slowly Alice stepped inside. Who had been inside her flat? Alice wasn't a give-a-spare-key-to-a-neighbor kind of girl. No one in the world had access but her.

That was when she saw it: a note gingerly propped up on the side by the flowers.

Dear Miss Gunnersley,

You appear to be absent and we needed to clear the front desk from your deliveries. The flowers kept dying. I hope you don't mind that we delivered them to your flat.

Yours sincerely,
Jim Broach
Head of Maintenance

Well, that was one question answered.

Alice reached for the card next to the note. She recognized the handwriting but couldn't quite place where from.

Dear Alice,
Sending you lots of get well soon wishes and
good energy for your recovery. We all miss you and
are thinking of you.
Love, Lyla & Arnold

P.S. I hope you like the potted plant. Arnold thought it
would be better than flowers as it will last longer (only if you
water it, though!).

P.P.S. I made Henry order you a weekly bunch of flowers.
Serves him right for being a tight bastard! x

Alice laughed. How she would have loved to see Lyla approach that conversation. Poor Henry wouldn't know what hit him! A rush of affection surged through her.

She picked off the card attached to the large bouquet of flowers.

Please find these regular flowers delivered to you
on behalf of your colleagues at Coleman and Chase.
Get well soon.

Lyla hadn't been lying—she really had got Henry to pay out! The final card all but broke her.

AL!
Welcome home, my love.

Here is a little something to make you smile /
please don't kill them straight away!
Miss you always
Sarah and Raph xxx

No matter how much she pushed or how fiercely she de-
nied it, right now Alice couldn't help but feel anything but
loved.

These people cared. They really cared. How had she
taken it for granted for so long?

Alice texted Sarah to let her know she was home safe, put
a wash on, and then sat in the middle of the floor and cried
herself to sleep.

The next morning she woke up a little disoriented and very
much in pain. Her back ached and she could barely move
her body. Crying on the floor was one thing, but sleeping on
it all night was another thing entirely. Part of her wondered if
she could just lie there all day. No one would notice. What
else was she planning to do with her time?

She decided to kill a good hour doing an online shop. As
much as she hated to admit it, she needed food. The only
surviving items in her fridge were an unopened jar of pickled
onions and some jam—and even an unaccomplished chef
like Alice knew that they did not go well together. Twenty-
four ready meals and every flavor of Ben & Jerry's ordered—
and still it was only 10 a.m.

This is going to be hell.

True, there wasn't endless excitement on the ward, but
she'd always had Alfie to distract her.

Alfie.

She lay back on her sofa and allowed herself to imagine all the things he could be getting up to right this very moment. Thoughts of his mum force-feeding him plate after plate of brownies while his friends sat around him and tried their best to insult one another kept her amused for a while. Then she remembered it was 10:30 a.m. on a Wednesday. He was probably at work.

Work.

She hadn't been in touch with the firm for months! There was absolutely no way that she was ready to go back yet, but looking at the colorful roses on her kitchen table she couldn't help but feel duty-bound to at least let them know she was safe.

Message to Henry Boss • August 22, 10:34 a.m.
Hi Henry, it's Alice. I thought I'd drop you a text to let you know I've formally been discharged from the hospital and am back at home. Thank you for the flowers, they are lovely. Let me know if we need to discuss a return to work date, conscious it's been some time.

Thanks
Alice

She regretted it as soon as she'd sent it.

What if he replies and demands that I come into the office this week?

On the other hand—what if I don't have a job anymore?

What will I do for money?

She nearly jumped out of her skin when she felt the phone buzz in her hand.

Oh God. Oh God oh God oh God.

Message from Henry Boss • August 22, 10:47 a.m.

What the hell was wrong with her? Since when had she become so afraid of everything?

In one quick swipe, she opened the message.

Hi, Alice. Great to hear from you and glad you are back home. No need to rush back. Please take as much time as you need. Henry

She closed her eyes and let out a long, slow sigh. A wave of relief washed over her. She was safe! At least for a few more weeks she could stay hidden away and pretend that real life wasn't just around the corner waiting for her. She sank back and buried herself deeper into the sofa. If only Henry could see her now—holed up in the flat she barely used to sleep in, afraid of her own reflection. Would he even recognize her?

A single tear tracked down her cheek.

Why would he? You don't even recognize yourself.

Chapter 65

ALFIE

"So, big guy, what's the plan?" Matty flopped down on the sofa next to Alfie.

By the end of his first month home, the crowds of visitors had slowly reduced to a trickle and Alfie found himself spending more and more time on his own. Some things hadn't changed, however, and Matty's weekly visits had continued religiously. Every Wednesday the pair would spend the afternoon together, often doing as little as humanly possible in the pleasure of each other's company.

"I don't know." Alfie shrugged. "Xbox?" His monosyllabic responses were becoming the norm now and not just reserved for his mother's phone calls.

"I don't mean now, you idiot. I meant for your birthday."

Shit. How the hell had that come around so quickly?

"There isn't one at the moment, mate." Alfie picked at the red, raw hangnail on his thumb. "I'm not really bothered this year."

"What!"

Alfie looked at Matty's shocked face.

"Come *on*! Not that long ago you were in the hospital in a complete and utter pit of despair. I'm sorry to remind you, but it's true. Now look at you! Back in your own flat, single man walking again . . . we have to celebrate!"

Time was a weird and wonderful thing. How could a few months already have passed since the accident? It felt like only yesterday he was leaving the hospital, yet a lifetime since he'd woken up this morning. Every minute felt like wading through treacle. Doing anything other than sitting felt arduous. Had his life been switched to slow motion?

"I don't know, Matty." Alfie resumed picking the skin from his thumb.

The thought of doing anything more social than this made Alfie feel strangely on edge. He'd spoken to enough people over the past month to last him a lifetime, and he increasingly found the thought of social interaction unbearable. Even having Matty over was a strain at times. No. All he wanted was to sit in his flat in peace. Why couldn't anyone respect that?

"Don't be boring, Alf, it will do you good to get everyone together!"

Matty was not letting this go. Alfie was well aware that there were some battles not worth fighting, and this was definitely one of them. Maybe it was best to let go of any semblance of control and just go with it. He could always cancel last-minute anyway.

"Well, why don't you organize it? I'll go along with whatever." Surely there was only so much the man could do in the next few days?

"Leave it with me, my man, leave it with me!"

Looking at Matty rubbing his hands together with glee did not fill Alfie with much confidence.

"Anyway, I better be off, I'm picking the kids up from swimming and if I'm late again I will be in the shit with Mel." Alfie knew that Mel was not a woman to cross and so wasn't surprised at the pace at which Matty said good-bye. "See you later, mate," he called as the door slammed shut.

Alfie didn't even bother to respond. He simply sat once again staring at the TV, letting the sounds and colors pass mindlessly through his brain.

What is wrong with you?

He knew his behavior was getting worse. Every day he felt his moods growing darker and those old, familiar black clouds were back, hovering ominously in his mind, threatening to consume him completely.

Get a grip.

Just as Alfie was about to try to distract himself with another round of puzzles, the doorbell went.

Of course Matty had forgotten something, he could be the most useless human at times.

"Hold on, I'm coming."

But as he got closer, he knew straightaway that it wasn't Matty. Funny how distinctive someone's silhouette could be.

"Hey, Alfie. It's me, Tom."

This time his visitor knocked.

Tom? Who is Tom? His mind was spinning, trying to place this name and voice.

"From Heartlands High . . ."

Oh, *that* Tom.

Why on earth is he here?

"Yeah, give me a second, this lock's a bit funny." Biding

his time, Alfie mustered his best *I'm doing completely fine* smile before he opened the door.

"Sorry for dropping in on you like this, I just thought I'd pop round and see how you're doing?"

Alfie looked at the man in front of him—shirt, tie, shiny shoes—and was suddenly very aware of his own odd socks, dirty Adidas tracksuit, and stained T-shirt. Had he even showered today?

"I'm doing okay." *Keep it short and sweet, that's the plan.*

"I haven't got long, just came on my lunch break actually. Don't mind if I come in and eat my sandwiches, do you?"

Alfie laughed. After all this time, Tom's wife was still packing him lunch every day. At first he'd found it weird and a little too much, but over time Alfie had come to find it quite sweet. No one apart from his mum had ever made his sandwiches.

"Sure. Come in."

This was the first time anyone from work had ever been inside Alfie's flat. Although he'd made good friends at the school, it always felt just one step too far inviting them back to see the place where he slept each night and walked around naked every morning.

Tom perching hesitantly on his sofa was quite a sight. This man didn't belong here amid Alfie's chaos, with his straight lines and neat edges. It was a meeting of worlds that did not align.

"So, how's everything been?" Tom looked around as if he knew the answer already. The pile of dirty underwear in the corner was probably a big enough giveaway.

"Yeah, like I said, okay. Just trying to get used to things, I guess."

Alfie hadn't sat down; he wasn't ready to accept that this conversation was going to last longer than five minutes.

"Of course. Must feel pretty weird, right?"

Obviously it's weird, Tom. "Mm-hmm" was all he managed.

Tom sheepishly took a bite out of his sandwich. Wow, he really was going to eat his lunch here. Alfie had suspected that was just a ploy. "Fancy one?" He held up a limp ham sandwich.

"Nah, you're all right."

God, when was this going to be over? Why was Tom willingly prolonging the awkwardness?

"A few people have been asking me if I've heard from you. We miss you at school. Everyone does."

Alfie felt the sharp pang of guilt. The kids. God, how he missed the kids.

"I know the office has said they've tried to call but not got a response. We are worried about you, Alfie. No one has heard from you in weeks. Before the accident we could barely get you to leave the school, and now it's radio silence."

Aha. They sent poor Tom in to check how the invalid is doing. Sweet, Alfie thought, *but completely unnecessary.*

"I'm fine. There's just a lot going on, you know, I only moved back a few weeks ago so I'm taking it slowly, that's all."

He thought he'd sounded confident enough, but the look on Tom's face suggested otherwise.

"The thing is, I had a bit of a shit time a few months back, and I kind of lost myself for a bit," Tom said. "It got pretty bad and there were times I wasn't sure I'd make it, to be honest."

Wow, he wasn't expecting that. The ever so well put-together and immaculate Tom had a secret personal crisis of his own.

Remember—never judge a book by its cover.

"It took me a while to realize, but when I did and"—Tom suddenly looked nervous—"and I got help for it, things really started to turn around for me."

"Got help?"

"Yeah . . . you know." Tom nibbled cautiously at the crust of his sandwich. "Professional help."

The penny dropped.

"You're telling me you think I need to see a shrink." Alfie had been here many times before, and he wasn't ready to entertain going back there again.

"It's just a suggestion." Tom held his hands up in defense. "I won't pretend I know half the things you're going through, but I just wanted you to know that you don't have to do everything on your own. Sometimes just talking about stuff can help take off the load, you know?"

"Appreciate it, mate, but I'm genuinely fine. In fact, I'm meant to be meeting someone in a few minutes, so, if you don't mind, you're going to have to take your lunch back to school if that's okay?"

He was already at the door before Tom could protest.

"Of course. Not at all. Like I said, I just thought I'd check in."

"Thanks, mate. See you soon."

Alfie practically hurled Tom and his half-eaten sandwiches out the door. He looked around his flat. So what if he hadn't tidied up in a while? It wasn't his fault he'd been in a life-threatening accident and lost his leg. It took time to adjust back to reality. He kicked the pile of dirty washing in frustration.

Don't need to do this alone.

Who the fuck does he think he is?

I'm fine on my own.

Maybe being alone was the easiest way to live. Maybe Alice had been right all along.

Chapter 66

ALICE

It had been eight days.

Eight days since Alice had left the flat.

At first she'd justified it as "integration time," the chance to get used to being out of the hospital and back in her old surroundings. It was a big adjustment and not one that could be rushed. Plus with the help of online shopping and Deliveroo, Alice really had no need to venture outside. She was safe and warm and content in her flat. To be honest, it was the most amount of time she'd ever spent there since buying it—at least she was finally getting value for her money.

On the ninth day of isolation, her self-pitying routine was interrupted.

Message from Sarah BFF • August 30, 7:35 a.m.
Hey, Al. I've got an evening off (about bloody time!). Can we FaceTime? Love you. xxx

Alice stared at the message for a whole fifteen minutes.

Message to Sarah BFF • August 30, 7:50 a.m.
Can't we just phone call? Wi-Fi isn't great. xxx

Message from Sarah BFF • August 30, 7:52 a.m.
Alice, don't be ridiculous. I'm calling you in 10. Be ready. xxx

Alice knew deep down that it wasn't a big deal. Sarah had seen her at her worst. So what was the problem? Guilt started to gnaw at her insides. It wasn't that she'd lied before. She might have just been a bit hazy on some of the details whenever Sarah asked about the operation. She had been meaning to tell her, but it sort of felt easier to avoid it. The thought of explaining it all and having to relive the shame and disappointment was too much to bear. It felt nice keeping the secret to herself; in Sarah's mind all was good in the world, and Alice liked having the chance to pretend alongside her. Luckily they mainly texted back and forth, with the rare phone call added in for variety. But FaceTime—that was a brand-new dimension. She couldn't hide any longer.

As Alice sat there trying to find excuses not to answer, it dawned on her that not only would she have to face up to telling Sarah the truth but she'd also have to face herself again. The morning after she'd got home from the hospital, Alice had taken down every single mirror she owned. Even the thought of walking past and catching her reflection worried her. Now she was about to see it reflected back to her on the screen.

Sarah Mansfield would like FaceTime

Alice clasped the phone tightly.

For Christ's sake, Alice. Get a grip.

She closed her eyes and hit answer.

"Aha, she lives!"

"Only just . . ." She was suddenly aware of how disheveled she looked. Would Sarah be able to tell she hadn't left the house in over a week?

"How's it all been? Please tell me you've left the house at least once?"

Fuck.

"Erm." Alice smiled coyly.

"Alice Gunnersley!"

"I'm sorry, I'm sorry." As hard as she tried, she couldn't stop looking at the little image of herself in the top right-hand corner of the screen. In miniature form she didn't look so bad, especially if she held the phone as far away from her face as possible.

"So come on then, show me the new and improved you. I can barely see anything in that light." Sarah's face was beaming with excitement.

"The thing is . . ." Her words felt like glue in her mouth.

"Stop making excuses and show me! I know what you're like, Alice, you're just being hard on yourself."

Tell her.

Just say it now.

"It didn't work!" She practically screamed the words out.

"What?" Sarah's face twisted in confusion. "What didn't work?"

Alice could barely see the screen through her tears. "The operation. They had to abandon it. It didn't work, Sarah. I practically have the same mess of a face that you left me with. The scarring has gone a little and it's less red in places, but . . . I'm still a freak."

"Don't you *dare*, Alice." Sarah was angry now; Alice didn't even need to see her to know that. "You are not a freak. Do you hear me? You are more than your looks, you always have been, and you always will be."

"That's easy for you to say."

And with that, Alice hung up.

Barely two seconds passed before the screen flashed brightly.

Incoming Call Sarah Mansfield

It took every drop of energy to answer.

"Come on, Al. You don't even need to look at me — just please talk to me."

"I don't know. I just don't know what to do with myself. I feel like everything is the same but I don't quite fit properly, if that makes sense? Part of me wants to be back at work and distracted, and then another part is terrified of showing my face outside. I feel completely and utterly trapped. I had these stupid fantasies that this operation would fix me. That I'd return to normal in some miraculous fucking transformation, but no. Instead I'm stuck like this, and it breaks my heart."

As soon as the words were out of her mouth, Alice could feel the weight lifting ever so slightly from her shoulders.

"I'm so sorry, Alice. I really, *really* am." Sarah's voice cracked. "But I'm guessing that's completely normal and all part of the process, right? You're adjusting. It's going to take time. But whether you choose to go back to work is irrelevant right now; the most important thing is accepting that you can't hide away in your flat forever. Even if you just go and stand outside your building for five minutes every day, at least that's something! You have to take it one step at a time, my love."

Resistance suddenly rose up inside of her. Why couldn't she stay hidden away all the time?

Something jogged in her memory.

Alfie.

What had she said to him?

"You're saying that you'd rather I spend the rest of my life hiding? Hiding away from people, from new places, new experiences? Hiding behind these fucking hideous curtains? I want more, Alfie. I never thought I'd say it, but I do."

"Al, you still there, or have you hung up on me again?"

"No, sorry, I'm still here. I was just thinking about something."

"Let me guess . . . Alfie?" Alice could practically see the Cheshire cat smile creep onto Sarah's face. "Have you spoken to him since he left the hospital?"

"No." Alice wanted to move off this subject as quickly as possible. "And I don't want to."

"Okay. Well, you know what I think, don't you?"

"Go on. . . ." Alice was grateful Sarah had moved on but could sense the hint of mischief in her voice.

"I think you should file an insurance claim against your office building's maintenance, get a massive payout, and come and stay with me in Australia! Fuck staying in miserable London!"

Alice laughed. "And then you could build me a granny flat and I become a permanent third wheel?"

"I'm serious! Okay, maybe not about the granny flat, but I've been thinking about it. I even asked Raph, and he said you'd have a good chance of winning a case."

Oh, shit—she really was serious.

"Thanks, but I can't think about that right now. Maybe let's prioritize me exiting my building first? Small steps and all that."

"Fine. But if you want advice, Raph is more than happy to chat."

Alice knew it wasn't fine and that Sarah wouldn't be letting this go anytime soon. "Okay, thank you. Anyway . . . fill me in on life in Oz. What's new?"

As Sarah launched into a full-blown day-by-day account of her life, Alice let her mind wander.

She was finding it hard to fit neatly into her life as it had been before the accident—but maybe, just maybe that wasn't the answer.

Maybe she did need to create a new life.

A new life surrounded by the people who loved her.

Alfie.

Sarah's words flashed in front of her eyes.

He loves you. You know he does.

Alice hated how every time she thought of him, any hope she held about meeting him would be extinguished by the cynicism. How could he have loved her without ever seeing her? That was the fantasy of movies and fiction. And even *if* he had, Alice was pretty certain that love would disappear the moment he laid eyes on her. Alice needed to forget him. And if she wanted to move on and away to the other side of the world, she needed to forget him fast.

Chapter 67

ALFIE

"Sweetheart, are you sure you're doing okay? You haven't come over in weeks and we can barely get hold of you on the phone."

This was exactly why Alfie had been avoiding her; it hurt too much to hear how much his mum cared. It also made the guilt one hundred times worse.

"Sorry, I'm just so caught up with planning my return to work that I can't seem to keep track of time."

No. The lying was why he avoided her. He hated lying to her.

She paused. He could already sense the hesitation.

"It's just, we actually phoned the school"—*shit*—"and they said they haven't heard from you at all."

"Alfie?"

His mind frantically searched for excuses and cover-ups, but came up blank.

"You know, it's okay if something's happened. You can tell me. You don't have to pretend to be okay if you're not."

His mind flashed back to Alice. How many times had he told her the very same thing? How many times had he tried to let her know that being upset didn't make you weak, or small, or feeble? And yet here he was doing the exact opposite.

"Alfie, say something, please. You're scaring me."

He knew the game was up. He didn't want to put his mum through any more pain—she'd had a life too full of that already—but there was no hiding from it now.

"Mum, I think I need help."

As much as hearing the words out loud made him want to crawl into a hole and cry, the moment they were out of his mouth he couldn't ignore the sense of relief that washed over him.

"Oh, Alfie, can I come over?"

"Yes, please." There was an urgency in his voice that surprised even himself.

"Give me twenty minutes."

And there she was, twenty minutes later, armed with chocolate biscuits and hot coffee. He had to hand it to her: this woman knew how to handle a crisis.

"Come in, it's, erm, it's a bit of a mess." Alfie knew there was no need for the warning; one look at the state of him was enough. The reason he hadn't asked for help was that by now, everything had gone too far. He'd let the dishes pile too high, the clothes get too dirty, his world grow too messy. How could he bear to let anyone see this?

The shame increased with every step they took inside the flat, but not once did his mum make a comment. Not when she saw him for the first time, unwashed and unkempt. Not even when she had to pick her way through the piles of empty takeaway boxes and dirty underwear. Jane Mack kept her eyes up and a smile on her face.

"Right." She stood in the middle of the living room, finally able to survey the full extent of the chaos. "Quite honestly, Alfie, you look awful. How about you take a shower and get to bed while I sort things out down here?"

"Don't be silly, I can't let you do that."

"You don't have a choice. There's no way you can help anyone smelling like that." She smiled and pulled him into her arms.

"Thanks, Mum."

"Go rest. I'll be down here waiting when you're ready."

Alfie dragged himself into his bathroom. He'd been wearing the same outfit for so long that he practically had to peel the clothes off. Just as he was about to step into the shower, he caught a glimpse of himself in the mirror. How long had it been since he'd properly looked at himself? It was a sobering moment, to say the least. Standing before him wasn't a man he recognized. His hair was long and greasy. His skin was dry and almost gray. Where had the life gone? Where had his sparkle gone? It was if he were staring at a drawing of himself, familiar but flat and slightly off somehow.

Imagine if Alice turned up now! What the hell would she think of me?

He shook the thoughts from his head and maneuvered himself under the hot, welcoming water.

One long shower and a two-hour nap later, both Alfie and the flat had been transformed.

"Alfie, honey, wake up. I've got some food on the table."

Of course she had. Not only had his mum cleaned the entire flat and put two loads of washing in, but she'd also managed to bake lasagna from a fridge full of nothing.

"Mum, what have you done?"

"A thank-you will do. Now, sit down, shut up, and eat some actual food for once. If I even smell another chow mein, I might vomit." She ruffled his now clean hair and forced a pile of steaming tomato goodness in front of him.

The moment the food hit his stomach, a wave of comfort radiated through him. "Did you think you'd still be looking after me after all this time?"

"I knew I'd signed up for life the moment I had you."

There was no resentment in her eyes, just pure, undying love. Alfie couldn't stand to look at it for too long; he knew the guilt was just waiting to strike.

"Honestly, thank you." He knew the words weren't enough, but it was the only thing he had to offer her. "I'll make it up to you, I promise."

"You'll make it up to me by telling me what's going on. As soon as you're done eating, you're going to sit with me and explain everything. No more excuses. I need you to help me understand, okay?"

"Okay."

It was finally time to start facing his problems.

"Good. Now, have another plate, you look famished."

Chapter 68

ALICE

On day ten, she left the flat.

It might have been in the dead of night and in complete and utter darkness, but still she'd done it.

One of the downsides of staying cooped up inside the flat for days at a time was that sleep became elusive. Her body clock was completely out of sync, and she had become so used to doing nothing that by the time the sun clocked off its shift and bedtime called, Alice could do nothing but lie wide awake. For hours she would lie there, watching the minutes crawl by on her clock. No matter how hard she prayed for sleep to come and take her, it always remained hidden and just out of reach.

In her old life, Alice had practically thrived on no sleep. She needed four hours maximum to be able to function at her peak, and sometimes with the help of an extra espresso she could manage on less than three. Then again, that old

Alice was full of life. There was so much to do and so many things to achieve that when her head finally hit the pillow at the end of each day, she would instantly black out. Now she was just a shell of existence. Stuck in a constant haze of sleep-deprived lethargy, it seemed the only activity she got now was listening to the racing thoughts churning through her mind.

Go outside.

No.

Yes.

It's pitch-black.

Exactly! It's perfect.

I can't go outside now.

Why?

It's dangerous.

Is slowly rotting away alone in your flat any less dangerous?

Why wasn't there a way to mute your own thoughts? Surely someone had invented an off switch for the brain by now?

Go on. Just for five minutes.

Try it.

This isn't living, Alice. This is a slow death.

Perhaps it was sleep deprivation or insanity, but whatever it was, before she knew it she was standing at her front door with her coat thrown over her pajamas.

If you're going to do it, just do it.

Her hand reached for the door handle. Her head felt dizzy with adrenaline, and every last drop of moisture had evaporated from her mouth.

"Fuck it."

And for the first time in ten days, Alice stepped outside of her flat. The lights in the hallway flashed on and the brightness burnt her eyes.

Good God, what the hell was she doing?

You're here now, just go!

She ran to the lift in a panic, jabbing the call button relentlessly. The moment the doors opened she practically threw herself in, like a woman possessed. As the lift jolted into life, Alice closed her eyes tightly.

Breathe.

All you need to do is breathe.

Was it always this slow? Claustrophobia began to set in. She squeezed her palms tightly, fingernails digging into her skin.

As soon as the lift opened again, Alice hurled herself out and through the front doors.

The fresh air hit her immediately, its chill catching in her chest and stealing the breath from her lungs. She gasped, gulping desperately for more. She stared upwards at the sky, the stars thrown haphazardly on the velvet backdrop casting their pins of light onto her. The wind whipped through her hair and grazed her bare flesh. She closed her eyes and simply stood with arms out wide, head thrown upwards, begging for the breeze to lift her up and carry her away.

"You okay, miss?"

Alice's heart dropped. She snapped her eyes open and frantically tried to search out who'd spoken.

"Sorry, didn't mean to scare you."

As her eyes adjusted to the darkness, she clocked the outline of a person walking towards her.

"I don't mean any harm. I just want to check you're okay?"

She stumbled backwards and farther into the shadows. "I'm fine," she croaked, sounding anything but fine. "I just needed some air."

"You and me both. Lucky I've got Bruno here as an excuse to get outdoors."

The cold, wet nose of a dog sniffled at her feet.

"Holy shit!"

"You're not scared of dogs, are you? Sorry, it's hard to see where he's gone at night. Bruno, come back here, you bloody idiot."

If she weren't so petrified of being seen Alice would have laughed at the ridiculousness of this situation. Her heightened senses from the ward kicked back in as she tried to paint a picture of this man by his voice. He was old, definitely. Frail but with a deep resistance to admitting it. There was a fire in him that Alice could feel burning through the cold night.

"I'm Fred, by the way. I live just over there on the new estate. Bruno's getting on a bit now, but every time I can't sleep I like to come out and give him a quick walk. Good for clearing the head, you know. How come you're out so late?"

How come I always attract the talkers?

"Couldn't sleep," she murmured.

"Ever since my wife passed I've barely managed to get a solid hour a night. God bless her. Married for more than fifty years, and then just like that she's gone."

Alice's mind instantly went to Mr. Peterson and Agnes. Her heart strained in her chest at the thought of them. "I'm sorry for your loss." She really was.

"Thank you. On the whole it's fine, me and Bruno make a good pair, but I guess I just get a bit lonely, you know?"

I do know. More than she'd ever care to admit.

"So, now, what's the real reason a young lady like yourself is standing outside in the middle of the night?"

Alice wasn't entirely sure what made her do it. Could fresh air make you delirious? Perhaps the rush of oxygen to her brain was causing reckless abandonment, or maybe the chill of the night had numbed her fear temporarily.

"I was in an accident a few months ago. I got discharged from the hospital nearly two weeks ago, and tonight is the first time I've left the house. Think I was at risk of going stir-crazy holed up in my flat."

"Can I ask what happened?"

He hadn't moved from his spot, and she was grateful for the distance that remained between them.

"There was a fire in my office building and I got caught in it. Badly."

"I see."

"I'm sorry. You don't need to hear any of this, you don't even know me!" She desperately looked round for the quickest way back inside.

"I asked you the question! You're simply doing me the honor of answering it."

Alice smiled. "I guess so."

"Can I ask you another question?" There was such frailty in his voice that it made Alice want to bundle him up and get him inside for safety.

"Okay. . . ."

"What do you see when you look at that tree over there?"

She saw his dark figure point in the direction of a giant, gnarled oak tree standing tall in the center of the front lawn.

Maybe I'm not the only crazy one around here.

"I'm not really sure, to be honest. I just see a tree." Alice was starting to panic. Maybe he was insane. Was she safe? Should she run?

"Okay, well, how would you *describe* the big tree over there?"

Alice looked harder at the twisted branches, the flaking bark, the giant roots bursting through the earth.

"Wise. Majestic. Powerful. Beautiful." As she spoke the

words, her body began to relax. Mother Nature really was an artist.

"Exactly. You don't look at that damaged, weathered, worn-out tree and see it flawed, do you? Our scars are simply the marks of our stories. They show we've lived a great life, and most of all that we have survived it. Don't hide your story away in the shadows."

The words hit her with physical force. She felt the ground beneath her shift as waves of emotion crashed over her one after another, relentless and unyielding. The rawness and vulnerability of his words had blindsided her. She hadn't been prepared for it, and she found herself unraveling right there and then.

Without thinking, Alice stepped boldly out of the shadows. The orange haze of the streetlights washed over her, and she saw the old man move tentatively towards her.

"Ah, just as I thought. You have a wonderful story to tell."

He bowed ever so slightly, then turned to leave. Alice watched his tiny figure disappear into the endless darkness. She stood there until her fingers turned numb and the sun began to rise.

It seemed the kindness of strangers would save her once more. Maybe it was time to close the book on her old life and start a new chapter completely.

Chapter 69

ALFIE

"Hi, Alfie. Thanks for joining me today."

"No problem at all. I'm paying for it, so might as well show up, right?"

Idiot.

Rule number one: don't joke with therapists.

She offered him an awkward smile, at least. "So. It says in your notes that you've been suffering with depression since your accident. Is that right?"

"Erm, well, that's what the doctors said."

That awkward smile was already becoming unbearable.

"And would you agree?"

"I mean, some days are harder than others. At first I thought it was just a case of me adjusting back to reality. The hospital became a strange little family, I guess. Being without them is more difficult than I imagined."

"Them?"

"Huh?"

"You said *them*. I was wondering if you meant anyone specifically."

"Oh, I just meant the other patients on the ward. The nurses. Everyone, really."

"Have you spoken to any of them since you've been home? I'm sure you can still visit and check in from time to time?"

"No, not really. A few people have called but . . . but there's some people I can't see."

"Really? Why's that?"

He wished she wouldn't look at him like that. So innocent, yet so blatantly aware there was something to be uncovered if she just pushed a little more.

"Well, one of them died."

"I'm sorry to hear that. And the other?"

"Well. It's a bit of an odd situation, really."

Could he change the subject without her knowing?

She's a shrink. She probably already knows you're thinking about doing that right this second.

"Go on. . . ."

Alfie took a deep breath. Maybe it was finally time to talk about her. Maybe this stranger, with her notepad and stern glasses, could be the one person to finally help him let her go. For so long he'd tried to bury her away, putting all thoughts of Alice into a box at the back of his mind. But no matter how hard he tried and how fiercely he fought, she always seemed to find a way out. He hadn't spoken to a soul about her since he'd left. He was too afraid and, if he was being honest with himself, a little embarrassed. How could anyone understand what they'd had? The experiences they had shared and the intensity of his feelings? The only person he'd touched on the subject with was Mr. Peterson, and even that had left him feeling exposed and unsure.

He'd promised his mum that he would be honest in these sessions. That he would use this time to release anything and everything he was holding on to. This was his chance to move forward—and he knew deep down that if he was going to do that, Alice had to be the first thing to go.

He fixed his eyes firmly on the floor by her feet.

"I met this girl . . . she moved into the bed next to me on the ward . . . her name was Alice . . . and I think . . . I think I fell in love with her. . . ."

Chapter 70

ALICE

Today was a big day. There was so much to be done on the schedule that Alice felt exhausted looking at it.

Start at the top and just work your way down.

Simple.

The schedules had only been meant to be a temporary fix, but now she seemed unable to live her life without them. Her midnight chat with the dog-walking stranger had set the wheels in motion. His words would play over and over in her mind, willing her to find a way to live, and so, taking inspiration from Alfie's schedule, she'd begun by creating a very small to-do list to get her up, moving, and productive again. The first few had been laughable.

TO DO:

- *Eat breakfast*
- *Eat lunch*
- *Go to reception*

- *Eat dinner*
- *Message one person*

How basic could it get? But to begin with, even these tiny tasks felt unbelievably difficult. The anxiety that would consume her merely walking to the lift sometimes was enough to render her speechless. Those three meters felt like three miles on some days.

The first trip she'd taken in broad daylight had been a huge milestone. Remembering it now still sent faint shivers of anxiety through her body.

You can do this, Alice.

It's just out the door, into the lift, out, and back up.

Simple.

If it was so goddamn simple, then why did it feel like she was about to run a marathon, blindfolded, with a gun to her head?

It took four attempts at opening the door, five to step outside of her flat, and three to actually get in the lift and down; but eventually Alice had found herself at the front desk staring into the face of Rita, the new concierge.

"How may I help you, miss?"

There was staring, but no repulsion.

Maybe she's a very good actress.

Or maybe she doesn't care?

"Can I help you?" Rita prompted again.

Alice realized that in fact she was the one who was staring blankly at this woman.

"Any post for flat twenty?"

"Let me check, one moment."

The instant her back was turned, Alice wanted to run. She could have got an emergency phone call; she could have forgotten something important upstairs. Maybe she could say she'd left the gas on?

You are insane, Alice. Wait!

Then, just like that, Rita was back with no post and still no judgment on her face.

"Nothing for you today, Miss Gunnersley."

Relief swept through her. Imagine if she'd had to take a parcel from Rita's hand? God, no. She couldn't stand the thought of a stranger having to touch her just yet.

You let Alfie touch you.

That was different

Was it?

Yes, now stop thinking about him.

"Thanks." She'd gone before the word had actually left her mouth.

Back in the safety of the flat, she couldn't quite believe how hard her heart was beating. The fear was still bubbling under the surface of her skin and every nerve felt as though it had been cut open and exposed. But amongst all of that chaos Alice had realized that buried away in the corner of her chest was a tiny shard of pride glowing ever so slightly. She'd done it. Step one on her road to recovery completed, and Alice felt like a small child who had written her name for the very first time.

Even though the lists had grown longer and the distance she could comfortably travel had increased, the anxiety still reared its head. She decided that actually she didn't really mind when people stared. She supposed if the shoe were on the other foot, she'd probably do the exact same thing; curiosity was part and parcel of human nature, after all. What she couldn't stand, however, was the pointing and the whispering. That was the stuff that hurt. At first she'd look for it everywhere, seeking out the groups of people muttering about her in their hushed tones; but after a while she resigned herself to the fact that looking for it did nothing but make it hurt more. Let them point. Let them whisper. It wasn't nice, and it probably never would be, but Alice knew she had the resolve and strength to see it, acknowledge it, and move past it. In fact, she found now that these experiences, the source of her fear, were becoming her main motivation for doing something. Proving that in spite of everything she was up and living her life was a delicious victory that she got to experience nearly every day.

She'd been waiting for this next task all week. The timing had to be right, as there was a lot at stake and multiple things to organize, but now it was all coming together perfectly.

Message to Sarah BFF • September 29, 7:23 a.m.
Hello! What are you doing two weeks on Saturday? Love you. xxx

Message from Sarah BFF • September 29, 8:15 a.m.
You know very well that it's my birthday! And embarrassingly at the moment we have 0 plans. Who knew 33 could be so depressing! Why? You want to be my Skype date? Love you. xxx

Message to Sarah BFF • September 29, 9:17 a.m.
How about you pick me up from the airport and we can have a proper date?! Surprise. I got the payout. I'm coming to stay for two weeks! Happy birthday my love. xxx

Message from Sarah BFF • September 29, 9:18 a.m.
Oh my God. Yes yes a million times yes. Unless this is a joke. In which case I will have to immediately get on a plane and kill you. I love you and can't WAIT to see you. xxx

Alice's smug feeling lasted about five minutes before it dawned on her. What was she going to wear? The only parts of her body Alice had revealed outside of her own bathroom were her feet and, at a push, the bottoms of her calves. If she was lucky, she probably had a swimsuit stuffed into the back of her wardrobe, a pathetic souvenir from a half-arsed attempt at a triathlon about three years ago.

Everything had happened so fast, she didn't know if she was coming or going these days. The claim against the maintenance company had been processed surprisingly quickly. Whether they simply wanted to wash their hands of it or if deep down they knew they didn't stand a chance of winning didn't really matter to Alice. She'd gotten her payout, and now she had the financial freedom to do what she wanted. First stop was always going to be a holiday in Australia.

In a mild panic, Alice ran into her bedroom and flung open her wardrobe doors.

Suits, suits, and more suits. Mostly black, with a few odd navy pieces and one beige cardigan. Holy shit, the situation was more dire than she'd imagined. She started to rummage through the clothes, praying that somewhere tucked away at the back would be at least one suitable outfit, when suddenly her hands clasped around something bulky.

She reached in a little farther and pulled out a cloth bag.

PROPERTY OF ST. FRANCIS'S HOSPITAL

Of course! Her hospital bag. She must have thrown it in the cupboard when she first got back. It was a painful token of the accident and an embarrassing reminder that, without family or friends to bring her a bag from home, Alice had been forced to keep her belongings in a donated hospital wash bag.

Intrigued, she peered inside.

Toothpaste.

Toothbrush.

Discharge leaflets.

Hospital slippers.

Then she saw it. A small rectangular package, wrapped in brown paper. Confused, Alice turned it over in her hands, looking for clues as to where it could have come from. She sat on the floor and started to unwrap it. As the last bit of paper fell, Alice drew a sharp breath. In her hands she was holding a book. A puzzle book. The cover was hand-drawn in a familiar scrawl.

Alice Gunnersley's Very Special Book
of Very Hard Puzzles

Her heartbeat quickened. She tried desperately to keep her mind from flashing back to the ward, to him, to his voice. She had to focus.

Why did I not see this before?

Then something clicked. There was a memory there. What was it?

Of course!

Alice reached back into the bag, frantically searching until at last she felt it. His letter. What had he said right at the end . . . ?

Her eyes scanned anxiously for that one line she knew she'd seen somewhere before. YES! There it was.

P.S. Enjoy the puzzles!

The present she'd stuffed away and completely forgotten about! Alice took a few breaths, closed her eyes, and just held the book in her hands for a moment.

He made this for me.

This is a part of him in my hands right here, right now.

She reached for a discarded pen in one of her drawers and opened to the first page. A dot-to-dot . . . of course! She quickly set to work, letting the pen reveal the secrets of the puzzle.

It was the shape of an eye.

Come on, Alfie, you can do better than this.

She turned to the next page. Another dot-to-dot.

A very accurately drawn human heart.

Okay, this really was slightly random. Although what was she expecting? A hidden message? She laughed to herself and carried on overleaf.

Another dot-to-dot. *No points for imagination,* she thought.

A sheep.

Just as she was about to give up, she noticed a little note at the bottom of the page.

Put those together and what do you get, Alice?

There it was, clear as day on the page.

I LOVE YOU

She felt like she hadn't taken a breath for an eternity. She turned over to the next puzzle.

I. STILL. LOVE. YOU.

She couldn't believe what she was seeing. Every page she turned to had a similar pattern. There it was—fifteen pages of *I love you*—until she reached the very last page.

Her heart must have stopped completely when she saw it.

Alice, I don't know if I've made it clear enough yet, but I have completely and utterly fallen in love with you. If you feel the tiniest spark of anything towards me, please come and find me. Let's meet, let's talk, let's read Harry Potter *together! I will forever be hopeful. Yours, Alfie x*

Without thinking she jumped to her feet. Her entire body vibrated as adrenaline flooded her veins. There was so much energy moving through her that she could barely think, let alone sit still. She needed to go somewhere.

But where?

She smiled, clocking the tiny scrawled address at the bottom of the letter.

Chapter 71

ALFIE

Alfie had known physical exertion. He'd played sports his whole life; he'd learnt to walk again, for heaven's sake—but therapy. Now, that was a whole new level of tired.

Five sessions in, and he still hadn't wrapped his head around it. How could the hardest part of his entire recovery process involve sitting in a room for forty-five minutes talking? After every session he'd leave completely and utterly devoid of energy, as though someone had pulled the plug and let the life drain out of him. It required effort simply to keep his eyes open, let alone walk home from the station. But he did it. Because he'd promised he would, and because ultimately he knew it was helping.

Today's session had been especially difficult. Once again they'd come back round to Alfie's incessant need to please people. To be the hero and to make people laugh. Deep-rooted patterns were being pulled up and exposed over and over, inspected and analyzed in minute detail. By the time he got home, the only thing he could think about was sitting in his wonderfully tidy flat and watching mind-numbing TV until Matty arrived. Turned out that not coming home to piles of your own dirty laundry and moldy takeaway cartons really did make a difference. At last he felt settled in his flat, and he relished being able to call it home again.

He heard the doorbell go just as he sat down on the sofa. For the first time in his entire existence, Matty had decided to show up early. He had asked to come over to talk through the stag-party weekend he wanted to plan for one of the boys, which, considering his early arrival, filled Alfie with dread.

Throughout their entire friendship he'd never seen this side of Matty. How excited could one man get over organizing events? He'd been the same about Alfie's birthday, although he'd known that event was slightly different. Alfie's party had been a celebration of much more than just his birthday. It had marked a new start in his life. It was honoring all that had been and all that was to come. Alfie had been carefully piecing the lost parts of himself back together. It wasn't quick or easy or even enjoyable, but it had changed his world completely.

"Sorry, Matty, I'm coming!"

A part of him didn't want to know what plans were being concocted—but the sooner he got wind of the ideas, the easier it would be to steer Matty off course.

"I may be half robot, but I'm still a slow mover!"

Silence.

Strange, Alfie thought, Matty never missed an opportunity to come back with a hilarious insult.

"Matty, you all right, mate?"

As he came closer, he realized it wasn't Matty at the door; the silhouette was too slight and too female.

"Sorry, I was expecting someone else. . . ." he apologized, feeling just a little embarrassed for shouting at this stranger. He wrestled with the lock and pulled back the door.

The first thing he saw was her auburn hair.

The second thing was her hand.

Chapter 72

ALICE

Before she even had time to think, the door opened.

And just like that, there he was. A mass of dark curly hair, broad shoulders, and dangerously chiseled cheekbones.

It was Alfie Mack.

In the flesh.

She'd pictured his face a thousand times, but seeing him in front of her was beyond anything she could ever have imagined. Affection surged through her; her skin tingled with an energy she'd never felt before. Her whole body radiated with heat. Feelings were bubbling up from somewhere deep down, a rush of longing and desire and fear and anxiety filling her heart. This was what she'd read about in books but brushed off as fiction. This was what she'd watched in films and laughed at as fantasy. This was it. This was how it felt. A lifetime of emotions hitting her in one single moment.

Alice tried to smile, but her face felt frozen; all she could do was stare blankly at him.

His eyes narrowed just a little—those curious mismatched eyes he'd talked about. The eyes she'd tried to imagine so many times, on so many different faces.

Was it recognition she could sense? Confusion? Or was it downright disgust?

The thoughts crowded her mind, filling it with chatter. She couldn't catch hold of one before it was pushed out by another. She felt sick. Her breath seemed to be stuck somewhere in the middle of her chest. Her head felt dizzy, her body suddenly hit with a wave of nausea.

Alice took a slight step back.

Why had she come here? Really, what had she been expecting? She'd told herself over and over that this was a stupid idea. She'd gotten on and off the bus four times, had turned back at the end of his road twice and very nearly ordered an Uber home—but now that she was standing here, the reality felt much worse. She had to go.

Why weren't her legs moving?

This was all too much; the silence was suffocating.

She forced herself to take another step back but was unable to tear her eyes away from him. She wanted to drink in as much as of him as possible. This would be the first and last time she ever got to see him, and she wanted to imprint as much of it into her mind as she could.

His body shifted forward a fraction.

Turn and go.

Don't even look back, Alice.

Just leave!

As she finally turned to run, she felt something grab her.

His hand had found hers. The hand she'd held so many times before.

God, how she'd missed his touch.

She felt her body turn back instinctively to face him again. "Wait."

God, how she'd missed that sound.

The sound of him.

She tried to pull her hand away, but he only held it tighter and squeezed. This was what home had felt like all along.

"Alice?" He raised an eyebrow and flashed her a wicked smile. "What the hell took you so long?"

Epilogue

ALFIE

Five years later

"Mr. Mack! But what happens wh—"

"Kaleb. Remember, we don't shout out over each other. If we want to say something, we have to raise our hand," Alfie reminded him gently.

"Sorry, sir." Kaleb's eyes flashed in panic at the realization that he'd once again spoken without his hand up, which subsequently flew high up in the air, arm straight as an arrow.

The little boy looked as though he were about to explode at any moment if he wasn't relieved of the burning question that he was holding between his puffed-out cheeks. Alfie managed to stifle a laugh. "Yes, Kaleb. What would you like to ask?"

"What happens if people *do* say mean things to you? Don't you get upset?" Kaleb's voice faltered and his gaze dropped to his lap.

Even though Alfie had been running these after-school sessions for nearly a year now, they never got any easier.

Talking about *his* experiences didn't bother him much these days. He'd had enough practice of reliving every stomach-wrenching, heartbreaking moment of his life in his therapy sessions with Linda. So speaking about his mental health to schoolchildren was a dream in comparison to that. No. What got him the most, what kept him awake at night, was knowing just how many children were suffering in silence. He could recognize the signs immediately. The way they asked certain questions, the glances around the room to check that they weren't going to be laughed at, or dragged round the back of the school later and beaten because they'd dared to voice an opinion. Sometimes all Alfie had to do was look into their eyes and he'd see the pain—the humiliation swimming be-hind the glazed-over stares. But no matter how difficult and uncomfortable he found running the discussion groups to be, he had never felt prouder of anything in his life.

"Well." Alfie straightened up and looked directly into Ka-leb's anxious face. "When people say mean things to me, the first thing I do is take a deep breath. Sometimes, I close my eyes and just take a moment to sit with how those words made me feel. Then I name those feelings: maybe it's anger, or sadness, or shame. Sometimes that's enough for them to disappear. Other times, if they are very strong, I'll take myself away from the situation and write down what happened. Ev-erything. My thoughts, what I was wearing, what the other person was wearing, how I felt, what I wanted to say. I get it all out of my head and onto the paper. Then I usually tell someone I love what happened and we talk about it. Do you have someone you can talk to, Kaleb?"

The little boy's face lit up instantly. "My big brother. I can tell him anything. He's my best friend."

Alfie's insides melted and his heart surged in gratitude.

"Good. Then remember, if you ever find yourself in those situations, you can always talk to your brother. You're never alone, okay?" He tore his eyes away from Kaleb and surveyed the entire room. "And . . . even if you don't have an older brother, or sister, or someone you can talk to in your family, you always have me. Always." The sea of worried little faces nodded in unison, and Alfie prayed that they believed him.

A pale hand shot up into the air. "Yes, Mandy?" Alfie asked.

"Who do you talk to, sir?"

Alfie's face broke into a wide grin. Even after all this time, the very thought of her sent electricity through his body.

"Most of the time, I talk to my wife, Alice."

Hushed excitement rolled over the children in waves. "Can we meet her, sir?" Mandy chirped.

"Maybe one day. She's a very busy woman, but I'm sure she'd love to meet you all."

"What does she do, sir?" another shrill voice called out.

"Actually, she runs her own business. She's the clever one out of the two of us." He smiled. "But don't tell her I said that! Anyway, are there any more questions, or are we good to finish for the day?"

Another small hand reached into the air.

"Yes, Annie?"

"Is she pretty, sir?"

Alfie couldn't hold back his laugh this time. "Any questions *not* about my wife?"

The moment the last set of feet had filed out of the classroom, Alfie reached for his phone. He'd made a promise to himself that he would finish on time today. He couldn't bear to spend a minute longer than needed with his phone on silent.

"Shit," he cursed, seeing the time.

How was it already 4:45? The session had overrun, as it always did. He was trying not to worry, or to let his constant anxiety bubble to the surface and reveal itself to Alice, but he was struggling. The closer they got to the date, the stronger the nerves grew, and the more frustrated she became with him. She'd practically had to hurl him out of the door this morning, for fear he'd voluntarily take a day off sick to be with her. If there was one thing Alfie knew about his wife, it was that she was perfectly capable of handling almost anything by herself. It didn't stop him fretting, though.

Alfie's heart lurched when he saw his screen flash.

Message from Mum • May 30, 3:45 p.m.
Alfie, call me when you can. Don't panic, but you just
need to get to the hospital as soon as you can. Love you x

His heart was already trying to force its way out of his chest. He knew he should have stayed home. He could tell she was feeling off, even under the persistent smiles and reassurances. Shaking, he dialed his mum's number and hurtled out of the room.

"Mum, what's happening?" he shouted the second she picked up. He tore down the corridor, nodding frantically at teachers and students as he passed.

"Jesus! At last! Thank goodness I took my phone with me to the café today, otherwise who knows what would have happened," his mum babbled on. Alfie tried to keep his cool, but he could feel the pressure mounting in his head.

"Is she okay? Tell me she's okay?"

"Oh, she's fine. Nothing to worry about. They just had to bring her in sooner than expected." Alfie appreciated how

calm his mum was being, but even he could sense the apprehension in her voice. "How quickly can you get here?"

"I'm on my way. I won't be long." He didn't even wait for
a goodbye before hanging up and rushing out of the door.

She'll be fine.

She's in the best possible hands.

Breathe, Alfie. Just breathe.

Thoughts were racing through his mind and he knew if he
was ever going to be able to drive, he needed to calm down. As
he flung himself into his car, he rested his hands on the steering wheel and closed his eyes. What was it Linda had taught
him to do in these moments? Breathe in for four. Hold for four.
Out for four. Hold for four. He managed two rounds before the
adrenaline coursed through his veins once more and he knew
there was no more time to waste. He had to get to Alice.

Unfortunately, the early-evening traffic rush had other ideas.
The usual twenty-minute journey ended up taking just over
an hour. The entire time, Alfie had to force himself to remain
in the car and not abandon all rationale and attempt to run
there. Thankfully, the moment he arrived, he knew exactly
where to go. Sometimes he wondered whether he would ever
be able to forget the layout of the hospital that had once been
his home. They had chosen St Francis's not only because it
was the closest to them, but because they both knew deep
down that they wouldn't have been able to go anywhere else.

As he hurried through the foyer, sweat poured from every
inch of him and his leg with the prosthesis was starting to
ache. But he didn't stop. Not even to apologize to the people
he banged into as he unceremoniously pushed his way
through the crowded reception and along the corridors. His

phone continued to vibrate in his pocket but there was no time to answer. He needed to see her. He needed to make sure she was okay.

"Excuse me, sir, are you all right?" a nurse called out after him.

"Yes, sorry, just need to find my wife," he shouted back, not even bothering to turn his head to look at her. Then he saw it. The sign above the door at the end of the corridor. He'd made it. But what would he find on the other side?

Don't think like that, Alfie.

That doesn't help anyone.

He slowed to a brisk walk, desperately trying to catch his breath. Forcing mouthfuls of oxygen down his throat and into his lungs. He needed to at least *look* in control. He placed his hand gently on the double door and pushed.

"Alfie!" His mum ran over to him, pulling him into a fierce embrace. Squeezing all of the air out of him once again. "You made it! She's in delivery suite 3."

Alfie's body sagged in relief, and he barely had time to form any words before his mother started leading him towards a room at the far end of the ward.

"Alice, honey." She placed her hand on the door and knocked tentatively. "Alfie's here!"

"About fucking time," a familiar voice cried out. "Alfie Mack, get in here NOW!"

"That's my Alice." He smiled anxiously at his mum and stepped inside.

The instant Alfie laid eyes on the tiny human being in Alice's arms, his world shifted. It was as though every thought, worry, or care before that very moment in time had been dissolved.

Melted away and reduced to nothing. The only thing that mattered, the only thing he needed to think about, was that tiny bundle of life and the woman holding him.

"Trust you to nearly miss the whole thing," Alice purred as she lay her head on Alfie's shoulder.

He kissed her auburn hair, still a little damp with effort, and breathed in the smell of her. "Well, trust you to deliver our baby ahead of schedule! Always the overachiever, aren't you, Alice?" She nudged him hard in the ribs. "Ouch!"

"You think that hurts? Try going through labor, and then you'll know pain." She looked up at him and grinned.

"Ah." He nestled himself closer to her warm, full body. "Can't argue with that. Although it was worth it, right? For this little guy." Alfie leant over and placed a gentle kiss on his son's forehead. "Hello there, little Euan. Do you know you're named after some of the greatest men who ever lived?" He cooed softly. "Euan Arthur Stephen Mack. You're going to make them all so proud." He felt a wave of grief lap at his heart. "And you have your daddy's beautiful eyes. God, you're going to be a heartbreaker, aren't you?"

"Well, hopefully you won't have daddy's awful sense of humor," Alice whispered into the soft down of their son's head.

"Hey. It got me the girl in the end, didn't it? As long as he doesn't inherit your silver tongue, then I think we'll be okay!"

Alice's brown eyes widened gleefully. "Oh, shush. You wouldn't have me any other way."

Alfie looked at Alice cradling their baby in her arms. His wife and his son. His entire world right there in front of him. Everything he'd lost had led him to everything he'd ever wanted. His heart grew so big in his chest that for a second, he forgot to breathe.

"Alice Mack, I wouldn't change this for the world."

ACKNOWLEDGMENTS

To my three rocks, Mum, Dad, and Katie—so much of me is because of you and so much of me is on these pages, so thank you. And to Rod and Cathy—thank you for showing me the true meaning of family.

To the incredible team of people I have been lucky enough to work with—none of this could have happened without you! Special thanks go to Claire, Molly, Amelia, Victoria, Viv, Joal, Sara, and all the teams at Transworld and Gallery. You have welcomed me in with open arms and it has been a dream come true to work with you.

To Jenny Bent in the US, Bastian Schlueck and Kathrin Nehm in Germany, and everyone else involved in my foreign sales—thank you for enabling Alice and Alfie's story to be shared across the world.

I want to say a huge and heartfelt thank-you to my UK editor, Sally Williamson. Your calm patience and unwavering support throughout this journey has been incredible. You have given me the confidence and guidance to elevate my writing and this story to brand-new heights. What an honor it has been, and from the bottom of my heart—thank you!

Also to Kate Dresser, thank you for taking on the story of Alice and Alfie with such care. Your thoughts and perspective were instrumental in this creation and it has been an absolute pleasure to work with you.

To Sarah Hornsley, a gift from the universe, a serendipitous crossing of paths, a blast from the past! Thank you for being the most brilliant agent and organized human being I know. Your support and dedication is unrivaled and I am blessed to have you in my corner.

To Dr. Nagla Elfaki, Dr. Tom Stonier, and Dr. Naomi Cairns, who were, despite saving lives and working unbelievably long hours, always on hand for medical fact-checking and advice! I do have to say creative license was still taken with the book, but without their knowledge and support the authenticity and understanding of the characters' journeys would not have been the same.

And finally (last but not least!) to my incredible family and friends. You know who you are. Your love and excitement for this next chapter of my life has been overwhelming and I am forever grateful. Alfie and Alice are a reflection of so many parts of me and without you they would never exist. I love you all.

ABOUT THE AUTHOR

Emily Houghton is an ex–digital specialist and full-time creative writer. She originally comes from Essex but has been living in London for the past eight years. A trained yoga and spin teacher, Emily is completely obsessed with dogs and has dreamt of being an author ever since she could hold a pen.